EVERYMAN,

I WILL GO WITH THEE,

AND BE THY GUIDE,

IN THY MOST NEED

TO GO BY THY SIDE

EVERYMAN'S POCKET CLASSICS

STORIES FROM THE KITCHEN

EDITED BY DIANA SECKER TESDELL

EVERYMAN'S POCKET CLASSICS
Alfred A. Knopf New York London Toronto

THIS IS A BORZOI BOOK
PUBLISHED BY ALFRED A. KNOPF

This selection by Diana Secker Tesdell first published in
Everyman's Library, 2015
Copyright © 2015 by Everyman's Library
A list of acknowledgments to copyright owners appears at the back
of this volume.
Second printing (US)

All rights reserved. Published in the United States by Alfred A. Knopf,
a division of Penguin Random House LLC, New York, and in
Canada by Penguin Random House Canada Limited, Toronto.
Distributed by Penguin Random House LLC, New York. Published
in the United Kingdom by Everyman's Library, 50 Albemarle Street,
London W1S 4BD, and distributed by Penguin Random House UK,
20 Vauxhall Bridge Road, London SW1V 2SA.

www.randomhouse.com/everymans
www.everymanslibrary.co.uk

ISBN: 978-1-101-90759-7 (US)
978-1-84159-619-8 (UK)

A CIP catalogue reference for this book is available from the
British Library

Typography by Peter B. Willberg
Typeset in the UK by Input Data Services Ltd, Bridgwater, Somerset
Printed and bound in Germany by GGP Media GmbH, Pössneck

STORIES FROM
THE KITCHEN

Contents

FOOD AND LOVE

CHARLES DICKENS
Love and Oysters — 13

GUY DE MAUPASSANT
From *Bel Ami* — 23

SAKI
Tea — 35

M. F. K. FISHER
A Kitchen Allegory — 43

ISAAC BASHEVIS SINGER
Short Friday — 51

NORA EPHRON
Potatoes and Love from *Heartburn* — 69

LARA VAPNYAR
A Bunch of Broccoli on the Third Shelf — 75

ELISSA SCHAPPELL
The Joy of Cooking — 93

MEMORABLE MEALS

JEAN ANTHELME BRILLAT-SAVARIN
   On the Pleasures of the Table   129

ANTON CHEKHOV
   On Mortality   137

VIRGINIA WOOLF
   From *To the Lighthouse*   141

EVELYN WAUGH
   The Manager of "The Kremlin"   175

ISAK DINESEN
   Babette's Feast   185

GERALD DURRELL
   Owls and Aristocracy   227

SHIRLEY JACKSON
   Like Mother Used to Make   245

AMY TAN
   Best Quality   263

CULINARY ALCHEMY

EMILE ZOLA
The Cheese Symphony from *The Belly of Paris* — 281

MARCEL PROUST
From *Swann's Way* — 303

ALICE B. TOKLAS
Murder in the Kitchen — 309

GÜNTER GRASS
The Last Meal from *The Flounder* — 319

T. C. BOYLE
Sorry Fugu — 327

JOHN LANCHESTER
A Winter Menu from *The Debt to Pleasure* — 353

ERICA BAUERMEISTER
Lillian — 379

JIM CRACE
#45 from *The Devil's Larder* — 401

ACKNOWLEDGMENTS — 407

FOOD AND LOVE

"Sharing food with another human being is an intimate act that should not be indulged in lightly."

—M.F.K. Fisher, *An Alphabet for Gourmets*

CHARLES DICKENS

LOVE AND OYSTERS

IF WE HAD to make a classification of society, there is a particular kind of men whom we should immediately set down under the head of "Old Boys", and a column of most extensive dimensions the old boys would require. To what precise causes the rapid advance of old-boy population is to be traced, we are unable to determine. It would be an interesting and curious speculation, but, as we have not sufficient space to devote to it here, we simply state the fact that the numbers of the old boys have been gradually augmenting within the last few years, and that they are at this moment alarmingly on the increase.

Upon a general review of the subject, and without considering it minutely in detail, we should be disposed to subdivide the old boys into two distinct classes—the gay old boys, and the steady old boys. The gay old boys are paunchy old men in the disguise of young ones, who frequent the Quadrant and Regent-street in the day-time: the theatres (especially theatres under lady management) at night; and who assume all the foppishness and levity of boys, without the excuse of youth or inexperience. The steady old boys are certain stout old gentlemen of clean appearance, who are always to be seen in the same taverns, at the same hours every evening, smoking and drinking in the same company.

There was once a fine collection of old boys to be seen round the circular table at Offley's every night, between the hours of half-past eight and half-past eleven. We have lost sight of them for some time. There were, and may be still, for aught we know, two splendid specimens in full blossom at the Rainbow Tavern in Fleet-street, who always used to sit in the box nearest the fireplace, and smoked long cherry-stick pipes which went under the table, with the bowls resting on the floor. Grand old boys they were—fat, red-faced, white-headed old fellows—always there—one on one side the table, and the other opposite—puffing and drinking away in great state. Everybody knew them, and it was supposed by some people that they were both immortal.

Mr. John Dounce was an old boy of the latter class (we don't mean immortal, but steady), a retired glove and braces maker, a widower, resident with three daughters—all grown up, and all unmarried—in Cursitor-street, Chancery-lane. He was a short, round, large-faced, tubbish sort of man, with a broad-brimmed hat, and a square coat; and had that grave, but confident, kind of roll, peculiar to old boys in general. Regular as clockwork—breakfast at nine—dress and titivate a little—down to the Sir Somebody's Head—a glass of ale and the paper—come back again, and take daughters out for a walk—dinner at three—glass of grog and pipe—nap—tea —little walk—Sir Somebody's Head again—capital house— delightful evenings. There were Mr. Harris, the law-stationer, and Mr. Jennings, the robe-maker (two jolly young fellows like himself), and Jones, the barrister's clerk—rum fellow that Jones—capital company—full of anecdote!— and there they sat every night till just ten minutes before twelve, drinking their brandy-and-water, and smoking their pipes, and telling stories, and enjoying themselves with a kind of solemn joviality particularly edifying.

Sometimes Jones would propose a half-price visit to Drury Lane or Covent Garden, to see two acts of a five-act play, and a new farce, perhaps, or a ballet, on which occasions the whole four of them went together: none of your hurrying and nonsense, but having their brandy-and-water first, comfortably, and ordering a steak and some oysters for their supper against they came back, and then walking coolly into the pit, when the "rush" had gone in, as all sensible people do, and did when Mr. Dounce was a young man, except when the celebrated Master Betty was at the height of his popularity, and then, sir,—then—Mr. Dounce perfectly well remembered getting a holiday from business; and going to the pit doors at eleven o'clock in the forenoon, and waiting there, till six in the afternoon, with some sandwiches in a pocket-handkerchief and some wine in a phial; and fainting after all, with the heat and fatigue, before the play began; in which situation he was lifted out of the pit, into one of the dress boxes, sir, by five of the finest women of that day, sir, who compassionated his situation and administered restoratives, and sent a black servant, six foot high, in blue and silver livery, next morning with their compliments, and to know how he found himself, sir—by G—! Between the acts Mr. Dounce and Mr. Harris, and Mr. Jennings, used to stand up, and look round the house, and Jones—knowing fellow that Jones—knew everybody—pointed out the fashionable and celebrated Lady So-and-So in the boxes, at the mention of whose name Mr. Dounce, after brushing up his hair, and adjusting his neckerchief, would inspect the aforesaid Lady So-and-So through an immense glass, and remark, either, that she was a "fine woman—very fine woman, indeed," or that "there might be a little more of her, eh, Jones?" Just as the case might happen to be. When the dancing began, John Dounce and the other old boys were particularly anxious to see what was going forward on the stage, and Jones—wicked dog that Jones—whispered little critical remarks into the ears of John Dounce, which John Dounce retailed to Mr. Harris and Mr. Harris to Mr. Jennings; and then they all four laughed, until the tears ran down out of their eyes.

When the curtain fell, they walked back together, two and two, to the steaks and oysters; and when they came to the second glass of brandy-and-water, Jones—hoaxing scamp, that Jones—used to recount how he had observed a lady in white feathers, in one of the pit boxes, gazing intently on Mr. Dounce all the evening, and how he had caught Mr. Dounce, whenever he thought no one was looking at him, bestowing ardent looks of intense devotion on the lady in return; on which Mr. Harris and Mr. Jennings used to laugh very heartily, and John Dounce more heartily than either of them, acknowledging, however, that the time HAD been when he MIGHT have done such things; upon which Mr. Jones used to poke him in the ribs, and tell him he had been a sad dog in his time, which John Dounce with chuckles confessed. And after Mr. Harris and Mr. Jennings had preferred their claims to the character of having been sad dogs too, they separated harmoniously, and trotted home.

The decrees of Fate, and the means by which they are brought about, are mysterious and inscrutable. John Dounce had led this life for twenty years and upwards, without wish for change, or care for variety, when his whole social system was suddenly upset and turned completely topsy-turvy—not by an earthquake, or some other dreadful convulsion of nature, as the reader would be inclined to suppose, but by the simple agency of an oyster; and thus it happened.

Mr. John Dounce was returning one night from the Sir Somebody's Head, to his residence in Cursitor-street—not tipsy, but rather excited, for it was Mr. Jennings's birthday, and they had had a brace of partridges for supper, and a brace of extra glasses afterwards, and Jones had been more than ordinarily amusing—when his eyes rested on a newly-opened oyster-shop, on a magnificent scale, with natives laid, one deep, in circular marble basins in the windows, together with little round barrels of oysters directed to Lords and Baronets, and Colonels and Captains, in every part of the habitable globe.

Behind the natives were the barrels, and behind the barrels was a young lady of about five-and-twenty, all in blue, and all alone—splendid creature, charming face and lovely figure! It is difficult to say whether Mr. John Dounce's red countenance, illuminated as it was by the flickering gas-light in the window before which he paused, excited the lady's risibility, or whether a natural exuberance of animal spirits proved too much for that staidness of demeanour which the forms of society rather dictatorially prescribe. But certain it is, that the lady smiled; then put her finger upon her lip, with a striking recollection of what was due to herself; and finally retired, in oyster-like bashfulness, to the very back of the counter. The sad-dog sort of feeling came strongly upon John Dounce: he lingered—the lady in blue made no sign. He coughed—still she came not. He entered the shop.

"Can you open me an oyster, my dear?" said Mr. John Dounce.

"Dare say I can, sir," replied the lady in blue, with playfulness. And Mr. John Dounce ate one oyster, and then looked at the young lady, and then ate another, and then squeezed the young lady's hand as she was opening the third, and so forth, until he had devoured a dozen of those at eightpence in less than no time.

"Can you open me half-a-dozen more, my dear?" inquired Mr. John Dounce.

"I'll see what I can do for you, sir," replied the young lady in blue, even more bewitchingly than before; and Mr. John Dounce ate half-a-dozen more of those at eightpence.

"You couldn't manage to get me a glass of brandy-and-water, my dear, I suppose?" said Mr. John Dounce, when he had finished the oysters: in a tone which clearly implied his supposition that she could.

"I'll see, sir," said the young lady: and away she ran out of the shop, and down the street, her long auburn ringlets shaking in the wind in the most enchanting manner; and back she came again, tripping over the coal-cellar lids like a whipping-top, with a tumbler of brandy-and-water, which Mr. John Dounce insisted on her taking a share of, as it was regular ladies' grog—hot, strong, sweet, and plenty of it.

So, the young lady sat down with Mr. John Dounce, in a little red box with a green curtain, and took a small sip of the brandy-and-water, and a small look at Mr. John Dounce, and then turned her head away, and went through various other serio-pantomimic fascinations, which forcibly reminded Mr. John Dounce of the first time he courted his first wife, and which made him feel more affectionate than ever; in pursuance of which affection, and actuated by which feeling, Mr. John Dounce sounded the young lady on her matrimonial engagements, when the young lady denied having formed any such engagements at all—she couldn't abear the men, they were such deceivers; thereupon Mr. John Dounce inquired whether this sweeping condemnation was meant to include other than very young men; on which the young lady blushed deeply—at least she turned away her head, and said Mr. John Dounce had made her blush, so of course she DID blush—and Mr. John Dounce was a long time drinking the brandy-and-water; and, at last, John Dounce went home to bed, and dreamed of his first wife, and his second wife, and the young lady, and partridges, and oysters, and brandy-and-water, and disinterested attachments.

The next morning, John Dounce was rather feverish with the extra brandy-and-water of the previous night; and, partly in the hope of cooling himself with an oyster, and partly with the view of ascertaining whether he owed the young lady anything, or not, went back to the oyster-shop. If the young lady had appeared beautiful by night, she was perfectly irresistible by day; and, from this time forward, a change came over the spirit of John Dounce's dream. He bought shirt-pins; wore a ring on his third finger; read poetry; bribed a cheap miniature-painter to perpetrate a faint resemblance to a youthful face, with a curtain over his head, six large books in the background, and an open country in the distance (this he called his portrait); "went on" altogether in such an uproarious manner, that the three Miss Dounces went off on small pensions, he having made the tenement in Cursitor-street too warm to contain them; and in short, comported and demeaned himself in every respect like an unmitigated old Saracen, as he was.

As to his ancient friends, the other old boys, at the Sir Somebody's Head, he dropped off from them by gradual degrees; for, even when he did go there, Jones—vulgar fellow that Jones—persisted in asking "when it was to be?" and "whether he was to have any gloves?" together with other inquiries of an equally offensive nature: at which not only Harris laughed, but Jennings also; so, he cut the two, altogether, and attached himself solely to the blue young lady at the smart oyster-shop.

Now comes the moral of the story—for it has a moral after all. The last-mentioned young lady, having derived sufficient profit and emolument from John Dounce's attachment, not only refused, when matters came to a crisis, to take him for better for worse, but expressly declared, to use her own forcible words, that she "wouldn't have him at no price"; and John Dounce, having lost his old friends, alienated his relations, and rendered himself ridiculous to everybody, made offers successively to a schoolmistress, a landlady, a feminine tobacconist, and a housekeeper; and, being directly rejected by each and every of them, was accepted by his cook, with whom he now lives, a henpecked husband, a melancholy monument of antiquated misery, and a living warning to all uxorious old boys.

GUY DE MAUPASSANT

FROM *BEL AMI*

Translated by Ernest Boyd

AS SOON AS they were alone, Madame de Marelle lowered her voice. "You do not know, but I have a grand scheme, and I have thought of you. This is it. As I dine every week at the Forestiers, I return their hospitality from time to time at some restaurant. I do not like to entertain company at home, my household is not arranged for that, and besides, I do not understand anything about domestic affairs, anything about the kitchen, anything at all. I like to live anyhow. So I entertain them now and then at a restaurant, but it is not very lively when there are only three, and my own acquaintances scarcely go well with them. I tell you all this in order to explain a somewhat irregular invitation. You understand, do you not, that I want you to make one of us on Saturday at the Café Riche, at half-past seven. You know the place?"

He accepted with pleasure, and she went on: "There will be only us four. These little outings are very amusing to us women who are not accustomed to them."

She was wearing a dark brown dress, which showed off the lines of her waist, her hips, her bosom, and her arm in a coquettishly provocative way. Duroy felt confusedly astonished at the lack of harmony between this carefully refined elegance and her evident carelessness as regarded her dwelling. All that clothed her body, all that closely and directly touched her flesh was fine and delicate, but that which surrounded her did not matter to her.

He left her, retaining, as before, the sense of her continued presence in species of hallucination of the senses. And he awaited the day of the dinner with growing impatience.

Having hired, for the second time, a dress suit—his funds not yet allowing him to buy one—he arrived first at the rendezvous, a few minutes before the time. He was ushered up to the second story, and into a small private dining-room hung with red and white, its single window opening into the boulevard. A square table, laid for four, displaying its white cloth, so shining that it seemed to be varnished, and the glasses and the silver glittered brightly in the light of the twelve candles of two tall candelabra. Without was a broad patch of light green, due to the leaves of a tree lit up by the bright light from the dining-rooms.

Duroy sat down on a very low sofa, upholstered in red to match the hangings on the walls. The worn springs yielding beneath him caused him to feel as though sinking into a hole. He heard throughout the huge house a confused murmur, the murmur of a large restaurant, made up of the clattering of glass and silver, the hurried steps of the waiters, deadened by the carpets in the passages, and the opening of doors letting out the sound of voices from the numerous private rooms in which people were dining. Forestier came in and shook hands with him, with a cordial familiarity which he never displayed at the offices of the "Vie Française."

"The ladies are coming together," said he; "these little dinners are very pleasant."

Then he glanced at the table, turned a gas jet that was feebly burning completely off, closed one sash of the window on account of the draught, and chose a sheltered place for himself, with a remark: "I must be careful; I have been better for a month, and now I am queer again these last few days. I must have caught cold on Tuesday, coming out of the theatre."

The door was opened, and, followed by a waiter, the two ladies appeared, veiled, muffled, reserved, with that charmingly mysterious bearing they assume in such places, where the surroundings are suspicious.

As Duroy bowed to Madame Forestier she scolded him for not having come to see her again; then she added with a smile, in the direction of her friend: "I know what it is; you prefer Madame de Marelle, you can find time to visit her."

They sat down to the table, and the waiter having handed the wine card to Forestier, Madame de Marelle exclaimed: "Give these gentlemen whatever they like, but for us iced champagne, the best, sweet champagne, mind—nothing else." And the man having withdrawn, she added with an excited laugh: "I am going to get tight this evening; we will have a spree—a regular spree."

Forestier, who did not seem to have heard, said: "Would you mind the window being closed? My chest has been rather queer the last few days."

"No, not at all."

He pushed the sash that was left open, and returned to his place with a reassured and tranquil countenance. His wife said nothing. Seemingly lost in thought, and with her eyes lowered towards the table, she smiled at the glasses with that vague smile which seemed always to promise and never to grant.

The Ostend oysters were brought in, tiny and plump like little ears enclosed in shells, and melting between the tongue and the palate like salt bonbons. Then, after the soup, was served a trout as rose-tinted as a young girl, and the guests began to talk.

They spoke at first of a current scandal; the story of a lady of position, surprised by one of her husband's friends supping in a private room with a foreign prince. Forestier laughed a great deal at the adventure; the two ladies declared that the indiscreet gossip was nothing less than a blackguard and a coward. Duroy was of their opinion, and loudly proclaimed that it is the duty of a man in these matters, whether he be actor, confidant, or simple spectator, to be silent as the grave. He added: "How full life would be of pleasant things if we could reckon upon the absolute discretion of one another. That which often, almost always, checks women is the fear of the secret being revealed. Come, is it not true?" he continued. "How many are there who would yield to a sudden desire, the caprice of an hour, a passing fancy, did they not fear to pay for a short-lived and fleeting pleasure by an irremediable scandal and painful tears?"

He spoke with catching conviction, as though pleading a cause, his own cause, as though he had said: "It is not with me that one would have to dread such dangers. Try me and see."

They both looked at him approvingly, holding that he spoke rightly and justly, confessing by their friendly silence that their flexible morality as Parisians would not have held out long before the certainty of secrecy. And Forestier, leaning back in his place on the divan, one leg bent under him, and his napkin thrust into his waistcoat, suddenly said with the satisfied laugh of a skeptic: "The deuce! yes, they would all go in for it if they were certain of silence. Poor husbands!"

And they began to talk of love. Without admitting it to be eternal, Duroy understood it as lasting, creating a bond, a tender friendship, a confidence. The union of the senses was only a seal to the union of hearts. But he was angry at the outrageous jealousies, melodramatic scenes, and unpleasantness which almost always accompany ruptures.

When he ceased speaking, Madame de Marelle replied:

"Yes, it is the only pleasant thing in life, and we often spoil it by preposterous unreasonableness."

Madame Forestier, who was toying with her knife, added: "Yes—yes—it is pleasant to be loved."

And she seemed to be carrying her dream further, to be thinking things that she dared not give words to.

As the first *entrée* was slow in coming, they sipped from time to time a mouthful of champagne, and nibbled bits of crust which they broke off the rolls. And the idea of love, entering into them, slowly intoxicated their souls, as the bright wine, rolling drop by drop down their throats, fired their blood and perturbed their minds.

The waiter brought in some lamb cutlets, delicate and tender, upon a thick bed of asparagus tips.

"Ah! this is good," exclaimed Forestier; and they ate slowly, savouring the delicate meat and vegetables as smooth as cream.

Duroy resumed: "For my part, when I love a woman everything else in the world disappears." He said this in a tone of conviction, becoming enthusiastic at the thought of the pleasures of love, while he enjoyed the pleasures of the table.

Madame Forestier murmured, with her air of indifference: "There is no happiness comparable to that of the first handclasp, when the one asks, 'Do you love me?' and the other replies, 'Yes.'"

Madame de Marelle, who had just tossed a fresh glass of champagne off at a draught, said gayly, as she put down her glass: "For my part, I am not so Platonic."

And all began to smile with kindling eyes at these words.

Forestier, stretched out in his seat on the divan, opened his arms, rested them on the cushions, and said in a serious tone: "This frankness does you honour, and proves that you are a practical woman. But may one ask you what is the opinion of Monsieur de Marelle?"

She shrugged her shoulders slightly, with infinite and prolonged disdain; and then in a decided tone remarked: "Monsieur de Marelle has no opinions on this point. He only has—abstentions."

And the conversation, descending from the elevated theories, concerning love, strayed into the flowery garden of refined indecency. It was the moment of clever double meanings; veils raised by words, as petticoats are lifted by the wind; tricks of language; clever disguised audacities; sentences which reveal nude images in covered phrases; which cause the vision of all that may not be said to flit rapidly before the eye and the mind, and allow the well-bred people the enjoyment of a kind of subtle and mysterious love, a species of impure mental contact, due to the simultaneous evocation of secret, shameful, and longed-for pleasures. The roast, consisting of partridges flanked by quails, had been served; then a dish of green peas, and then a terrine of foie gras, accompanied by a curly-leaved salad, filling a salad bowl as though with green foam. They had partaken of all these things without tasting them, without knowing, solely taken up by what they were talking of, plunged as it were in a bath of love.

The two ladies were now going it strong in their remarks. Madame de Marelle, with a native audacity which resembled a direct provocation, and Madame Forestier with a charming reserve, a modesty in her tone, voice, smile, and bearing that underlined while seeming to soften the bold remarks falling from her lips. Forestier, leaning quite back on the cushions, laughed, drank and ate without leaving off, and sometimes threw in a word so risqué or so crude that the ladies, somewhat shocked by its appearance, and for appearance sake, put on a little air of embarrassment that lasted two or three seconds. When he had given vent to something a little too coarse, he added: "You are going ahead nicely, my children. If you go on like that you will end by making fools of yourselves."

Dessert came, and then coffee; and the liqueurs poured a warmer and heavier intoxication into their excited minds.

As she had announced on sitting down to table, Madame de Marelle was intoxicated, and acknowledged it in the lively and graceful chatter of a woman emphasizing, in order to amuse her guests, a very real degree of tipsiness.

Madame Forestier was silent now, perhaps out of prudence, and Duroy, feeling himself too much excited not to be in danger of compromising himself, maintained a prudent reserve.

Cigarettes were lit, and all at once Forestier began to cough. It was a terrible fit, that seemed to tear his chest, and with red face and forehead damp with perspiration, he choked behind his napkin. When the fit was over he growled angrily: "These entertainments are very bad for me; they are ridiculous." All his good humour had vanished before his terror of the illness that haunted his thoughts. "Let us go home," said he.

Madame de Marelle rang for the waiter, and asked for the bill. It was brought almost immediately. She tried to read it, but the figures danced before her eyes, and she passed it to Duroy, saying: "Here, pay for me; I can't see, I am too full."

And at the same time she threw him her purse. The bill amounted to one hundred and thirty francs. Duroy checked it, and then handed over two notes and received back the change, saying in a low tone: "What shall I give the waiter?"

"What you like; I do not know."

He put five francs on the salver, and handed back the purse, saying: "Shall I see you to your door?"

"Certainly. I am incapable of finding my way home."

They shook hands with the Forestiers, and Duroy found himself alone with Madame de Marelle in a cab. He felt her close to him, so close, in this dark box, suddenly lit up for a moment by the lamps on the sidewalk. He felt through his sleeve the warmth of her shoulder, and he could find nothing to say to her, absolutely nothing, his mind being paralyzed by the imperative desire to seize her in his arms.

"If I dared to, what would she do?" he thought. The recollection of all the things uttered during dinner emboldened him, but the fear of scandal restrained him at the same time.

Nor did she say anything either, but remained motionless in her corner. He would have thought that she was asleep if he had not seen her eyes glitter every time that a ray of light entered the carriage.

"What was she thinking?" He felt that he must not speak, that a word, a single word, breaking this silence would destroy his chance; yet courage failed him, the courage needed for abrupt and brutal action. All at once he felt her foot move. She had made a movement, a quick, nervous movement of impatience, perhaps of appeal. This almost imperceptible gesture caused a thrill to run through him from head to foot, and he threw himself upon her, seeking her mouth with his lips, her bare body with his hands.

But the cab having shortly stopped before the house in which she resided, Duroy, surprised, had no time to seek passionate phrases to thank her, and express his grateful love. However, stunned by what had taken place, she did not rise, she did not stir. Then he was afraid that the driver might suspect something, and got out first to help her alight.

At length she got out of the cab, staggering and without

saying a word. He rang the bell, and as the door opened, said, tremblingly: "When shall I see you again?"

She murmured so softly that he scarcely heard it: "Come and lunch with me to-morrow." And she disappeared in the entry, pushed to the heavy door, which closed with a noise like that of a cannon. He gave the driver five francs, and began to walk along with rapid and triumphant steps, and heart overflowing with joy.

He had won at last—a married woman, a lady. How easy and unexpected it had all been. He had fancied up till then that to assail and conquer one of these so greatly longed-for beings, infinite pains, interminable expectations, a skillful siege carried on by means of gallant attentions, words of love, sighs, and gifts were needed. And, lo! suddenly, at the faintest attack, the first whom he had encountered had yielded to him so quickly that he was stupefied at it.

SAKI

TEA

JAMES CUSHAT-PRINKLY was a young man who had always had a settled conviction that one of these days he would marry; up to the age of thirty-four he had done nothing to justify that conviction. He liked and admired a great many women collectively and dispassionately without singling out one for especial matrimonial consideration, just as one might admire the Alps without feeling that one wanted any particular peak as one's own private property. His lack of initiative in this matter aroused a certain amount of impatience among the sentimentally minded women-folk of his home circle; his mother, his sisters, an aunt-in-residence, and two or three intimate matronly friends regarded his dilatory approach to the married state with a disapproval that was far from being inarticulate. His most innocent flirtations were watched with the straining eagerness which a group of unexercised terriers concentrates on the slightest movements of a human being who may be reasonably considered likely to take them for a walk. No decent-souled mortal can long resist the pleading of several pairs of walk-beseeching dog-eyes; James Cushat-Prinkly was not sufficiently obstinate or indifferent to home influences to disregard the obviously expressed wish of his family that he should become enamoured of some nice marriageable girl, and when his Uncle Jules departed this life and bequeathed him a comfortable little legacy it really seemed the correct thing to do to set about discovering some one to share it with him. The process of discovery was carried on more by the force of suggestion and the weight of public opinion than by any initiative of his own; a clear working majority of his female relatives and the aforesaid matronly friends had pitched on Joan Sebastable as the most suitable young woman in his range of acquaintance to whom he might propose marriage, and James became gradually accustomed to the idea that he and Joan would go together through the prescribed stages of congratulations, present-receiving, Norwegian or Mediterranean hotels, and eventual domesticity. It was necessary, however, to ask the lady what she thought about the matter; the family had so far conducted and directed the flirtation with ability and discretion, but the actual proposal would have to be an individual effort.

Cushat-Prinkly walked across the Park towards the Sebastable residence in a frame of mind that was moderately complacent. As the thing was going to be done he was glad to feel that he was going to get it settled and off his mind that afternoon. Proposing marriage, even to a nice girl like Joan, was a rather irksome business, but one could not have a honeymoon in Minorca and a subsequent life of married happiness without such preliminary. He wondered what Minorca was really like as a place to stop in; in his mind's eye it was an island in perpetual half-mourning, with black or white Minorca hens running all over it. Probably it would not be a bit like that when one came to examine it. People who had been in Russia had told him that they did not remember having seen any Muscovy ducks there, so it was possible that there would be no Minorca fowls on the island.

His Mediterranean musings were interrupted by the sound of a clock striking the half-hour. Half-past four. A frown of dissatisfaction settled on his face. He would arrive at the Sebastable mansion just at the hour of afternoon tea.

Joan would be seated at a low table, spread with an array of silver kettles and cream-jugs and delicate porcelain teacups, behind which her voice would tinkle pleasantly in a series of little friendly questions about weak or strong tea, how much, if any, sugar, milk, cream, and so forth. "Is it one lump? I forgot. You do take milk, don't you? Would you like some more hot water, if it's too strong?"

Cushat-Prinkly had read of such things in scores of novels, and hundreds of actual experiences had told him that they were true to life. Thousands of women, at this solemn afternoon hour, were sitting behind dainty porcelain and silver fittings, with their voices tinkling pleasantly in a cascade of solicitous little questions. Cushat-Prinkly detested the whole system of afternoon tea. According to his theory of life a woman should lie on a divan or couch, talking with incomparable charm or looking unutterable thoughts, or merely silent as a thing to be looked on, and from behind a silken curtain a small Nubian page should silently bring in a tray with cups and dainties, to be accepted silently, as a matter of course, without drawn-out chatter about cream and sugar and hot water. If one's soul was really enslaved at one's mistress's feet, how could one talk coherently about weakened tea? Cushat-Prinkly had never expounded his views on the subject to his mother; all her life she had been accustomed to tinkle pleasantly at tea-time behind dainty porcelain and silver, and if he had spoken to her about divans and Nubian pages she would have urged him to take a week's holiday at the seaside. Now, as he passed through a tangle of small streets that led indirectly to the elegant Mayfair terrace for which he was bound, a horror at the idea of confronting Joan Sebastable at her tea-table seized on him. A momentary deliverance presented itself; on one floor of a narrow little house at the noisier end of Esquimault Street lived Rhoda

Ellam, a sort of remote cousin, who made a living by creating hats out of costly materials. The hats really looked as if they had come from Paris; the cheques she got for them unfortunately never looked as if they were going to Paris. However, Rhoda appeared to find life amusing and to have a fairly good time in spite of her straitened circumstances. Cushat-Prinkly decided to climb up to her floor and defer by half-an-hour or so the important business which lay before him; by spinning out his visit he could contrive to reach the Sebastable mansion after the last vestiges of dainty porcelain had been cleared away.

Rhoda welcomed him into a room that seemed to do duty as workshop, sitting-room, and kitchen combined, and to be wonderfully clean and comfortable at the same time.

"I'm having a picnic meal," she announced. "There's caviare in that jar at your elbow. Begin on that brown bread-and-butter while I cut some more. Find yourself a cup; the teapot is behind you. Now tell me about hundreds of things."

She made no other allusion to food, but talked amusingly and made her visitor talk amusingly too. At the same time she cut the bread-and-butter with a masterly skill and produced red pepper and sliced lemon, where so many women would merely have produced reasons and regrets for not having any. Cushat-Prinkly found that he was enjoying an excellent tea without having to answer as many questions about it as a Minister for Agriculture might be called on to reply to during an outbreak of cattle plague.

"And now tell me why you have come to see me," said Rhoda suddenly. "You arouse not merely my curiosity but my business instincts. I hope you've come about hats. I heard that you had come into a legacy the other day, and, of course, it struck me that it would be a beautiful and desirable thing for you to celebrate the event by buying brilliantly expensive hats for all your sisters. They may not have said anything about it, but I feel sure the same idea has occurred to them. Of course, with Goodwood on us, I am rather rushed just now, but in my business we're accustomed to that; we live in a series of rushes—like the infant Moses."

"I didn't come about hats," said her visitor. "In fact, I don't think I really came about anything. I was passing and I just thought I'd look in and see you. Since I've been sitting talking to you, however, a rather important idea has occurred to me. If you'll forget Goodwood for a moment and listen to me, I'll tell you what it is."

Some forty minutes later James Cushat-Prinkly returned to the bosom of his family, bearing an important piece of news.

"I'm engaged to be married," he announced.

A rapturous outbreak of congratulation and self-applause broke out.

"Ah, we knew! We saw it coming! We foretold it weeks ago!"

"I'll bet you didn't," said Cushat-Prinkly. "If any one had told me at lunch-time today that I was going to ask Rhoda Ellam to marry me and that she was going to accept me, I would have laughed at the idea."

The romantic suddenness of the affair in some measure compensated James's women-folk for the ruthless negation of all their patient effort and skilled diplomacy. It was rather trying to have to deflect their enthusiasm at a moment's notice from Joan Sebastable to Rhoda Ellam; but, after all, it was James's wife who was in question, and his tastes had some claim to be considered.

On a September afternoon of the same year, after the honeymoon in Minorca had ended, Cushat-Prinkly came into the drawing-room of his new house in Granchester

Square. Rhoda was seated at a low table, behind a service of dainty porcelain and gleaming silver. There was a pleasant tinkling note in her voice as she handed him a cup.

"You like it weaker than that, don't you? Shall I put some more hot water to it? No?"

M. F. K. FISHER

A KITCHEN ALLEGORY

MRS. QUAYLE WAS an agreeable and reasonable woman —in her private estimation, at least—who finally lived alone after a full life of raising her own and other people's families. Little by little, she slipped or propelled herself into somewhat eccentric habits, especially about eating. To her, no matter what the pattern was at the moment, it seemed logical.

For a time, for instance, since she was alone and could not puzzle anyone but herself, she arose early, made herself two large cups of strong tea, and then floated through the morning on a *far-niente* cloud of theine, which at noon she cut earthward by the equally deliberate absorption of one-quarter pound of raw chopped steak and a few stalks of celery. And so on. There were several other systems, which she followed with a detached fervor and dedication until something new sounded better, although she never really asked either "Better than what?" or "Better *for* what?," being in excellent health.

Once, early in her culinary solitude, there was a period of mashing three ripe bananas with some agar-agar and milk into a pale porridge. Mrs. Quayle did not find out for several years that this was the way she had permanently alienated a close friend, who had had to face her morning consumption of such a chilly mess during a short visit. Her own intrinsic naïveté, Mrs. Quayle decided, was perhaps why people faded out of her life, and why and how, on one weekend, there was a final adieu to her two dearest—her last daughter and small grandson. She would never know whether she offered too much or, on the other hand, too little during those packed, bungled hours.

In her peculiar dietary pattern, it was a gastronomical event to plan for someone else's hunger. By now, she was living on a salutary mishmash of green beans, zucchini, parsley, and celery, which she made once or twice a day in a pressure cooker. She drained the juices from this concoction and drank them when she felt queer, between bowlsful of the main bulk. She believed, temporarily anyway, that she got everything she needed—whatever that was—from this regime, and she lost pounds and felt rather pure and noble. But, in a pseudo-protective flutter, the day before her darling girl was to arrive for what might be a whole weekend, she went marketing in several stores she had long ignored, on a kind of spree.

She bought madly and stupidly, more than could possibly be eaten in a week by five people, in a masochistic flurry of wishful child-feeding. Her daughter was already set in her own paths of behavior, staying slim, abjuring fats-sugars-starches and unobtrusively watching her pocket calorie chart. Mrs. Quayle, who well knew this, bought cartons full of affront to her child's philosophy, so that by the time the little family was together there was a newly dusted cookie jar full of strange rich temptations, all loaded with butter and sweetness; there was bread for toast, which she herself had not eaten for months; marmalade and strawberry preserves were ready to the hand. In the crammed icebox, there were bowls of freshly chopped beef, prawns cooked correctly (which is to say in the *family* fashion) and peeled and ready, fresh mayonnaise, and far at the back a lost bowl of her own mashed vegetables. Clean lettuces lay ready in the crisping drawers. Did the girl want coffee overroast, freshly ground, decaffeinized, powdered? It was in the cupboard. There was milk, both homogenized and "slim." There were pounds of sweet butter, of course. And on the sideboard there were bananas and papayas and lemons and tangelos for the dear little boy. There was a box of Russian mints. There were little new pink potatoes to cook in their luminous skins. There was some really fine garden-green asparagus, which Mrs. Quayle's daughter used to love, and then a block of excellent Teleme Jack cheese—something of a rarity. There were fresh bright strawberries in a bowl, ready to be washed at the last minute, but in case the girl's old passion for tapioca pudding still waxed, four little Chinese bowls of it were ready, too, and a couple of bottles of white wine, the favorite ones, and a Grignolino on the counter when the time came for a *bœuf tartare* or a grilled hamburger. And in the freezer ...

The whole thing was sad. What was Mrs. Quayle asking for? Whatever it was, she got it.

The bus arrived with the two beautiful young creatures on it, and then, after some communal intercourse or at least exchange of quiet talk, but not a great deal—perhaps six hours of it—the bus went off again, and the mother walked home and there was all that food, and although she knew that two people had been there, she could see little sign of it. In the icebox, the bowls of everything still sat. All the fruit, except maybe one banana, ripened subtly upon the sideboard. Once more, guests had come and gone, this time a last beloved child and her son, but often before a lover, a fiendish enemy, a mother, someone needed. They, too, had vanished, long before Mrs. Quayle meant them to. It was bewildering to her as she sat listening to the icebox that hummed in the kitchen. She wondered what started the whole business. How did it end? What did she want for supper?

She heard again the bus whining off into the dark, and saw through its blue window glass the tiny hand, like a sea anemone, of her grandson. Behind him, a more earthly flower, was her dear child, the purposeful shadow of a fine relationship. "Until soon," she called into the glass. They made mouths back at her, compassionately. And then she returned to the confrontation with her stores of unwanted, uneaten, unneeded nourishment. She had bought them willfully. They would rot. Her girl had found the half-hidden bowl of mashed green vegetables, and eaten it with voluptuous fuss about its rare fresh taste, its good feeling within her. But the rest of the provender must be destroyed, before it could hurt other people with its quick sly decay. And Mrs. Quayle herself would return to her mishmash three times a day and the greenish broth between meals, and forget the finality of her adieus, for as if her bones were steel cold she acknowledged that the girl was leaving with the baby to join life again, far away, where other things would feed her.

The suddenly very old-feeling woman went to the kitchen to clean it out, to ready the dead supplies for the morning's collection of refuse, to make herself a pot of vegetables and go to bed with a warm stomach and copies of *John O'London's* and *Vogue*. Instead, she made a little drink first, and then, without paying any attention, she started the water for her special way of making asparagus on toast, somewhat intricate but worth the bother, and a meal in itself. She opened the bottle of Folle Blanche, and put it back in the icebox to wait until she finished her gin-and-It, and then set a place nicely at the kitchen table, with two wineglasses in case she wanted a little Grignolino after the white. She made a salad from the hearts of the lettuces she had cleaned. (She loved the hearts best, but most of her life had given them to other people because they did, too, and they were dependent on her.)

Then she deftly put together a *bœuf tartare* as she had done for a thousand years. She would boil some of the little potatoes tomorrow, or perhaps tonight to eat cold. ... All the time, she was thinking in a frozen way about saying goodbye ... goodbyes.

As she chopped herbs and sliced asparagus and poured boiling water and added the magic dash of brandy to the mixed soft meat, she kept thinking, but not in a frantic way at all, about never seeing two more people again. She wondered with strange calm why her child had not told her before that they were going away, flying to a far land and a new life with a new husband. She felt sorry that they had been so hurried, almost evasive. It was odd: all she wanted to do was make them full of her love, her food, but they could not swallow it. Even the tiny boy ate almost nothing. Her girl drank tea, and smoked many cigarettes, and did not really look at her.

Mrs. Quayle smiled a little, recognizing that she seemed to have absorbed some of the passive detachment of the past hours and that it felt good. She went through the routine movements of boiling the asparagus three-times-three, an old trick, and all the little saucepans and pots were at their right temperatures on the bright stove. A plate arranged almost correctly in the Japanese style was at her place on the table, with five prawns, three halves of green olives, and a curl of celery upon it to amuse her. The *bœuf tartare*, bound with olive oil and seasoning, with the yolk of an egg in its half shell on top like a jaundiced eye, waited on the sideboard. There was buttered toast in the warm oven, for the asparagus. Mrs. Quayle poured Folle Blanche for the shrimps, and opened the Grignolino for the meat, perhaps between the two cold courses? And then there were the little puddings, still four of them—the ones her last girl had always loved. Or perhaps a bowl of cool strawberries? Later, she would make coffee, and eat one of the candies, a tricky little block of mint and black chocolate.

She thought that she would sit a long time at the table. There was no reason not to. There was nobody wanting to get up early in the morning except herself, and *she* did not want to, truthfully. There was nobody in the house with measles or a cold, to be listened for or to hear *her*. There was, in fact, nobody to cook for, not even herself. In all this facing of the situation, she did not feel any self-pity, which was a proof of something—perhaps her wisdom, or at least her sense of self-preservation.

Suddenly she wondered with real violence, like walking head on into a closed door in the dark, why her girl had not told her before about that new marriage and that new man and that leaving. It seemed very selfish. Mrs. Quayle permitted herself a few seconds of anger, and then she looked at the nicely set table and the simmering things on the stove, and she listened to the icebox humming to keep the other supplies dormant, and she decided, without further thought or doubt, to turn off the whole silly business and go to bed. This is what she did, in almost no time at all.

In the morning, after a good peaceful sleep except for one small dream about an anemone waving this way and that way in blue water and then turning into a mouth that wanted to eat her, she made herself a pressure cooker full of mishmash, salvaged most of the unused food to take to friends who were getting too stiff to do their own marketing, and read a new book about a system to hold off the aging process, or arthritis or cancer or almost anything, by the use of iodides in the diet. She must get some Japanese seaweed, she thought—go to the *natural* sources for her strengths in the battle.

ISAAC BASHEVIS SINGER
SHORT FRIDAY

IN THE VILLAGE of Lapschitz lived a tailor named Shmul-Leibele with his wife, Shoshe. Shmul-Leibele was half tailor, half furrier, and a complete pauper. He had never mastered his trade. When filling an order for a jacket or a gaberdine, he inevitably made the garment either too short or too tight. The belt in the back would hang either too high or too low, the lapels never matched, the vent was off center. It was said that he had once sewn a pair of trousers with the fly off to one side. Shmul-Leibele could not count the wealthy citizens among his customers. Common people brought him their shabby garments to have patched and turned, and the peasants gave him their old pelts to reverse. As is usual with bunglers, he was also slow. He would dawdle over a garment for weeks at a time. Yet despite his shortcomings, it must be said that Shmul-Leibele was an honorable man. He used only strong thread and none of his seams ever gave. If one ordered a lining from Shmul-Leibele, even one of common sackcloth or cotton, he bought only the very best material, and thus lost most of his profit. Unlike other tailors who hoarded every last bit of remaining cloth, he returned all scraps to his customers.

Had it not been for his competent wife, Shmul-Leibele would certainly have starved to death. Shoshe helped him in whatever way she could. On Thursdays she hired herself out to wealthy families to knead dough, and on summer days went off to the forest to gather berries and mushrooms, as well as pinecones and twigs for the stove. In winter she plucked down for brides' featherbeds. She was also a better tailor than her husband, and when he began to sigh, or dally and mumble to himself, an indication that he could no longer muddle through, she would take the chalk from his hand and show him how to continue. Shoshe had no children, but it was common knowledge that it wasn't she who was barren, but rather her husband who was sterile, since all of her sisters had borne children, while his only brother was likewise childless. The townswomen repeatedly urged Shoshe to divorce him, but she turned a deaf ear, for the couple loved one another with a great love.

Shmul-Leibele was small and clumsy. His hands and feet were too large for his body, and his forehead bulged on either side as is common in simpletons. His cheeks, red as apples, were bare of whiskers, and but a few hairs sprouted from his chin. He had scarcely any neck at all; his head sat upon his shoulders like a snowman's. When he walked, he scraped his shoes along the ground so that every step could be heard far away. He hummed continuously and there was always an amiable smile on his face. Both winter and summer he wore the same caftan and sheepskin cap with earlaps. Whenever there was any need for a messenger, it was always Shmul-Leibele who was pressed into service, and however far away he was sent, he always went willingly. The wags saddled him with a variety of nicknames and made him the butt of all sorts of pranks, but he never took offense. When others scolded his tormentors, he would merely observe: "What do I care? Let them have their fun. They're only children, after all. . . ."

Sometimes he would present one or another of the mischief makers with a piece of candy or a nut. This he did without any ulterior motive, but simply out of goodheartedness.

Shoshe towered over him by a head. In her younger days she had been considered a beauty, and in the households where she worked as a servant they spoke highly of her honesty and diligence. Many young men had vied for her hand, but she had selected Shmul-Leibele because he was quiet and because he never joined the other town boys who gathered on the Lublin road at noon Saturdays to flirt with the girls. His piety and retiring nature pleased her. Even as a girl Shoshe had taken pleasure in studying the Pentateuch, in nursing the infirm at the almshouse, in listening to the tales of the old women who sat before their houses darning stockings. She would fast on the last day of each month, the Minor Day of Atonement, and often attended the services at the women's synagogue. The other servant girls mocked her and thought her old-fashioned. Immediately following her wedding she shaved her head and fastened a kerchief firmly over her ears, never permitting a stray strand of hair from her matron's wig to show as did some of the other young women. The bath attendant praised her because she never frolicked at the ritual bath, but performed her ablutions according to the laws. She purchased only indisputably kosher meat, though it was a half-cent more per pound, and when she was in doubt about the dietary laws she sought out the rabbi's advice. More than once she had not hesitated to throw out all the food and even to smash the earthen crockery. In short, she was a capable, God-fearing woman, and more than one man envied Shmul-Leibele his jewel of a wife.

Above all of life's blessings the couple revered the Sabbath. Every Friday noon Shmul-Leibele would lay aside his tools and cease all work. He was always among the first at the ritual bath, and he immersed himself in the water four times for the four letters of the Holy Name. He also helped the beadle set the candles in the chandeliers and the candelabra. Shoshe scrimped throughout the week, but on the Sabbath she was lavish. Into the heated oven went cakes, cookies and the Sabbath loaf. In winter, she prepared puddings made of chicken's neck stuffed with dough and rendered fat. In summer she made puddings with rice or noodles, greased with chicken fat and sprinkled with sugar or cinnamon. The main dish consisted of potatoes and buckwheat, or pearl barley with beans, in the midst of which she never failed to set a marrowbone. To insure that the dish would be well cooked, she sealed the oven with loose dough. Shmul-Leibele treasured every mouthful, and at every Sabbath meal he would remark: "Ah, Shoshe love, it's food fit for a king! Nothing less than a taste of Paradise!" to which Shoshe replied, "Eat hearty. May it bring you good health."

Although Shmul-Leibele was a poor scholar, unable to memorize a chapter of the Mishnah, he was well versed in all the laws. He and his wife frequently studied *The Good Heart* in Yiddish. On half-holidays, holidays and on each free day, he studied the Bible in Yiddish. He never missed a sermon, and though a pauper, he bought from peddlers all sorts of books of moral instructions and religious tales, which he then read together with his wife. He never wearied of reciting sacred phrases. As soon as he arose in the morning he washed his hands and began to mouth the preamble to the prayers. Then he would walk over to the study house and worship as one of the quorum. Every day he recited a few chapters of the Psalms, as well as those prayers which the less serious tended to skip over. From his father he had inherited a thick prayer book with wooden covers, which contained the rites and laws pertaining to each day of the year. Shmul-Leibele and his wife heeded each and every one of these. Often he would observe to his wife: "I shall surely end up in Gehenna, since there'll be no one on earth to say Kaddish over me."

"Bite your tongue, Shmul-Leibele," she would counter. "For one, everything is possible under God. Secondly, you'll live until the Messiah comes. Thirdly, it's just possible that I will die before you and you will marry a young woman who'll bear you a dozen children." When Shoshe said this, Shmul-Leibele would shout: "God forbid! You must remain in good health. I'd rather rot in Gehenna!"

Although Shmul-Leibele and Shoshe relished every Sabbath, their greatest satisfaction came from the Sabbaths in wintertime. Since the day before the Sabbath evening was a short one, and since Shoshe was busy until late Thursday at her work, the couple usually stayed up all of Thursday night. Shoshe kneaded dough in the trough, covering it with cloth and a pillow so that it might ferment. She heated the oven with kindling-wood and dry twigs. The shutters in the room were kept closed, the door shut. The bed and bench-bed remained unmade, for at daybreak the couple would take a nap. As long as it was dark Shoshe prepared the Sabbath meal by the light of a candle. She plucked a chicken or a goose (if she had managed to come by one cheaply), soaked it, salted it and scraped the fat from it. She roasted a liver for Shmul-Leibele over the glowing coals and baked a small Sabbath loaf for him. Occasionally she would inscribe her name upon the loaf with letters of dough, and then Shmul-Leibele would tease her: "Shoshe, I am eating you up. Shoshe, I have already swallowed you." Shmul-Leibele loved warmth, and he would climb up on the oven and from there look down as his spouse cooked, baked, washed, rinsed, pounded and carved. The Sabbath loaf would turn out round and brown. Shoshe braided the loaf so swiftly that it seemed to dance before Shmul-Leibele's eyes. She bustled about efficiently with spatulas, pokers, ladles and goosewing dusters, and at times even snatched up a live coal with her bare fingers. The pots perked and bubbled. Occasionally a drop of soup would spill and the hot tin would hiss and squeal. And all the while the cricket continued its chirping. Although Shmul-Leibele had finished his supper by this time, his appetite would be whetted afresh, and Shoshe would throw him a knish, a chicken gizzard, a cookie, a plum from the plum stew or a chunk of the pot-roast. At the same time she would chide him, saying that he was a glutton. When he attempted to defend himself she would cry: "Oh, the sin is upon me, I have allowed you to starve. . . ."

At dawn they would both lie down in utter exhaustion. But because of their efforts Shoshe would not have to run herself ragged the following day, and she could make the benediction over the candles a quarter of an hour before sunset.

The Friday on which this story took place was the shortest Friday of the year. Outside, the snow had been falling all night and had blanketed the house up to the windows and barricaded the door. As usual, the couple had stayed up until morning, then had lain down to sleep. They had arisen later than usual, for they hadn't heard the rooster's crow, and since the windows were covered with snow and frost, the day seemed as dark as night. After whispering, "I thank Thee," Shmul-Leibele went outside with a broom and shovel to clear a path, after which he took a bucket and fetched water from the well. Then, as he had no pressing work, he decided to lay off for the whole day. He went to the study house for the morning prayers, and after breakfast wended his way to the bathhouse. Because of the cold outside, the patrons kept up an eternal plaint: "A bucket! A bucket!" and the bath attendant poured more and more water over the glowing stones so that the steam grew constantly denser. Shmul-Leibele located a scraggly willow-broom, mounted to the highest bench and whipped himself until his skin glowed red. From the bathhouse, he hurried over to the study house where the beadle had already swept and sprinkled the floor with sand. Shmul-Leibele set the candles and helped spread the tablecloths over the tables. Then he went home again and changed into his Sabbath clothes. His boots, resoled but a few days before, no longer let the wet through. Shoshe had done her washing for the week, and had given him a fresh shirt, underdrawers, a fringed garment, even a clean pair of stockings. She had already performed the benediction over the candles, and the spirit of the Sabbath emanated from every corner of the room. She was wearing her silk kerchief with the silver spangles, a yellow-and-gray dress, and shoes with gleaming, pointed tips. On her throat hung the chain that Shmul-Leibele's mother, peace be with her, had given her to celebrate the signing of the wedding contract. The marriage band sparkled on her index finger. The candlelight reflected in the window panes, and Shmul-Leibele fancied that there was a duplicate of this room outside and that another Shoshe was out there lighting the Sabbath candles. He yearned to tell his wife how full of grace she was, but there was no time for it, since it is specifically stated in the prayer book that it is fitting and proper to be amongst the first ten worshipers at the synagogue; as it so happened, going off to prayers he was the tenth man to arrive. After the congregation had intoned the Song of Songs, the cantor sang, "Give thanks," and "O come, let us exult." Shmul-Leibele prayed with fervor. The words were sweet upon his tongue, they seemed to fall from his lips with a life of their own, and he felt that they soared to the eastern wall, rose above the embroidered curtain of the Holy Ark, the gilded lions, and the tablets, and floated up to the ceiling with its painting of the twelve constellations. From there, the prayers surely ascended to the Throne of Glory.

The cantor chanted, "Come, my beloved," and Shmul-Leibele trumpeted along in accompaniment. Then came the prayers, and the men recited "It is our duty to praise ... " to which Shmul-Leibele added a "Lord of the Universe." Afterwards, he wished everyone a good Sabbath: the rabbi, the ritual slaughterer, the head of the community, the assistant rabbi, everyone present. The *cheder* lads shouted, "Good Sabbath, Shmul-Leibele," while they mocked him with gestures and grimaces, but Shmul-Leibele answered them all with a smile, even occasionally pinched a boy's cheek affectionately. Then he was off for home. The snow was piled high so that one could barely make out the contours of the roofs, as if the entire settlement had been immersed in white. The sky, which had hung low and overcast all day, now grew clear. From among white clouds a full moon peered down, casting a daylike brilliance over the snow. In the west, the edge of a cloud still held the glint of sunset. The stars on this Friday seemed larger and sharper, and through some miracle Lapschitz seemed to have blended with the sky. Shmul-Leibele's hut, which was situated not far from the synagogue, now hung suspended in space, as it is written: "He suspendeth the earth on nothingness." Shmul-Leibele walked slowly since, according to law, one must not hurry when coming from a holy place. Yet he longed to be home. "Who knows?" he thought. "Perhaps Shoshe has become ill? Maybe she's gone to fetch water and, God forbid, has fallen into the well? Heaven save us, what a lot of troubles can befall a man."

On the threshold he stamped his feet to shake off the snow, then opened the door and saw Shoshe. The room made him think of Paradise. The oven had been freshly whitewashed, the candles in the brass candelabras cast a Sabbath glow. The aromas coming from the sealed oven blended with the scents of the Sabbath supper. Shoshe sat on the bench-bed apparently awaiting him, her cheeks shining with the freshness of a young girl's. Shmul-Leibele wished her a happy Sabbath and she in turn wished him a good year. He began to hum, "Peace upon ye minstering angels ... " and after he had said his farewells to the invisible angels that accompany each Jew leaving the synagogue, he recited: "That worthy woman." How well he understood the meaning of these words, for he had read them often in Yiddish, and each time reflected anew on how aptly they seemed to fit Shoshe.

Shoshe was aware that these holy sentences were being said in her honor, and thought to herself, "Here am I, a simple woman, an orphan, and yet God has chosen to bless me with a devoted husband who praises me in the holy tongue."

Both of them had eaten sparingly during the day so that they would have an appetite for the Sabbath meal. Shmul-Leibele said the benediction over the raisin wine and gave Shoshe the cup so that she might drink. Afterwards, he rinsed his fingers from a tin dipper, then she washed hers, and they both dried their hands with a single towel, each at either end. Shmul-Leibele lifted the Sabbath loaf and cut it with the bread knife, a slice for himself and one for his wife.

He immediately informed her that the loaf was just right, and she countered: "Go on, you say that every Sabbath."

"But it happens to be the truth," he replied.

Although it was hard to obtain fish during the cold weather, Shoshe had purchased three-fourths of a pound of pike from the fishmonger. She had chopped it with onions, added an egg, salt and pepper and cooked it with carrots and parsley. It took Shmul-Leibele's breath away, and after it he had to drink a tumbler of whiskey. When he began the table chants, Shoshe accompanied him quietly. Then came the chicken soup with noodles and tiny circlets of fat which glowed on the surface like golden ducats. Between the soup and the main course, Shmul-Leibele again sang Sabbath hymns. Since goose was cheap at this time of year, Shoshe gave Shmul-Leibele an extra leg for good measure. After the dessert, Shmul-Leibele washed for the last time and made a benediction. When he came to the words: "Let us not be in need either of the gifts of flesh and blood nor of their loans," he rolled his eyes upward and brandished his fists. He never stopped praying that he be allowed to continue to earn his own livelihood and not, God forbid, become an object of charity.

After grace, he said yet another chapter of the Mishnah, and all sorts of other prayers which were found in his large prayer book. Then he sat down to read the weekly portion of the Pentateuch twice in Hebrew and once in Aramaic. He enunciated every word and took care to make no mistake in the difficult Aramaic paragraphs of the Onkelos. When he reached the last section, he began to yawn and tears gathered in his eyes. Utter exhaustion overcame him. He could barely keep his eyes open and between one passage and the next he dozed off for a second or two. When Shoshe noticed this, she made up the bench-bed for him and prepared her own featherbed with clean sheets. Shmul-Leibele barely managed to say the retiring prayers and began to undress. When he was already lying on his bench-bed he said: "A good Sabbath, my pious wife. I am very tired. . . ." and turning to the wall, he promptly began to snore.

Shoshe sat a while longer gazing at the Sabbath candles

which had already begun to smoke and flicker. Before getting into bed, she placed a pitcher of water and a basin at Shmul-Leibele's bedstead so that he would not rise the following morning without water to wash with. Then she, too, lay down and fell asleep.

They had slept an hour or two or possibly three—what does it matter, actually?—when suddenly Shoshe heard Shmul-Leibele's voice. He waked her and whispered her name. She opened one eye and asked, "What is it?"

"Are you clean?" he mumbled.

She thought for a moment and replied, "Yes."

He rose and came to her. Presently he was in bed with her. A desire for her flesh had roused him. His heart pounded rapidly, the blood coursed in his veins. He felt a pressure in his loins. His urge was to mate with her immediately, but he remembered the law which admonished a man not to copulate with a woman until he had first spoken affectionately to her, and he now began to speak of his love for her and how this mating could possibly result in a male child.

"And a girl you wouldn't accept?" Shoshe chided him, and he replied, "Whatever God deigns to bestow would be welcome."

"I fear this privilege isn't mine anymore," she said with a sigh.

"Why not?" he demanded. "Our mother Sarah was far older than you."

"How can one compare oneself to Sarah? Far better you divorce me and marry another."

He interrupted her, stopping her mouth with his hand. "Were I sure that I could sire the twelve tribes of Israel with another, I still would not leave you. I cannot even imagine myself with another woman. You are the jewel of my crown."

"And what if I were to die?" she asked.

"God forbid! I would simply perish from sorrow. They would bury us both on the same day."

"Don't speak blasphemy. May you outlive my bones. You are a man. You would find somebody else. But what would I do without you?"

He wanted to answer her, but she sealed his lips with a kiss. He went to her then. He loved her body. Each time she gave herself to him, the wonder of it astonished him anew. How was it possible, he would think, that he, Shmul-Leibele, should have such a treasure all to himself? He knew the law, one dared not surrender to lust for pleasure. But somewhere in a sacred book he had read that it was permissible to kiss and embrace a wife to whom one had been wed according to the laws of Moses and Israel, and he now caressed her face, her throat and her breasts. She warned him that this was frivolity. He replied, "So I'll lie on the torture rack. The great saints also loved their wives." Nevertheless, he promised himself to attend to ritual bath the following morning, to intone psalms and to pledge a sum to charity. Since she loved him also and enjoyed his caresses, she let him do his will.

After he had satiated his desire, he wanted to return to his own bed, but a heavy sleepiness came over him. He felt a pain in his temples. Shoshe's head ached as well. She suddenly said, "I'm afraid something is burning in the oven. Maybe I should open the flue?"

"Go on, you're imagining it," he replied. "It'll become too cold in here."

And so complete was his weariness that he fell asleep, as did she.

That night Shmul-Leibele suffered an eerie dream. He imagined that he had passed away. The Burial-Society brethren came by, picked him up, lit candles by his head, opened the windows, intoned the prayer to justify God's ordainment. Afterwards, they washed him on the ablution board, carried him on a stretcher to the cemetery. There they buried him as the gravedigger said Kaddish over his body.

"That's odd," he thought, "I hear nothing of Shoshe lamenting or begging forgiveness. Is it possible that she would so quickly grow unfaithful? Or has she, God forbid, been overcome by grief?"

He wanted to call her name, but he was unable to. He tried to tear free of the grave, but his limbs were powerless. All of a sudden he awoke.

"What a horrible nightmare!" he thought. "I hope I come out of it all right."

At that moment Shoshe also awoke. When he related his dream to her, she did not speak for a while. Then she said, "Woe is me. I had the very same dream."

"Really? You too?" asked Shmul-Leibele, now frightened. "This I don't like."

He tried to sit up, but he could not. It was as if he had been shorn of all his strength. He looked towards the window to see if it were day already, but there was no window visible, nor any window pane. Darkness loomed everywhere. He cocked his ears. Usually, he would be able to hear the chirping of a cricket, the scurrying of a mouse, but this time only a dead silence prevailed. He wanted to reach out to Shoshe, but his hand seemed lifeless.

"Shoshe," he said quietly. "I've grown paralyzed."

"Woe is me, so have I," she said. "I cannot move a limb."

They lay there for a long while, silently, feeling their numbness. Then Shoshe spoke: "I fear that we are already in our graves for good."

"I'm afraid you're right," Shmul-Leibele replied in a voice that was not of the living.

"Pity me, when did it happen? How?" Shoshe asked. "After all, we went to sleep hale and hearty."

"We must have been asphyxiated by the fumes from the stove," Shmul-Leibele said.

"But I said I wanted to open the flue."

"Well, it's too late for that now."

"God have mercy upon us, what do we do now? We were still young people . . . ."

"It's no use. Apparently it was fated."

"Why? We arranged a proper Sabbath. I prepared such a tasty meal. An entire chicken neck and tripe."

"We have no further need of food."

Shoshe did not immediately reply. She was trying to sense her own entrails. No, she felt no appetite. Not even for a chicken neck and tripe. She wanted to weep, but she could not.

"Shmul-Leibele, they've buried us already. It's all over."

"Yes, Shoshe, praised be the true Judge! We are in God's hands."

"Will you be able to recite the passage attributed to your name before the Angel Dumah?"

"Yes."

"It's good that we are lying side by side," she muttered.

"Yes, Shoshe," he said, recalling a verse: *Lovely and pleasant in their lives, and in their death they were not divided.*

"And what will become of our hut? You did not even leave a will."

"It will undoubtedly go to your sister."

Shoshe wished to ask something else, but she was ashamed. She was curious about the Sabbath meal. Had it been removed from the oven? Who had eaten it? But she felt that such a query would not be fitting of a corpse. She was no longer Shoshe the dough-kneader, but a pure, shrouded corpse with shards covering her eyes, a cowl over her head and myrtle twigs between her fingers. The Angel Dumah would appear at any moment with his fiery staff, and she would have to be ready to give an account of herself.

Yes, the brief years of turmoil and temptation had come to an end. Shmul-Leibele and Shoshe had reached the true world. Man and wife grew silent. In the stillness they heard the flapping of wings, a quiet singing. An angel of God had come to guide Shmul-Leibele the tailor and his wife, Shoshe, into Paradise.

NORA EPHRON

POTATOES AND LOVE

From *Heartburn*

The beginning

I HAVE FRIENDS who begin with pasta, and friends who begin with rice, but whenever I fall in love, I begin with potatoes. Sometimes meat and potatoes and sometimes fish and potatoes, but always potatoes. I have made a lot of mistakes falling in love, and regretted most of them, but never the potatoes that went with them.

Not just any potato will do when it comes to love. There are people who go on about the virtues of plain potatoes—plain boiled new potatoes with a little parsley or dill, or plain baked potatoes with crackling skins—but my own feeling is that a taste for plain potatoes coincides with cultural antecedents I do not possess, and that in any case, the time for plain potatoes—if there is ever a time for plain potatoes—is never at the beginning of something. It is also, I should add, never at the end of something. Perhaps you can get away with plain potatoes in the middle, although I have never been able to.

All right, then: I am talking about crisp potatoes. Crisp potatoes require an immense amount of labor. It's not just the peeling, which is one of the few kitchen chores no electric device has been invented to alleviate; it's also that the potatoes, once peeled, must be cut into whatever shape you intend them to be, put into water to be systematically prevented from turning a loathsome shade of bluish-brownish-black, and then meticulously dried to ensure that they crisp properly. All this takes time, and time, as any fool can tell you, is what true romance is about. In fact, one of the main reasons why you must make crisp potatoes in the beginning is that if you don't make them in the beginning, you never will. I'm sorry to be so cynical about this, but that's the truth.

There are two kinds of crisp potatoes that I prefer above all others. The first are called Swiss potatoes, and they're essentially a large potato pancake of perfect hash browns; the flipping of the pancake is so wildly dramatic that the potatoes themselves are almost beside the point. The second are called potatoes Anna; they are thin circles of potato cooked in a shallow pan in the oven and then turned onto a plate in a darling mound of crunchy brownness. Potatoes Anna is a classic French recipe, but there is something so homely and old-fashioned about them that they can usually be passed off as either an ancient family recipe or something you just made up.

For Swiss potatoes: Peel 3 large (or 4 small) russet potatoes (or all-purpose if you can't get russets) and put them in cold water to cover. Start 4 tablespoons butter and 1 tablespoon cooking oil melting in a nice heavy large frying pan. Working quickly, dry the potatoes and grate them on the grating disk of the Cuisinart. Put them into a colander and squeeze out as much water as you can. Then dry them again on paper towels. You will need more paper towels to do this than you ever thought possible. Dump the potatoes into the frying pan, patting them down with a spatula, and cook over medium heat for about 15 minutes, until the bottom of the pancake is brown. Then, while someone is watching, loosen the pancake and, with one incredibly deft motion, flip it over. Salt it generously. Cook 5 minutes more. Serves two.

For potatoes Anna: Peel 3 large (or 4 small) russet potatoes (or Idahos if you can't get russets) and put them in water. Working quickly, dry each potato and slice into 1/16-inch rounds. Dry them with paper towels, round by round. Put 1 tablespoon clarified butter into a cast-iron skillet and line the skillet with overlapping potatoes. Dribble clarified butter and salt and pepper over them. Repeat twice. Put into a 425° oven for 45 minutes, pressing the potatoes down now and then. Then turn up the oven to 500° and cook 10 more minutes. Flip onto a round platter. Serves two.

The middle (I)

One day the inevitable happens. I go to the potato drawer to make potatoes and discover that the little brown buggers I bought in a large sack a few weeks earlier have gotten soft and mushy and are sprouting long and quite uninteresting vines. In addition, one of them seems to have developed an odd brown leak, and the odd brown leak appears to be the cause of a terrible odor that in only a few seconds has permeated the entire kitchen. I throw out the potatoes and look in the cupboard for a box of pasta. This is the moment when the beginning ends and the middle begins.

The middle (II)

Sometimes, when a loved one announces that he has decided to go on a low-carbohydrate, low-fat, low-salt diet (thus ruling out the possibility of potatoes, should you have been so inclined), he is signaling that the middle is ending and the end is beginning.

The end

In the end, I always want potatoes. Mashed potatoes. Nothing like mashed potatoes when you're feeling blue.

Nothing like getting into bed with a bowl of hot mashed potatoes already loaded with butter, and methodically adding a thin cold slice of butter to every forkful. The problem with mashed potatoes, though, is that they require almost as much hard work as crisp potatoes, and when you're feeling blue the last thing you feel like is hard work. Of course, you can always get someone to make the mashed potatoes for you, but let's face it: the reason you're blue is that there *isn't* anyone to make them for you. As a result, most people do not have nearly enough mashed potatoes in their lives, and when they do, it's almost always at the wrong time.

(You can, of course, train children to mash potatoes, but you should know that Richard Nixon spent most of his childhood making mashed potatoes for his mother and was extremely methodical about getting the lumps out. A few lumps make mashed potatoes more authentic, if you ask me, but that's not the point. The point is that perhaps children should not be trained to mash potatoes.)

For mashed potatoes: Put 1 large (or 2 small) potatoes in a large pot of salted water and bring to a boil. Lower the heat and simmer for at least 20 minutes, until tender. Drain and place the potatoes back in the pot and shake over low heat to eliminate excess moisture. Peel. Put through a potato ricer and immediately add 1 tablespoon heavy cream and as much melted butter and salt and pepper as you feel like. Eat immediately. Serves one.

LARA VAPNYAR

A BUNCH OF BROCCOLI ON THE THIRD SHELF

"ANOTHER ONE, SEDUCED and abandoned," Nina's husband said, pulling a bunch of wilted broccoli from the refrigerator shelf. He held it with two fingers as if it stank, his handsome face scrunched in a grimace of disgust.

It doesn't stink, Nina thought. She blushed and hurried to take the broccoli—to throw it into the garbage. It isn't fresh, but you can't say that it stinks. She didn't say these thoughts aloud. She said she was sorry, she was busy all week and didn't have time for cooking. Nina worked in Manhattan. By the time she came home to Brooklyn, it was already seven thirty, sometimes eight, and she felt too tired to cook. The most she could do was fix a sandwich for her husband and herself or boil some meat dumplings from a Russian food store.

"Yes, I know," her husband said. "But why buy all these vegetables if you know you won't have time to cook them?" Nina shrugged. She liked shopping for vegetables.

Nina couldn't say when she'd first begun the habit of shopping for vegetables. Probably two years earlier, on her second day in America, when she and her husband left her sister's Brooklyn apartment to explore the nearest shopping street. Her sister, who'd lived in America for fourteen years, called herself an American. She thought Nina would be impatient to see everything. "Go, go," her sister said. "But don't buy anything. To survive in America, there are two rules you have to remember. First: Never buy anything in expensive stores unless they have a fifty-percent-off sale. Second: Never *ever* buy anything in cheap stores."

On the street with the unimaginative name Avenue M, they walked through narrow stores that all looked alike to Nina, no matter what they sold: food, electronics, clothes, or hardware. After a while, it seemed that they were walking in and out of the same store over and over, just to hear the chime of its bell. The February morning was cold, and the sunlight was pale. Nina hid her reddened nose in the fur collar of her Russian coat. She clutched her husband's elbow and carefully stepped over piles of garbage, reluctant to look up or sideways at the ashen sky or the motley signs of the shops. She felt dizzy and a little nauseated from the flight and the all-night talk with her sister. Only one place attracted her attention: a small Korean grocery with fruits and vegetables set outside on plywood stands—colorful piles of oranges, tomatoes, and cucumbers, almost unnaturally clean and bright. Nina read the sign on the box of tomatoes: SUNRIPE. She was still learning English, and every new expression seemed exciting and full of great meaning. SUNRIPE brought to mind a vegetable patch on a summer afternoon, the smell of the rich soil heated by the sun, pale-green branches sagging under heavy tomatoes bursting with juice. SUNRIPE reminded her of her family's tiny vegetable garden when she was little. Nina wanted to touch the tomatoes in the box, hoping that their surface would still be a little warm from all the sun that shined on them while they ripened. She was reaching for one when her husband dragged her away to another store.

Now Nina shopped alone for vegetables every Saturday morning while her husband slept late. Nina drove to 86th Street to visit the Korean and Russian vegetables stores between 22nd and 23rd avenues. The assortment in the stores was generally the same, but Nina liked to explore each of them, hoping to find something surprising, such as the occasional white asparagus, or plastic baskets of gooseberries, or tiny nutlike new potatoes. On days when there weren't any new or exciting items, it was still interesting to compare the stores. In one store the onions could be large and shiny, but the bunches of lettuce wilted and colorless. Another store could boast of the freshest, brightest lettuce, while the squashy gray onions hid timidly in string bags.

Nina felt a thrill as soon as she climbed out of the car by a store entrance, her feet touching a sidewalk littered with bits of lettuce, onion peel, and broken tomatoes. Inside, she walked between the produce shelves, touching the fruit and vegetables and marveling at how different their surfaces felt. She ran her fingers over the tomatoes; they felt smooth and glossy like polished furniture. She cupped oranges, feeling their lumpy skins in her palms. Sometimes she would hook an orange peel with her nail so it would sputter a little of its pungent, spicy juice on her finger. She avoided the hairy egg-shaped kiwis and wormlike string beans. She liked to stroke the light, feathery bunches of dill and parsley, and to squeeze artichokes, which felt like pine cones, but soft ones. She liked to pat cantaloupes and tap watermelons with her index finger to hear the hollow sound they made. Most of all, Nina loved broccoli. It smelled of young spring grass, and it looked like a spring tree with its solid stem and luxuriant crown of tight grainy florets that resembled recently blossomed leaves.

Regardless of the other vegetables she bought, Nina took home a bunch of broccoli every week. She carried the heavy brown bags proudly to the car with the firm belief that this weekend she would find time to cook. There was the rest of Saturday afternoon ahead, and all of Sunday. She would wash the vegetables as soon as she got home and then cook something on Sunday, maybe spinach gnocchi, or grilled zucchini, or broccoli topped with a three-cheese sauce.

Somehow, Nina invariably managed to forget both the errands she had to run on Sundays and the Saturday-night parties at her husband's friend's. As soon as she came home, Nina immediately found herself in a whirl of things to do. She had to shower in a hurry, hot-curl her hair, brush it down if it turned out too frizzy, try on and reject various sweaters and pants, put on her makeup, find her husband's socks, iron his shirt, tell him where his other sock was, check if the gas was off, and lock the door.

In what seemed like only a minute, Nina found herself back in the car on the way to the party. She alternately glanced at her husband in the driver's seat and at her reflection in the mirror. Her husband seemed distant and deep in his thoughts, which was natural, she told herself, because he was driving. And her own reflection seemed unsatisfying. Her hair was still too frizzy, her soft-featured round face required a different type of makeup, and her blue angora pullover cut into her armpits. The thing about clothes bought at fifty-percent-off sales was that they were either the wrong size or the wrong design. In the car, Nina didn't think about vegetables. They lay abandoned on the refrigerator shelves, where Nina had shoved them in a hurry: tomatoes squashed under zucchini, lettuce leaves jammed against the edge of the vegetable basket, a bunch of broccoli that didn't fit anywhere else placed all by itself on the third shelf.

The parties were held at Pavlik's place, Nina's husband's friend from work, whose wife had divorced him a few years earlier. Pavlik was a heavy man with an uneven ginger-colored beard. He wore ill-fitting trousers and unclean shirts. He loved to laugh heartily and smack his friends on the back.

"Don't mind the mess!" he yelled, as his guests wandered through the dusty labyrinth of his house, stumbling on mismatched furniture, broken electronic equipment, heavy volumes of Russian books, and slippery magazines. It seemed to Nina that Pavlik's function as a host was limited to yelling, "Don't mind the mess!" He didn't feed or entertain his guests. People came to him with their own food and wine, their own plastic dinnerware, their own guitars, and sometimes their own poems written in notebooks.

Not one of Pavlik's guests was a professional poet or musician, though. Most of them worked as computer programmers, the occupation they took up in America, finding it easier and more profitable than trying to prove the value of their Russian degrees in science or the arts. Some of them, Nina's husband included, adopted a condescending, slightly snobbish attitude to their new profession, as something easy and boring, something beneath them. "A computer programmer, like everybody else," they answered reluctantly, when asked about their present profession. "But that's not what I used to be in my previous life." They preferred to talk about art or music or their exciting hobbies, such as mountain climbing, rafting, or photographing Alaskan sunsets.

Nina was a computer programmer too, but unlike everybody else she'd also been a computer programmer in her "previous life." What was worse, she didn't know much about poetry or music, and she didn't have any exciting talents or hobbies.

"My wife is a vegetable lover," Nina's husband said, introducing her to Pavlik's circle.

Nina didn't like Pavlik's guests. The men were untidy and unattractive. They piled up their paper plates with cold cuts, smoked too much, and laughed with their mouths full. They repeated the same things over and over, and it seemed to

Nina that there was always a piece of ham or salami hanging from their mouths while they talked.

The women, on the other hand, with the exception of one or two, were attractive but in a wrong, unpleasant way. They were thin and sophisticated, with straight hair and strong hands with long powerful fingers, toughened by playing either the piano or the guitar. They had soulful eyes, sad from all the poetry they read, and wore expressions of eternal fatigue. They had everything that Nina lacked.

Nina usually sat through the whole evening in the corner of Pavlik's stiff sofa, away from the other guests, who sat on the floor by the cold fireplace, and away from her husband. The sounds of their laughter, their singing, and their reading floated around the room but didn't seem to reach her. The food and wine on a rickety folding table by the window were more accessible from the sofa. Nina made frequent trips to that table, where cold cuts lay on paper plates, loaves of bread stood on cutting boards, and pickles swam in glass jars with a fork invariably stuck into one of them. There were usually a few unopened bottles of vodka, and a five-liter box of Burgundy or Chablis. The wine often dripped from the plastic spigot right onto the beige carpet, making intricate patterns, so that by the end of the party Pavlik's modest carpet looked like a fancy Turkish rug.

When they first started going to Pavlik's parties, Nina sat by the fireplace with the others. She loved to sit across from her husband and watch his face while he played. His neck was bent down, the bangs of his dark hair fallen over his half-closed eyes. From time to time he glanced at her, and then his eyes flickered through the forest of his hair like two tiny lightning bugs. At those moments Nina felt he was playing for her, and then the music touched her, making her skin prickle and her throat hurt.

With time, Nina noticed that she wasn't the only one staring at her husband while he played. Nina saw how the faces of other women lit up just like hers under his fleeting gaze. Each of them must have felt that he was playing for her. Sometimes Nina thought those women had more right to be looked at by her husband. Sometimes those women threw quick looks at Nina, and then Nina felt that she was changing in size; she was growing, bloating up, turning into an enormous exhibit: a dull, untalented woman wearing the wrong clothes and the wrong makeup. She thought that all of them must have wondered why this interesting, talented man had married her.

Her sister didn't wonder. "You were his ticket to America," she often reminded Nina, having first said it on Nina's arrival in New York. "Can you disprove that?"

Nina couldn't.

It was true that Nina's husband had always wanted to emigrate but couldn't obtain a visa. He didn't have close relatives in the United States. It was true that, having married Nina, he had gotten his visa. And it was true that Nina hadn't wanted to emigrate but yielded to her husband's wishes. But it wasn't true that he had married Nina just for that, and it wasn't true that he didn't love her. Nina's sister didn't know what Nina knew. She didn't know that when Nina was in the hospital after appendix surgery, her husband wouldn't leave her room even for a minute. She begged him to go and have some coffee or to take a breath of fresh air, but he refused. He held Nina's hand and squeezed it every time she moaned. Nina's sister didn't know how sometimes he would hug Nina from behind, bury his face in her hair, and whisper, "There is nothing like it. Nothing in the world." She could feel his sharp nose and his hot breath on the nape of her neck, and her eyes would grow moist. And Nina's sister didn't know that he often said the same words when they were making love.

It was a relief to come home after the party and find herself in bed, next to her husband, with a book. Nina had covered the nightstand with cookbooks bought at a fifty-percent discount at Barnes & Noble. She read lying on her back, using her stomach to prop up her book. The thick, glossy pages rustled against Nina's satin nightgowns (fifty-percent off at Victoria's Secret). She loved the rustling sound as much as she loved the prickly sensation in her feet when they touched her husband's hairy legs from time to time. She also loved the euphoric feeling roused in her by lustrous photographs of okra and tomato stew in rustic clay bowls, grilled zucchini parcels on ceramic trays, and baskets of fresh vegetables against a background of meadows or olive groves. Her favorite book, *Italian Cuisine: The Taste of the Sun*, included step-by-step photographs of the cooking process. In the photos, smooth light-skinned female hands with evenly trimmed fingernails performed all the magical actions on the vegetables. They looked like Nina's hands, and Nina fantasized that they were hers. It was she, Nina, who made those perfect curled carrot slices. It was she who pushed the hard, stubborn stuffing into the bell peppers, or rinsed grit off lettuce leaves, or chopped broccoli florets, scattering tiny green crumbs all over the table. Nina's lips moved, forming the rich, passionate words of the cooking instructions: "Brush with olive oil," "bring to a boil and simmer gently," "serve hot," "scoop out the pulp," "chop," "slice," "crush," "squash." When eventually she put the book away, cuddled against her husband's back, and closed her eyes, her lips continued moving for some time.

Nina's husband left her during the middle of September,

when the vegetable stores on 86th Street were full of tomatoes and zucchinis. There was an abundance of them in Nina's refrigerator when her sister opened it.

"The fifth week is the worst. The first four weeks it hasn't sunk in yet. You feel the shock, but you don't feel the pain. It's like you're numb. But the fifth week. ... Brace yourself for the fifth week." Nina's sister crouched in front of the refrigerator, unloading the food she had brought. She came to console Nina with four large bags from a Russian food store.

Nina felt tired. She sat at the table, staring at her sister's broad back. Nina thought that if you tried to hit it with a hammer it would produce a loud ringing sound, as if her sister's back were made of hardwood. The refrigerator shelves filled quickly: bright cartons of currant juice—"Currant juice saved my life; I basically lived on it when Volodya left me"—cream cheese, farmer's cheese, soft cheese, Swiss cheese, bread—"Always keep bread in the refrigerator, it preserves much better this way"—pickles, a jar of cherry compote.

"Nina!" her sister suddenly shrieked. "What is this?" She pulled out a vegetable basket. Inside was a pile of mushy tomatoes with a white beard of mold where the skin split, oozing dark juice; zucchini covered with brown splotches; dark, slimy bunches of collard greens. "You've got the whole vegetable graveyard in here." Her sister emptied the basket into the garbage can, where the vegetables made a squashing sound.

The faint rotten smell stayed in the kitchen for a long time after Nina's sister left. The smell wasn't unpleasant. It was a simple, cozy kitchen smell, like vegetable soup simmering on the stove, the kind Nina's mother used to make.

Contrary to her sister's prediction, the fifth week didn't

bring Nina any extreme pain but only added to her fatigue. Nina felt as if she were recovering from a long, exhausting illness. She tried to do as few household chores as possible. She didn't shop for vegetables anymore. She still read her cookbooks after work, but she was too tired to decipher the recipes. Instead, she ran her finger over the index pages, which were filled with neat columns of letters. The austere phrases were logical and easy to read: "Broccoli: gratin, 17; macaroni with, 71; penne and, 79." She had no desire to look up the recipe on the referred page, she simply went on to the next entry that caught her eye: "Eggplant: braised chicken with orange and, 137."

Pavlik's booming voice on the old, creaky answering machine broke into the elegant sequence of string bean recipes. Nina had turned off the ringer on the phone weeks earlier and now only listened to messages as they came through her machine. Most often they were from Nina's sister, who called to ask if Nina was eating well and to tell her the latest news: that Nina's husband had been seen on Brighton Beach with some "dried herring," then that he was moving to Boston, then that he had already moved. Her sister's voice seemed to Nina distant and somewhat unnatural.

Pavlik's voice made her jump. "Hey! Nina! Are you home?" he shouted.

On impulse, Nina looked at the front door. It was hard to believe that all that roaring came from a modest plastic box on the kitchen counter. Pavlik's voice suddenly went low, and it became hard to make out his words. "Don't disappear," he said, if Nina heard him correctly.

Pavlik's Place looked different. Nina saw it as soon as she stepped into his living room, but she couldn't quite figure out why. The rickety food table still stood on the "Turkish" rug, the fireplace was crammed with piles of old magazines, Pavlik's hulking figure was shaking with laughter, and the vacant sofa was waiting for Nina in the corner. Everything was there, everything was in the same place, yet something was undeniably different. The size—it's become bigger, Nina decided, taking her seat between the sofa cushions. Pavlik's place had more space and more air.

A thin, delicate woman's voice sang something about a little path in the woods that meandered among the trees. Just like the words in this song, Nina thought. She liked the song. When it ended, the singer put her guitar down and walked to the food table. She was wearing a long gray cardigan with drooping pockets. There wasn't anything mysterious about her. A balding man with a closely trimmed gray beard took over the guitar. Nina's eyes traveled from the man's outstretched elbow protruding through his shabby corduroy sleeve, to his stooped shoulder, to the greasy line of his hair. Nina suddenly saw that his untidiness wasn't some kind of snobbish fashion statement but a sign of loneliness, of being uncared for. She saw that the women sitting in a circle were watching the man just as they used to watch her husband. They were tired, lonely women, just as she was. There wasn't anything mysterious about them either. Nina also noticed that she wasn't the only one sitting outside the singing circle. In fact, only a few people sat in the circle, while others were scattered all around Pavlik's house. A lonely figure here and there sat quietly on a chair, an old box, or a windowsill, or wandered around the room. From time to time the paths of the lonely figures intersected, and then conversations were struck: awkward yet hopeful conversations, just as the one Nina was having now.

"You are a vegetable lover, aren't you?" a man asked, having seated himself in the opposite corner of Nina's sofa.

Nina nodded.

"Yes, I thought I heard that from somebody. Do you like to cook vegetables?"

Nina nodded again.

"You know, I love vegetables myself. My wife hates it when I cook, though." The man rolled his eyes, making Nina smile. He was short, with thin rusty-red hair and a very pale complexion. A tiny piece of toilet paper with a spot of dried blood stuck to his cheek.

"Are you a computer programmer like everybody else?" Nina asked.

The man nodded with a smile.

"And in your previous life?"

"A physics teacher in high school. But I can't say that I miss it. I was terrified of my students."

Nina laughed. It was easy to talk to him. Nina looked at his smiling eyes, then down at his hands—short fingernails, white fingers; red hair on the knuckles. She tried to imagine what it would be like if a hand like this brushed against her breast. Accidentally.

Nina wiped the little beads of sweat off her nose. He was a strange, married, and not particularly attractive man. He introduced himself as Andrei.

"So, what's your favorite vegetable?" Nina asked.

"I would say fennel. Fennel has an incredible flavor. Reminds me of a wild apple and, oddly enough, freshly sawed wood. Do you like fennel?"

Nina nodded. She liked fennel. It had a funny, slightly ribbed surface, and it was heavy and spouted weird green shoots that seemed to grow out of nowhere. Nina'd never tasted fennel. "I like broccoli," she said.

"Oh, broccoli! I love how they cook it in Chinese places. How do you cook it?"

This man with the piece of tissue stuck to his cheek looked safe enough to confide in. "I've never cooked broccoli—or any other vegetable," Nina said.

"Let's have a cooking date," Andrei offered.

A cooking date! Nina couldn't remember ever feeling so excited. She was sure she had been as excited sometime before, she just couldn't remember when. So the better part of the following Saturday Nina spent shopping for cooking utensils. She went to Macy's and abandoned the fifty-percent-discount rule for the first time, buying two drastically overpriced skillets, a set of shiny stainless steel saucepans, a steamer, and a pretty wooden spoon with a carved handle.

"Do you want it wrapped as a wedding present?" the cashier asked.

Halfway home, Nina realized that she hadn't bought nearly enough. Knives! She needed knives! And a cutting board, and a colander, and God knows what else. She swerved her car in the direction of Avenue M, where, abandoning the second rule about never ever buying anything in cheap stores, she bought a set of knives, two wooden cutting boards and one plastic, a colander, a curved grapefruit knife just because it looked so cute, a vegetable peeler, a set of stainless steel bowls, and two aprons with a picture of wild mushrooms on a yellow background. In a grocery store next door Nina bought a bottle of olive oil, black pepper, chili pepper, and a jar of something dry and dark-green with Chinese letters on it.

Well before three o'clock—the time of their cooking date—Nina had everything ready. The sparkling saucepans and the skillet stood proudly on the stove. The bowls, the colander, the cutting boards, and the knives were arranged on the kitchen counter in careful disarray around the centerpiece: the opened *Italian Cuisine: The Taste of the Sun*. Nina observed her kitchen, trying to shake off the embarrassing excess of excitement.

Andrei came on time, even earlier. At five minutes to three he already stood in Nina's hall, removing his bulky leather jacket and his leather cap sprinkled with raindrops. He smelled of wet leather. He handed Nina a bottle of wine and a baguette in a sodden paper bag. "In movies, when a man hands a woman a baguette and a bottle of wine, it always seems chic, doesn't it?" he said.

Nina nodded. Andrei looked more homely than she remembered. Nina's memory somehow had managed to erase the red spots on his pasty cheeks, to color his brows and eyelashes, to make him slimmer, and add an inch or two to his height. It was strange seeing him in her house, especially in her tiny hall, where every object was familiar, its place carefully considered. He clashed with the surroundings like a bad piece of furniture. Nina hurried to lead him into the kitchen.

"So, are we cooking broccoli today?" Andrei asked. He began leafing through *Italian Cuisine: The Taste of the Sun*, his freshly washed hands still smelling of Nina's soap.

"Broccoli, yes," Nina mumbled. She was suddenly struck by a dreadful suspicion, which was immediately confirmed upon opening the refrigerator.

In all her shopping frenzy, she had forgotten to buy any vegetables.

She jerked out the vegetable basket, faintly hoping for a miracle. The basket was empty and sparklingly clean, wiped with a kitchen towel moistened in Clorox by her sister's firm hand. There was only a tiny strip of onion skin stuck between the edge of the basket and the shelf above. Nina turned to Andrei, motioning to the empty basket. Her throat felt as if someone were squeezing it. Suddenly everything seemed hopeless and absurd: the counter crammed with gleaming, artificial sets of kitchenware; the barren vegetable basket; this perfect stranger, who came to cook in her kitchen; Nina herself, with all her energy and excitement of moments ago, now pressing her forehead against the cold vinyl of the refrigerator door.

"Do you want me to drive to a supermarket?" Andrei asked.

Nina shook her head. She knew it would never work now, after everything had been exposed to her in all its absurdity.

"What's this?" Andrei asked. He was looking toward the back of the refrigerator. A bunch of broccoli was stuck between the third shelf and the refrigerator wall. It hung upside down, the florets nearly touching the shelf below. The bunch wasn't yellowed or covered with rotten slime. On the contrary, for the weeks that it lay between the shelves, it had become darker and dryer. A few more weeks and it would have turned into a broccoli mummy. It smelled okay, or rather it didn't smell at all. "I'm sure we can still cook it," Andrei said. He began showing Nina what to do.

Nina ran cold water over the florets, then shook the bunch fiercely, letting out a shower of green drops. She chopped off the stem, then cut off the base of each floret, watching with fascination how they split into new tiny bunches of broccoli. She then peeled the stem and cut it into even, star-shaped slices. Some things turned out to be different from Nina's cooking fantasies, others exactly the same. Some were disappointing, others better than she ever imagined. The best thing of all was that, when the broccoli was already on the stove, sputtering boiling water from under the shiny lid, Andrei pulled one of her kitchen chairs close to the stove and suggested she stand on it.

"Climb up and inhale," he said. "The hot air travels up. The strongest aroma should be right under the ceiling." He stood back, giving her room.

Nina stood on the chair, her hair just grazing the ceiling. She closed her eyes, lifted her nose, and breathed in deep. The warm aroma of broccoli rose up, caressing Nina's face, enveloping the whole of her.

ELISSA SCHAPPELL

THE JOY OF COOKING

I WAS HALFWAY out the door when the phone rang. Another person would have let the machine pick up, but you know how it is when you're a mother.

"Thank God you're there," my daughter Emily said, sounding out of breath.

"I am, but sweetie," I said, "I'm in a bit of a rush ... "

"No, no, wait! Don't go," she cried. "Please, *Mommy*? I'm begging you. I just need one thing, I promise."

I looked at the clock: 4:00. Yoga started at 4:30. My doctor had recommended it for stress reduction, and the pain I'd been having in my hips. After yoga, provided I wasn't bleeding or paralyzed, I was planning to pop into the drugstore and buy new lipstick. Something youthful but sophisticated with shimmer. My mother always said that a woman should have a signature lipstick the way a man had a signature cocktail. I'd married and divorced Emily's father, Terry, in Cherries in the Snow. After that, I was going to treat myself to an overdue haircut at Sheer Delight. Something new, possibly even a little racy. I'd been toying with the idea of bangs. Then, at 6:30, I was meeting Hugo, the new man shelving the philosophy section at the bookstore, where for the last fifteen years I'd been working as a cashier and bookkeeper. It was just coffee, but let's just say it had been a long time between cups of coffee: 1,825 days to be exact. Five years. Not that I was counting.

It isn't easy to meet men, let alone carry on a relationship when, for all practical purposes, you're a single mother. Even though Terry was around, it wasn't like Emily and Paige lived with their father, or he ever took care of them. Not that I'm complaining. My daughters have always come first. I have no regrets.

The girl who'd picked up my shift for the afternoon was named Bea. Last month, she and her boyfriend had decided, on a whim, to drive to Arizona and back over the long weekend, but his car broke down in the desert. She'd called the store collect from a payphone. I'd accepted the charges without thinking. I'm lucky that, of all the things I have to worry about, my girls running off with a man is not one of them. Bea's trip didn't sound at all romantic, but I understood. I'd have gone anywhere with Terry when I was twenty-two. It took me back—which might explain why I'd been flirting with Hugo. Why I had shaved my legs.

Emily cleared her throat theatrically. "Well, you'll just have to wait a minute, as I have an announcement to make. Today," she paused, "I became a woman."

Emily was twenty-four.

"I bought a chicken. I did. With legs and everything."

"Really?"

Emily didn't cook. She chopped salads, sliced fruit, and poured brewer's yeast on popcorn. She went to restaurants where she tortured the waiters with special orders, everything steamed or boiled, sauce on the side, then ultimately returned half of it. Emily had been anorexic for almost half her life.

I assumed she meant a dead chicken.

"I have a suitor!"

It sounded like she said: *suture*. Slap a steak on a black eye, a chicken breast on stitches. I wish I didn't think this way.

"A *suitor*, Mommy. A gentleman caller." She sighed as if

she might faint from the mere pleasure of saying the word. Emily had often lectured her sister, Paige, and me on the subject of love, saying, "When Percy Shelley, the *poet*, drowned, Mary Shelley carried his burnt-up heart in her handbag for the rest of her life. *In her handbag!* That's real love. That's what I'm waiting for."

I wondered, *How long before that heart started to stink?*

"You mean, a boyfriend?" Emily had admirers, mostly older men she'd met through the art museum where she worked. Elderly patrons who enjoyed the company of a slight, pale-skinned girl with long dark pre-Raphaelite hair, able to converse about romantic poetry, renaissance art, and classical music through drinks and intermission. But she never had boyfriends. It was understood that she didn't like to be touched.

She had always told me everything. Kissing was sublime, but the rest of it—she'd shudder—reliving the feel of a man's hot hairy hands on her body, his breath on her neck—was disgusting. After her freshman year in the dorms at Sarah Lawrence (zero privacy, a roommate who looked like a dairy maid and whistled in her sleep, boys loitering in the halls night and day like pimps on street corners), she'd come back home to live with me. Or she had, until last year when her therapist insisted that in order for her to *separate* she had to move out. It was ridiculous. Now she was in a snug fourth-floor walk-up that I could afford, three blocks away. She didn't mind the stairs. She liked stairs. All that mattered, she said, was that it was close to me. Close enough to run over in her pajamas to borrow a cup of sugar.

"He's been wooing me for a few weeks now, and I thought it was time I made him dinner, because that's what you're supposed to do, right? Cook?" She took a breath. "Which is why I called. I need you to give me the family recipe."

I could tell that she was biting her nails. Biting them down to the pink. She'd eat her nails, chew the skin off her fingers. But you couldn't get her to eat a hot dog.

"Mommy? Is there something wrong?"

"No. I'm just surprised." A few weeks? We spoke every day, two sometimes three times a day, and she never once mentioned she was dating someone.

"You promise? Otherwise, I'd have to throw myself under a train, or walk into a river with stones in my pockets, or something." *Or something.*

"I promise. I'm your mother. You just caught me with one foot out the door. And I'm meeting *someone* tonight for a drink." I waited for an interrogation. *Someone Who?* Emily had a gift for zeroing in on the shortcomings in men I'd normally turn a blind eye to. Imitating the strut of the attorney who, despite being round and balding, retained the arrogance of a once-beautiful person; mimicking the nervous throat clearing habit of the accountant; pointing out the receding chin and mustache of the college professor. "Only stagecoach robbers, rednecks, and the cop in the Village People should have mustaches," she said. "I just could never trust a man with a mustache!" But I wasn't twenty-four anymore. And he was separated from his wife.

"So, can you give it to me? Now?"

"I don't know what you're talking about."

"Seriously, Mother. Are you claiming there *is* no family recipe? Because Paige told me there was," Emily said, as though she'd caught me in a lie. "Paige told me that the other night when the two of you were having dinner alone together"—she paused meaningfully, jealousy lurking in her voice like a maniac with a hammer—"*she* said you gave it to her."

It was true Paige and I had dinner alone. She wanted to

stop by and pick up some books—poetry books I'd owned in college. Back then I always had a copy of Dante or Rilke in my bag and a pack of cigarettes. I was surprised that Paige, who was pre-med (a fact I was very proud of) even wanted them. She seemed surprised to find I owned them.

She'd discovered them on the bottom shelf of the bookcase in my bedroom. When I found her, sitting on my bed, running her finger down their spines like she was checking for scoliosis, she demanded to know, *Whose are these? Where did they come from?*

"My old piano teacher used to say that you don't know a culture until you read their poetry. . . . It sounds silly now, but when I was your age I'd wanted to be a classical pianist, playing concerts all across Europe . . . "

"I believe that too," Paige said, a hungry look in her eye.

When she called the next day to ask if she could borrow them, I told her she could have them. They were gibberish to me now. "Come," I said, "and you can stay for dinner."

The chicken I'd made for Paige wasn't from a family recipe, or even out of a cookbook—just something I'd seen a friend's mother do years ago. I was surprised I remembered it. The closest I had come to inheriting a recipe from my mother was rescuing her copy of the *Joy of Cooking* out of a box she'd packed up to donate to the church after my father died. "Ha," my mother said, "they ought to call that one *No Joy of Cooking*."

It had been the only cookbook my mother ever needed while my father was alive. All of the dishes he required—beef stroganoff, pork chops, and Hawaiian chicken, even the vanilla ice box cake, which my mother made for my birthday year after year, insisting that it was *my* favorite—all four had come from that book.

"Is this recipe something grandma used to make?" Paige asked, as she helped herself to seconds of chicken and stuffing.

"My *mother*? No. Your grandmother wasn't really the homemaking type." I topped off our wineglasses. "Cooking, cleaning, children. She felt it was a kind of servitude, I think."

"I can totally see that." Paige nodded, as though her grandmother's chafing at motherhood was a point of pride. "Who can blame her?" She licked her fingers. "She wanted more."

It wasn't like I didn't want more, too. I'd always planned to go back to piano. I thought I could wait until the girls went to school, until they didn't need me so much. But then they kept on needing me. Well, one of them, anyway.

After dinner, and deep into a second bottle of wine, Paige asked if she could smoke. I had no idea she smoked, and didn't know whether to scold her or, because we were having such fun, ask if I could bum one. It had been years, but I did neither.

She told me about a friend of hers who'd purposefully had sex with a man in order to contract crabs.

"Although, because she was pre-med," Paige said, "she preferred the term 'pubic lice' or in Latin, *phthirus pubis*."

These crabs, Paige explained, weren't ordinary civilian crabs, but rock 'n' roll royalty crabs, having been passed, via groupies, from the Rolling Stones to Aerosmith to Guns N' Roses, for decades. It made her feel connected to something larger, a part of history.

"Like those sourdough starters that were so popular in the seventies," I said. "Mine was supposedly a direct descendant of one that Alice Waters started in Berkeley."

"Or what about herpes?" Paige winced. "Herpes is the worst—like an old rock star, herpes never really dies, it just fades away."

The recipe for the chicken I made Paige was so simple I could have just told it to her. In her first year of pre-med she'd memorized all 206 bones in the human body, including the ones babies are born with that then disappear. Still, I'd written it out on a recipe card carefully, in my very best *keep-this-for-posterity* script.

Secret: Puncture a lemon several times with a fork and insert it inside the bird—this will keep it moist. Paige wouldn't know about the lemon. That was something I could give my daughter who didn't need me. *A lemon.*

She looked pleased. "Thanks," she said, then careful not to bend it slid the recipe carefully into her handbag.

"Do you even have a roasting pan?"

If she didn't I'd get her one for Christmas.

"I'm sure I can manage," she patted the pocket where she'd put the recipe for safekeeping. "Don't worry."

"I practically had to stalk Paige to get the recipe," Emily complained. "I literally had to call her ten times, god knows where she was. Finally, at seven in the morning, she picked up. Even so, she said all she could remember were the ingredients, not the proportions. So you see, Mommy, you have to help me."

I shrugged off my coat and put my keys on the kitchen counter.

"Did you get the lemon?"

"What lemon?" Emily said, sounding dismayed. "She left out the lemon. That is *so* like her."

"It's just a silly lemon. It's not important." If Paige forgot, it was most likely tiredness, although it could have been spite.

"No. It has to be good—just as good as the recipe you gave Paige. No, better."

"It will be. I promise." For Emily it would always have to be better.

"You are the best mommy in the world, you know that?"

"I'll make it easy."

"Good, because remember, I'm no good with numbers."

This, I knew, was a lie. Emily was obsessed with numbers. The lower the better. For years the goal was to keep herself under 200 calories a day. She'd tried to stop counting, but it was hard. Old habits don't die with sudden-aneurysm efficiency. They go in and out of comas, existing on life-support for years.

"Why don't I just come over?"

"No. I can do it," she said firmly. Then she shrieked. "Eek! It's slimy. Its legs won't stay closed—I'm putting on rubber gloves—bad chicken, slutty chicken. Oh god, it's disgusting. I can't even look at it. I think I'm going to be sick."

My Emily, who loved horror movies, who giggled through the shower scene in *Psycho*, was horrified at the sight of a raw chicken.

"Hold it steady in the sink," I said. "Turn on the water, not too hot, just lukewarm, and wash it. Gently. There's no need to scrub."

"Soap?"

"No soap. Just pat it dry." I could have been teaching her how to wash a baby. Then there was a loud thud and the sound of the phone being dropped.

"Oh no, oh no, I dropped it! It squirted right out of my hands."

"Just pick it up and start over." Good thing it wasn't a baby.

There was the thump of the chicken being dumped into the sink.

Her voice broke, "I can't do this."

"Yes, you can." I wanted her to do it herself. It was time. She ought to be able to make a damn chicken. "You'll need to preheat the oven, 350 degrees." I stopped, it was my call waiting, loud and insistent. I knew Emily could hear it too.

"Did you ever cook for Daddy? When you were courting?" she pressed on, ignoring the sound, as she always did.

I checked my caller ID. It was Paige.

"Of course," I said. "We did that sort of thing back then."

"You think chicken is good, right?"

"Chicken is good." The phone beeped once more, then stopped. I poured myself some wine.

"Good, I thought so." Emily's voice eased.

"*Coq au vin*," I said. "That was the first meal I ever made your father." He'd come to my apartment. It was tiny, with a galley kitchen not even big enough for two people to stand. "I made it from a recipe in a women's magazine. The pearl onions, the red wine, the French name—it all seemed so sophisticated. Until the chicken turned purple."

Emily groaned. "Well, that's completely and utterly disgusting."

"I misread the directions, and poured in three times the amount of Cabernet," I said. "Your father and I got drunk on that meat."

"I'm sorry, Mother, but that's not exactly romantic."

It was, though. Terry was the most charming, handsomest man who ever wanted me. He played guitar and dreamed of sailing around the world. He kissed my ears. He called me baby. He was rich with million-dollar ideas.

We married at twenty-three. It was the seventies; even then it seemed young. The marriage lasted thirteen years.

Thirteen is the lace anniversary. My husband gave me a divorce. My mother and father were married at twenty-three, it was the forties, so it would have seemed old. The marriage lasted forty years. Forty is the ruby anniversary. Forty trumps thirteen. My mother got a gold necklace with a ruby drop, a bead of blood at her throat.

For forty years my mother ignored my father tooting his horn and whistling at women on the street, endured him placing his hand on the behinds of hundreds of waitresses and shop girls. Forty years she held her tongue, twisted her napkin in her lap, glaring murderously at me when I dared to look at her with anything close to pity.

I am forty-eight and I can still fit into my old wedding dress. Every year, I try it on to gauge how my body has changed. It's a little tight around the middle, but if I gave up my nightly glass or two of wine, started running again, or did yoga, it would fit.

At twenty-four, Emily is one year older than I was when I had her. Paige is two years younger than Emily. Paige kayaks and sails and ran a marathon for fun. I never worry about her. Emily boasts of her great eating habits, attention to nutrition, she walks everywhere. I worry about her breaking a bone.

Estimated number of times a week Emily calls me? Twenty. Exact number of times a week she calls her father? One. On Sunday—long-distance from my house. Zero is the number of times Emily has, to my knowledge, entertained a man in her apartment. The number of times Emily has cooked for me? Also zero.

I do the math. It all adds up.

"Okey, dokey," Emily says, "step one of the stuffing completed. I'm done with the carrots and celery." Celery is a staple of Emily's diet. It has six calories, and chewing burns ten. If you stop eating sugar, carrots taste like candy.

"So now the onion," I say. I hear her blade, cutting fast, like she thinks if she chops fast, she can out-distance the tears. I'm afraid she's going to cut herself.

"Gee, this is such fun," Emily says with a happy sniffle, "or maybe it only feels that way because I'm in love."

"Love?" It stuck in my throat like a bone.

"I despise the word *stuffing*. Don't you, Mommy? Why would anyone eat anything that promised to stuff you?" I sensed her shiver. "So, now I'm just supposed to pack this mess into that hole?"

"Don't over fill it—it expands."

She laughed. "Will it explode?"

I almost wished that would happen. What would Prince Charming do? Laugh it off, take her in his arms and tell her not to worry? Would he insist they salvage the bird, and then, afterward, tell her: *Baby, it was delicious*. Or would he judge her? Scowl as he made a mental note: *Not wife material. Can't have poultry blowing up left and right! Someone could lose an eye!*

"Emily," I said, fighting my annoyance, "maybe I could just tell the recipe to you and you could just write it down . . . "

"Oh pardon me, I just thought, in light of these *extraordinary* circumstances, you might want to help."

"I do want to. I'm sorry. The phone. It's just hard this way."

"Forget it, Mother. I'm letting it go." She took a deep breath. "Because," she said, "did I mention that I'm in love?"

Fifty was the estimated number of lovers Terry had during our marriage. He didn't offer this number with remorse, or grief, or pride, more like a seasoned tax attorney. He delivered the information to me because, he said, "It's been weighing on my conscience for too long." As though his conscience were a beach chair, groaning under the fat ass of his indiscretion.

Every year for a decade after we split, I got an AIDS test. *Did I mention that I'm in love?*

Terry's second wife is thirty-five. Thirteen years younger than me. They have two boys. Emily, Paige, and I, we call them the Toxic Test Tube Twins. They are in grade school and, Emily says, "blond as Nazis." Terry told the girls the divorce was my idea. I was inflexible, demanding. No fun. I told them zero about his screwing around. I was ashamed to admit that, no matter how much and how good I gave, it wasn't enough. Two hours was the amount of time the lifeguard at the YMCA estimated Emily had been swimming before she passed out last year and nearly drowned. Five minutes was the amount of time Emily estimated she was unconscious. One second is how far away Emily swears she was from going into the light.

Because Emily wasn't living with me, and had long ago stopped recording her gains and losses on a piece of graph paper taped on the bathroom wall, I didn't know until then that she'd dropped below seventy-five pounds. Seventy-five pounds was the magic number. It meant she could be checked into the eating disorders wing of the Melrose Institute—that made two times in six years.

Sixteen days after she was released she moved into her own apartment. She'd bought her own scale, light and high tech that measured with digital precision, down to the ounce, as well as calculated your body fat. In comparison, my own scale, a large gray slab with a needle that wavered uncertainly, seemed out of the Stone Age, as precise as using a sundial for a stopwatch.

The hospital is one hour and forty-five minutes away. I bought the complete works of Stephen King on CD for the car ride back and forth. Vampires, witches, ghosts; tales of the undead dead terrorizing the innocent. Each day another monster claimed another victim and the hero got closer to slaying it.

The hospital where my mother is bedridden is twenty minutes from my home. She sleeps a lot. Some days all she will eat is a gallon of vanilla Häagen Dazs. She has a sweet tooth. When I visit we sit outside the hospital on a bench so she can smoke, three cigarettes an hour—her tank of oxygen, which she drags everywhere, sitting just inside the door, like a chaperone past caring.

When I told my mother that Emily was in the hospital too, she sighed. "It's such a shame you weren't able to keep that husband of yours. He was so dashing. He made a mean Old Fashioned too," she said, shaking her head with grave disappointment. "Those poor, poor girls. But, you know, you did spoil them. I told you, if you pick up a baby every time it cries, it will grow up thinking every time it cries someone will pick them up." She put her hand on my leg. "Now, look at you. Look how well you turned out."

I know she's old. Sick, too. Still, it wouldn't be the worst thing to never see my mother again. Amount of money I'd inherit: zero. Amount of money Emily's ninety-day stay cost me: $40,000. Amount my insurance company would pay: $10,000.

Five was the number of group therapy sessions Emily took part in each week. Four the number of one-on-one sessions with a psychiatrist. Three meetings with a nutritionist. The number of times she was tied to her bed during her stay? One.

Given her medical history, Emily's chances of ever being able to have a baby are one in one hundred. The internist at Melrose was the first of three doctors to tell me that. I wanted to cry. How could Emily not have a daughter someday? It was like hearing your child would never be happy. The age of the unmarried doctor who so glibly gave us this news? Maybe twenty-six. Number of children? You can bet zero.

Emily might have dated him. It happened all the time. Pretty girl, cute doctor. I liked the idea. A doctor-husband, one who could perform CPR, set broken bones, prescribe painkillers. Someone I could trust to take care of her. At twenty-three, she was one of the older girls in the program—a seasoned pro among teenagers. During group therapy, the mothers and daughters sat in a circle. You could tell that the mothers had made an effort to look nice. No sweats or sneakers. The mothers wear lipstick. We do our hair. We don't look like the parents visiting children in other parts of the hospital. The daughters, dressed in regulation blue gowns that hit just below the knee, stared icily at us, like gang members cracking their knuckles, shivs made from melted-down toothbrushes hidden in their thick wooly socks. Their matching hospital bands like friendship bracelets.

For us, the girls recalled—in poetic detail—their inaugural purge. They did so with the nostalgia of a first kiss. Masters now, some boasted that the simple act of kneeling and bringing two fingers toward their mouths could trigger their gag reflex. One said she could make herself vomit by just thinking the word *meatball*.

They talked shop: Amphetamines. Ipecac. Enemas. Emily flashed her scars. Showed off the tooth she'd chipped bingeing on frozen éclairs. Even here—especially here—it was a competition. A race. Simple math. The one who'd lost the most weight won. The thing is, to win was to die. You didn't even get the trophy.

We weren't allowed to cry. Just witness. "This isn't about you right now," the group leader would remind us. How was it not about us?

Did I mention that I'm in love?

"Now we're ready to butter the skin."

"Excuse me? No, *we're* not. The skin? You've got to be kidding me. I was just starting to pull it off."

"Stop. Stop now. If you remove the skin, the meat will dry out."

"But it's disgusting."

"It's flavor."

"It's fat."

It had always been like this. She'd ask for my advice, listen intently, nod her head, and then ignore it.

I heard my call waiting, again. I checked the number. Paige. She'd have to wait. "Well," I said, "you have to weigh the two evils against each other. If you don't follow the recipe, you can't control the outcome. You don't know what could happen. It could be a disaster. Now get the butter. Use a whole stick. Cover the bird—in around the legs—don't be shy."

"Ugh. I can't believe I am doing this. It's making me gag. What is the exact amount of butter the recipe calls for?" Emily asked, suspicious.

I was getting tired. I wasn't going to offer to go over there again. If she wanted me, she'd have to ask me. Beg.

"Does every recipe require you to crayon disgusting fat all over the bird?"

"So, tell me about this boy," I said: "I mean *man*." Maybe if I distracted her, she'd butter the entire chicken without noticing.

"Well," she said, excited. "He's terribly handsome—"

I knew the type. Vain. The kind of man who can't resist catching sight of his own reflection, admiring his profile in the back of a spoon.

"—and an actor."

He was poor. I knew it, poor, and short, probably a dwarf.

"How did the two of you meet?"

"Ah," Emily said, as though she imagined one day she'd be telling this story to their children. "It was at the Social Security office. I lost my card."

"Really?"

"I'd been trapped in that circle of hell for what felt like eternity, literally, clinging to Jane Austen for life, waiting and waiting for my number to be called, when out of nowhere this gentlemen appears before me—"

I could picture him—square chin, arrogant.

"—and begins to mime picking roses."

"How romantic," I said.

It was easy to see Emily feeding off all that attention. The good-looking man, all those people. Her cheeks flushed, hands clasped at her chest, her eyes wide and sparkling. Intoxicated.

"It was! He even pricked his finger on a thorn. It was so sweet. Then he presented me with this bouquet and the whole place positively erupted in applause. It was so—"

"He's a mime?" I said, fighting laughter. I poured myself two more inches of wine.

"He's an actor," she countered, suddenly irritable. "Extraordinarily gifted too. Wait until I show you the review of the last play he was in. It was a small role, off-off Broadway, but the critic singled him out, he called him a *promising young thespian.*"

"*Sounds* promising," I said. "Have you finished buttering the skin?"

"And Mommy, he's got the face of a poet. *Byronic.* It's beautiful. You've got to see us. Everyone says how fantastic we look together."

I chew on the inside of my lip. Everyone? *Who are these people you've shown him to, before introducing him to your mother?*

"And he does magic."

"That's a plus."

"After filling my arms with these enchanting roses, he made a silver dollar appear from behind my ear. Right there in the middle of the Social Security office. It was glorious. He swore he'd stand there all day long pulling silver pieces out of my ear until I agreed to have coffee with him. He said, *I'll lose my job, go broke, fall into poverty, and it will be all your fault . . .* "

"Did he really?"

Falling into poverty made it sound like an accident, a slip off a bridge into a sinkhole of threadbare coats, government cheese, and wonder bread wrappers that did double duty as galoshes. I wanted to say, *People don't fall into poverty—they're pushed.* I'd peered over that precipice when the hospital bills started mounting and Terry stopped sending us checks. I protected my girls, because that is what a mother does. I made sure they still had designer jeans, department store makeup, expensive haircuts. I didn't, but they did.

"I hope you got to keep the silver dollar," I said.

"I knew it!" Emily snapped. "Oh, I just knew it. I knew you'd act like this. I should never have told you! Why do you insist on criticizing me all the time?"

"I'm not criticizing you," I said. "What do you mean?"

Then, just like that, she hung up on me.

Emily celebrated her Sweet 16 with lime Jell-O, in bed, on the children's wing at Mercy General. She was so small, and the hospital mattress, in comparison, so thick it reminded me of the fairy tale *The Princess and the Pea*. Paige and I stuck a candle in a low-fat iced carrot muffin, even though we weren't allowed to light it, and sang to her. She wouldn't eat either the Jell-O or the muffin.

The year she turned fifteen, Emily insisted she didn't want to celebrate, then was disappointed we hadn't thrown her a surprise party. She licked her fingers and ate her cake—angel food, raspberry sauce on the side—crumb by crumb by crumb. In a joking voice she sang, "It's My Party and I'll Cry if I Want To." When Terry came to pick the girls up to take them to his place for the weekend, I asked him if he didn't think Emily looked a little thin. Her periods had stopped. A fact which filled her with glee.

"I'm a little concerned," I said.

"Nah," he said, "she looks great. You're just jealous."

Fifteen was the year Emily started complaining about not being able to find clothes that fit. "Why don't they make double o sizes?" she'd ask saleswomen, whose expressions of barely disguised jealousy made them look bloated with envy.

ooEmily, license to purge.

In her size o jeans Emily sat on the floor with Paige playing slapjack, trying to teach her how to eat an M&M by first cracking the shell with her teeth.

"You can't eat just one," she said, digging her hand into the pocket of her sweater, where she'd dumped half the bowl of candy. When she stood the pocket hung down like a teat.

Her own breasts had disappeared.

* * *

At fourteen Emily said she wanted butterfly cupcakes, just like when she was eleven. Exactly the same. So I'd dug through my cookbooks, my recipe box, and the kitchen drawers until I found it.

She'd insisted on a new party dress, a manicure, an arrangement of pink roses, a lace tablecloth, my wedding china, and silver. "Everything," she kept saying, "has to be perfect." She was so excited, she couldn't stop running in circles. She must have kissed me ten times.

One hour before the guests arrived, she was in tears. The balloons looked stupid, the dress made her look fat. Paige stroked her hair trying to comfort her. Even though it was just three girls for pizza, cupcakes, and a scary movie, *An American Werewolf in London*—Emily said it was too much. But when they showed up, presents in hand, she was suddenly all smiles. In her bedroom, the girls giggled and danced to the Bee Gees' "Staying Alive," striking poses in the mirror. That night Emily complained of a stomachache—too much junk food—and asked to save her cupcake for the next day.

On her thirteenth birthday, faced with a vanilla cake with white icing and fresh daisies, she stood over me as I cut and warned, "Not too much." I felt a pang. Here she was, like a grown woman demurring, "Just a sliver for me."

While Emily and ten of her best friends sat in a circle on the floor playing Telephone, Terry sat beside me on the sofa. As the girls whispered into each other's ears, passing along the message, I murmured, "You smell like perfume."

He didn't miss a beat.

"I stopped at Macy's on the way over, thinking that perfume might be appropriate for the occasion—you realize she's not a baby anymore, but you know what it's like—the beauty department. It's a jungle out there. It's dangerous.

I tell you it's no place for a man. The saleswomen popping up from behind every counter like the Viet Cong, shooting eau de toilette like tear gas."

"Did you get her something?"

"Are you kidding me?"

I laughed, relieved. Later, I'd think, *booby-traps left and right*.

At twelve Emily requested yellow layer cake with rainbow sprinkles in the batter. This was the cake all the popular girls were having at their parties. The slice was a four-inch wedge and she ate it with a fork. Terry's phone had rung in the middle of singing "Happy Birthday," the sound of a funky jazz trumpet coming from his pants pocket. Before Emily had even blown out her candles, he'd stepped out into the hall to take the call.

Twelve was the year of counting calories. Sit-ups. It didn't seem that abnormal. It didn't make me happy, but I thought it was just a stage, like drinking Long Island Ice teas and smoking clove cigarettes. Anyway, Kate Moss-thin was in and Terry was right: Emily was a little pudgy.

The year Emily turned ten I made her chocolate devil's food with chocolate icing, in the shape of an Arabian stallion. I used black licorice whips for the mane. Emily ate two pieces in record time, and got frosting on her nose. Terry laughed, "Hey, whoa Bessie! No one's going to take it away from you!"

By accident, Paige swallowed three pennies. Terry joked, "These too shall pass."

At five it didn't really matter what flavor her cake was. What mattered was that Terry made a precious miniature merry-go-round to go on top. It actually moved, the girls took turns spinning it. Paige tried to eat one of the carousel horses. Terry and I kissed. We whispered to each other that we were the luckiest people alive.

On her first birthday I made my baby girl a carrot cake and she fed herself with her fist. She squealed with delight. I thought: *So, this is love.*

How many hundreds of times had I thought about that cake?

"Did you just hang up on me? Did you really just—" I was furious.

"Oh my gosh, Mommy, I'm so sorry, I got another call," Emily said, unfazed by my anger, and not sounding sorry at all.

"Don't do that ever again. I mean it," I said, but she wasn't listening.

"You'll never guess who that was. Jenny. And guess what? She's actually thinking of moving here in a couple of weeks—isn't that fantastic? It is. I promise you if she doesn't escape the clutches of her evil mother, someone will die. I told her she *had* to stay with me until she finds a place, it'll be like a sleepover. Oh my gosh. *Jenny.* We'll make s'mores and stay up late watching scary movies, and do facials. I've never had a real roommate."

Emily and I had done all these things, countless times. Snuggled in my bed, a bowl of popcorn between us, we watched the Terminator cut a murderous swath through humanity, with typical cyborg savoir-faire. It became a joke between us, whenever one of us left the room, we'd say, mimicking that Bavarian monotone, *I'll be back.*

"I don't know who that is."

I hoped she wasn't one of those girls whose arms and legs were covered with thin white scars, like they'd taken some shrapnel. Or one who stuck out her boney chest proudly like she expected someone to pin a medal on her.

"*Jenny*, I can't believe you. She was one of my best friends at Melrose, Mother. She was dear to me. You must remember her. Tennis player? I took her under my wing."

There might have been a girl named Jenny who talked into her lap so softly that you had to lean in to hear her, whose mother kept reaching over to adjust her gown, and touch her hair to fix her up.

"The one who was in the car accident?"

"No. You're thinking of Charlotte—the one who got raped," she said. I confess I felt a flicker of jealousy. As terrible as that was, at least there was an answer to *why*.

"She didn't belong there. She was a wannarexic, a lowly Thanksgiving bulimic, not committed at all. And suiciding on aspirin? Please. How J.V. Her mother was a piece of work, wasn't she? With her Stage 4 tan and Nancy Reagan helmet hair. Anytime her daughter opened her mouth to speak, she'd start shaking her head. Did she think no one noticed?"

I winced.

"I'm sorry, I don't remember her," I said.

"Honestly?"

I knew exactly who she meant. I wasn't going to pick at her bones.

I never spoke to that mother. We had waited for the elevator together, however, the tacit understanding that we were undercover demanded we only acknowledge each other with a nearly imperceptible nod. She always waited until she got off the elevator to remove her sunglasses. I remembered the mother, but not their story. But it was always the same. The daughter battled her anorexia on her own. She was, everybody said it, a survivor. It was such an inspiration to see how she'd grown, like a pink flowering cherry tree, out of the cold barren soil of her childhood. She'd flourished. She'd blossomed. While in the eyes of the world, her *mother*, the poisonous root of all this evil would stay just that—a stone-hard immutable root buried in dirt. No one saw how much the mother hurt. No one knew, or cared, what she'd lost.

"Have you got salt?" I asked.

"Salt is bad for you," Emily said.

"Everyone needs salt. You'd die without it."

"It causes bloating."

"It tenderizes the meat, and brings out the flavor. You need it."

"Fine, fine," she said.

"Pour the salt in your hand," I said. "You'll need more than you think."

"Ouch." She whimpered.

"More," I said. "You'll want to salt the inside too."

"But it stings. It's burning my fingers." I knew how raw the skin around her cuticles must have been. "I mean it, Mommy. It really hurts."

Did I mention that I'm in love.

"Your grandmother always cut out the wishbone before roasting a bird. Your grandfather thought it made it easier to carve."

Emily gasped. "That doesn't seem right. The wishbone? How could she? That's terrible. Did she just throw it away?"

I couldn't remember ever breaking a wishbone with anyone until I met Terry.

"Most likely. Do your fingers still hurt?"

It's the wrists that give the girls away, one of first things the mothers always mentioned. They'd say: *I had no idea. She hid it. She always wore baggy pants and sweatshirts, you know, it's the style, and then one day she pushed up her sleeves to dry the dishes and I saw her wrists . . .*

Even in summertime Emily wore long-sleeved shirts and layered sweaters, pulling the sleeves down over her hands because she was cold. Always cold, even in July. She'd grab my hands to prove it. "Feel how cold I am."

I'd say, "Cold hands, warm heart." But I was thinking: *I bet I could break Emily's wrists if I wanted to*. Later, at the coffee urn that had been set up down the hall away from the meeting room so we couldn't hear our daughters, we talked about their spines, and the way their clavicles stood out like Victorian ruffed collars, and how we counted their ribs. What poor protection they seemed for their heart and lungs. We called our daughters skeletal. Skeletal. A word that, when spoken, felt like eating something soft with bones. One mother described the sight of her daughter in a bathing suit as Auschwitz on the Jersey Shore. Out of courtesy, I laughed, though no one else did.

Standing at the table, we dumped creamers flavored with vanilla, hazelnut, and Irish crème into the weak coffee so it tasted like hot melted ice cream. Sweet and thick and disgusting. Some days there were powdered sugar donuts.

One donut has 270 calories.

"So you've salted the skin, and stuffed it?"

"Yes, Mommy—it's completely, disgustingly stuffed."

"You buttered the bird? Around the legs."

"Um, yes."

"Did you *really* get in there?"

"Yes. Enough."

"Do you have your string ready?"

"String?"

"A needle would be best. You don't want the stuffing to fall out, do you?"

She groaned.

"I'm just trying to help you. If you can't sew it up, you can just tie the legs together."

"This dinner has to be perfect, mother. Do you understand me? Perfect."

"It will be."

"So, I'll do it the right way. Properly. I don't have string, but I've got lots of yarn, and yarn is prettier anyway."

At Melrose they taught the girls to knit. Cast on twenty, knit, knit, knit, purl, purl, purl. It kept their hands busy and their minds off food. Over the years, Emily had knit Paige and me sweaters. We'd open them with trepidation, admire the stitchery, try to resist her pleas for us to model them, but she wouldn't let up. It was always the same. In her mind we were gargantuan, and the sweaters resembled woolen sleeping bags. Humiliated, she'd tearfully demand them back, promising to fix them. Every time, I assured her they'd be perfect if we just washed them and threw them in the dryer. They were so pretty, and we wanted them so badly, but it didn't matter.

"Do you have a needle with a big enough eye for yarn?"

"Mother, I have more stuff like that here than you can imagine. Hold on." I waited for several minutes before Emily came back on the line. "All right," she said, sounding nervous. "I'm threaded and ready."

"Then start sewing the hole closed."

There was no sound.

"No, no I can't. I can't. It's too scary."

You don't know scary, I thought. For ten years I'd kept a pair of slip-on sneakers in the coat closet by the front door, and a twenty-dollar bill in the inside pocket of my car coat just in case of emergencies.

"Stop talking, Emily, and start making stitches."

She was twenty-one when I'd found her in the tub. I just knew. Like the cliché: *A mother knows.*

In the waiting room of the E.R., Emily sat with her arms wrapped in white bath towels, moving between belligerence—*Why did you save me?*—and begging me to forgive her. *I'm so sorry. I didn't mean it. I love you. I never want to leave you.* When other sick or injured people came staggering into the waiting room and fell into seats beside us, she looked embarrassed at not being dead.

"Don't tell Dad," she said. Then, "Have you called Dad yet?"

Three hours later, Emily and I were behind a blue cloth curtain. She was lying down and I was sitting beside her bed, focusing on the green and white tiles behind her head, the perfect squares like a map of Manhattan. I decided I'd take Emily to New York City on her birthday to go shopping. Because it's a grid of numbered streets, running east and west, we could always figure out where we were. If she got lost, I could find her.

It occurred to me thousands of people would come through this hospital, lie on this bed, hundreds of mothers would sit in this chair, and some of the people they loved would die. But that couldn't happen to us.

Emily lifted her head. Her hair looked matted. "Mommy, are you there?"

"Always," I said.

She was groggy from the Valium they'd given her so she'd stay still while they stitched up her wrists. The thread looked black and stiff as hair. I counted the stitches. Ten in each wrist. People always remembered how many stitches.

"Thankfully," the doctor had said, "she cut across the veins, not up and down. Beginner's luck."

"*Voilà!*" Emily shouted. "I did it. Triumph is mine! I really did it and it's a masterpiece. Aren't you proud of me?"

"I am. That was fast. How many stitches did you do?"
"Three."
"Three? That's all?"
"Well, that's all there is room for. But I do have enough thread left to embroider hearts and flowers on the breast."

Calmly I asked her, "How many pounds is the chicken, sweetheart?"

"I don't know. I didn't weigh it, mother. Two or three."

It wasn't a chicken—it was a Cornish game hen.

"What? What's wrong?" Her voice was climbing, scrabbling like an animal with tiny toenails. "Tell me, tell me now. Oh no. It's too small, isn't it?"

"Don't worry," I said. "It'll be enough."

I could see this tiny, pitiful bird lying bound on the plate between my daughter and the man she loved, each of them eyeing it, trying to figure their meager share. I could almost laugh.

"It doesn't matter," she said quickly. "I wasn't going to eat that much anyway."

She'd been a fat baby, eight pounds ten ounces. I remember the picture Terry had taken of newborn Emily and me outside the hospital with his new camera. I don't know if it was the flash or sunlight bouncing off the windows, but the bundle in my arms was brilliant white, like it had just exploded. I'm squinting down at her, temporarily blinded perhaps, but not surprised.

Twenty-two years later, seventy-seven pounds heavier, I brought my baby home again. On the way back, we sang along to Carole King's "I Feel the Earth Move" and she talked nonstop. "I can't wait to sleep in my own bed with my comforter, see my books, and take a bath." I flinched. Her lip trembled, "Oh but I'm going to miss my friends so unbearably much. You can't even begin to imagine. I miss them already and it hasn't even been one hour—the pain is exquisite." She threw her head back against the seat and closed her eyes like she was fighting tears.

"Oh baby," I said, reaching out to squeeze her shoulder, but before I could, she turned away.

"You can't possibly understand. They're like family to me. Family I've chosen, in *my heart*," she gasped. "I don't want to cry anymore. I can't. I'm spent." She sniffled. "How is Paige?"

"Good. I haven't seen her in a while. She's so busy with schoolwork. She's got a new boyfriend, he's in law, and very tall she says."

"Have you been in touch with Dad? Did you tell him I was coming home today?"

"He knows."

"It doesn't matter," Emily said. "No one in the world gets it—gets *me*—like *they* do," she said. "They accept me for who I am, and love me unconditionally."

"I love you," I said. "You can't begin to know how much I love you. You can't." After I parked, before I got out, she'd grabbed my arm.

"I promise that will never happen again. I promise," she said, then leaned over and rested her head on my shoulder, rubbing her nose against my neck. She smelled like vanilla, Vaseline, and rubbing alcohol.

"Am I still your baby?" she asked in a small voice.

"You're always my baby."

"Your *first*," she said, as though this were an accomplishment.

"Always the first."

"But," she sighed, "not the only."

"No," I said, touching her cheek. "But first. First always."

* * *

"You did a great job, Em," I said, knowing how dismayed she must be about the chicken. "You're home-free now. When are you expecting him?"

I had no idea how much time had passed. When was the last time I'd eaten?

"He's supposed to arrive at six, and he's very punctual, which you know I appreciate. I despise rude people."

"So put it in a half an hour before you think you want to eat, and just check on it."

"Do you think it's going to be good? Really good? It is, right? It's going to be wonderful. No, it doesn't matter, right? It doesn't matter."

I thought again of the purple chicken I'd made for Terry. How excited I'd been to cook for him. To show him how worthy I was of his love. The memory of how young and romantic I'd been—unforgivably romantic—had grown less painful over the years. Lately, I'd become nostalgic for the days when I felt hopeful.

"I just want everything to be perfect," she said. "Did I tell you I bought these beautiful linen napkins and—"

"You won't forget to set the timer, will you?"

"Mommy ... " I could hear her beginning to chew her cuticles again. "Mommy, no matter what, *no matter what*, you'll always love me, right? You'll always be there? You'll always help me? Like this."

"Of course. I'm your mother."

"Promise me. Even if I ran off to Fez to be a belly dancer, or moved to California, you'd still—" she spat out a piece of finger skin.

I laughed. "You'd hate California. No one reads. And there are earthquakes," I said, aware of a sour taste in the back of my throat, the pressure of a headache from drinking wine on an empty stomach gathering behind my eyes.

"Don't say that, don't be silly," Emily squeaked. "Oh, Mommy... I don't know how to tell you this, but we've been talking about moving to Los Angeles. Running away together. Isn't that divine? Not this week, of course, but soon. Can you even believe it?"

California was more than two thousand miles away.

"There are, of course, so many more opportunities for thespians on the coast."

"You can't possibly be serious."

I heard her inhale sharply. "Oh my god, I forgot candles! How could I possibly forget candles? What am I going to do? Oh no, no, no. This is horrendous! I had it all planned out—crimson tapers. I set the table this morning, lovely lace tablecloth, wineglasses. How could I be so stupid? I'm not ready at all. I've got to hang up, Mommy, right this instant!"

"Don't forget the bird!" I cried. "You have to tend to it, Emily. Watch it. Baste it. It's a small bird."

"Oh god," she wailed, "this is a colossal mistake, isn't it?"

"No. It's good. It's normal. It's right."

"I really ought to say good-bye now."

The phone felt warm and heavy in my palm. I stared at my ringless fingers. Hands get thinner with age. My mother's hands seemed smaller every time I saw her.

"So," I said, trying to sound casual, "when will I see you again?"

"I'm not really sure. I'm pretty busy." She sounded distracted. Was she thinking about what she was going to wear, or gazing at her pretty table, wondering if she could do without candles?

"I'm free in the afternoon on Saturday, or—"

"Mommy, I'd love to keep talking, but I really have to go. Why don't you call Paige?"

"I said I can't tonight, I have *a date*."

There was a long silence, as though Emily had only just realized she had no idea who I was going out with, or where I was going.

"Wow," she said. "I did it, didn't I?"

"You did," I said. "I'm glad." Was it terrible that some part of me wanted her evening to fail?

One day she'll cook for me, I thought, *and we'll eat again together.* I knew it. I knew it the way I knew I'd always be hungry. Like Emily, only different.

MEMORABLE MEALS

"DINNER: A major daily activity, which can be accomplished in worthy fashion only by intelligent people. It is not enough to eat. To dine, there must be diversified, calm conversation. It should sparkle with the rubies of the wine between courses, be deliciously suave with the sweetness of dessert, and acquire true profundity with the coffee."

—Alexandre Dumas, *The Grand Dictionary of Cuisine*

JEAN ANTHELME BRILLAT-SAVARIN

ON THE PLEASURES OF THE TABLE

Translated by M. F. K. Fisher

I HAVE ALREADY said that the pleasures of the table, as I conceive of them, can go on for a rather long period of time; I am going to prove this now by giving a detailed and faithful account of the lengthiest meal I ever ate in my life; it is a little bonbon which I shall pop into my reader's mouth as a reward for having read me thus far with such agreeable politeness. Here it is:

I used to have, at the end of the Rue du Bac, a family of cousins composed of the following: Doctor Dubois, seventy-eight years old; the captain, seventy-six; their sister Jeannette, who was seventy-four. I went now and then to pay them a visit, and they always received me very graciously.

"By George!" the doctor said one day to me, standing on tiptoe to slap me on the shoulder. "For a long time now you've been boasting of your *fondues* (eggs scrambled with cheese), and you always manage to keep our mouths watering. It's time to stop all this. The captain and I are coming soon to have breakfast with you, to see what it's all about." (It was, I believe, in 1801 that he thus teased me.)

"Gladly," I replied. "You'll taste it in all its glory, for I myself will make it. Your idea is completely delightful to me. So ... tomorrow at ten sharp, military style!"*

---

*Whenever a meal is announced in this way, it must be served on the stroke of the hour: latecomers are treated as deserters.

At the appointed hour I saw my guests arrive, freshly shaved, their hair carefully arranged and well-powdered: two little old men who were still spry and healthy.

They smiled with pleasure when they saw the table ready, spread with white linen, three places laid, and at each of them two dozen oysters and a gleaming golden lemon.

At both ends of the table rose up bottles of Sauterne, carefully wiped clean except for the corks, which indicated in no uncertain way that it was a long time that the wine had rested there.

Alas, in my life-span I have almost seen the last of those oyster breakfasts, so frequent and so gay in the old days, where the molluscs were swallowed by the thousands! They have disappeared with the abbés, who never ate less than a gross apiece, and with the chevaliers, who went on eating them forever. I regret them, in a philosophical way: if time can change governments, how much more influence has it over our simple customs!

After the oysters, which were found to be deliciously fresh, grilled skewered kidneys were served, a deep pastry shell of truffled *foie gras*, and finally the *fondue*.

All its ingredients had been mixed in a casserole, which was brought to the table with an alcohol lamp. I performed on this battlefield, and my cousins did not miss a single one of my gestures.

They exclaimed with delight on the charms of the whole procedure, and asked for my recipe, which I promised to give them, the while I told the two anecdotes on the subject which my reader will perhaps find further on.

After the *fondue* came seasonable fresh fruits and sweetmeats, a cup of real Mocha made *à la Dubelloy*, a method which was then beginning to be known, and finally two kinds of liqueurs, one sharp for refreshing the palate and the other oily for soothing it.

The breakfast being well-ended, I suggested to my guests that we take a little exercise, and that it consist of inspecting my apartment, quarters which are far from elegant but which are spacious and comfortable, and which pleased my company especially since the ceilings and gildings date from the middle of the reign of Louis XV.

I showed them the clay original of the bust of my lovely cousin Mme. Récamier by Chinard, and her portrait in miniature by Augustin; they were so delighted by these that the doctor kissed the portrait with his full fleshy lips, and the captain permitted himself to take such liberty with the statue that I slapped him away; for if all the admirers of the original did likewise, that breast so voluptuously shaped would soon be in the same state as the big toe of Saint Peter in Rome, which pilgrims have worn to a nubbin with their kisses.

Then I showed them a few casts from the works of the best antique sculptors, some paintings which were not without merit, my guns, my musical instruments, and a few fine first editions, as many of them French as foreign.

In this little excursion into such varied arts they did not forget my kitchen. I showed them my economical stockpot, my roasting-shell, my clockwork spit, and my steamcooker. They inspected everything with the most finicky curiosity, and were all the more astonished since in their own kitchens everything was still done as it had been during the Regency.

At the very moment we re-entered my drawing room, the clock struck two. "Bother!" the doctor exclaimed. "Here it is dinner time; and sister Jeannette will be waiting for us! We must hurry back to her. I must confess I feel no real hunger, but still I must have my bowl of soup. It is an old habit with me, and when I go for a day without taking it I have to say with Titus, *Diem perdidi.*"

"My dear doctor," I said to him, "why go so far for what is right here at hand? I'll send someone to the kitchen to give warning that you will stay awhile longer with me, and that you will give me the great pleasure of accepting a dinner toward which I know you will be charitable, since it will not have all the finish of such a meal prepared with more leisure."

A kind of oculary consultation took place at this point between the two brothers, followed by a formal acceptance. I then sent a messenger posthaste to the Faubourg Saint-Germain, and exchanged a word or two with my master cook; and after a remarkably short interval, and thanks partly to his own resources and partly to the help of neighboring restaurants, he served us a very neatly turned out little dinner, and a delectable one to boot.

It gave me deep satisfaction to observe the poise and aplomb with which my two friends seated themselves, pulled nearer to the table, spread out their napkins, and prepared for action.

They were subjected to two surprises which I myself had not intended for them; for first I served them Parmesan cheese with the soup, and then I offered them a glass of dry Madeira. These were novelties but lately imported by Prince Talleyrand, the leader of all our diplomats, to whom we owe so many witticisms, so many epigrams and profundities, and the man so long followed by the public's devout attention, whether in the days of his power or of his retirement.

Dinner went off very well in both its accessory and its main parts, and my cousins reflected as much pleasure as gaiety.

Afterwards I suggested a game of piquet, which they

refused; they preferred the sweet siesta, the *far niente*, of the Italians, the captain told me; and therefore we made a little circle close to the hearth.

In spite of the delights of a postprandial doze, I have always felt that nothing lends more calm pleasure to the conversation than an occupation of whatever kind, so long as it does not absorb the attention. Therefore I proposed a cup of tea.

Tea in itself was an innovation to the old die-hard patriots. Nevertheless it was accepted. I made it before their eyes, and they drank down several cups of it with all the more pleasure since they had always before considered it a remedy.

Long practice has taught me that one pleasure leads to another, and that once headed along this path a man loses the power of refusal. Therefore it was that in an almost imperative voice I spoke of finishing the afternoon with a bowl of punch.

"But you will kill us!" the doctor said.

"Or at least make us tipsy!" the captain added.

To all this I replied only by calling vociferously for lemons, for sugar, for rum.

I concocted the punch then, and while I was busy with it, I had made for me some beautifully thin, delicately buttered, and perfectly salted slices of zwiebach (TOAST).

This time there was a little protest. My cousins assured me that they had already eaten very well indeed, and that they would not touch another thing; but since I am acquainted with the temptations of this completely simple dish, I replied with only one remark, that I hoped I had made enough of it. And sure enough, soon afterwards the captain took the last slice, and I caught him peeking to see if there were still a little more or if it was really the last. I ordered another plateful immediately.

During all this, time had passed, and my watch showed me it was past eight o'clock.

"We must get out of here!" my guests exclaimed. "We are absolutely obliged to go home and eat at least a bit of salad with our poor sister, who has not set eyes on us today!"

I had no real objection to this; faithful to the duties of hospitality when it is concerned with two such delightful old fellows, I accompanied them to their carriage, and watched them be driven away.

Someone may ask if boredom did not show itself now and then in such a long séance.

I shall reply in the negative: the attention of my guests was fixed by my making the *fondue*, by the little trip around the apartment, by a few things which were new to them in the dinner, by the tea, and above all by the punch, which they had never before tasted.

Moreover the doctor knew the genealogy and the bits of gossip of all Paris; the captain had passed part of his life in Italy, both as a soldier and as an envoy to the Parman court; I myself have traveled a great deal; we chatted without affectation, and listened to one another with delight. Not even that much is needed to make time pass with grace and rapidity.

The next morning I received a letter from the doctor; he wished to inform me that the little debauch of the night before had done them no harm at all; quite to the contrary, after the sweetest of sleeps, the two old men had arisen refreshed, feeling both able and eager to begin anew.

ANTON CHEKHOV

ON MORTALITY:
A CARNIVAL TALE

Translated by Peter Constantine

COURT COUNSELOR SEMYON Petrovitch Podtikin sat down at the table, spread a napkin across his chest, and quivering with impatience, awaited the moment the blini would appear. Before him, as before a general surveying a battlefield, a vista unfolded: rank upon rank of bottles, from the middle of the table right up to the front line—three types of vodka, Kiev brandy, Château La Rose, Rhine wine, and even a big-bellied flask of priestly Benedictine. Crowding around the liquors in artful disarray were platters of sprats, sardines in hot sauce, sour cream, caviar (at three rubles forty kopecks a pound), fresh salmon, and so on. Podtikin greedily ran his eyes over the food. His eyes melted like butter; his face oozed with lust.

Frowning, he turned to his wife.

"What's taking so long? Katya!" he called to the cook. "Hurry up!"

Finally, the cook arrived with the blini. At the risk of scorching his fingers, Semyon Petrovitch snatched up two of the hottest from the top of the pile and slapped them onto his plate with gusto. The blini were crisp, lacy, and as plump as the shoulders of a merchant's daughter. Podtikin smiled affably, hiccupped with pleasure, and doused the blini in hot butter. Then, as if to tease his appetite, luxuriating in anticipation, he slowly, deliberately heaped them with caviar. He poured sour cream over the places the caviar left bare. Now he had only to eat, right? Wrong! Contemplating his creation, Podtikin was not quite satisfied. After a moment's thought, he topped the blini with the oiliest slice of salmon he could find, and a sprat, and a sardine; then, no longer able to hold back, trembling with delight and gasping, he rolled up the two blini, downed a shot of vodka, wheezed, opened his mouth—and was struck by an apoplectic fit.

VIRGINIA WOOLF

FROM
TO THE
LIGHTHOUSE

BUT WHAT HAVE I done with my life? thought Mrs. Ramsay, taking her place at the head of the table, and looking at all the plates making white circles on it. "William, sit by me," she said. "Lily," she said, wearily, "over there." They had that—Paul Rayley and Minta Doyle—she, only this—an infinitely long table and plates and knives. At the far end, was her husband, sitting down, all in a heap, frowning. What at? She did not know. She did not mind. She could not understand how she had ever felt any emotion or affection for him. She had a sense of being past everything, through everything, out of everything, as she helped the soup, as if there was an eddy—there—and one could be in it, or one could be out of it, and she was out of it. It's all come to an end, she thought, while they came in one after another, Charles Tansley—"Sit there, please," she said—Augustus Carmichael—and sat down. And meanwhile she waited, passively, for some one to answer her, for something to happen. But this is not a thing, she thought, ladling out soup, that one says.

Raising her eyebrows at the discrepancy—that was what she was thinking, this was what she was doing—ladling out soup—she felt, more and more strongly, outside that eddy; or as if a shade had fallen, and, robbed of colour, she saw things truly. The room (she looked round it) was very shabby. There was no beauty anywhere. She forbore to look at Mr. Tansley. Nothing seemed to have merged. They all sat separate. And the whole of the effort of merging and flowing and creating rested on her. Again she felt, as a fact without hostility, the sterility of men, for if she did not do it nobody would do it, and so, giving herself the little shake that one gives a watch that has stopped, the old familiar pulse began beating, as the watch begins ticking—one, two, three, one, two, three. And so on and so on, she repeated, listening to it, sheltering and fostering the still feeble pulse as one might guard a weak flame with a newspaper. And so then, she concluded, addressing herself by bending silently in his direction to William Bankes—poor man! who had no wife, and no children and dined alone in lodgings except for tonight; and in pity for him, life being now strong enough to bear her on again, she began all this business, as a sailor not without weariness sees the wind fill his sail and yet hardly wants to be off again and thinks how, had the ship sunk, he would have whirled round and round and found rest on the floor of the sea.

"Did you find your letters? I told them to put them in the hall for you," she said to William Bankes.

Lily Briscoe watched her drifting into that strange no-man's land where to follow people is impossible and yet their going inflicts such a chill on those who watch them that they always try at least to follow them with their eyes as one follows a fading ship until the sails have sunk beneath the horizon.

How old she looks, how worn she looks, Lily thought, and how remote. Then when she turned to William Bankes, smiling, it was as if the ship had turned and the sun had struck its sails again, and Lily thought with some amusement because she was relieved, Why does she pity him? For that was the impression she gave, when she told him that his letters were in the hall. Poor William Bankes, she seemed to be saying, as if her own weariness had been partly pitying people, and the life in her, her resolve to live again, had been stirred by pity. And it was not true, Lily thought; it was one of those misjudgements of hers that seemed to be instinctive and to arise from some need of her own rather than of other people's. He is not in the least pitiable. He has his work, Lily said to herself. She remembered, all of a sudden as if she had found a treasure, that she had her work. In a flash, she saw her picture, and thought, Yes, I shall put the tree further in the middle; then I shall avoid that awkward space. That's what I shall do. That's what has been puzzling me. She took up the salt cellar and put it down again on a flower in pattern in the table-cloth, so as to remind herself to move the tree.

"It's odd that one scarcely gets anything worth having by post, yet one always wants one's letters," said Mr. Bankes.

What damned rot they talk, thought Charles Tansley, laying down his spoon precisely in the middle of his plate, which he had swept clean, as if, Lily thought (he sat opposite to her with his back to the window precisely in the middle of view), he were determined to make sure of his meals. Everything about him had that meagre fixity, that bare unloveliness. But nevertheless, the fact remained, it was almost impossible to dislike any one if one looked at them. She liked his eyes; they were blue, deep set, frightening.

"Do you write many letters, Mr. Tansley?" asked Mrs. Ramsay, pitying him too, Lily supposed; for that was true of Mrs. Ramsay—she pitied men always as if they lacked something—women never, as if they had something. He wrote to his mother; otherwise he did not suppose he wrote one letter a month, said Mr. Tansley, shortly.

For he was not going to talk the sort of rot these people wanted him to talk. He was not going to be condescended to by these silly women. He had been reading in his room, and now he came down and it all seemed to him silly, superficial, flimsy. Why did they dress? He had come down in his ordinary clothes. He had not got any dress clothes. "One never gets anything worth having by post"—that was the sort of thing they were always saying. They made men say that sort of thing. Yes, it was pretty well true, he thought. They never got anything worth having from one year's end to another. They did nothing but talk, talk, talk, eat, eat, eat. It was the women's fault. Women made civilization impossible with all their "charm," all their silliness.

"No going to the Lighthouse tomorrow, Mrs. Ramsay," he said, asserting himself. He liked her; he admired her; he still thought of the man in the drain-pipe looking up at her; but he felt it necessary to assert himself.

He was really, Lily Briscoe thought, in spite of his eyes, but then look at his nose, look at his hands, the most uncharming human being she had ever met. Then why did she mind what he said? Women can't write, women can't paint—what did that matter coming from him, since clearly it was not true to him but for some reason helpful to him, and that was why he said it? Why did her whole being bow, like corn under a wind, and erect itself again from this abasement only with a great and rather painful effort? She must make it once more. There's the sprig on the table-cloth; there's my painting; I must move the tree to the middle; that matters—nothing else. Could she not hold fast to that, she asked herself, and not lose her temper, and not argue; and if she wanted revenge take it by laughing at him?

"Oh, Mr. Tansley," she said, "do take me to the Lighthouse with you. I should so love it."

She was telling lies he could see. She was saying what she did not mean to annoy him, for some reason. She was laughing at him. He was in his old flannel trousers. He had no others. He felt very rough and isolated and lonely. He knew that she was trying to tease him for some reason; she didn't want to go to the Lighthouse with him; she despised him: so did Prue Ramsay; so did they all. But he was not going to be made a fool of by women, so he turned deliberately in his chair and looked out of the window and said, all in a jerk, very rudely, it would be too rough for her tomorrow. She would be sick.

It annoyed him that she should have made him speak like that, with Mrs. Ramsay listening. If only he could be alone in his room working, he thought, among his books. That was where he felt at his ease. And he had never run a penny into debt; he had never cost his father a penny since he was fifteen; he had helped them at home out of his savings; he was educating his sister. Still, he wished he had known how to answer Miss Briscoe properly; he wished it had not come out all in a jerk like that. "You'd be sick." He wished he could think of something to say to Mrs. Ramsay, something which would show her he was not just a dry prig. That was what they all thought him. He turned to her. But Mrs. Ramsay was talking about people he had never heard of to William Bankes.

"Yes, take it away," she said briefly, interrupting what she was saying to Mr. Bankes to speak to the maid. "It must have been fifteen—no, twenty years ago—that I last saw her," she was saying, turning back to him again as if she could not lose a moment of their talk, for she was absorbed by what they were saying. So he had actually heard from her this evening! And was Carrie still living at Marlow, and was everything still the same? Oh, she could remember as if it were yesterday—going on the river, feeling very cold. But if the Mannings made a plan they stuck to it. Never should she forget

Herbert killing a wasp with a teaspoon on the bank! And it was still going on, Mrs. Ramsay mused, gliding like a ghost among the chairs and tables of that drawing-room on the banks of the Thames where she had been so very, very cold twenty years ago; but now she went among them like a ghost; and it fascinated her, as if, while she had changed, that particular day, now become very still and beautiful, had remained there, all these years. Had Carrie written to him herself? she asked.

"Yes. She says they're building a new billiard room," he said. No! No! That was out of the question! Building a billiard room! It seemed to her impossible.

Mr. Bankes could not see that there was anything very odd about it. They were very well off now. Should he give her love to Carrie?

"Oh," said Mrs. Ramsay with a little start. "No," she added, reflecting that she did not know this Carrie who built a new billiard room. But how strange, she repeated, to Mr. Bankes's amusement, that they should be going on there still. For it was extraordinary to think that they had been capable of going on living all these years when she had not thought of them more than once all that time. How eventful her own life had been, during those same years. Yet perhaps Carrie Manning had not thought about her either. The thought was strange and distasteful.

"People soon drift apart," said Mr. Bankes, feeling, however, some satisfaction when he thought that after all he knew both the Mannings and the Ramsays. He had not drifted apart he thought, laying down his spoon and wiping his clean-shaven lips punctiliously. But perhaps he was rather unusual, he thought, in this; he never let himself get into a groove. He had friends in all circles ... Mrs. Ramsay had to break off here to tell the maid something about keeping food hot. That was why he preferred dining alone. All those interruptions annoyed him. Well, thought William Bankes, preserving a demeanour of exquisite courtesy and merely spreading the fingers of his left hand on the table-cloth as a mechanic examines a tool beautifully polished and ready for use in an interval of leisure, such are the sacrifices one's friends ask of one. It would have hurt her if he had refused to come. But it was not worth it for him. Looking at his hand he thought that if he had been alone dinner would have been almost over now; he would have been free to work. Yes, he thought, it is a terrible waste of time. The children were dropping in still. "I wish one of you would run up to Roger's room," Mrs. Ramsay was saying. How trifling it all is, how boring it all is, he thought, compared with the other thing—work. Here he sat drumming his fingers on the table-cloth when he might have been—he took a flashing bird's-eye view of his work. What a waste of time it all was to be sure! Yet, he thought, she is one of my oldest friends. I am by way of being devoted to her. Yet now, at this moment her presence meant absolutely nothing to him: her beauty meant nothing to him; her sitting with her little boy at the window—nothing, nothing. He wished only to be alone and to take up that book. He felt uncomfortable; he felt treacherous, that he could sit by her side and feel nothing for her. The truth was that he did not enjoy family life. It was in this sort of state that one asked oneself, What does one live for? Why, one asked oneself, does one take all these pains for the human race to go on? Is it so very desirable? Are we attractive as a species? Not so very, he thought, looking at those rather untidy boys. His favourite, Cam, was in bed, he supposed. Foolish questions, vain questions, questions one never asked if one was occupied. Is human life this? Is human life that? One never had time to think about it. But here he was asking himself that sort of question, because Mrs. Ramsay was giving orders to servants, and also because it had struck him, thinking how surprised Mrs. Ramsay was that Carrie Manning should still exist, that friendships, even the best of them, are frail things. One drifts apart. He reproached himself again. He was sitting beside Mrs. Ramsay and he had nothing in the world to say to her.

"I'm so sorry," said Mrs. Ramsay, turning to him at last. He felt rigid and barren, like a pair of boots that have been soaked and gone dry so that you can hardly force your feet into them. Yet he must force his feet into them. He must make himself talk. Unless he were very careful, she would find out this treachery of his; that he did not care a straw for her, and that would not be at all pleasant, he thought. So he bent his head courteously in her direction.

"How you must detest dining in this bear garden," she said, making use, as she did when she was distracted, of her social manner. So, when there is a strife of tongues, at some meeting, the chairman, to obtain unity, suggests that every one shall speak in French. Perhaps it is bad French; French may not contain the words that express the speaker's thoughts; nevertheless speaking French imposes some order, some uniformity. Replying to her in the same language, Mr. Bankes said, "No, not at all," and Mr. Tansley, who had no knowledge of this language, even spoken thus in words of one syllable, at once suspected its insincerity. They did talk nonsense, he thought, the Ramsays; and he pounced on this fresh instance with joy, making a note which, one of these days, he would read aloud, to one or two friends. There, in a society where one could say what one liked he would sarcastically describe "staying with the Ramsays" and what nonsense they talked. It was worth while doing it once, he would say; but not again. The women bored one so, he would say.

Of course Ramsay had dished himself by marrying a beautiful woman and having eight children. It would shape itself something like that, but now, at this moment, sitting stuck there with an empty seat beside him, nothing had shaped itself at all. It was all in scraps and fragments. He felt extremely, even physically, uncomfortable. He wanted somebody to give him a chance of asserting himself. He wanted it so urgently that he fidgeted in his chair, looked at this person, then at that person, tried to break into their talk, opened his mouth and shut it again. They were talking about the fishing industry. Why did no one ask him his opinion? What did they know about the fishing industry?

Lily Briscoe knew all that. Sitting opposite him, could she not see, as in an X-ray photograph, the ribs and thigh bones of the young man's desire to impress himself, lying dark in the mist of his flesh—that thin mist which convention had laid over his burning desire to break into the conversation? But, she thought, screwing up her Chinese eyes, and remembering how he sneered at women, "can't paint, can't write," why should I help him to relieve himself?

There is a code of behaviour, she knew, whose seventh article (it may be) says that on occasions of this sort it behooves the woman, whatever her own occupation may be, to go to the help of the young man opposite so that he may expose and relieve the thigh bones, the ribs, of his vanity, of his urgent desire to assert himself; as indeed it is their duty, she reflected, in her old maidenly fairness, to help us, suppose the Tube were to burst into flames. Then, she thought, I should certainly expect Mr. Tansley to get me out. But how would it be, she thought, if neither of us did either of these things? So she sat there smiling.

"You're not planning to go to the Lighthouse, are you, Lily," said Mrs. Ramsay. "Remember poor Mr. Langley; he had been round the world dozens of times, but he told me he never suffered as he did when my husband took him there. Are you a good sailor, Mr. Tansley?" she asked.

Mr. Tansley raised a hammer: swung it high in air; but realizing, as it descended, that he could not smite that butterfly with such an instrument as this, said only that he had never been sick in his life. But in that one sentence lay compact, like gunpowder, that his grandfather was a fisherman; his father a chemist; that he had worked his way up entirely himself; that he was proud of it; that he was Charles Tansley—a fact that nobody there seemed to realize; but one of these days every single person would know it. He scowled ahead of him. He could almost pity these mild cultivated people, who would be blown sky high, like bales of wool and barrels of apples, one of these days by the gunpowder that was in him.

"Will you take me, Mr. Tansley?" said Lily, quickly, kindly, for, of course, if Mrs. Ramsay said to her, as in effect she did, "I am drowning, my dear, in seas of fire. Unless you apply some balm to the anguish of this hour and say something nice to that young man there, life will run upon the rocks—indeed I hear the grating and the growling at this minute. My nerves are taut as fiddle strings. Another touch and they will snap"—when Mrs. Ramsay said all this, as the glance in her eyes said it, of course for the hundred and fiftieth time Lily Briscoe had to renounce the experiment—what happens if one is not nice to that young man there—and be nice.

Judging the turn in her mood correctly—that she was friendly to him now—he was relieved of his egotism, and told her how he had been thrown out of a boat when he was a baby; how his father used to fish him out with a boat-hook; that was how he had learnt to swim. One of his uncles kept the light on some rock or other off the Scottish coast, he said. He had been there with him in a storm. This was said loudly in a pause. They had to listen to him when he said that he had been with his uncle in a lighthouse in a storm. Ah, thought Lily Briscoe, as the conversation took this auspicious turn, and she felt Mrs. Ramsay's gratitude (for Mrs. Ramsay was free now to talk for a moment herself), ah, she thought, but what haven't I paid to get it for you? She had not been sincere.

She had done the usual trick—been nice. She would never know him. He would never know her. Human relations were all like that, she thought, and the worst (if it had not been for Mr. Bankes) were between men and women. Inevitably these were extremely insincere she thought. Then her eye caught the salt cellar, which she had placed there to remind her, and she remembered that next morning she would move the tree further towards the middle, and her spirits rose so high at the thought of painting tomorrow that she laughed out loud at what Mr. Tansley was saying. Let him talk all night if he liked it.

"But how long do they leave men on a Lighthouse?" she asked. He told her. He was amazingly well informed. And as he was grateful, and as he liked her, and as he was beginning to enjoy himself, so now, Mrs. Ramsay thought, she could return to that dream land, that unreal but fascinating place, the Mannings' drawing-room at Marlow twenty years ago; where one moved about without haste or anxiety, for there was no future to worry about. She knew what had happened to them, what to her. It was like reading a good book again, for she knew the end of that story, since it had happened twenty years ago, and life, which shot down even from this dining-room table in cascades, heaven knows where, was sealed up there, and lay, like a lake, placidly between its banks. He said they had built a billiard room—was it possible? Would William go on talking about the Mannings? She wanted him to. But, no—for some reason he was no longer in the mood. She tried. He did not respond. She could not force him. She was disappointed.

"The children are disgraceful," she said, sighing. He said something about punctuality being one of the minor virtues which we do not acquire until later in life.

"If at all," said Mrs. Ramsay merely to fill up space, thinking what an old maid William was becoming. Conscious of his treachery, conscious of her wish to talk about something more intimate, yet out of mood for it at present, he felt come over him the disagreeableness of life, sitting there, waiting. Perhaps the others were saying something interesting? What were they saying?

That the fishing season was bad; that the men were emigrating. They were talking about wages and unemployment. The young man was abusing the government. William Bankes, thinking what a relief it was to catch on to something of this sort when private life was disagreeable, heard him say something about "one of the most scandalous acts of the present government." Lily was listening; Mrs. Ramsay was listening; they were all listening. But already bored, Lily felt that something was lacking; Mr. Bankes felt that something was lacking. Pulling her shawl round her Mrs. Ramsay felt that something was lacking. All of them bending themselves to listen thought, "Pray heaven that the inside of my mind may not be exposed," for each thought, "The others are feeling this. They are outraged and indignant with the government about the fishermen. Whereas, I feel nothing at all." But perhaps, thought Mr. Bankes, as he looked at Mr. Tansley, here is the man. One was always waiting for the man. There was always a chance. At any moment the leader might arise; the man of genius, in politics as in anything else. Probably he will be extremely disagreeable to us old fogies, thought Mr. Bankes, doing his best to make allowances, for he knew by some curious physical sensation, as of nerves erect in his spine, that he was jealous, for himself partly, partly more probably for his work, for his point of view, for his science; and therefore he was not entirely open-minded or altogether fair, for Mr. Tansley seemed to be saying, You have wasted your lives. You are all of you wrong. Poor old fogies, you're hopelessly behind the times. He seemed to be rather cocksure, this young man; and his manners were bad. But Mr. Bankes bade himself observe, he had courage; he had ability; he was extremely well up in the facts. Probably, Mr. Bankes thought, as Tansley abused the government, there is a good deal in what he says.

"Tell me now . . . " he said. So they argued about politics, and Lily looked at the leaf on the table-cloth; and Mrs. Ramsay, leaving the argument entirely in the hands of the two men, wondered why she was so bored by this talk, and wished, looking at her husband at the other end of the table, that he would say something. One word, she said to herself. For if he said a thing, it would make all the difference. He went to the heart of things. He cared about fishermen and their wages. He could not sleep for thinking of them. It was altogether different when he spoke; one did not feel then, pray heaven you don't see how little I care, because one did care. Then, realizing that it was because she admired him so much that she was waiting for him to speak, she felt as if somebody had been praising her husband to her and their marriage, and she glowed all over without realizing that it was she herself who had praised him. She looked at him thinking to find this in his face; he would be looking magnificent.... But not in the least! He was screwing his face up, he was scowling and frowning, and flushing with anger. What on earth was it about? she wondered. What could be the matter? Only that poor old Augustus had asked for another plate of soup—that was all. It was unthinkable, it was detestable (so he signalled to her across the table) that Augustus should be beginning his soup over again. He loathed people eating when he had finished. She saw his anger fly like a pack of hounds into his eyes, his brow, and she knew that in a moment something violent would explode, and then—thank goodness! she saw him clutch himself and clap a brake on the wheel, and the whole of his body seemed to emit sparks but not words. He sat there scowling. He had said nothing, he would have her observe. Let her give him the credit for that! But why after all should poor Augustus not ask for another plate of soup? He had merely touched Ellen's arm and said:

"Ellen, please, another plate of soup," and then Mr. Ramsay scowled like that.

And why not? Mrs. Ramsay demanded. Surely they could let Augustus have his soup if he wanted it. He hated people wallowing in food, Mr. Ramsay frowned at her. He hated everything dragging on for hours like this. But he had controlled himself, Mr. Ramsay would have her observe, disgusting though the sight was. But why show it so plainly, Mrs. Ramsay demanded (they looked at each other down the long table sending these questions and answers across, each knowing exactly what the other felt). Everybody could see, Mrs. Ramsay thought. There was Rose gazing at her father, there was Roger gazing at his father; both would be off in spasms of laughter in another second, she knew, and so she said promptly (indeed it was time):

"Light the candles," and they jumped up instantly and went and fumbled at the sideboard.

Why could he never conceal his feelings? Mrs. Ramsay wondered, and she wondered if Augustus Carmichael had noticed. Perhaps he had; perhaps he had not. She could not help respecting the composure with which he sat there, drinking his soup. If he wanted soup, he asked for soup. Whether people laughed at him or were angry with him he was the same. He did not like her, she knew that; but partly for that very reason she respected him, and looking at him, drinking soup, very large and calm in the failing light, and monumental, and contemplative, she wondered what he did feel then, and why he was always content and dignified; and she thought how devoted he was to Andrew, and would call him into his room and, Andrew said, "show him things." And there he would lie all day long on the lawn brooding presumably over his poetry, till he reminded one of a cat watching birds, and then he clapped his paws together when he had found the word, and her husband said, "Poor old Augustus—he's a true poet," which was high praise from her husband.

Now eight candles were stood down the table, and after the first stoop the flames stood upright and drew with them into visibility the long table entire, and in the middle a yellow and purple dish of fruit. What had she done with it, Mrs. Ramsay wondered, for Rose's arrangement of the grapes and pears, of the horny pink-lined shell, of the bananas, made her think of a trophy fetched from the bottom of the sea, of Neptune's banquet, of the bunch that hangs with vine leaves over the shoulder of Bacchus (in some picture), among the leopard skins and the torches lolloping red and gold. ... Thus brought up suddenly into the light it seemed possessed of great size and depth, was like a world in which one could take one's staff and climb hills, she thought, and go down into valleys, and to her pleasure (for it brought them into sympathy momentarily) she saw that Augustus too feasted his eyes on the same plate of fruit, plunged in, broke off a bloom there, a tassel here, and returned, after feasting, to his hive. That was his way of looking, different from hers. But looking together united them.

Now all the candles were lit up, and the faces on both sides of the table were brought nearer by the candlelight, and composed, as they had not been in the twilight, into a party round a table, for the night was now shut off by panes of glass, which, far from giving any accurate view of the outside world, rippled it so strangely that here, inside the room, seemed to be order and dry land; there, outside, a reflection in which things wavered and vanished, waterily.

Some change at once went through them all, as if this had really happened, and they were all conscious of making a party together in a hollow, on an island; had their common cause against that fluidity out there. Mrs. Ramsay, who had been uneasy, waiting for Paul and Minta to come in, and unable, she felt, to settle to things, now felt her uneasiness changed to expectation. For now they must come, and Lily Briscoe, trying to analyse the cause of the sudden exhilaration, compared it with that moment on the tennis lawn, when solidity suddenly vanished, and such vast spaces lay between them; and now the same effect was got by the many candles in the sparely furnished room, and the uncurtained windows, and the bright mask-like look of faces seen by candlelight. Some weight was taken off them; anything might happen, she felt. They must come now, Mrs. Ramsay thought, looking at the door, and at that instant, Minta Doyle, Paul Rayley, and a maid carrying a great dish in her hands came in together. They were awfully late; they were horribly late, Minta said, as they found their way to different ends of the table.

"I lost my brooch—my grandmother's brooch," said Minta with a sound of lamentation in her voice, and a suffusion in her large brown eyes, looking down, looking up, as she sat by Mr. Ramsay, which roused his chivalry so that he bantered her.

How could she be such a goose, he asked, as to scramble about the rocks in jewels?

She was by way of being terrified of him—he was so fearfully clever, and the first night when she had sat by him, and he talked about George Eliot, she had been really frightened, for she had left the third volume of *Middlemarch* in the train and she never knew what happened in the end; but afterwards she got on perfectly, and made herself out even more ignorant than she was, because he liked telling her she was a fool. And so tonight, directly he laughed at her, she was not frightened. Besides, she knew, directly she came into the room that the miracle had happened; she wore her golden haze. Sometimes she had it; sometimes not. She never knew why it came or why it went, or if she had it until she came into the room and then she knew instantly by the way some man looked at her. Yes, tonight she had it, tremendously; she knew that by the way Mr. Ramsay told her not to be a fool. She sat beside him, smiling.

It must have happened then, thought Mrs. Ramsay; they are engaged. And for a moment she felt what she had never expected to feel again—jealousy. For he, her husband, felt it too—Minta's glow; he liked these girls, these golden-reddish girls, with something flying, something a little wild and harum-scarum about them, who didn't "scrape their hair off," weren't, as he said about poor Lily Briscoe, ". . . skimpy." There was some quality which she herself had not; some lustre, some richness, which attracted him, amused him, led him to make favourites of girls like Minta. They might cut his hair from him, plait him watch-chains, or interrupt him at his work, hailing him (she heard them), "Come along, Mr. Ramsay; it's our turn to beat them now," and out he came to play tennis.

But indeed she was not jealous, only, now and then, when she made herself look in her glass a little resentful that she had grown old, perhaps, by her own fault. (The bill for the greenhouse and all the rest of it.) She was grateful to them for laughing at him. ("How many pipes have you smoked today, Mr. Ramsay?" and so on), till he seemed a young man; a man very attractive to women, not burdened, not weighed down with the greatness of his labours and the sorrows of the world and his fame or his failure, but again as she had first known him, gaunt but gallant; helping her out of a boat, she remembered; with delightful ways, like that (she looked at him, and he looked astonishingly young, teasing Minta). For herself—"Put it down there," she said, helping the Swiss girl to place gently before her the huge brown pot in which was the Bœuf en Daube—for her own part she liked her boobies. Paul must sit by her. She had kept a place for him. Really, she sometimes thought she liked the boobies best. They did not bother one with their dissertations. How much they missed, after all, these very clever men! How dried up they did become, to be sure. There was something, she thought as he sat down, very charming about Paul. His manners were delightful to her, and his sharp-cut nose and his bright blue eyes. He was so considerate. Would he tell her—now that they were all talking again—what had happened?

"We went back to look for Minta's brooch," he said, sitting down by her. "We"—that was enough. She knew from the effort, the rise in his voice to surmount a difficult word that it was the first time he had said "we." "We did this, we did that." They'll say that all their lives, she thought, and an exquisite scent of olives and oil and juice rose from the great brown dish as Marthe, with a little flourish, took the cover off. The cook had spent three days over that dish. And she must take great care, Mrs. Ramsay thought, diving into the soft mass, to choose a specially tender piece for William Bankes. And she peered into the dish, with its shiny walls and its confusion of savoury brown and yellow meats and its bay leaves and its wine, and thought, This will celebrate the occasion—a curious sense rising in her, at once freakish and tender, of celebrating a festival, as if two emotions were called up in her, one profound—for what could be more serious than the love of man for woman, what more commanding, more impressive, bearing in its bosom the seeds of death; at the same time these lovers, these people entering into illusion glittering eyed, must be danced round with mockery, decorated with garlands.

"It is a triumph," said Mr. Bankes, laying his knife down for a moment. He had eaten attentively. It was rich; it was tender. It was perfectly cooked. How did she manage these things in the depths of the country? he asked her. She was a wonderful woman. All his love, all his reverence, had returned; and she knew it.

"It is a French recipe of my grandmother's," said Mrs. Ramsay, speaking with a ring of great pleasure in her voice. Of course it was French. What passes for cookery in England is an abomination (they agreed). It is putting cabbages in water. It is roasting meat till it is like leather. It is cutting off the delicious skins of vegetables. "In which," said Mr. Bankes, "all the virtue of the vegetable is contained." And the waste, said Mrs. Ramsay. A whole French family could live on what an English cook throws away. Spurred on by her sense that William's affection had come back to her, and that everything was all right again, and that her suspense was over, and that now she was free both to triumph and to mock, she laughed, she gesticulated, till Lily thought, How childlike, how absurd she was, sitting up there with all her beauty opened again in her, talking about the skins of vegetables. There was something frightening about her. She was irresistible. Always she got her own way in the end, Lily thought. Now she had brought this off—Paul and Minta, one might suppose, were engaged. Mr. Bankes was dining here. She put a spell on them all, by wishing, so simply, so directly, and Lily contrasted that abundance with her own poverty of spirit, and supposed that it was partly that belief (for her face was all lit up—without looking young, she looked radiant) in this strange, this terrifying thing, which made Paul Rayley, sitting at her side, all of a tremor, yet abstract, absorbed, silent. Mrs. Ramsay, Lily felt, as she talked about the skins of vegetables, exalted that, worshipped that; held her hands over it to warm them, to protect it, and yet, having brought it all about, somehow laughed, led her victims, Lily felt, to the altar. It came over her too now—the emotion, the vibration, of love. How inconspicuous she felt herself by Paul's side! He, glowing, burning; she, aloof, satirical; he, bound for adventure; she, moored to the shore; he, launched, incautious; she, solitary, left out—and, ready to implore a share, if it were disaster, in his disaster, she said shyly:

"When did Minta lose her brooch?"

He smiled the most exquisite smile, veiled by memory, tinged by dreams. He shook his head. "On the beach," he said.

"I'm going to find it," he said, "I'm getting up early." This being kept secret from Minta, he lowered his voice, and turned his eyes to where she sat, laughing, beside Mr. Ramsay.

Lily wanted to protest violently and outrageously her desire to help him, envisaging how in the dawn on the beach she would be the one to pounce on the brooch half-hidden by some stone, and thus herself be included among the sailors and adventurers. But what did he reply to her offer? She actually said with an emotion that she seldom let appear, "Let me come with you," and he laughed. He meant yes or no—either perhaps. But it was not his meaning—it was the odd chuckle he gave, as if he had said, Throw yourself over the cliff if you like, I don't care. He turned on her cheek the heat of love, its horror, its cruelty, its unscrupulosity. It scorched her, and Lily, looking at Minta, being charming to Mr. Ramsay at the other end of the table, flinched for her exposed to these fangs, and was thankful. For at any rate, she said to herself, catching sight of the salt cellar on the pattern, she need not marry, thank Heaven: she need not undergo that degradation. She was saved from that dilution. She would move the tree rather more to the middle.

Such was the complexity of things. For what happened to her, especially staying with the Ramsays, was to be made to feel violently two opposite things at the same time; that's what you feel, was one; that's what I feel, was the other, and then they fought together in her mind, as now. It is so beautiful, so exciting, this love, that I tremble on the verge of it, and offer, quite out of my own habit, to look for a brooch on a beach; also it is the stupidest, the most barbaric of human passions, and turns a nice young man, with a profile like a gem's (Paul's was exquisite) into a bully with a crowbar (he was swaggering, he was insolent) in the Mile End Road. Yet, she said to herself, from the dawn of time odes have been sung to love; wreaths heaped and roses; and if you asked nine people out of ten they would say they wanted nothing but this—love; while the women, judging from her own experience, would all the time be feeling, This is not what we want; there is nothing more tedious, puerile, and inhumane than this; yet it is also beautiful and necessary. Well then, well then? she asked, somehow expecting the others to go on with the argument, as if in an argument like this one threw one's own little bolt which fell short obviously and left the others to carry it on. So she listened again to what they were saying in case they should throw any light upon the question of love.

"Then," said Mr. Bankes, "there is that liquid the English call coffee."

"Oh, coffee!" said Mrs. Ramsay. But it was much rather a question (she was thoroughly roused, Lily could see, and talked very emphatically) of real butter and clean milk. Speaking with warmth and eloquence, she described the iniquity of the English dairy system, and in what state milk was delivered at the door, and was about to prove her charges, for she had gone into the matter, when all round the table, beginning with Andrew in the middle, like a fire leaping from tuft to tuft of furze, her children laughed; her husband laughed; she was laughed at, fire-encircled, and forced to veil her crest, dismount her batteries, and only retaliate by displaying the raillery and ridicule of the table to Mr. Bankes as an example of what one suffered if one attacked the prejudices of the British Public.

Purposely, however, for she had it on her mind that Lily, who had helped her with Mr. Tansley, was out of things, she exempted her from the rest; said "Lily anyhow agrees with me," and so drew her in, a little fluttered, a little startled. (For she was thinking about love.) They were both out of things, Mrs. Ramsay had been thinking, both Lily and Charles Tansley. Both suffered from the glow of the other two. He, it was clear, felt himself utterly in the cold; no woman would look at him with Paul Rayley in the room. Poor fellow! Still, he had his dissertation, the influence of somebody upon something: he could take care of himself. With Lily it was different. She faded, under Minta's glow; became more inconspicuous than ever, in her little grey dress with her little puckered face and her little Chinese eyes. Everything about her was so small. Yet, thought Mrs. Ramsay, comparing her with Minta, as she claimed her help (for Lily should bear her out, she talked no more about her dairies than her husband did about his boots—he would talk by the hour about his boots) of the two, Lily at forty will be the better. There was in Lily a thread of something; a flare of something; something of her own which Mrs. Ramsay liked very much indeed, but no man would, she feared. Obviously, not, unless it were a much older man, like William Bankes. But then he cared, well, Mrs. Ramsay sometimes thought that he cared, since his wife's death, perhaps for her. He was not "in love" of course; it was one of those unclassified affections of which there are so many. Oh, but nonsense, she thought; William must marry Lily. They have so many things in common. Lily is so fond of flowers. They are both cold and aloof and rather self-sufficing. She must arrange for them to take a long walk together.

Foolishly, she had set them opposite each other. That could be remedied tomorrow. If it were fine, they should go for a picnic. Everything seemed possible. Everything seemed right. Just now (but this cannot last, she thought, dissociating herself from the moment while they were all talking about boots) just now she had reached security; she hovered like a hawk suspended; like a flag floated in an element of joy which filled every nerve of her body fully and sweetly, not noisily, solemnly rather, for it arose, she thought, looking at them all eating there, from husband and children and friends; all of which rising in this profound stillness (she was helping William Bankes to one very small piece more, and peered into the depths of the earthenware pot) seemed now for no special reason to stay there like a smoke, like a fume rising upwards, holding them safe together. Nothing need be said; nothing could be said. There it was, all round them. It partook, she felt, carefully helping Mr. Bankes to a specially tender piece, of eternity; as she had already felt about something different once before that afternoon; there is a coherence in things, a stability; something, she meant, is immune from change, and shines out (she glanced at the window with its ripple of reflected lights) in the face of the flowing, the fleeting, the spectral, like a ruby; so that again tonight she had the feeling she had had once today, already, of peace, of rest. Of such moments, she thought, the thing is made that endures.

"Yes," she assured William Bankes, "there is plenty for everybody."

"Andrew," she said, "hold your plate lower, or I shall spill it." (The Bœuf en Daube was a perfect triumph.) Here, she felt, putting the spoon down, was the still space that lies about the heart of things, where one could move or rest; could wait now (they were all helped) listening; could then, like a hawk which lapses suddenly from its high station, flaunt and sink on laughter easily, resting her whole weight upon what at the other end of the table her husband was saying about the square root of one thousand two hundred and fifty-three. That was the number, it seemed, on his watch.

What did it all mean? To this day she had no notion. A square root? What was that? Her sons knew. She leant on them; on cubes and square roots; that was what they were talking about now; on Voltaire and Madame de Staël; on the character of Napoleon; on the French system of land tenure; on Lord Rosebery; on Creevey's Memoirs: she let it uphold her and sustain her, this admirable fabric of the masculine intelligence, which ran up and down, crossed this way and that, like iron girders spanning the swaying fabric, upholding the world, so that she could trust herself to it utterly, even shut her eyes, or flicker them for a moment, as a child staring up from its pillow winks at the myriad layers of the leaves of a tree. Then she woke up. It was still being fabricated. William Bankes was praising the Waverley novels.

He read one of them every six months, he said. And why should that make Charles Tansley angry? He rushed in (all, thought Mrs. Ramsay, because Prue will not be nice to him) and denounced the Waverley novels when he knew nothing about it, nothing about it whatsoever, Mrs. Ramsay thought, observing him rather than listening to what he said. She could see how it was from his manner—he wanted to assert himself, and so it would always be with him till he got his Professorship or married his wife, and so need not be always saying, "I – I – I." For that was what his criticism of poor Sir Walter, or perhaps it was Jane Austen, amounted to. "I – I – I." He was thinking of himself and the impression he was making, as she could tell by the sound of his voice, and his emphasis and his uneasiness. Success would be good for him. At any rate they were off again. Now she need not listen. It could not last, she knew, but at the moment her eyes were so clear that they seemed to go round the table unveiling each of these people, and their thoughts and their feelings, without effort like a light stealing under water so that its ripples and the reeds in it and the minnows balancing themselves, and the sudden silent trout are all lit up hanging, trembling. So she saw them; she heard them; but whatever they said had also this quality, as if what they said was like the movement of a trout when, at the same time, one can see the ripple and the gravel, something to the right, something to the left; and the whole is held together; for whereas in active life she would be netting and separating one thing from another; she would be saying she liked the Waverley novels or had not read them; she would be urging herself forward; now she said nothing. For the moment, she hung suspended.

"Ah, but how long do you think it'll last?" said somebody. It was as if she had antennæ trembling out from her, which, intercepting certain sentences, forced them upon her attention. This was one of them. She scented danger for her husband. A question like that would lead, almost certainly, to something being said which reminded him of his own failure. How long would he be read—he would think at once. William Bankes (who was entirely free from all such vanity) laughed, and said he attached no importance to changes in fashion. Who could tell what was going to last—in literature or indeed in anything else?

"Let us enjoy what we do enjoy," he said. His integrity seemed to Mrs. Ramsay quite admirable. He never seemed for a moment to think, But how does this affect me? But then if you had the other temperament, which must have praise, which must have encouragement, naturally you began (and she knew that Mr. Ramsay was beginning) to be uneasy; to want somebody to say, Oh, but your work will last, Mr. Ramsay, or something like that. He showed his uneasiness quite clearly now by saying, with some irritation, that, anyhow, Scott (or was it Shakespeare?) would last him his lifetime. He said it irritably. Everybody, she thought, felt a little uncomfortable, without knowing why. Then Minta Doyle, whose instinct was fine, said bluffly, absurdly, that she did not believe that any one really enjoyed reading Shakespeare. Mr. Ramsay said grimly (but his mind was turned away again) that very few people liked it as much as they said they did. But, he added, there is considerable merit in some of the plays nevertheless, and Mrs. Ramsay saw that it would be all right for the moment anyhow; he would laugh at Minta, and she, Mrs. Ramsay saw, realizing his extreme anxiety about himself, would, in her own way, see that he was taken care of, and praise him, somehow or other. But she wished it was not necessary: perhaps it was her fault that it was necessary. Anyhow, she was free now to listen to what Paul Rayley was trying to say about books one had read as a boy. They lasted, he said. He had read some of Tolstoi at school. There was one he always remembered, but he had forgotten the name. Russian names were impossible, said Mrs. Ramsay. "Vronsky," said Paul. He remembered that because he always thought it such a good name for a villain. "Vronsky," said Mrs. Ramsay; "Oh, *Anna Karenina*," but that did not take them very far; books were not in their line. No, Charles Tansley would put them both right in a second about books, but it was all so mixed up with, Am I saying the right thing? Am I making a good impression? that, after all, one knew more about him than about Tolstoi, whereas, what Paul said was about the thing, simply, not himself, nothing else. Like all stupid people, he had a kind of modesty too, a consideration for what you were feeling, which, once in a way at least, she found attractive. Now he was thinking, not about himself or about Tolstoi, but whether she was cold, whether she felt a draught, whether she would like a pear.

No, she said, she did not want a pear. Indeed she had been keeping guard over the dish of fruit (without realizing it) jealously, hoping that nobody would touch it. Her eyes had been going in and out among the curves and shadows of the fruit, among the rich purples of the lowland grapes, then over the horny ridge of the shell, putting a yellow against a purple, a curved shape against a round shape, without knowing why she did it, or why, every time she did it, she felt more and more serene; until, oh, what a pity that they should do it—a hand reached out, took a pear, and spoilt the whole thing. In sympathy she looked at Rose. She looked at Rose sitting between Jasper and Prue. How odd that one's child should do that!

How odd to see them sitting there, in a row, her children, Jasper, Rose, Prue, Andrew, almost silent, but with some joke of their own going on, she guessed, from the twitching at their lips. It was something quite apart from everything else, something they were hoarding up to laugh over in their own room. It was not about their father, she hoped. No, she thought not. What was it, she wondered, sadly rather, for it seemed to her that they would laugh when she was not there. There was all that hoarded behind those rather set, still, mask-like faces, for they did not join in easily; they were like watchers, surveyors, a little raised or set apart from the grown-up people. But when she looked at Prue tonight, she saw that this was not now quite true of her. She was just beginning, just moving, just descending. The faintest light was on her face, as if the glow of Minta opposite, some excitement, some anticipation of happiness was reflected in her, as if the sun of the love of men and women rose over the rim of the table-cloth, and without knowing what it was she bent towards it and greeted it. She kept looking at Minta, shyly, yet curiously, so that Mrs. Ramsay looked from one to the other and said, speaking to Prue in her own mind, You will be as happy as she is one of these days. You will be much happier, she added, because you are my daughter, she meant; her own daughter must be happier than other people's daughters. But dinner was over. It was time to go. They were only playing with things on their plates. She would wait until they had done laughing at some story her husband was telling. He was having a joke with Minta about a bet. Then she would get up.

She liked Charles Tansley, she thought, suddenly; she liked his laugh. She liked him for being so angry with Paul and Minta. She liked his awkwardness. There was a lot in that young man after all. And Lily, she thought, putting her napkin beside her plate, she always has some joke of her own. One need never bother about Lily. She waited. She tucked her napkin under the edge of her plate. Well, were they done now? No. That story had led to another story. Her husband was in great spirits tonight, and wishing, she supposed, to make it all right with old Augustus after that scene about the soup, had drawn him in—they were telling stories about some one they had both known at college. She looked at the window in which the candle flames burnt brighter now that the panes were black, and looking at that outside the voices came to her very strangely, as if they were voices at a service in a cathedral, for she did not listen to the words. The sudden bursts of laughter and then one voice (Minta's) speaking alone, reminded her of men and boys crying out the Latin words of a service in some Roman Catholic cathedral. She waited. Her husband spoke. He was repeating something, and she knew it was poetry from the rhythm and the ring of exultation, and melancholy in his voice:

> *Come out and climb the garden path,*
> *Luriana Lurilee.*
> *The China rose is all abloom and buzzing with the*
> *yellow bee.*

The words (she was looking at the window) sounded as if they were floating like flowers on water out there, cut off from them all, as if no one had said them, but they had come into existence of themselves.

"And all the lives we ever lived and all the lives to be are full of trees and changing leaves." She did not know what they meant, but, like music, the words seemed to be spoken by her own voice, outside her self, saying quite easily and naturally what had been in her mind the whole evening while she said different things. She knew, without looking round, that every one at the table was listening to the voice saying:

> *I wonder if it seems to you,*
> *Luriana, Lurilee*

with the same sort of relief and pleasure that she had, as if this were, at last, the natural thing to say, this were their own voice speaking.

But the voice stopped. She looked round. She made herself get up. Augustus Carmichael had risen and, holding his table napkin so that it looked like a long white robe he stood chanting:

> *To see the Kings go riding by*
> *Over lawn and daisy lea*
> *With their palm leaves and cedar sheaves,*
> *Luriana, Lurilee,*

and as she passed him, he turned slightly towards her repeating the last words:

> *Luriana, Lurilee*

and bowed to her as if he did her homage. Without knowing why, she felt that he liked her better than he had ever done before; and with a feeling of relief and gratitude she returned his bow and passed through the door which he held open for her.

It was necessary now to carry everything a step further. With her foot on the threshold she waited a moment longer in a scene which was vanishing even as she looked, and then, as she moved and took Minta's arm and left the room, it changed, it shaped itself differently; it had become, she knew, giving one last look at it over her shoulder, already the past.

EVELYN WAUGH

THE MANAGER OF "THE KREMLIN"

THIS STORY WAS told me in Paris very early in the morning by the manager of a famous night club, and I am fairly certain that it is true.

I shall not tell you the real name of the manager or of his club, because it is not the sort of advertisement he would like, but I will call them, instead, Boris and "The Kremlin."

"The Kremlin" occupies a position of its own.

Your hat and coat are taken at the door by a perfectly genuine Cossack of ferocious appearance; he wears riding-boots and spurs, and the parts of his face that are not hidden by beard are cut and scarred like that of a pre-war German student.

The interior is hung with rugs and red, woven stuff to represent a tent. There is a very good *tsigain* band playing gipsy music, and a very good jazz-band which plays when people want to dance.

The waiters are chosen for their height. They wear magnificent Russian liveries, and carry round flaming skewers on which are spitted onions between rounds of meat. Most of them are ex-officers of the Imperial Guard.

Boris, the manager, is quite a young man; he is 6 ft. $5\frac{1}{2}$ in. in height. He wears a Russian silk blouse, loose trousers and top boots, and goes from table to table seeing that everything is all right.

From two in the morning until dawn "The Kremlin" is invariably full, and the American visitors, looking wistfully at their bills, often remark that Boris must be "making a good thing out of it." So he is.

Fashions change very quickly in Montmartre, but if his present popularity lasts for another season, he talks of retiring to a villa on the Riviera.

One Saturday night, or rather a Sunday morning, Boris did me the honour of coming to sit at my table and take a glass of wine with me. It was then that Boris told his story.

His father was a general, and when the war broke out Boris was a cadet at the military academy.

He was too young to fight, and was forced to watch, from behind the lines, the collapse of the Imperial Government.

Then came the confused period when the Great War was over, and various scattered remnants of the royalist army, with half-hearted support from their former allies, were engaged in a losing fight against the Bolshevists.

Boris was eighteen years old. His father had been killed and his mother had already escaped to America.

The military academy was being closed down, and with several of his fellow cadets Boris decided to join the last royalist army which, under Kolchak, was holding the Bolshevists at bay in Siberia.

It was a very odd kind of army. There were dismounted cavalry and sailors who had left their ships, officers whose regiments had mutinied, frontier garrisons and aides-de-camp, veterans of the Russo-Japanese war, and boys like Boris who were seeing action for the first time.

Besides these, there were units from the Allied Powers, who seemed to have been sent there by their capricious Governments and forgotten; there was a corps of British engineers and some French artillery; there were also liaison officers and military attachés to the General Headquarters Staff.

Among the latter was a French cavalry officer a few years

older than Boris. To most educated Russians before the war French was as familiar as their own language.

Boris and the French attaché became close friends. They used to smoke together and talk of Moscow and Paris before the war.

As the weeks passed it became clear that Kolchak's campaign could end in nothing but disaster.

Eventually a council of officers decided that the only course open was to break through to the east coast and attempt to escape to Europe.

A force had to be left behind to cover the retreat, and Boris and his French friend found themselves detailed to remain with this rearguard. In the action which followed, the small covering force was completely routed.

Alone among the officers Boris and his friend escaped with their lives, but their condition was almost desperate.

Their baggage was lost and they found themselves isolated in a waste land, patrolled by enemy troops and inhabited by savage Asiatic tribesmen.

Left to himself, the Frenchman's chances of escape were negligible, but a certain prestige still attached to the uniform of a Russian officer in the outlying villages.

Boris lent him his military overcoat to cover his uniform, and together they struggled through the snow, begging their way to the frontier.

Eventually they arrived in Japanese territory. Here all Russians were suspect, and it devolved on the Frenchman to get them safe conduct to the nearest French Consulate.

Boris' chief aim now was to join his mother in America. His friend had to return to report himself in Paris, so here they parted.

They took an affectionate farewell, promising to see each other again when their various affairs were settled. But each in his heart doubted whether chance would ever bring them together again.

Two years elapsed, and then one day in spring a poorly-dressed young Russian found himself in Paris, with three hundred francs in his pocket and all his worldly possessions in a kitbag.

He was very different from the debonair Boris who had left the military academy for Kolchak's army. America had proved to be something very different from the Land of Opportunity he had imagined.

His mother sold the jewels and a few personal possessions she had been able to bring away with her, and had started a small dressmaking business.

There seemed no chance of permanent employment for Boris, so after two or three months of casual jobs he worked his passage to England.

During the months that followed, Boris obtained temporary employment as a waiter, a chauffeur, a professional dancing-partner, a dock-labourer, and he came very near to starvation.

Finally, he came across an old friend of his father's, a former first secretary in the diplomatic corps, who was now working as a hairdresser.

This friend advised him to try Paris, where a large Russian colony had already formed, and gave him his fare.

It was thus that one morning, as the buds were just beginning to break in the Champs Elysées and the *couturiers* were exhibiting their Spring fashions, Boris found himself, ill-dressed and friendless, in another strange city.

His total capital was the equivalent of about thirty shillings; and so, being uncertain of what was to become of him, he decided to have luncheon.

An Englishman finding himself in this predicament would no doubt have made careful calculations.

He would have decided what was the longest time that his money would last him, and would have methodically kept within his budget while he started again "looking for a job."

But as Boris stood working out this depressing sum, something seemed suddenly to snap in his head.

With the utmost privation he could hardly hope to subsist for more than two or three weeks.

At the end of that time he would be in exactly the same position, a fortnight older, with all his money spent and no nearer a job.

Why not now as well as in a fortnight's time? He was in Paris, about which he had read and heard so much. He made up his mind to have one good meal and leave the rest to chance.

He had often heard his father speak of a restaurant called Larne. He had no idea where it was, so he took a taxi.

He entered the restaurant and sat down in one of the red-plush seats, while the waiters eyed his clothes with suspicion.

He looked about him in an unembarrassed way. It was quieter and less showy in appearance than the big restaurants he had passed in New York and London, but a glance at the menu told him that it was not a place where poor people often went.

Then he began ordering his luncheon, and the waiter's manner quickly changed as he realized that this eccentrically dressed customer did not need any advice about choosing his food and wine.

He ate fresh caviare and *ortolansan porto* and *crêpes suzettes*; he drank a bottle of vintage claret and a glass of very old *fine champagne*, and he examined several boxes of cigars before he found one in perfect condition.

When he had finished, he asked for his bill. It was 260 francs. He gave the waiter a tip of 26 francs and 4 francs to the man at the door who had taken his hat and kitbag. His taxi had cost 7 francs.

Half a minute later he stood on the kerb with exactly 3 francs in the world. But it had been a magnificent lunch, and he did not regret it.

As he stood there, meditating what he could do, his arm was suddenly taken from behind, and turning he saw a smartly dressed Frenchman, who had evidently just left the restaurant. It was his friend the military attaché.

"I was sitting at the table behind you," he said. "You never noticed me, you were so intent on your food."

"It is probably my last meal for some time," Boris explained, and his friend laughed at what he took to be a joke.

They walked up the street together, talking rapidly. The Frenchman described how he had left the army when his time of service was up, and was now a director of a prosperous motor business.

"And you, too," he said. "I am delighted to see that you also have been doing well."

"Doing well? At the moment I have exactly 3 francs in the world."

"My dear fellow, people with 3 francs in the world do not eat caviare at Larne."

Then for the first time he noticed Boris' frayed clothes. He had only known him in a war-worn uniform and it had seemed natural at first to find him dressed as he was.

Now he realized that these were not the clothes which prosperous young men usually wear.

"My dear friend," he said, "forgive me for laughing.

I didn't realize. ... Come and dine with me this evening at my flat, and we will talk about what is to be done."

"And so," concluded Boris, "I became the manager of 'The Kremlin.' *If I had not gone to Larne that day it is about certain we should never have met!*

"My friend said that I might have a part in his motor business, but that he thought anyone who could spend his last 300 francs on one meal was ordained by God to keep a restaurant.

"So it has been. He financed me. I collected some of my old friends to work with us. Now, you see, I am comparatively a rich man."

The last visitors had paid their bill and risen, rather unsteadily, to go. Boris rose, too, to bow them out. The daylight shone into the room as they lifted the curtain to go out.

Suddenly, in the new light, all the decorations looked bogus and tawdry; the waiters hurried away to change their sham liveries. Boris understood what I was feeling.

"I know," he said. "It is not Russian. It is not anything even to own a popular night club when one has lost one's country."

ISAK DINESEN
BABETTE'S FEAST

I. TWO LADIES OF BERLEVAAG

IN NORWAY THERE is a fjord—a long narrow arm of the sea between tall mountains—named Berlevaag Fjord. At the foot of the mountains the small town of Berlevaag looks like a child's toy-town of little wooden pieces painted gray, yellow, pink and many other colors.

Sixty-five years ago two elderly ladies lived in one of the yellow houses. Other ladies at that time wore a bustle, and the two sisters might have worn it as gracefully as any of them, for they were tall and willowy. But they had never possessed any article of fashion; they had dressed demurely in gray or black all their lives. They were christened Martine and Philippa, after Martin Luther and his friend Philip Melanchton. Their father had been a Dean and a prophet, the founder of a pious ecclesiastic party or sect, which was known and looked up to in all the country of Norway. Its members renounced the pleasures of this world, for the earth and all that it held to them was but a kind of illusion, and the true reality was the New Jerusalem toward which they were longing. They swore not at all, but their communication was yea yea and nay nay, and they called one another Brother and Sister.

The Dean had married late in life and by now had long been dead. His disciples were becoming fewer in number every year, whiter or balder and harder of hearing; they were even becoming somewhat querulous and quarrelsome, so that sad little schisms would arise in the congregation. But they still gathered together to read and interpret the Word. They had all known the Dean's daughters as little girls; to them they were even now very small sisters, precious for their dear father's sake. In the yellow house they felt that their Master's spirit was with them; here they were at home and at peace.

These two ladies had a French maid-of-all-work, Babette.

It was a strange thing for a couple of Puritan women in a small Norwegian town; it might even seem to call for an explanation. The people of Berlevaag found the explanation in the sisters' piety and kindness of heart. For the old Dean's daughters spent their time and their small income in works of charity; no sorrowful or distressed creature knocked on their door in vain. And Babette had come to that door twelve years ago as a friendless fugitive, almost mad with grief and fear.

But the true reason for Babette's presence in the two sisters' house was to be found further back in time and deeper down in the domain of human hearts.

II. MARTINE'S LOVER

As young girls, Martine and Philippa had been extraordinarily pretty, with the almost supernatural fairness of flowering fruit trees or perpetual snow. They were never to be seen at balls or parties, but people turned when they passed in the streets, and the young men of Berlevaag went to church to watch them walk up the aisle. The younger sister also had a lovely voice, which on Sundays filled the church with sweetness. To the Dean's congregation earthly love, and marriage with it, were trivial matters, in themselves nothing but illusions; still it is possible that more than one of the elderly Brothers had been prizing the maidens far above rubies and had suggested as much to their father. But the Dean had declared that to him in his calling his daughters were his right and left hand. Who could want to bereave him of them? And the fair girls had been brought up to an ideal of heavenly love; they were all filled with it and did not let themselves be touched by the flames of this world.

All the same they had upset the peace of heart of two gentlemen from the great world outside Berlevaag.

There was a young officer named Lorens Loewenhielm, who had led a gay life in his garrison town and had run into debt. In the year of 1854, when Martine was eighteen and Philippa seventeen, his angry father sent him on a month's visit to his aunt in her old country house of Fossum near Berlevaag, where he would have time to meditate and to better his ways. One day he rode into town and met Martine in the marketplace. He looked down at the pretty girl, and she looked up at the fine horseman. When she had passed him and disappeared he was not certain whether he was to believe his own eyes.

In the Loewenhielm family there existed a legend to the effect that long ago a gentleman of the name had married a Huldre, a female mountain spirit of Norway, who is so fair that the air round her shines and quivers. Since then, from time to time, members of the family had been second-sighted. Young Lorens till now had not been aware of any particular spiritual gift in his own nature. But at this one moment there rose before his eyes a sudden, mighty vision of a higher and purer life, with no creditors, dunning letters or parental lectures, with no secret, unpleasant pangs of conscience and with a gentle, golden-haired angel to guide and reward him.

Through his pious aunt he got admission to the Dean's house, and saw that Martine was even lovelier without a bonnet. He followed her slim figure with adoring eyes, but he loathed and despised the figure which he himself cut in her nearness. He was amazed and shocked by the fact that he could find nothing at all to say, and no inspiration in the glass of water before him. "Mercy and Truth, dear brethren, have met together," said the Dean. "Righteousness and Bliss have kissed one another." And the young man's thoughts were with the moment when Lorens and Martine should be kissing each other. He repeated his visit time after time, and each time seemed to himself to grow smaller and more insignificant and contemptible.

When in the evening he came back to his aunt's house he kicked his shining riding-boots to the corners of his room; he even laid his head on the table and wept.

On the last day of his stay he made a last attempt to communicate his feelings to Martine. Till now it had been easy for him to tell a pretty girl that he loved her, but the tender words stuck in his throat as he looked into this maiden's face. When he had said good-bye to the party, Martine saw him to the door with a candlestick in her hand. The light shone on her mouth and threw upwards the shadows of her long eyelashes. He was about to leave in dumb despair when on the threshold he suddenly seized her hand and pressed it to his lips.

"I am going away forever!" he cried. "I shall never, never see you again! For I have learned here that Fate is hard, and that in this world there are things which are impossible!"

When he was once more back in his garrison town he thought his adventure over, and found that he did not like to think of it at all. While the other young officers talked of their love affairs, he was silent on his. For seen from the officers' mess, and so to say with its eyes, it was a pitiful business. How had it come to pass that a lieutenant of the hussars had let himself be defeated and frustrated by a set of long-faced sectarians, in the bare-floored rooms of an old Dean's house?

Then he became afraid; panic fell upon him. Was it the family madness which made him still carry with him the dream-like picture of a maiden so fair that she made the air round her shine with purity and holiness? He did not want to be a dreamer; he wanted to be like his brother-officers.

So he pulled himself together, and in the greatest effort of his young life made up his mind to forget what had happened to him in Berlevaag. From now on, he resolved, he would look forward, not back. He would concentrate on his career, and the day was to come when he would cut a brilliant figure in a brilliant world.

His mother was pleased with the result of his visit to Fossum, and in her letters expressed her gratitude to his aunt. She did not know by what queer, winding roads her son had reached his happy moral standpoint.

The ambitious young officer soon caught the attention of his superiors and made unusually quick advancement. He was sent to France and to Russia, and on his return he married a lady-in-waiting to Queen Sophia. In these high circles he moved with grace and ease, pleased with his surroundings and with himself. He even in the course of time benefited from words and turns which had stuck in his mind from the Dean's house, for piety was now in fashion at Court.

In the yellow house of Berlevaag, Philippa sometimes turned the talk to the handsome, silent young man who had so suddenly made his appearance, and so suddenly disappeared again. Her elder sister would then answer her gently, with a still, clear face, and find other things to discuss.

III. PHILIPPA'S LOVER

A year later a more distinguished person even than Lieutenant Loewenhielm came to Berlevaag.

The great singer Achille Papin of Paris had sung for a week at the Royal Opera of Stockholm, and had carried away his audience there as everywhere. One evening a lady of the Court, who had been dreaming of a romance with the artist, had described to him the wild, grandiose scenery of Norway. His own romantic nature was stirred by the narration, and he had laid his way back to France round the Norwegian coast. But he felt small in the sublime surroundings; with nobody to talk to he fell into that melancholy in which he saw himself as an old man, at the end of his career, till on a Sunday, when he could think of nothing else to do, he went to church and heard Philippa sing.

Then in one single moment he knew and understood all. For here were the snowy summits, the wild flowers and the white Nordic nights, translated into his own language of music, and brought him in a young woman's voice. Like Lorens Loewenhielm he had a vision.

"Almighty God," he thought, "Thy power is without end, and Thy mercy reacheth unto the clouds! And here is a prima donna of the opera who will lay Paris at her feet."

Achille Papin at this time was a handsome man of forty, with curly black hair and a red mouth. The idolization of nations had not spoilt him; he was a kind-hearted person and honest toward himself.

He went straight to the yellow house, gave his name—which told the Dean nothing—and explained that he was staying in Berlevaag for his health, and the while would be happy to take on the young lady as a pupil.

He did not mention the Opera of Paris, but described at length how beautifully Miss Philippa would come to sing in church, to the glory of God.

For a moment he forgot himself, for when the Dean asked whether he was a Roman Catholic he answered according to truth, and the old clergyman, who had never seen a live Roman Catholic, grew a little pale. All the same the Dean was pleased to speak French, which reminded him of his young days when he had studied the works of the great French Lutheran writer, Lefèvre d'Etaples. And as nobody could long withstand Achille Papin when he had really set his heart on a matter, in the end the father gave his consent, and remarked to his daughter: "God's paths run across the sea and the snowy mountains, where man's eye sees no track."

So the great French singer and the young Norwegian novice set to work together. Achille's expectation grew into certainty and his certainty into ecstasy. He thought: "I have been wrong in believing that I was growing old. My greatest triumphs are before me! The world will once more believe in miracles when she and I sing together!"

After a while he could not keep his dreams to himself, but told Philippa about them.

She would, he said, rise like a star above any diva of the past or present. The Emperor and Empress, the Princes, great ladies and *bels esprits* of Paris would listen to her, and shed tears. The common people too would worship her, and she would bring consolation and strength to the wronged and oppressed. When she left the Grand Opera upon her master's arm, the crowd would unharness her horses, and themselves draw her to the Café Anglais, where a magnificent supper awaited her.

Philippa did not repeat these prospects to her father or her sister, and this was the first time in her life that she had had a secret from them.

The teacher now gave his pupil the part of Zerlina in Mozart's opera *Don Giovanni* to study. He himself, as often before, sang Don Giovanni's part.

He had never in his life sung as now. In the duet of the second act—which is called the seduction duet—he was swept off his feet by the heavenly music and the heavenly voices. As the last melting note died away he seized Philippa's hands, drew her toward him and kissed her solemnly, as a bridegroom might kiss his bride before the altar. Then he let her go. For the moment was too sublime for any further word or movement; Mozart himself was looking down on the two.

Philippa went home, told her father that she did not want any more singing lessons and asked him to write and tell Monsieur Papin so.

The Dean said: "And God's paths run across the rivers, my child."

When Achille got the Dean's letter he sat immovable for an hour. He thought: "I have been wrong. My day is over. Never again shall I be the divine Papin. And this poor weedy garden of the world has lost its nightingale!"

A little later he thought: "I wonder what is the matter with that hussy? Did I kiss her, by any chance?"

In the end he thought: "I have lost my life for a kiss, and I have no remembrance at all of the kiss! Don Giovanni kissed Zerlina, and Achille Papin pays for it! Such is the fate of the artist!"

In the Dean's house Martine felt that the matter was deeper than it looked, and searched her sister's face. For a moment, slightly trembling, she too imagined that the Roman Catholic gentleman might have tried to kiss Philippa. She did not imagine that her sister might have been surprised and frightened by something in her own nature.

Achille Papin took the first boat from Berlevaag.

Of this visitor from the great world the sisters spoke but little; they lacked the words with which to discuss him.

IV. A LETTER FROM PARIS

Fifteen years later, on a rainy June night of 1871, the bell-rope of the yellow house was pulled violently three times. The mistresses of the house opened the door to a massive, dark, deadly pale woman with a bundle on her arm, who stared at them, took a step forward and fell down on the doorstep in a dead swoon. When the frightened ladies had restored her to life she sat up, gave them one more glance from her sunken eyes and, all the time without a word, fumbled in her wet clothes and brought out a letter which she handed to them.

The letter was addressed to them all right, but it was written in French. The sisters put their heads together and read it. It ran as follows:

Ladies!

Do you remember me? Ah, when I think of you I have the heart filled with wild lilies-of-the-valley! Will the memory of a Frenchman's devotion bend your hearts to save the life of a Frenchwoman?

The bearer of this letter, Madame Babette Hersant, like my beautiful Empress herself, has had to flee from Paris. Civil war has raged in our streets. French hands have shed French blood. The noble Communards, standing up for the Rights of Man, have been crushed and annihilated. Madame Hersant's husband and son, both eminent ladies' hairdressers, have been shot. She herself was arrested as a Pétroleuse—(which word is used here for women who set fire to houses with petroleum)—and has narrowly escaped the bloodstained hands of General Galliffet. She has lost all she possessed and dares not remain in France.

A nephew of hers is cook to the boat Anna Colbioernsson, *bound for Christiania*—(as I believe, the capital of Norway)—and he has obtained shipping opportunity for his aunt. This is now her last sad resort!

Knowing that I was once a visitor to your magnificent country she comes to me, asks me if there be any good people in Norway and begs me, if it be so, to supply her with a letter to them. The two words of "good people" immediately bring before my eyes your picture, sacred to my heart. I send her to you. How she is to get from Christiania to Berlevaag I know not, having forgotten the map of Norway. But she is a Frenchwoman, and you will find that in her misery she has still got resourcefulness, majesty and true stoicism.

I envy her in her despair: she is to see your faces.

As you receive her mercifully, send a merciful thought back to France.

For fifteen years, Miss Philippa, I have grieved that your voice should never fill the Grand Opera of Paris. When tonight I think of you, no doubt surrounded by a gay and loving family, and of myself: gray, lonely, forgotten by those who once applauded and adored me, I feel that you may have chosen the better part in life. What is fame? What is glory? The grave awaits us all!

And yet, my lost Zerlina, and yet, soprano of the snow! As I write this I feel that the grave is not the end. In

Paradise I shall hear your voice again. There you will sing, without fears or scruples, as God meant you to sing. There you will be the great artist that God meant you to be. Ah! How you will enchant the angels.

Babette can cook.

Deign to receive, my ladies, the humble homage of the friend who was once

Achille Papin

At the bottom of the page, as a P.S. were neatly printed the first two bars of the duet between Don Giovanni and Zerlina, like this:

The two sisters till now had kept only a small servant of fifteen to help them in the house and they felt that they could not possibly afford to take on an elderly, experienced housekeeper. But Babette told them that she would serve Monsieur Papin's good people for nothing, and that she would take service with nobody else. If they sent her away she must die. Babette remained in the house of the Dean's daughters for twelve years, until the time of this tale.

V. STILL LIFE

Babette had arrived haggard and wild-eyed like a hunted animal, but in her new, friendly surroundings she soon acquired all the appearance of a respectable and trusted servant. She had appeared to be a beggar; she turned out to be a conqueror. Her quiet countenance and her steady, deep glance had magnetic qualities; under her eyes things moved, noiselessly, into their proper places.

Her mistresses at first had trembled a little, just as the Dean had once done, at the idea of receiving a Papist under their roof. But they did not like to worry a hard-tried fellow-creature with catechization; neither were they quite sure of their French. They silently agreed that the example of a good Lutheran life would be the best means of converting their servant. In this way Babette's presence in the house became, so to say, a moral spur to its inhabitants.

They had distrusted Monsieur Papin's assertion that Babette could cook. In France, they knew, people ate frogs. They showed Babette how to prepare a split cod and an ale-and-bread-soup; during the demonstration the French-woman's face became absolutely expressionless. But within a week Babette cooked a split cod and an ale-and-bread-soup as well as anybody born and bred in Berlevaag.

The idea of French luxury and extravagance next had alarmed and dismayed the Dean's daughters. The first day after Babette had entered their service they took her before them and explained to her that they were poor and that to them luxurious fare was sinful. Their own food must be as plain as possible; it was the soup-pails and baskets for their poor that signified. Babette nodded her head; as a girl, she informed her ladies, she had been cook to an old priest who was a saint. Upon this the sisters resolved to surpass the French priest in asceticism. And they soon found that from the day when Babette took over the housekeeping its cost was miraculously reduced, and the soup-pails and baskets acquired a new, mysterious power to stimulate and strengthen their poor and sick.

The world outside the yellow house also came to

acknowledge Babette's excellence. The refugee never learned to speak the language of her new country, but in her broken Norwegian she beat down the prices of Berlevaag's flintiest tradesmen. She was held in awe on the quay and in the marketplace.

The old Brothers and Sisters, who had first looked askance at the foreign woman in their midst, felt a happy change in their little sisters' life, rejoiced at it and benefited by it. They found that troubles and cares had been conjured away from their existence, and that now they had money to give away, time for the confidences and complaints of their old friends and peace for meditating on heavenly matters. In the course of time not a few of the brotherhood included Babette's name in their prayers, and thanked God for the speechless stranger, the dark Martha in the house of their two fair Marys. The stone which the builders had almost refused had become the headstone of the corner.

The ladies of the yellow house were the only ones to know that their cornerstone had a mysterious and alarming feature to it, as if it was somehow related to the Black Stone of Mecca, the Kaaba itself.

Hardly ever did Babette refer to her past life. When in early days the sisters had gently condoled her upon her losses, they had been met with that majesty and stoicism of which Monsieur Papin had written. "What will you ladies?" she had answered, shrugging her shoulders. "It is Fate."

But one day she suddenly informed them that she had for many years held a ticket in a French lottery, and that a faithful friend in Paris was still renewing it for her every year. Some time she might win the *grand prix* of ten thousand francs. At that they felt that their cook's old carpetbag was made from a magic carpet; at a given moment she might mount it and be carried off, back to Paris.

And it happened when Martine or Philippa spoke to Babette that they would get no answer, and would wonder if she had even heard what they said. They would find her in the kitchen, her elbows on the table and her temples on her hands, lost in the study of a heavy black book which they secretly suspected to be a popish prayer-book. Or she would sit immovable on the three-legged kitchen chair, her strong hands in her lap and her dark eyes wide open, as enigmatical and fatal as a Pythia upon her tripod. At such moments they realized that Babette was deep, and that in the soundings of her being there were passions, there were memories and longings of which they knew nothing at all.

A little cold shiver ran through them, and in their hearts they thought: "Perhaps after all she had indeed been a Pétroleuse."

VI. BABETTE'S GOOD LUCK

The fifteenth of December was the Dean's hundredth anniversary.

His daughters had long been looking forward to this day and had wished to celebrate it, as if their dear father were still among his disciples. Therefore it had been to them a sad and incomprehensible thing that in this last year discord and dissension had been raising their heads in his flock. They had endeavored to make peace, but they were aware that they had failed. It was as if the fine and lovable vigor of their father's personality had been evaporating, the way Hoffmann's anodyne will evaporate when left on the shelf in a bottle without a cork. And his departure had left the door ajar to things hitherto unknown to the two sisters, much younger than his spiritual children. From a past half a century back, when the unshepherded sheep had been running astray in the mountains, uninvited dismal guests pressed through the opening on the heels of the worshippers and seemed to darken the little rooms and to let in the cold. The sins of old Brothers and Sisters came, with late piercing repentance like a toothache, and the sins of others against them came back with bitter resentment, like a poisoning of the blood.

There were in the congregation two old women who before their conversion had spread slander upon each other, and thereby to each other ruined a marriage and an inheritance. Today they could not remember happenings of yesterday or a week ago, but they remembered this forty-year-old wrong and kept going through the ancient accounts; they scowled at each other. There was an old Brother who suddenly called to mind how another Brother, forty-five years ago, had cheated him in a deal; he could have wished to dismiss the matter from his mind, but it stuck there like a deep-seated, festering splinter. There was a gray, honest skipper and a furrowed, pious widow, who in their young days, while she was the wife of another man, had been sweethearts. Of late each had begun to grieve, while shifting the burden of guilt from his own shoulders to those of the other and back again, and to worry about the possible terrible consequences, through all eternity, to himself, brought upon him by one who had pretended to hold him dear. They grew pale at the meetings in the yellow house and avoided each other's eyes.

As the birthday drew nearer, Martine and Philippa felt the responsibility growing heavier. Would their ever-faithful father look down to his daughters and call them by name as unjust stewards? Between them they talked matters over and repeated their father's saying: that God's paths were running even across the salt sea, and the snow-clad mountains, where man's eye sees no track.

One day of this summer the post brought a letter from France to Madame Babette Hersant. This in itself was a surprising thing, for during these twelve years Babette had received no letter. What, her mistresses wondered, could it contain? They took it into the kitchen to watch her open and read it. Babette opened it, read it, lifted her eyes from it to her ladies' faces and told them that her number in the French lottery had come out. She had won ten thousand francs.

The news made such an impression on the two sisters that for a full minute they could not speak a word. They themselves were used to receiving their modest pension in small instalments; it was difficult to them even to imagine the sum of ten thousand francs in a pile. Then they pressed Babette's hand, their own hands trembling a little. They had never before pressed the hand of a person who the moment before had come into possession of ten thousand francs.

After a while they realized that the happenings concerned themselves as well as Babette. The country of France, they felt, was slowly rising before their servant's horizon, and correspondingly their own existence was sinking beneath their feet. The ten thousand francs which made her rich—how poor did they not make the house she had served! One by one old forgotten cares and worries began to peep out at them from the four corners of the kitchen. The congratulations died on their lips, and the two pious women were ashamed of their own silence.

During the following days they announced the news to their friends with joyous faces, but it did them good to see these friends' faces grow sad as they listened to them. Nobody, it was felt in the Brotherhood, could really blame Babette: birds will return to their nests and human beings to the country of their birth. But did that good and faithful servant realize that in going away from Berlevaag she would be leaving many old and poor people in distress? Their little sisters would have no more time for the sick and sorrowful. Indeed, indeed, lotteries were ungodly affairs.

In due time the money arrived through offices in Christiania and Berlevaag. The two ladies helped Babette to count it, and gave her a box to keep it in. They handled, and became familiar with, the ominous bits of paper.

They dared not question Babette upon the date of her departure. Dared they hope that she would remain with them over the fifteenth of December?

The mistresses had never been quite certain how much of their private conversation the cook followed or understood. So they were surprised when on a September evening Babette came into the drawing room, more humble or subdued than they had ever seen her, to ask a favor. She begged them, she said, to let her cook a celebration dinner on the Dean's birthday.

The ladies had not intended to have any dinner at all. A very plain supper with a cup of coffee was the most sumptuous meal to which they had ever asked any guest to sit down. But Babette's dark eyes were as eager and pleading as a dog's; they agreed to let her have her way. At this the cook's face lighted up.

But she had more to say. She wanted, she said, to cook a French dinner, a real French dinner, for this one time. Martine and Philippa looked at each other. They did not like the idea; they felt that they did not know what it might imply. But the very strangeness of the request disarmed them. They had no arguments wherewith to meet the proposition of cooking a real French dinner.

Babette drew a long sigh of happiness, but still she did not move. She had one more prayer to make. She begged that her mistresses would allow her to pay for the French dinner with her own money.

"No, Babette!" the ladies exclaimed. How could she imagine such a thing? Did she believe that they would allow her to spend her precious money on food and drink—or on them? No, Babette, indeed.

Babette took a step forward. There was something formidable in the move, like a wave rising. Had she stepped forth like this, in 1871, to plant a red flag on a barricade? She spoke, in her queer Norwegian, with classical French eloquence. Her voice was like a song.

Ladies! Had she ever, during twelve years, asked you a favor? No! And why not? Ladies, you who say your prayers every day, can you imagine what it means to a human heart to have no prayer to make? What would Babette have had to pray for? Nothing! Tonight she had a prayer to make, from the bottom of her heart. Do you not then feel tonight, my ladies, that it becomes you to grant it her, with such joy as that with which the good God has granted you your own?

The ladies for a while said nothing. Babette was right; it was her first request these twelve years; very likely it would be her last. They thought the matter over. After all, they told themselves, their cook was now better off than they, and a dinner could make no difference to a person who owned ten thousand francs.

Their consent in the end completely changed Babette. They saw that as a young woman she had been beautiful. And they wondered whether in this hour they themselves had not, for the very first time, become to her the "good people" of Achille Papin's letter.

VII. THE TURTLE

In November Babette went for a journey.

She had preparations to make, she told her mistresses, and would need a leave of a week or ten days. Her nephew, who had once got her to Christiania, was still sailing to that town; she must see him and talk things over with him. Babette was a bad sailor; she had spoken of her one sea-voyage, from France to Norway, as of the most horrible experience of her life. Now she was strangely collected; the ladies felt that her heart was already in France.

After ten days she came back to Berlevaag.

Had she got things arranged as she wished? the ladies asked. Yes, she answered, she had seen her nephew and given him a list of the goods which he was to bring her from France. To Martine and Philippa this was a dark saying, but they did not care to talk of her departure, so they asked her no more questions.

Babette was somewhat nervous during the next weeks. But one December day she triumphantly announced to her mistresses that the goods had come to Christiania, had been transshipped there, and on this very day had arrived at Berlevaag. She had, she added, engaged an old man with a wheelbarrow to have them conveyed from the harbor to the house.

But what goods, Babette? the ladies asked. Why, Mesdames, Babette replied, the ingredients for the birthday dinner. Praise be to God, they had all arrived in good condition from Paris.

By this time Babette, like the bottled demon of the fairy tale, had swelled and grown to such dimensions that her mistresses felt small before her. They now saw the French dinner coming upon them, a thing of incalculable nature and range. But they had never in their life broken a promise; they gave themselves into their cook's hands.

All the same when Martine saw a barrow load of bottles wheeled into the kitchen, she stood still. She touched the bottles and lifted up one. "What is there in this bottle, Babette?" she asked in a low voice. "Not wine?" "Wine, Madame!" Babette answered. "No, Madame. It is a Clos Vougeot 1846!" After a moment she added: "From Philippe, in Rue Montorgueil!" Martine had never suspected that wines could have names to them, and was put to silence.

Late in the evening she opened the door to a ring, and was once more faced with the wheelbarrow, this time with a red-haired sailor-boy behind it, as if the old man had by this time been worn out. The youth grinned at her as he lifted a big, undefinable object from the barrow. In the light of the lamp it looked like some greenish-black stone, but when set down on the kitchen floor it suddenly shot out a snake-like head and moved it slightly from side to side. Martine had seen pictures of tortoises, and had even as a child owned a pet tortoise, but this thing was monstrous in size and terrible to behold. She backed out of the kitchen without a word.

She dared not tell her sister what she had seen. She passed an almost sleepless night; she thought of her father and felt that on his very birthday she and her sister were lending his house to a witches' sabbath. When at last she fell asleep she had a terrible dream, in which she saw Babette poisoning the old Brothers and Sisters, Philippa and herself.

Early in the morning she got up, put on her gray cloak and went out in the dark street. She walked from house to house, opened her heart to her Brothers and Sisters, and confessed her guilt. She and Philippa, she said, had meant no harm; they had granted their servant a prayer and had not foreseen what might come of it. Now she could not tell what, on her father's birthday, her guests would be given to eat or drink. She did not actually mention the turtle, but it was present in her face and voice.

The old people, as has already been told, had all known Martine and Philippa as little girls; they had seen them cry bitterly over a broken doll. Martine's tears brought tears into their own eyes. They gathered in the afternoon and talked the problem over.

Before they again parted they promised one another that for their little sisters' sake they would, on the great day, be silent upon all matters of food and drink. Nothing that might be set before them, be it even frogs or snails, should wring a word from their lips.

"Even so," said a white-bearded Brother, "the tongue is a little member and boasteth great things. The tongue can no man tame; it is an unruly evil, full of deadly poison. On the day of our Master we will cleanse our tongues of all taste and purify them of all delight or disgust of the senses, keeping and preserving them for the higher things of praise and thanksgiving."

So few things ever happened in the quiet existence of the Berlevaag brotherhood that they were at this moment deeply moved and elevated. They shook hands on their vow, and it was to them as if they were doing so before the face of their Master.

VIII. THE HYMN

On Sunday morning it began to snow. The white flakes fell fast and thick; the small windowpanes of the yellow house became pasted with snow.

Early in the day a groom from Fossum brought the two

sisters a note. Old Mrs. Loewenhielm still resided in her country house. She was now ninety years old and stone-deaf, and she had lost all sense of smell or taste. But she had been one of the Dean's first supporters, and neither her infirmity nor the sledge journey would keep her from doing honor to his memory. Now, she wrote, her nephew, General Lorens Loewenhielm, had unexpectedly come on a visit; he had spoken with deep veneration of the Dean, and she begged permission to bring him with her. It would do him good, for the dear boy seemed to be in somewhat low spirits.

Martine and Philippa at this remembered the young officer and his visits; it relieved their present anxiety to talk of old happy days. They wrote back that General Loewenhielm would be welcome. They also called in Babette to inform her that they would now be twelve for dinner; they added that their latest guest had lived in Paris for several years. Babette seemed pleased with the news, and assured them that there would be food enough.

The hostesses made their little preparations in the sitting room. They dared not set foot in the kitchen, for Babette had mysteriously nosed out a cook's mate from a ship in the harbor—the same boy, Martine realized, who had brought in the turtle—to assist her in the kitchen and to wait at table, and now the dark woman and the red-haired boy, like some witch with her familiar spirit, had taken possession of these regions. The ladies could not tell what fires had been burning or what cauldrons bubbling there from before daybreak.

Table linen and plate had been magically mangled and polished, glasses and decanters brought, Babette only knew from where. The Dean's house did not possess twelve dining-room chairs, the long horsehair-covered sofa had been moved from the parlor to the dining room, and the parlor, ever sparsely furnished, now looked strangely bare and big without it.

Martine and Philippa did their best to embellish the domain left to them. Whatever troubles might be in wait for their guests, in any case they should not be cold; all day the sisters fed the towering old stove with birch-knots. They hung a garland of juniper round their father's portrait on the wall, and placed candlesticks on their mother's small working table beneath it; they burned juniper-twigs to make the room smell nice. The while they wondered if in this weather the sledge from Fossum would get through. In the end they put on their old black best frocks and their confirmation gold crosses. They sat down, folded their hands in their laps and committed themselves unto God.

The old Brothers and Sisters arrived in small groups and entered the room slowly and solemnly.

This low room with its bare floor and scanty furniture was dear to the Dean's disciples. Outside its windows lay the great world. Seen from in here the great world in its winter-whiteness was ever prettily bordered in pink, blue and red by the row of hyacinths on the window-sills. And in summer, when the windows were open, the great world had a softly moving frame of white muslin curtains to it.

Tonight the guests were met on the doorstep with warmth and sweet smell, and they were looking into the face of their beloved Master, wreathed with evergreen. Their hearts like their numb fingers thawed.

One very old Brother, after a few moments' silence, in his trembling voice struck up one of the Master's own hymns:

> *"Jerusalem, my happy home*
> *name ever dear to me ... "*

One by one the other voices fell in, thin quivering women's voices, ancient seafaring Brothers' deep growls, and above them all Philippa's clear soprano, a little worn with age but still angelic. Unwittingly the choir had seized one another's hands. They sang the hymn to the end, but could not bear to cease and joined in another:

> *"Take not thought for food or raiment*
> *careful one, so anxiously . . . "*

The mistresses of the house somewhat reassured by it, the words of the third verse:

> *"Wouldst thou give a stone, a reptile*
> *to thy pleading child for food? . . . "*

went straight to Martine's heart and inspired her with hope.

In the middle of this hymn sledge bells were heard outside; the guests from Fossum had arrived.

Martine and Philippa went to receive them and saw them into the parlor. Mrs. Loewenhielm with age had become quite small, her face colorless like parchment, and very still. By her side General Loewenhielm, tall, broad and ruddy, in his bright uniform, his breast covered with decorations, strutted and shone like an ornamental bird, a golden pheasant or a peacock, in this sedate party of black crows and jackdaws.

IX. GENERAL LOEWENHIELM

General Loewenhielm had been driving from Fossum to Berlevaag in a strange mood. He had not visited this part of the country for thirty years. He had come now to get a rest from his busy life at Court, and he had found no rest. The old house of Fossum was peaceful enough and seemed somehow pathetically small after the Tuileries and the Winter Palace. But it held one disquieting figure: young Lieutenant Loewenhielm walked in its rooms.

General Loewenhielm saw the handsome, slim figure pass close by him. And as he passed the boy gave the elder man a short glance and a smile, the haughty, arrogant smile which youth gives to age. The General might have smiled back, kindly and a little sadly, as age smiles at youth, if it had not been that he was really in no mood to smile; he was, as his aunt had written, in low spirits.

General Loewenhielm had obtained everything that he had striven for in life and was admired and envied by everyone. Only he himself knew of a queer fact, which jarred with his prosperous existence: that he was not perfectly happy. Something was wrong somewhere, and he carefully felt his mental self all over, as one feels a finger over to determine the place of a deep-seated, invisible thorn.

He was in high favor with royalty, he had done well in his calling, he had friends everywhere. The thorn sat in none of these places.

His wife was a brilliant woman and still good-looking. Perhaps she neglected her own house a little for her visits and parties; she changed her servants every three months and the General's meals at home were served unpunctually. The General, who valued good food highly in life, here felt a slight bitterness against the lady, and secretly blamed her for the indigestion from which he sometimes suffered. Still the thorn was not here either.

Nay, but an absurd thing had lately been happening to General Loewenhielm: he would find himself worrying about his immortal soul. Did he have any reason for doing so? He was a moral person, loyal to his king, his wife and his friends, an example to everybody. But there were moments when it seemed to him that the world was not a moral, but a mystic, concern. He looked into the mirror, examined the row of decorations on his breast and sighed to himself: "Vanity, vanity, all is vanity!"

The strange meeting at Fossum had compelled him to make out the balance-sheet of his life.

Young Lorens Loewenhielm had attracted dreams and fancies as a flower attracts bees and butterflies. He had fought to free himself of them; he had fled and they had followed. He had been scared of the Huldre of the family legend and had declined her invitation to come into the mountain; he had firmly refused the gift of second sight.

The elderly Lorens Loewenhielm found himself wishing that one little dream would come his way, and a gray moth of dusk look him up before nightfall. He found himself longing for the faculty of second sight, as a blind man will long for the normal faculty of vision.

Can the sum of a row of victories in many years and in many countries be a defeat? General Loewenhielm had fulfilled Lieutenant Loewenhielm's wishes and had more than satisfied his ambitions. It might be held that he had gained the whole world. And it had come to this, that the stately, worldly-wise older man now turned toward the naïve young figure to ask him, gravely, even bitterly, in what he had profited? Somewhere something had been lost.

When Mrs. Loewenhielm had told her nephew of the Dean's anniversary and he had made up his mind to go with her to Berlevaag, his decision had not been an ordinary acceptance of a dinner invitation.

He would, he resolved, tonight make up his account with

young Lorens Loewenhielm, who had felt himself to be a shy and sorry figure in the house of the Dean, and who in the end had shaken its dust off his riding boots. He would let the youth prove to him, once and for all, that thirty-one years ago he had made the right choice. The low rooms, the haddock and the glass of water on the table before him should all be called in to bear evidence that in their milieu the existence of Lorens Loewenhielm would very soon have become sheer misery.

He let his mind stray far away. In Paris he had once won a *concours hippique* and had been feted by high French cavalry officers, princes and dukes among them. A dinner had been given in his honor at the finest restaurant of the city. Opposite him at table was a noble lady, a famous beauty whom he had long been courting. In the midst of dinner she had lifted her dark velvet eyes above the rim of her champagne glass and without words had promised to make him happy. In the sledge he now all of a sudden remembered that he had then, for a second, seen Martine's face before him and had rejected it. For a while he listened to the tinkling of the sledge bells, then he smiled a little as he reflected how he would tonight come to dominate the conversation round that same table by which young Lorens Loewenhielm had sat mute.

Large snowflakes fell densely; behind the sledge the tracks were wiped out quickly. General Loewenhielm sat immovable by the side of his aunt, his chin sunk in the high fur collar of his coat.

X. BABETTE'S DINNER

As Babette's red-haired familiar opened the door to the dining room, and the guests slowly crossed the threshold, they let go one another's hands and became silent. But the silence was sweet, for in spirit they still held hands and were still singing.

Babette had set a row of candles down the middle of the table; the small flames shone on the black coats and frocks and on the one scarlet uniform, and were reflected in clear, moist eyes.

General Loewenhielm saw Martine's face in the candlelight as he had seen it when the two parted, thirty years ago. What traces would thirty years of Berlevaag life have left on it? The golden hair was now streaked with silver; the flowerlike face had slowly been turned into alabaster. But how serene was the forehead, how quietly trustful the eyes, how pure and sweet the mouth, as if no hasty word had ever passed its lips.

When all were seated, the eldest member of the congregation said grace in the Dean's own words:

> *"May my food my body maintain,*
> *may my body my soul sustain,*
> *may my soul in deed and word*
> *give thanks for all things to the Lord."*

At the word of "food" the guests, with their old heads bent over their folded hands, remembered how they had vowed not to utter a word about the subject, and in their hearts they reinforced the vow: they would not even give it a thought! They were sitting down to a meal, well, so had people done at the wedding of Cana. And grace has chosen to manifest itself there, in the very wine, as fully as anywhere.

Babette's boy filled a small glass before each of the party. They lifted it to their lips gravely, in confirmation of their resolution.

General Loewenhielm, somewhat suspicious of his wine, took a sip of it, startled, raised the glass first to his nose and then to his eyes, and sat it down bewildered. "This is very strange!" he thought. "Amontillado! And the finest Amontillado that I have ever tasted." After a moment, in order to test his senses, he took a small spoonful of his soup, took a second spoonful and laid down his spoon. "This is exceedingly strange!" he said to himself. "For surely I am eating turtle-soup—and what turtle-soup!" He was seized by a queer kind of panic and emptied his glass.

Usually in Berlevaag people did not speak much while they were eating. But somehow this evening tongues had been loosened. An old Brother told the story of his first meeting with the Dean. Another went through that sermon which sixty years ago had brought about his conversion. An aged woman, the one to whom Martine had first confided her distress, reminded her friends how in all afflictions any Brother or Sister was ready to share the burden of any other.

General Loewenhielm, who was to dominate the conversation of the dinner table, related how the Dean's collection of sermons was a favorite book of the Queen's. But as a new dish was served he was silenced. "Incredible!" he told himself. "It is Blinis Demidoff!" He looked round at his fellow-diners. They were all quietly eating their Blinis Demidoff without any sign of either surprise or approval, as if they had been doing so every day for thirty years.

A Sister on the other side of the table opened on the subject of strange happenings which had taken place while the Dean was still amongst his children, and which one might venture to call miracles. Did they remember, she asked, the time when he had promised a Christmas sermon in the village the other side of the fjord? For a fortnight the weather had been so bad that no skipper or fisherman would risk the crossing. The villagers were giving up hope, but the Dean told them that if no boat would take him, he would come to them walking upon the waves. And behold! Three days before Christmas the storm stopped, hard frost set in, and the fjord froze from shore to shore—and this was a thing which had not happened within the memory of man!

The boy once more filled the glasses. This time the Brothers and Sisters knew that what they were given to drink was not wine, for it sparkled. It must be some kind of lemonade. The lemonade agreed with their exalted state of mind and seemed to lift them off the ground, into a higher and purer sphere.

General Loewenhielm again set down his glass, turned to his neighbor on the right and said to him: "But surely this is a Veuve Cliquot 1860?" His neighbor looked at him kindly, smiled at him and made a remark about the weather.

Babette's boy had his instructions; he filled the glasses of the Brotherhood only once, but he refilled the General's glass as soon as it was emptied. The General emptied it quickly time after time. For how is a man of sense to behave when he cannot trust his senses? It is better to be drunk than mad.

Most often the people in Berlevaag during the course of a good meal would come to feel a little heavy. Tonight it was not so. The *convives* grew lighter in weight and lighter of heart the more they ate and drank. They no longer needed to remind themselves of their vow. It was, they realized, when man has not only altogether forgotten but has firmly renounced all ideas of food and drink that he eats and drinks in the right spirit.

General Loewenhielm stopped eating and sat immovable. Once more he was carried back to that dinner in Paris of which he had thought in the sledge. An incredibly recherché and palatable dish had been served there; he had asked its name from his fellow diner, Colonel Galliffet, and the Colonel had smilingly told him that it was named "Cailles en Sarcophage." He had further told him that the dish had been invented by the chef of the very café in which they were dining, a person known all over Paris as the greatest culinary genius of the age, and—most surprisingly—a woman! "And indeed," said Colonel Galliffet, "this woman is now turning a dinner at the Café Anglais into a kind of love affair—into a love affair of the noble and romantic category in which one no longer distinguishes between bodily and spiritual appetite or satiety! I have, before now, fought a duel for the sake of a fair lady. For no woman in all Paris, my young friend, would I more willingly shed my blood!" General Loewenhielm turned to his neighbor on the left and said to him: "But this is Cailles en Sarcophage!" The neighbor, who had been listening to the description of a miracle, looked at him absent-mindedly, then nodded his head and answered: "Yes, yes, certainly. What else would it be?"

From the Master's miracles the talk round the table had turned to the smaller miracles of kindliness and helpfulness daily performed by his daughters. The old Brother who had first struck up the hymn quoted the Dean's saying: "The only things which we may take with us from our life on earth are those which we have given away!" The guests smiled—what nabobs would not the poor, simple maidens become in the next world!

General Loewenhielm no longer wondered at anything. When a few minutes later he saw grapes, peaches and fresh figs before him, he laughed to his neighbor across the table and remarked: "Beautiful grapes!" His neighbor replied: "'And they came onto the brook of Eshcol, and cut down a branch with one cluster of grapes. And they bare it two upon a staff.'"

Then the General felt that the time had come to make a speech. He rose and stood up very straight.

Nobody else at the dinner table had stood up to speak. The old people lifted their eyes to the face above them in high, happy expectation. They were used to seeing sailors and vagabonds dead drunk with the crass gin of the country, but they did not recognize in a warrior and courtier the intoxication brought about by the noblest wine of the world.

XI. GENERAL LOEWENHIELM'S SPEECH

"Mercy and truth, my friends, have met together," said the General. "Righteousness and bliss shall kiss one another."

He spoke in a clear voice which had been trained in drill grounds and had echoed sweetly in royal halls, and yet he was speaking in a manner so new to himself and so strangely moving that after his first sentence he had to make a pause. For he was in the habit of forming his speeches with care, conscious of his purpose, but here, in the midst of the Dean's simple congregation, it was as if the whole figure of General Loewenhielm, his breast covered with decorations, were but a mouthpiece for a message which meant to be brought forth.

"Man, my friends," said General Loewenhielm, "is frail and foolish. We have all of us been told that grace is to be found in the universe. But in our human foolishness and short-sightedness we imagine divine grace to be finite. For this reason we tremble ... " Never till now had the General stated that he trembled; he was genuinely surprised and even shocked at hearing his own voice proclaim the fact. "We tremble before making our choice in life, and after having made it again tremble in fear of having chosen wrong. But the moment comes when our eyes are opened, and we see and realize that grace is infinite. Grace, my friends, demands nothing from us but that we shall await it with confidence and acknowledge it in gratitude. Grace, brothers, makes no conditions and singles out none of us in particular; grace takes us all to its bosom and proclaims general amnesty. See! that which we have chosen is given us, and that which we have refused is, also and at the same time, granted us. Ay, that which we have rejected is poured upon us abundantly. For mercy and truth have met together, and righteousness and bliss have kissed one another!"

The Brothers and Sisters had not altogether understood the General's speech, but his collected and inspired face and the sound of well-known and cherished words had seized and moved all hearts. In this way, after thirty-one years, General Loewenhielm succeeded in dominating the conversation at the Dean's dinner table.

Of what happened later in the evening nothing definite can here be stated. None of the guests later on had any clear remembrance of it. They only knew that the rooms had been filled with a heavenly light, as if a number of small halos had blended into one glorious radiance. Taciturn old people received the gift of tongues; ears that for years had been almost deaf were opened to it. Time itself had merged into eternity. Long after midnight the windows of the house shone like gold, and golden song flowed out into the winter air.

The two old women who had once slandered each other now in their hearts went back a long way, past the evil period in which they had been stuck, to those days of their early girlhood when together they had been preparing for confirmation and hand in hand had filled the roads round Berlevaag with singing. A Brother in the congregation gave another a knock in the ribs, like a rough caress between boys, and cried out: "You cheated me on that timber, you old scoundrel!" The Brother thus addressed almost collapsed in a heavenly burst of laughter, but tears ran from his eyes. "Yes, I did so, beloved Brother," he answered. "I did so." Skipper Halvorsen and Madam Oppegaarden suddenly found themselves close together in a corner and gave one another that long, long kiss, for which the secret uncertain love affair of their youth had never left them time.

The old Dean's flock were humble people. When later in life they thought of this evening it never occurred to any of them that they might have been exalted by their own merit. They realized that the infinite grace of which General Loewenhielm had spoken had been allotted to them, and they did not even wonder at the fact, for it had been but the fulfillment of an ever-present hope. The vain illusions of this earth had dissolved before their eyes like smoke, and they had seen the universe as it really is. They had been given one hour of the millennium.

Old Mrs. Loewenhielm was the first to leave. Her nephew accompanied her, and their hostesses lighted them out. While Philippa was helping the old lady into her many wraps, the General seized Martine's hand and held it for a long time without a word. At last he said:

"I have been with you every day of my life. You know, do you not, that it has been so?"

"Yes," said Martine, "I know that it has been so."

"And," he continued, "I shall be with you every day that is left to me. Every evening I shall sit down, if not in the flesh, which means nothing, in spirit, which is all, to dine with you, just like tonight. For tonight I have learned, dear sister, that in this world anything is possible."

"Yes, it is so, dear brother," said Martine. "In this world anything is possible."

Upon this they parted.

When at last the company broke up it had ceased to snow. The town and the mountains lay in white, unearthly splendor and the sky was bright with thousands of stars. In the street the snow was lying so deep that it had become difficult to walk. The guests from the yellow house wavered on their feet, staggered, sat down abruptly or fell forward on their knees and hands and were covered with snow, as if they had indeed had their sins washed white as wool, and in this regained innocent attire were gamboling like little lambs. It was, to each of them, blissful to have become as a small child; it was also a blessed joke to watch old Brothers and Sisters, who had been taking themselves so seriously, in this kind of celestial second childhood. They stumbled and got up, walked on or stood still, bodily as well as spiritually hand in hand, at moments performing the great chain of a beatified *lanciers.*

"Bless you, bless you, bless you," like an echo of the harmony of the spheres rang on all sides.

Martine and Philippa stood for a long time on the stone steps outside the house. They did not feel the cold. "The stars have come nearer," said Philippa.

"They will come every night," said Martine quietly. "Quite possibly it will never snow again."

In this, however, she was mistaken. An hour later it again began to snow, and such a heavy snowfall had never been known in Berlevaag. The next morning people could hardly push open their doors against the tall snowdrifts. The windows of the houses were so thickly covered with snow, it was told for years afterwards, that many good citizens of the town did not realize that daybreak had come, but slept on till late in the afternoon.

XII. THE GREAT ARTIST

When Martine and Philippa locked the door they remembered Babette. A little wave of tenderness and pity swept through them: Babette alone had had no share in the bliss of the evening.

So they went out into the kitchen, and Martine said to Babette: "It was quite a nice dinner, Babette."

Their hearts suddenly filled with gratitude. They realized that none of their guests had said a single word about the food. Indeed, try as they might, they could not themselves remember any of the dishes which had been served. Martine bethought herself of the turtle. It had not appeared at all, and now seemed very vague and far away; it was quite possible that it had been nothing but a nightmare.

Babette sat on the chopping block, surrounded by more black and greasy pots and pans than her mistresses had ever seen in their life. She was as white and as deadly exhausted as on the night when she first appeared and had fainted on their doorstep.

After a long time she looked straight at them and said: "I was once cook at the Café Anglais."

Martine said again: "They all thought that it was a nice dinner." And when Babette did not answer a word she added: "We will all remember this evening when you have gone back to Paris, Babette."

Babette said: "I am not going back to Paris."

"You are not going back to Paris?" Martine exclaimed.

"No," said Babette. "What will I do in Paris? They have all gone. I have lost them all, Mesdames."

The sisters' thoughts went to Monsieur Hersant and his son, and they said: "Oh, my poor Babette."

"Yes, they have all gone," said Babette. "The Duke of

Morny, the Duke of Decazes, Prince Narishkine, General Galliffet, Aurélian Scholl, Paul Daru, the Princesse Pauline! All!"

The strange names and titles of people lost to Babette faintly confused the two ladies, but there was such an infinite perspective of tragedy in her announcement that in their responsive state of mind they felt her losses as their own, and their eyes filled with tears.

At the end of another long silence Babette suddenly smiled slightly at them and said: "And how would I go back to Paris, Mesdames? I have no money."

"No money?" the sisters cried as with one mouth.

"No," said Babette.

"But the ten thousand francs?" the sisters asked in a horrified gasp.

"The ten thousand francs have been spent, Mesdames," said Babette.

The sisters sat down. For a full minute they could not speak.

"But ten thousand francs?" Martine slowly whispered.

"What will you, Mesdames," said Babette with great dignity. "A dinner for twelve at the Café Anglais would cost ten thousand francs."

The ladies still did not find a word to say. The piece of news was incomprehensible to them, but then many things tonight in one way or another had been beyond comprehension.

Martine remembered a tale told by a friend of her father's who had been a missionary in Africa. He had saved the life of an old chief's favorite wife, and to show his gratitude the chief had treated him to a rich meal. Only long afterwards the missionary learned from his own black servant that what he had partaken of was a small fat grandchild of the chief's, cooked in honor of the great Christian medicine man. She shuddered.

But Philippa's heart was melting in her bosom. It seemed that an unforgettable evening was to be finished off with an unforgettable proof of human loyalty and self-sacrifice.

"Dear Babette," she said softly, "you ought not to have given away all you had for our sake."

Babette gave her mistress a deep glance, a strange glance. Was there not pity, even scorn, at the bottom of it?

"For your sake?" she replied. "No. For my own."

She rose from the chopping block and stood up before the two sisters.

"I am a great artist!" she said.

She waited a moment and then repeated: "I am a great artist, Mesdames."

Again for a long time there was deep silence in the kitchen.

Then Martine said: "So you will be poor now all your life, Babette?"

"Poor?" said Babette. She smiled as if to herself. "No, I shall never be poor. I told you that I am a great artist. A great artist, Mesdames, is never poor. We have something, Mesdames, of which other people know nothing."

While the elder sister found nothing more to say, in Philippa's heart deep, forgotten chords vibrated. For she had heard, before now, long ago, of the Café Anglais. She had heard, before now, long ago, the names on Babette's tragic list. She rose and took a step toward her servant.

"But all those people whom you have mentioned," she said, "those princes and great people of Paris whom you named, Babette? You yourself fought against them. You were a Communard! The General you named had your husband and son shot! How can you grieve over them?"

Babette's dark eyes met Philippa's.

"Yes," she said, "I was a Communard. Thanks be to God, I was a Communard! And those people whom I named, Mesdames, were evil and cruel. They let the people of Paris starve; they oppressed and wronged the poor. Thanks be to God, I stood upon a barricade; I loaded the gun for my menfolk! But all the same, Mesdames, I shall not go back to Paris, now that those people of whom I have spoken are no longer there."

She stood immovable, lost in thought.

"You see, Mesdames," she said, at last, "those people belonged to me, they were mine. They had been brought up and trained, with greater expense than you, my little ladies, could ever imagine or believe, to understand what a great artist I am. I could make them happy. When I did my very best I could make them perfectly happy."

She paused for a moment.

"It was like that with Monsieur Papin too," she said.

"With Monsieur Papin?" Philippa asked.

"Yes, with your Monsieur Papin, my poor lady," said Babette. "He told me so himself: 'It is terrible and unbearable to an artist,' he said, 'to be encouraged to do, to be applauded for doing, his second best.' He said: 'Through all the world there goes one long cry from the heart of the artist: Give me leave to do my utmost!'"

Philippa went up to Babette and put her arms round her. She felt the cook's body like a marble monument against her own, but she herself shook and trembled from head to foot.

For a while she could not speak. Then she whispered:

"Yet this is not the end! I feel, Babette, that this is not the end. In Paradise you will be the great artist that God meant you to be! Ah!" she added, the tears streaming down her cheeks. "Ah, how you will enchant the angels!"

GERALD DURRELL

OWLS AND ARISTOCRACY

From *Birds, Beasts and Relatives*

NOW WINTER WAS upon us. Everything was redolent with the smoke of olive-wood fires. The shutters creaked and slapped the sides of the house as the wind caught them, and the birds and leaves were tumbled across a dark lowering sky. The brown mountains of the mainland wore tattered caps of snow and the rain filled the eroded, rocky valleys, turning them into foaming torrents that fled eagerly to the sea carrying mud and debris with them. Once they reached the sea they spread like yellow veins through the blue water, and the surface was dotted with squill bulbs, logs and twisted branches, dead beetles and butterflies, clumps of brown grass and splintered canes. Storms would be brewed in among the whitened spikes of the Albanian mountains and then tumble across to us, great black piles of cumulus, spitting a stinging rain, with sheet lightning blooming and dying like yellow ferns across the sky.

It was at the beginning of the winter that I received a letter.

Dear Gerald Durrell,

I understand from our mutual friend, Dr. Stephanides, that you are a keen naturalist and possess a number of pets. I was wondering, therefore, if you would care to have a white owl which my workmen found in an old shed they were demolishing? He has, unfortunately, a broken wing, but is otherwise in good health and feeding well.

If you would like him, I suggest you come to lunch on

Friday and take him with you when you return home. Perhaps you would be kind enough to let me know. A quarter to one, or one o'clock would be suitable.

Yours sincerely,
Countess Mavrodaki

This letter excited me for two reasons. Firstly, because I had always wanted a barn owl, for that was what it obviously was, and secondly, because the whole of Corfu society had been trying unavailingly for years to get to know the Countess. She was the recluse par excellence. Immensely wealthy, she lived in a gigantic, rambling, Venetian villa deep in the country and never entertained or saw anybody except the workmen on her vast estate. Her acquaintance with Theodore was due only to the fact that he was her medical adviser. The Countess was reputed to possess a large and valuable library and for this reason Larry had been most anxious to try to get himself invited to her villa, but without success.

"Dear God," he said bitterly when I showed him my invitation. "Here I've been trying for months to get that old harpy to let me see her books and she invites you to lunch—there's no justice in the world."

I said that after I had lunched with the Countess, maybe I could ask her if he could see her books.

"After she's had lunch with *you* I shouldn't think she would be willing to show me a copy of *The Times*, let alone her library," said Larry witheringly.

However, in spite of my brother's low opinion of my social graces, I was determined to put in a good word for him if I saw a suitable opportunity. It was, I felt, an important, even solemn occasion, and so I dressed with care. My shirt and shorts were carefully laundered and I had prevailed upon

Mother to buy me a new pair of sandals and a new straw hat. I rode on Sally—who had a new blanket as a saddle to honour the occasion—for the Countess's estate was some distance away.

The day was dark and the ground mushy under foot. It looked as though we would have a storm, but I hoped this would not be until after I had arrived, for the rain would spoil the crisp whiteness of my shirt. As we jogged along through the olives, the occasional woodcock zooming up from the myrtles in front of us, I became increasingly nervous. I discovered that I was ill-prepared for this occasion. To begin with, I had forgotten to bring my four-legged chicken in spirits. I had felt sure that the Countess would want to see this and in any case I felt it would provide a subject of conversation that would help us in the initial awkward stages of our meeting. Secondly, I had forgotten to consult anybody on the correct way to address a countess. "Your Majesty" would surely be too formal, I thought, especially as she was giving me an owl? Perhaps "Highness" would be better—or maybe just a simple "Mam"?

Puzzling over the intricacies of protocol, I had left Sally to her own devices, and so she had promptly fallen into a donkey-doze. Of all the beasts of burden, only the donkey seems capable of falling asleep while still moving. The result was that she ambled close to the ditch at the side of the road, suddenly stumbled and lurched and I, deep in thought, fell off her back into six inches of mud and water. Sally stared down at me with an expression of accusing astonishment that she always wore when she knew she was in the wrong. I was so furious, I could have strangled her. My new sandals oozed, my shorts and shirt—so crisp, so clean, so *well-behaved-looking* a moment before—were now bespattered with mud and bits of decaying water-weed. I could have wept with rage and frustration. We were too far from home to retrace our foot-steps so that I could change; there was nothing for it but to go on, damp and miserable, convinced now that it did not matter how I addressed the Countess. She would, I felt sure, take one look at my gypsy-like condition and order me home. Not only would I lose my owl, but any chance I had of getting Larry in to see her library. I was a fool, I thought bitterly. I should have walked instead of trusting myself to this hopeless creature, who was now trotting along at a brisk pace, her ears pricked like furry arum lilies.

Presently we came to the Countess's villa, lying deep in the olive groves, approached by a drive lined with tall green-and-pink-trunked eucalyptus trees. The entrance to the drive was guarded by two columns on which were perched a pair of white-winged lions who stared scornfully at Sally and me as we trotted down the drive. The house was immense, built in a hollow square. It had at one time been a lovely, rich, Venetian red, but this had now faded to a rose-pink, the plaster bulged and cracked in places by the damp, and I noticed that a number of brown tiles were missing from the roof. The eaves had slung under them more swallows' nests—now empty, like small, forgotten, brown ovens—than I had ever seen congregated in one spot before.

I tied Sally up under a convenient tree and made my way to the archway that led into the central patio. Here a rusty chain hung down and when I pulled it I heard a bell jangle faintly somewhere in the depths of the house. I waited patiently for some time and was just about to ring the bell again when the massive wooden doors were opened. There stood a man who looked to me exactly like a bandit. He was tall and powerful, with a great jutting hawk-nose, sweeping flamboyant white moustaches, and a mane of curling white hair. He was wearing a scarlet tarbush, a loose white blouse beautifully embroidered with scarlet-and-gold thread, baggy pleated black pants, and on his feet upturned *charukias* decorated with enormous red-and-white pom-poms. His brown face cracked into a grin and I saw that all his teeth were gold. It was like looking into a mint.

"*Kyrié* Durrell?" he inquired. "Welcome."

I followed him through the patio, full of magnolia trees and forlorn winter flower-beds, and into the house. He led me down a long corridor tiled in scarlet and blue, threw open a door, and ushered me into a great, gloomy room lined from ceiling to floor with bookshelves. At one end was a large fireplace in which a blaze flapped and hissed and crackled. Over the fire-place was an enormous gold-framed mirror, nearly black with age. Sitting by the fire on a long couch, almost obliterated by coloured shawls and cushions, was the Countess.

She was not a bit what I had expected. I had visualized her as being tall, gaunt, and rather forbidding, but as she rose to her feet and danced across the room to me I saw she was tiny, very fat, and as pink and dimpled as a rosebud. Her honey-coloured hair was piled high on her head in a pompadour style and her eyes, under permanently arched and surprised eyebrows, were as green and shiny as unripe olives. She took my hand in both her warm little pudgy ones and clasped it to her ample breast.

"How kind, how *kind* of you to come," she exclaimed in a musical, little girl's voice, exuding an overpowering odour of Parma violets and brandy in equal quantities. "How very, *very* kind. May I call you Gerry? Of course I may. My friends call me Matilda ... it isn't my *real* name, of course. That's Stephani Zinia ... so uncouth—like a patent medicine. I *much* prefer Matilda, don't you?"

I said, cautiously, that I thought Matilda a very nice name.

"Yes, a comforting *old-fashioned* name. Names are *so* important, don't you think? Now he there," she said, gesturing at the man who had shown me in, "*he* calls himself Demetrios. I call him Mustapha."

She glanced at the man and then leaned forward, nearly asphyxiating me with brandy and Parma violets, and hissed suddenly, in Greek, "He's a misbegotten Turk."

The man's face grew red and his moustache bristled, making him look more like a bandit than ever. "I am not a Turk," he snarled. "You lie."

"You are a Turk and your name's Mustapha," she retorted.

"It isn't . . . I'm not . . . It isn't . . . I'm not," said the man, almost incoherent with rage. "You are lying."

"I'm not."

"You are."

"I'm not."

"You are."

"I'm *not.*"

"You're a damned elderly liar."

"Elderly," she squeaked, her face growing red. "You dare to call me elderly . . . you . . . you *Turk* you."

"You are elderly and you're fat," said Demetrios-Mustapha coldly.

"That's too much," she screamed. "Elderly . . . fat . . . that's too much. You're sacked. Take a month's notice. No, leave this instant, you son of a misbegotten Turk."

Demetrios-Mustapha drew himself up regally.

"Very well," he said. "Do you wish me to serve the drinks and lunch before I go?"

"Of course," she said.

In silence he crossed the room and extracted a bottle of champagne from an ice bucket behind the sofa. He opened it and poured equal quantities of brandy and champagne into three large glasses. He handed us one each and lifted the third himself.

"I give you a toast," he said to me solemnly. "We will drink to the health of a fat, elderly liar."

I was in a quandary. If I drank the toast it would seem that I was concurring in his opinion of the Countess, and that would scarcely seem polite; and yet, if I did *not* drink the toast, he looked quite capable of doing me an injury. As I hesitated, the Countess, to my astonishment, burst into delighted giggles, her smooth fat cheeks dimpling charmingly.

"You mustn't tease our guest, Mustapha. But I must admit, the toast was a good touch," she said, gulping at her drink.

Demetrios-Mustapha grinned at me, his teeth glittering and winking in the fire-light.

"Drink, *kyrié*," he said. "Take no notice of us. She lives for food, drink, and fighting, and it is my job to provide all three."

"Nonsense," said the Countess, seizing my hand and leading me to the sofa, so that I felt as though I were hitched to a small, fat, pink cloud. "Nonsense, I live for a lot of things, a lot of things. Now, don't stand there drinking my drink, you drunkard. Go and see to the food."

Demetrios-Mustapha drained his glass and left the room, while the Countess seated herself on the sofa, clasping my hand in hers, and beamed at me.

"This *is* cosy," she said delightedly. "Just you and I. Tell me, do you always wear mud all over your clothes?"

I hastily and embarrassedly explained about Sally.

"So you came by *donkey*," she said, making it sound a very exotic form of transport. "How *wise* of you. I distrust motor-cars myself, noisy, uncontrollable things. Unreliable.

"I remember we had one when my husband was alive, a big yellow one. But my dear, it was a brute. It would obey my husband, but it would not do a thing I told it to do. One day it deliberately backed into a large stall containing fruit and vegetables—in spite of all I was trying to do to stop it— and then went over the edge of the harbour into the sea. When I came out of hospital, I said to my husband, 'Henri,' I said—that was his name—such a nice, *bourgeois* name, don't you think? Where was I? Oh, yes. Well, 'Henri,' I said, 'that car's malevolent,' I said. 'It's possessed of an evil spirit. You must sell it.' And so he did."

Brandy and champagne on an empty stomach combined with the fire to make me feel extremely mellow. My head whirled pleasantly and I nodded and smiled as the Countess chattered on eagerly.

"My husband was a very cultured man, very cultured indeed. He collected books, you know. Books, paintings, stamps, beer-bottle tops, anything cultural appealed to him. Just before he died, he started collecting busts of Napoleon. You would be surprised how many busts they had made of that horrible little Corsican. My husband had five hundred and eighty-two. 'Henri,' I said to him. 'Henri, this must stop. Either you give up collecting busts of Napoleon or I will leave you and go to St. Helena.' I said it as a joke, though, only as a joke, and you know what he said? He said he had been thinking about going to St. Helena for a holiday—with all his busts. My God, what dedication! It was not to be borne! I believe in a little bit of culture in its place, but not to become *obsessed* with it."

Demetrios-Mustapha came into the room, refilled our glasses and said, "Lunch in five minutes," and departed again.

"He was what you might call a *compulsive* collector, my

dear. The times that I trembled when I saw that fanatical gleam in his eye. At a state fair once he saw a combine harvester, simply immense it was, and I could *see* the gleam in his eyes, but I put my foot down. 'Henri,' I said to him. 'Henri, we are not going to have combine harvesters all over the place. If you must collect, why not something sensible? Jewels or furs or something?' It may seem harsh, my dear, but what could I do? If I had relaxed for an *instant* he would have had the whole house full of farm machinery."

Demetrios-Mustapha came into the room again. "Lunch is ready," he said.

Still chattering, the Countess led me by the hand out of the room, down the tiled corridor, then down some creaking wooden stairs into a huge kitchen in the cellars. The kitchen at our villa was enormous enough, but this kitchen simply dwarfed it. It was stone-flagged and at one end a positive battery of charcoal fires glowed and winked under the bubbling pots. The walls were covered with a great variety of copper pots, kettles, platters, coffee pots, huge serving dishes, and soup tureens. They all glowed with a pinky-red gleam in the fire-light, glinting and winking like tiger beetles. In the centre of the floor was a twelve-foot-long dining-table of beautiful polished walnut. This was carefully set for two with snowy-white serviettes and gleaming cutlery. In the centre of the table two giant silver candelabras each held a white forest of lighted candles. The whole effect of a kitchen and a state dining-room combined was very odd. It was very hot and so redolent with delicious smells they almost suffocated the Countess's scent.

"I hope you don't mind eating in the kitchen," said the Countess, making it sound as though it were really the most degrading thing to eat food in such humble surroundings.

I said I thought eating in the kitchen was a most sensible idea, especially in winter, as it was warmer.

"Quite right," said the Countess, seating herself as Demetrios-Mustapha held her chair for her. "And, you see, if we eat upstairs I get complaints from this elderly Turk about how far he has to walk."

"It isn't the distance I complain of, it's the weight of the food," said Demetrios-Mustapha, pouring a pale green-gold wine into our glasses. "If you didn't eat so much, it wouldn't be so bad."

"Oh, stop complaining and get on with serving," said the Countess plaintively, tucking her serviette carefully under her dimpled chin.

I, filled with champagne and brandy, was now more than a little drunk and ravenously hungry. I viewed with alarm the number of eating utensils that were flanking my plate, for I was not quite sure which to use first. I remembered Mother's maxim that you started on the outside and worked in, but there were so many utensils that I was uneasy. I decided to wait and see what the Countess used and then follow suit. It was an unwise decision for I soon discovered that she used any and every knife, fork, or spoon with a fine lack of discrimination and so, before long, I became so muddled I was doing the same.

The first course that Demetrios-Mustapha set before us was a fine, clear soup, sequined with tiny golden bubbles of fat, with fingernail-sized croutons floating like crisp little rafts on an amber sea. It was delicious, and the Countess had two helpings, scrunching up the croutons, the noise like someone walking over crisp leaves. Demetrios-Mustapha filled our glasses with more of the pale, musky wine and placed before us a platter of minute baby fish, each one fried a golden brown. Slices of yellow-green lemons in a large dish and a brimming sauce-boat of some exotic sauce unknown to me accompanied it. The Countess piled her plate high with fish, added a lava flow of sauce, and then squeezed lemon juice lavishly over the fish, the table, and herself. She beamed at me, her face now a bright rose-pink, her forehead slightly beaded with sweat. Her prodigious appetite did not appear to impair her conversational powers one jot, for she talked incessantly.

"Don't you love these little fish? Heavenly! Of course, it's such a pity that they should die so *young*, but there we are. *So* nice to be able to eat *all* of them without worrying about the bones. *Such* a relief! Henri, my husband, you know, started to collect skeletons once. My dear, the house looked and smelt like a mortuary. 'Henri,' I said to him. 'Henri, this must stop. This is an unhealthy death-wish you have developed. You must go and see a psychiatrist.'"

Demetrios-Mustapha removed our empty plates, poured for us a red wine, dark as the heart of a dragon, and then placed before us a dish in which lay snipe, the heads twisted round so that their long beaks could skewer themselves and their empty eye-sockets look at us accusingly. They were plump and brown with cooking, each having its own little square of toast. They were surrounded by thin wafers of fried potatoes like drifts of autumn leaves, pale greeny-white candles of asparagus and small peas.

"I simply cannot understand people who are vegetarians," said the Countess, banging vigorously at a snipe's skull with her fork so that she might crack it and get to the brain. "Henri once tried to be a vegetarian. Would you believe it? But I couldn't endure it. 'Henri,' I said to him, 'this must stop. We have enough food in the larder to feed an army, and I can't eat it single-handed.' Imagine, my dear, I had just ordered two dozen hares. 'Henri,' I said, 'you will have to give up this foolish fad.'"

It struck me that Henri, although obviously a bit of a trial as a husband, had nevertheless led a very frustrated existence.

Demetrios-Mustapha cleared away the debris of the snipe and poured out more wine. I was beginning to feel bloated with food and I hoped that there was not too much more to come. But there was still an army of knives and forks and spoons, unused, beside my plate, so it was with alarm I saw Demetrios-Mustapha approaching through the gloomy kitchen bearing a huge dish.

"Ah!" said the Countess, holding up her plump hands in excitement. "The main dish! What is it, Mustapha, what is it?"

"The wild boar that Makroyannis sent," said Demetrios-Mustapha.

"Oh, the boar! The *boar!*" squeaked the Countess, clasping her fat cheeks in her hands. "Oh, lovely! I had forgotten all about it. You do like wild boar, I hope?"

I said that it was one of my favourite meats, which was true, but could I have a very small helping, please?

"But of course you shall," she said, leaning over the great, brown, gravy-glistening haunch and starting to cut thick pink slabs of it. She placed three of these on a plate—obviously under the impression that this was, by anyone's standards, a small portion—and then proceeded to surround them with the accoutrements. There were piles of the lovely little golden wild mushrooms, chanterelles, with their delicate, almost winy flavour; tiny marrows stuffed with sour cream and capers; potatoes baked in their skins, neatly split and anointed with butter; carrots red as a frosty winter sun and great tree trunks of white leeks, poached in cream. I surveyed this dish of food and surreptitiously undid the top three buttons of my shorts.

"We used to get wild boar *such* a lot when Henri was alive. He used to go to Albania and shoot them, you know. But now we seldom have it. What a *treat!* Will you have some more mushrooms? No? So good for one. After this, I think we will have a pause. A pause is essential, I always think, for a good digestion," said the Countess, adding naïvely, "and it enables you to eat so much *more.*"

The wild boar was fragrant and succulent, having been marinaded well with herb-scented wine and stuffed with garlic cloves, but even so I only just managed to finish it. The Countess had two helpings, both identical in size, and then leaned back, her face congested to a pale puce colour, and mopped the sweat from her brow with an inadequate lace handkerchief.

"A pause, eh?" she said thickly, smiling at me. "A pause to marshal our resources."

I felt that I had not any resources to marshal, but I did not like to say so. I nodded and smiled and undid all the rest of the buttons on my shorts.

During the pause, the Countess smoked a long thin cheroot and ate salted peanuts, chatting on interminably about her husband. The pause did me good. I felt a little less solid and somnolent with food. When the Countess eventually decided that we had rested our internal organs sufficiently, she called for the next course, and Demetrios-Mustapha produced two mercifully small omelettes, crispy brown on the outside and liquid and succulent on the inside, stuffed with tiny pink shrimps.

"What have you got for a sweet?" inquired the Countess, her mouth full of omelette.

"I didn't make one," said Demetrios-Mustapha.

The Countess's eyes grew round and fixed.

"You didn't make a sweet?" she said, in tones of horror, as

though he were confessing to some heinous crime.

"I didn't have time," said Demetrios-Mustapha. "You can't expect me to do all this cooking and all the housework."

"But no *sweet*," said the Countess despairingly. "You can't have a lunch without a sweet."

"Well, I bought you some meringues," said Mustapha. "You'll have to make do with those."

"Oh, lovely!" said the Countess glowing and happy again. "Just what's needed."

It was the last thing I needed. The meringues were large and white and brittle as coral and stuffed to overflowing with cream. I wished fervently that I had brought Roger with me, as he could have sat under the table and accepted half my food, since the Countess was far too occupied with her own plate and her reminiscences really to concentrate on me.

"Now," she said at last, swallowing the last mouthful of meringue and brushing the white crumbs from her chin. "Now, do you feel replete? Or would you care for a little something more? Some fruit perhaps? Not that there's very much at this time of the year."

I said no thank you very much, I had had quite sufficient.

The Countess sighed and looked at me soulfully. I think nothing would have pleased her more than to ply me with another two or three courses.

"You don't eat enough," she said. "A growing boy like you should eat more. You're far too thin for your age. Does your Mother feed you properly?"

I could imagine Mother's wrath if she had heard this innuendo. I said yes, Mother was an excellent cook and we all fed like lords.

"I'm glad to hear it," said the Countess. "But you still look a little peaky to me."

I could not say so, but the reason I was beginning to look peaky was that the assault of food upon my stomach was beginning to make itself felt. I said, as politely as I could, that I thought I ought to be getting back.

"But of course, dear," said the Countess. "Dear me, a quarter past four already. How time flies!"

She sighed at the thought, then brightened perceptibly.

"However, it's nearly time for tea. Are you sure you wouldn't like to stay and have something?"

I said no, that Mother would be worried about me.

"Now, let me see," said the Countess. "What did you come for? Oh, yes, the owl. Mustapha, bring the boy his owl and bring me some coffee and some of those nice Turkish delights up in the lounge."

Mustapha appeared with a cardboard box done up with string and handed it to me.

"I wouldn't open it until you get home," he said. "That's a wild one, that."

I was overcome with the terrifying thought that if I did not hurry my departure, the Countess would ask me to partake of Turkish delight with her. So I thanked them both sincerely for my owl, and made my way to the front door.

"Well," said the Countess, "it has been enchanting having you, *absolutely enchanting*. You must come again. You must come in the spring or the summer when we have more choice of fruit and vegetables. Mustapha's got a way of cooking octopus which makes it simply melt in your mouth."

I said I would love to come again, making a mental vow that if I did, I would starve for three days in advance.

"Here," said the Countess, pressing an orange into my pocket, "take this. You might feel peckish on the way home."

As I mounted Sally and trotted off down the drive, she called, "Drive carefully."

Grim-faced, I sat there with the owl clasped to my bosom till we were outside the gates of the Countess's estate. Then the jogging I was subjected to on Sally's back was too much. I dismounted, went behind an olive tree, and was deliciously and flamboyantly sick.

When I got home I carried the owl up to my bedroom, untied the box and lifted him, struggling and beak-clicking, out onto the floor. The dogs, who had gathered round in a circle to view the new addition, backed away hurriedly. They knew what Ulysses could do when he was in a bad temper, and this owl was three times his size. He was, I thought, one of the most beautiful birds I had ever seen. The feathers on his back and wings were honeycomb golden, smudged with pale ash-grey; his breast was a spotless cream-white; and the mask of white feathers round his dark, strangely Oriental-looking eyes was as crisp and as starched-looking as any Elizabethan's ruff.

His wing was not as bad as I had feared. It was a clean break, and after half an hour's struggle, during which he managed to draw blood on several occasions, I had it splinted up to my satisfaction. The owl, which I had decided to call Lampadusa, simply because the name appealed to me, seemed to be belligerently scared of the dogs, totally unwilling to make friends with Ulysses, and viewed Augustus Tickletummy with undisguised loathing. I felt he might be happier, till he settled down, in a dark, secluded place, so I carried him up to the attic. One of the attic rooms was very tiny and lit by one small window which was so covered with cobwebs and dust that it allowed little light to penetrate the room. It was quiet and as dim as a cave, and I thought that here Lampadusa would enjoy his convalescence. I put him on the floor with a large saucer of chopped meat and locked the door carefully so that he would not be disturbed. That evening, when I went to visit him, taking him a dead mouse by way of a present, he seemed very much improved. He had eaten most of his meat and now hissed and beak-clicked at me with outspread wings and blazing eyes as he pitter-pattered about the floor. Encouraged by his obvious progress, I left him with his mouse and went to bed.

Some hours later I was awakened by the sound of voices emanating from Mother's room. Wondering, sleepily, what on earth the family could be doing at that hour, I got out of bed and stuck my head out of the bedroom door to listen.

"I tell you," Larry was saying, "it's a damned great poltergeist."

"It can't be a poltergeist, dear," said Mother. "Poltergeists throw things."

"Well, whatever it is, it's up there clanking its chains," said Larry, "and I want it exorcized. You and Margo are supposed to be the experts on the after-life. You go up and do it."

"I'm not going up there," said Margo tremulously. "It might be anything. It might be a malignant spirit."

"It's bloody malignant all right," said Larry. "It's been keeping me awake for the last hour."

"Are you sure it isn't the wind or something, dear?" asked Mother.

"I know the difference between wind and a damned ghost playing around with balls and chains," said Larry.

"Perhaps it's burglars," said Margo, more to give herself confidence than anything else. "Perhaps it's burglars and we ought to wake Leslie."

Half-asleep and still bee-drowsy from the liquor I had consumed that day, I could not think what the family were talking about. It seemed as intriguing as any of the other crises that they seemed capable of evoking at the most unexpected hours of the day or night, so I went to Mother's door and peered into the room. Larry was marching up and down, his dressing-gown swishing imperially.

"Something's got to be done," he said. "I can't sleep with rattling chains over my head, and if I can't sleep I can't write."

"I don't see what you expect *us* to do about it, dear," said Mother. "I'm sure it must be the wind."

"Yes, you can't expect us to go up there," said Margo. "You're a man, *you* go."

"Look," said Larry, "you are the one who came back from London covered with ectoplasm and talking about the infinite. It's probably some hellish thing you've conjured up from one of your séances that's followed you here. That makes it *your* pet. You go and deal with it."

The word "pet" penetrated. Surely it could not be Lampadusa? Like all owls, barn owls have wings as soft and as silent as dandelion clocks. Surely he could not be responsible for making a noise like a ball and chain?

I went into the room and inquired what they were all talking about.

"It's only a ghost, dear," said Mother. "Larry's found a ghost."

"It's in the attic," said Margo, excitedly. "Larry thinks it followed me from England. I wonder if it's Mawake?"

"We're not going to start *that* all over again," said Mother firmly.

"I don't care *who* it is," said Larry, "which one of your disembodied friends. I want it removed."

I said I thought there was just the faintest possibility that it might be Lampadusa.

"What's that?" inquired Mother.

I explained that it was the owl the Countess had given me.

"I might have known it," said Larry. "I might have known it. Why it didn't occur to me instantly, I don't know."

"Now, now, dear," said Mother. "It's only an owl."

"Only an owl!" said Larry. "It sounds like a battalion of tanks crashing about up there. Tell him to get it out of the loft."

I said I could not understand why Lampadusa was making a noise since owls were the quietest of things. . . . I said they drifted through the night on silent wings like flakes of ash. . . .

"This one hasn't got silent wings," said Larry. "It sounds like a one-owl jazz band. Go and get it *out*."

Hurriedly I took a lamp and made my way up to the attic. When I opened the door I saw at once what the trouble was. Lampadusa had devoured his mouse and then discovered that there was a long shred of meat still lying in his saucer. This, during the course of the long, hot day, had solidified and become welded to the surface of the saucer. Lampadusa, feeling that this shred of meat would do well as a light snack to keep body and soul together until dawn, had endeavoured to pick it off the plate. The curve of his sharp amber beak had gone through the meat, but the meat had refused to part company with the saucer, so that there he was, effectively trapped, flapping ineffectually round the floor, banging and clattering the saucer against the wooden boards in an effort to disentangle it from his beak. So I extricated him from this predicament and carried him down to my bedroom where I shut him in his cardboard box for safe-keeping.

SHIRLEY JACKSON

LIKE MOTHER
USED TO MAKE

DAVID TURNER, WHO did everything in small quick movements, hurried from the bus stop down the avenue toward his street. He reached the grocery on the corner and hesitated; there had been something. Butter, he remembered with relief; this morning, all the way up the avenue to his bus stop, he had been telling himself butter, don't forget butter coming home tonight, when you pass the grocery remember butter. He went into the grocery and waited his turn, examining the cans on the shelves. Canned pork sausage was back, and corned-beef hash. A tray full of rolls caught his eye, and then the woman ahead of him went out and the clerk turned to him.

"How much is butter?" David asked cautiously.

"Eighty-nine," the clerk said easily.

"Eighty-nine?" David frowned.

"That's what it is," the clerk said. He looked past David at the next customer.

"Quarter of a pound, please," David said. "And a half-dozen rolls."

Carrying his package home he thought, I really ought not to trade there any more; you'd think they'd know me well enough to be more courteous.

There was a letter from his mother in the mailbox. He stuck it into the top of the bag of rolls and went upstairs to the third floor. No light in Marcia's apartment, the only other apartment on the floor. David turned to his own door and unlocked it, snapping on the light as he came in the door. Tonight, as every night when he came home, the apartment looked warm and friendly and good; the little foyer, with the neat small table and four careful chairs, and the bowl of little marigolds against the pale green walls David had painted himself; beyond, the kitchenette, and beyond that, the big room where David read and slept and the ceiling of which was a perpetual trouble to him; the plaster was falling in one corner and no power on earth could make it less noticeable. David consoled himself for the plaster constantly with the thought that perhaps if he had not taken an apartment in an old brownstone the plaster would not be falling, but then, too, for the money he paid he could not have a foyer and a big room and a kitchenette, anywhere else.

He put his bag down on the table and put the butter away in the refrigerator and the rolls in the breadbox. He folded the empty bag and put it in a drawer in the kitchenette. Then he hung his coat in the hall closet and went into the big room, which he called his living-room, and lighted the desk light. His word for the room, in his own mind, was "charming." He had always been partial to yellows and browns, and he had painted the desk and the bookcases and the end tables himself, had even painted the walls, and had hunted around the city for the exact tweedish tan drapes he had in mind. The room satisfied him: the rug was a rich dark brown that picked up the darkest thread in the drapes, the furniture was almost yellow, the cover on the studio couch and the lampshades were orange. The rows of plants on the window sills gave the touch of green the room needed; right now David was looking for an ornament to set on the end table, but he had his heart set on a low translucent green bowl for more marigolds, and such things cost more than he could afford, after the silverware.

He could not come into this room without feeling that it was the most comfortable home he had ever had; tonight, as always, he let his eyes move slowly around the room, from couch to drapes to bookcase, imagined the green bowl on the end table, and sighed as he turned to the desk. He took his pen from the holder, and a sheet of the neat notepaper sitting in one of the desk cubbyholes, and wrote carefully: "Dear Marcia, don't forget you're coming for dinner tonight. I'll expect you about six." He signed the note with a "D" and picked up the key to Marcia's apartment which lay in the flat pencil tray on his desk. He had a key to Marcia's apartment because she was never home when her laundryman came, or when the man came to fix the refrigerator or the telephone or the windows, and someone had to let them in because the landlord was reluctant to climb three flights of stairs with the pass key. Marcia had never suggested having a key to David's apartment, and he had never offered her one; it pleased him to have only one key to his home, and that safely in his own pocket; it had a pleasant feeling to him, solid and small, the only way into his warm fine home.

He left his front door open and went down the dark hall to the other apartment. He opened the door with his key and turned on the light. This apartment was not agreeable for him to come into; it was exactly the same as his: foyer, kitchenette, living-room, and it reminded him constantly of his first day in his own apartment, when the thought of the careful home-making to be done had left him very close to despair. Marcia's home was bare and at random; an upright piano a friend had given her recently stood crookedly, half in the foyer, because the little room was too narrow and the big room was too cluttered for it to sit comfortably anywhere; Marcia's bed was unmade and a pile of dirty laundry lay on the floor. The window had been open all day and papers had blown wildly around the floor. David closed the window, hesitated over the papers, and then moved away quickly. He put the note on the piano keys and locked the door behind him.

In his own apartment he settled down happily to making dinner. He had made a little pot roast for dinner the night before; most of it was still in the refrigerator and he sliced it in fine thin slices and arranged it on a plate with parsley. His plates were orange, almost the same color as the couch cover, and it was pleasant to him to arrange a salad, with the lettuce on the orange plate, and the thin slices of cucumber. He put coffee on to cook, and sliced potatoes to fry, and then, with his dinner cooking agreeably and the window open to lose the odor of the frying potatoes, he set lovingly to arranging his table. First, the tablecloth, pale green, of course. And the two fresh green napkins. The orange plates and the precise cup and saucer at each place. The plate of rolls in the center, and the odd salt and pepper shakers, like two green frogs. Two glasses—they came from the five-and-ten, but they had thin green bands around them—and finally, with great care, the silverware. Gradually, tenderly, David was buying himself a complete set of silverware; starting out modestly with a service for two, he had added to it until now he had well over a service for four, although not quite a service for six, lacking salad forks and soup spoons. He had chosen a sedate, pretty pattern, one that would be fine with any sort of table setting, and each morning he gloried in a breakfast that started with a shining silver spoon for his grapefruit, and had a compact butter knife for his toast and a solid heavy knife to break his eggshell, and a fresh silver spoon for his coffee, which he sugared with a particular spoon meant only for sugar. The silverware lay in a tarnish-proof box on a high shelf all to itself, and David lifted it down carefully to take out a service for two. It made a lavish display set out on the table—knives, forks, salad forks, more forks for the pie, a spoon to each place, and the special serving pieces—the sugar spoon, the large serving spoons for the potatoes and the salad, the fork for the meat, and the pie fork. When the table held as much silverware as two people could possibly use he put the box back on the shelf and stood back, checking everything and admiring the table, shining and clean. Then he went into his living-room to read his mother's letter and wait for Marcia.

The potatoes were done before Marcia came, and then suddenly the door burst open and Marcia arrived with a shout and fresh air and disorder. She was a tall handsome girl with a loud voice, wearing a dirty raincoat, and she said, "I didn't forget, Davie, I'm just late as usual. What's for dinner? You're not mad, are you?"

David got up and came over to take her coat. "I left a note for you," he said.

"Didn't see it," Marcia said. "Haven't been home. Something smells good."

"Fried potatoes," David said. "Everything's ready."

"Golly." Marcia fell into a chair to sit with her legs stretched out in front of her and her arms hanging. "I'm tired," she said. "It's cold out."

"It was getting colder when I came home," David said. He was putting dinner on the table, the platter of meat, the salad, the bowl of fried potatoes. He walked quietly back and forth from the kitchenette to the table, avoiding Marcia's feet. "I don't believe you've been here since I got my silverware," he said.

Marcia swung around to the table and picked up a spoon. "It's beautiful," she said, running her finger along the pattern. "Pleasure to eat with it."

"Dinner's ready," David said. He pulled her chair out for her and waited for her to sit down.

Marcia was always hungry; she put meat and potatoes and salad on her plate without admiring the serving silver, and started to eat enthusiastically. "Everything's beautiful," she said once. "Food is wonderful, Davie."

"I'm glad you like it," David said. He liked the feel of the fork in his hand, even the sight of the fork moving up to Marcia's mouth.

Marcia waved her hand largely. "I mean everything," she said, "furniture, and nice place you have here, and dinner, and everything."

"I *like* things this way," David said.

"I know you do." Marcia's voice was mournful. "Someone should teach me, I guess."

"You *ought* to keep your home neater," David said. "You ought to get curtains at least, and keep your windows shut."

"I never remember," she said. "Davie, you are the most *wonderful* cook." She pushed her plate away, and sighed.

David blushed happily. "I'm glad you like it," he said again, and then he laughed. "I made a pie last night."

"A pie." Marcia looked at him for a minute and then she said, "Apple?"

David shook his head, and she said, "Pineapple?" and he shook his head again, and, because he could not wait to tell her, said, "Cherry."

"My *God*!" Marcia got up and followed him into the kitchen and looked over his shoulder while he took the pie carefully out of the breadbox. "Is this the first pie you ever made?"

"I've made two before," David admitted, "but this one turned out better than the others."

She watched happily while he cut large pieces of pie and

put them on other orange plates, and then she carried her own plate back to the table, tasted the pie, and made wordless gestures of appreciation. David tasted his pie and said critically, "I think it's a little sour. I ran out of sugar."

"It's perfect," Marcia said. "I always loved a cherry pie really sour. This isn't sour enough, even."

David cleared the table and poured the coffee, and as he was setting the coffeepot back on the stove Marcia said, "My doorbell's ringing." She opened the apartment door and listened, and they could both hear the ringing in her apartment. She pressed the buzzer in David's apartment that opened the downstairs door, and far away they could hear heavy footsteps starting up the stairs. Marcia left the apartment door open and came back to her coffee. "Landlord, most likely," she said. "I didn't pay my rent again." When the footsteps reached the top of the last staircase Marcia yelled, "Hello?" leaning back in her chair to see out the door into the hall. Then she said, "Why, Mr. Harris." She got up and went to the door and held out her hand. "Come in," she said.

"I just thought I'd stop by," Mr. Harris said. He was a very large man and his eyes rested curiously on the coffee cups and empty plates on the table. "I don't want to interrupt your dinner."

"*That's* all right," Marcia said, pulling him into the room. "It's just Davie. Davie, this is Mr. Harris, he works in my office. This is Mr. Turner."

"How do you do," David said politely, and the man looked at him carefully and said, "How do you do?"

"Sit down, sit down," Marcia was saying, pushing a chair forward. "Davie, how about another cup for Mr. Harris?"

"Please don't bother," Mr. Harris said quickly, "I just thought I'd stop by."

While David was taking out another cup and saucer and

getting a spoon down from the tarnish-proof silverbox, Marcia said, "You like homemade pie?"

"Say," Mr. Harris said admiringly, "I've forgotten what homemade pie *looks* like."

"Davie," Marcia called cheerfully, "how about cutting Mr. Harris a piece of that pie?"

Without answering, David took a fork out of the silverbox and got down an orange plate and put a piece of pie on it. His plans for the evening had been vague; they had involved perhaps a movie if it were not too cold out, and at least a short talk with Marcia about the state of her home; Mr. Harris was settling down in his chair and when David put the pie down silently in front of him he stared at it admiringly for a minute before he tasted it.

"Say," he said finally, "this is certainly some pie." He looked at Marcia. "This is really *good* pie," he said.

"You like it?" Marcia asked modestly. She looked up at David and smiled at him over Mr. Harris' head. "I haven't made but two, three pies before," she said.

David raised a hand to protest, but Mr. Harris turned to him and demanded, "Did you ever eat any better pie in your life?"

"I don't think Davie liked it much," Marcia said wickedly, "I think it was too sour for him."

"I *like* a sour pie," Mr. Harris said. He looked suspiciously at David. "A cherry pie's *got* to be sour."

"I'm glad you like it, anyway," Marcia said. Mr. Harris ate the last mouthful of pie, finished his coffee, and sat back. "I'm sure glad I dropped in," he said to Marcia.

David's desire to be rid of Mr. Harris had slid imperceptibly into an urgency to be rid of them both; his clean house, his nice silver, were not meant as vehicles for the kind of fatuous banter Marcia and Mr. Harris were playing at together;

almost roughly he took the coffee cup away from the arm Marcia had stretched across the table, took it out to the kitchenette and came back and put his hand on Mr. Harris' cup.

"Don't bother, Davie, honestly," Marcia said. She looked up, smiling again, as though she and David were conspirators against Mr. Harris. "I'll do them all tomorrow, honey," she said.

"Sure," Mr. Harris said. He stood up. "Let them wait. Let's go in and sit down where we can be comfortable."

Marcia got up and led him into the living-room and they sat down on the studio couch. "Come on in, Davie," Marcia called.

The sight of his pretty table covered with dirty dishes and cigarette ashes held David. He carried the plates and cups and silverware into the kitchenette and stacked them in the sink and then, because he could not endure the thought of their sitting there any longer, with the dirt gradually hardening on them, he tied an apron on and began to wash them carefully. Now and then, while he was washing them and drying them and putting them away, Marcia would call to him, sometimes, "Davie, what *are* you doing?" or, "Davie, won't you stop all that and come sit down?" Once she said, "Davie, I don't want you to wash all those dishes," and Mr. Harris said, "Let him work, he's happy."

David put the clean yellow cups and saucers back on the shelves—by now, Mr. Harris' cup was unrecognizable; you could not tell, from the clean rows of cups, which one he had used or which one had been stained with Marcia's lipstick or which one had held David's coffee which he had finished in the kitchenette—and finally, taking the tarnish-proof box down, he put the silverware away. First the forks all went together into the little grooves which held two forks each—

later, when the set was complete, each groove would hold four forks—and then the spoons, stacked up neatly one on top of another in their own grooves, and the knives in even order, all facing the same way, in the special tapes in the lid of the box. Butter knives and serving spoons and the pie knife all went into their own places, and then David put the lid down on the lovely shining set and put the box back on the shelf. After wringing out the dishcloth and hanging up the dish towel and taking off his apron he was through, and he went slowly into the living-room. Marcia and Mr. Harris were sitting close together on the studio couch, talking earnestly.

"My *father's* name was James," Marcia was saying as David came in, as though she were clinching an argument. She turned around when David came in and said, "Davie, you were so nice to do all those dishes yourself."

"That's all right," David said awkwardly. Mr. Harris was looking at him impatiently.

"I should have helped you," Marcia said. There was a silence, and then Marcia said, "Sit down, Davie, won't you?"

David recognized her tone; it was the one hostesses used when they didn't know what else to say to you, or when you had come too early or stayed too late. It was the tone he had expected to use on Mr. Harris.

"James and I were just talking about. . . ." Marcia began and then stopped and laughed. "What *were* we talking about?" she asked, turning to Mr. Harris.

"Nothing much," Mr. Harris said. He was still watching David.

"Well," Marcia said, letting her voice trail off. She turned to David and smiled brightly and then said, "Well," again.

Mr. Harris picked up the ashtray from the end table and

set it on the couch between himself and Marcia. He took a cigar out of his pocket and said to Marcia, "Do you mind cigars?" and when Marcia shook her head he unwrapped the cigar tenderly and bit off the end. "Cigar smoke's good for plants," he said thickly, around the cigar, as he lighted it, and Marcia laughed.

David stood up. For a minute he thought he was going to say something that might start, "Mr. Harris, I'll thank you to. . . ." but what he actually said, finally, with both Marcia and Mr. Harris looking at him, was, "Guess I better be getting along, Marcia."

Mr. Harris stood up and said heartily, "Certainly have enjoyed meeting you." He held out his hand and David shook hands limply.

"Guess I better be getting along," he said again to Marcia, and she stood up and said, "I'm sorry you have to leave so soon."

"Lots of work to do," David said, much more genially than he intended, and Marcia smiled at him again as though they were conspirators and went over to the desk and said, "Don't forget your key."

Surprised, David took the key of her apartment from her, said good night to Mr. Harris, and went to the outside door.

"Good night, Davie honey," Marcia called out, and David said "Thanks for a simply *wonderful* dinner, Marcia," and closed the door behind him.

He went down the hall and let himself into Marcia's apartment; the piano was still awry, the papers were still on the floor, the laundry scattered, the bed unmade. David sat down on the bed and looked around. It was cold, it was dirty, and as he thought miserably of his own warm home he heard faintly down the hall the sound of laughter and the scrape of a chair being moved. Then, still faintly, the sound of his radio. Wearily, David leaned over and picked up a paper from the floor, and then he began to gather them up one by one.

AMY TAN
BEST QUALITY

FIVE MONTHS AGO, after a crab dinner celebrating Chinese New Year, my mother gave me my "life's importance," a jade pendant on a gold chain. The pendant was not a piece of jewelry I would have chosen for myself. It was almost the size of my little finger, a mottled green and white color, intricately carved. To me, the whole effect looked wrong: too large, too green, too garishly ornate. I stuffed the necklace in my lacquer box and forgot about it.

But these days, I think about my life's importance. I wonder what it means, because my mother died three months ago, six days before my thirty-sixth birthday. And she's the only person I could have asked, to tell me about life's importance, to help me understand my grief.

I now wear that pendant every day. I think the carvings mean something, because shapes and details, which I never seem to notice until after they're pointed out to me, always mean something to Chinese people. I know I could ask Auntie Lindo, Auntie An-mei, or other Chinese friends, but I also know they would tell me a meaning that is different from what my mother intended. What if they tell me this curving line branching into three oval shapes is a pomegranate and that my mother was wishing me fertility and posterity? What if my mother really meant the carvings were a branch of pears to give me purity and honesty? Or ten-thousand-year droplets from the magic mountain, giving me my life's direction and a thousand years of fame and immortality?

And because I think about this all the time, I always notice other people wearing these same jade pendants—not the flat rectangular medallions or the round white ones with holes in the middle but ones like mine, a two-inch oblong of bright apple green. It's as though we were all sworn to the same secret covenant, so secret we don't even know what we belong to. Last weekend, for example, I saw a bartender wearing one. As I fingered mine, I asked him, "Where'd you get yours?"

"My mother gave it to me," he said.

I asked him why, which is a nosy question that only one Chinese person can ask another; in a crowd of Caucasians, two Chinese people are already like family.

"She gave it to me after I got divorced. I guess my mother's telling me I'm still worth something."

And I knew by the wonder in his voice that he had no idea what the pendant really meant.

At last year's Chinese New Year dinner, my mother had cooked eleven crabs, one crab for each person, plus an extra. She and I had bought them on Stockton Street in Chinatown. We had walked down the steep hill from my parents' flat, which was actually the first floor of a six-unit building they owned on Leavenworth near California. Their place was only six blocks from where I worked as a copywriter for a small ad agency, so two or three times a week I would drop by after work. My mother always had enough food to insist that I stay for dinner.

That year, Chinese New Year fell on a Thursday, so I got off work early to help my mother shop. My mother was seventy-one, but she still walked briskly along, her small body straight and purposeful, carrying a colorful flowery plastic bag. I dragged the metal shopping cart behind.

Every time I went with her to Chinatown, she pointed out other Chinese women her age. "Hong Kong ladies," she said, eyeing two finely dressed women in long, dark mink coats and perfect black hairdos. "Cantonese, village people," she whispered as we passed women in knitted caps, bent over in layers of padded tops and men's vests. And my mother—wearing light-blue polyester pants, a red sweater, and a child's green down jacket—she didn't look like anybody else. She had come here in 1949, at the end of a long journey that started in Kweilin in 1944; she had gone north to Chungking, where she met my father, and then they went southeast to Shanghai and fled farther south to Hong Kong, where the boat departed for San Francisco. My mother came from many different directions.

And now she was huffing complaints in rhythm to her walk downhill. "Even you don't want them, you stuck," she said. She was fuming again about the tenants who lived on the second floor. Two years ago, she had tried to evict them on the pretext that relatives from China were coming to live there. But the couple saw through her ruse to get around rent control. They said they wouldn't budge until she produced the relatives. And after that I had to listen to her recount every new injustice this couple inflicted on her.

My mother said the gray-haired man put too many bags in the garbage cans: "Cost me extra."

And the woman, a very elegant artist type with blond hair, had supposedly painted the apartment in terrible red and green colors. "Awful," moaned my mother. "And they take bath, two three times every day. Running the water, running, running, running, never stop!"

"Last week," she said, growing angrier at each step, "the *waigoren* accuse me." She referred to all Caucasians as *waigoren*, foreigners. "They say I put poison in a fish, kill that cat."

"What cat?" I asked, even though I knew exactly which one she was talking about. I had seen that cat many times. It was a big one-eared tom with gray stripes who had learned to jump on the outside sill of my mother's kitchen window. My mother would stand on her tiptoes and bang the kitchen window to scare the cat away. And the cat would stand his ground, hissing back in response to her shouts.

"That cat always raising his tail to put a stink on my door," complained my mother.

I once saw her chase him from her stairwell with a pot of boiling water. I was tempted to ask if she really had put poison in a fish, but I had learned never to take sides against my mother.

"So what happened to that cat?" I asked.

"That cat gone! Disappear!" She threw her hands in the air and smiled, looking pleased for a moment before the scowl came back. "And that man, he raise his hand like this, show me his ugly fist and call me worst Fukien landlady. I not from Fukien. Hunh! He know nothing!" she said, satisfied she had put him in his place.

On Stockton Street, we wandered from one fish store to another, looking for the liveliest crabs.

"Don't get a dead one," warned my mother in Chinese. "Even a beggar won't eat a dead one."

I poked the crabs with a pencil to see how feisty they were. If a crab grabbed on, I lifted it out and into a plastic sack. I lifted one crab this way, only to find one of its legs had been clamped onto by another crab. In the brief tug-of-war, my crab lost a limb.

"Put it back," whispered my mother. "A missing leg is a bad sign on a Chinese New Year."

But a man in a white smock came up to us. He started talking loudly to my mother in Cantonese, and my mother, who spoke Cantonese so poorly it sounded just like her Mandarin, was talking loudly back, pointing to the crab and its missing leg. And after more sharp words, that crab and its leg were put into our sack.

"Doesn't matter," said my mother. "This number eleven, extra one."

Back home, my mother unwrapped the crabs from their newspaper liners and then dumped them into a sinkful of cold water. She brought out her old wooden board and cleaver, then chopped the ginger and scallions, and poured soy sauce and sesame oil into a shallow dish. The kitchen smelled of wet newspapers and Chinese fragrances.

Then, one by one, she grabbed the crabs by their backs, hoisted them out of the sink and shook them dry and awake. The crabs flexed their legs in midair between sink and stove. She stacked the crabs in a multileveled steamer that sat over two burners on the stove, put a lid on top, and lit the burners. I couldn't bear to watch so I went into the dining room.

When I was eight, I had played with a crab my mother had brought home for my birthday dinner. I had poked it, and jumped back every time its claws reached out. And I determined that the crab and I had come to a great understanding when it finally heaved itself up and walked clear across the counter. But before I could even decide what to name my new pet, my mother had dropped it into a pot of cold water and placed it on the tall stove. I had watched with growing dread, as the water heated up and the pot began to clatter with this crab trying to tap his way out of his own hot soup. To this day, I remember that crab screaming as he thrust one bright red claw out over the side of the bubbling pot. It must have been my own voice, because now I know, of course, that crabs have no vocal cords. And I also try to convince myself that they don't have enough brains to know the difference between a hot bath and a slow death.

For our New Year celebration, my mother had invited her longtime friends Lindo and Tin Jong. Without even asking, my mother knew that meant including the Jongs' children: their son Vincent, who was thirty-eight years old and still living at home, and their daughter, Waverly, who was around my age. Vincent called to see if he could also bring his girlfriend, Lisa Lum. Waverly said she would bring her new fiancé, Rich Schields, who, like Waverly, was a tax attorney at Price Waterhouse. And she added that Shoshana, her four-year-old daughter from a previous marriage, wanted to know if my parents had a VCR so she could watch *Pinocchio*, just in case she got bored. My mother also reminded me to invite Mr. Chong, my old piano teacher, who still lived three blocks away at our old apartment.

Including my mother, father, and me, that made eleven people. But my mother had counted only ten, because to her way of thinking Shoshana was just a child and didn't count, at least not as far as crabs were concerned. She hadn't considered that Waverly might not think the same way.

When the platter of steaming crabs was passed around, Waverly was first and she picked the best crab, the brightest, the plumpest, and put it on her daughter's plate. And then she picked the next best for Rich and another good one for herself. And because she had learned this skill, of choosing the best, from her mother, it was only natural that her mother knew how to pick the next-best ones for her husband, her son, his girlfriend, and herself. And my mother, of course, considered the four remaining crabs and gave the one that looked the best to Old Chong, because he was nearly ninety and deserved that kind of respect, and then she picked another good one for my father. That left two on the platter: a large crab with a faded orange color, and number eleven, which had the torn-off leg.

My mother shook the platter in front of me. "Take it, already cold," said my mother.

I was not too fond of crab, ever since I saw my birthday crab boiled alive, but I knew I could not refuse. That's the way Chinese mothers show they love their children, not through hugs and kisses but with stern offerings of steamed dumplings, duck's gizzards, and crab.

I thought I was doing the right thing, taking the crab with the missing leg. But my mother cried, "No! No! Big one, you eat it. I cannot finish."

I remember the hungry sounds everybody else was making—cracking the shells, sucking the crab meat out, scraping out tidbits with the ends of chopsticks—and my mother's quiet plate. I was the only one who noticed her prying open the shell, sniffing the crab's body and then getting up to go to the kitchen, plate in hand. She returned, without the crab, but with more bowls of soy sauce, ginger, and scallions.

And then as stomachs filled, everybody started talking at once.

"Suyuan!" called Auntie Lindo to my mother. "Why you wear that color?" Auntie Lindo gestured with a crab leg to my mother's red sweater.

"How can you wear this color anymore? Too young!" she scolded.

My mother acted as though this were a compliment. "Emporium Capwell," she said. "Nineteen dollar. Cheaper than knit it myself."

Auntie Lindo nodded her head, as if the color were worth this price. And then she pointed her crab leg toward her future son-in-law, Rich, and said, "See how this one doesn't know how to eat Chinese food."

"Crab isn't Chinese," said Waverly in her complaining voice. It was amazing how Waverly still sounded the way she did twenty-five years ago, when we were ten and she had announced to me in that same voice, "You aren't a genius like me."

Auntie Lindo looked at her daughter with exasperation. "How do you know what is Chinese, what is not Chinese?" And then she turned to Rich and said with much authority, "Why you are not eating the best part?"

And I saw Rich smiling back, with amusement, and not humility, showing in his face. He had the same coloring as the crab on his plate: reddish hair, pale cream skin, and large dots of orange freckles. While he smirked, Auntie Lindo demonstrated the proper technique, poking her chopstick into the orange spongy part: "You have to dig in here, get this out. The brain is most tastiest, you try."

Waverly and Rich grimaced at each other, united in disgust. I heard Vincent and Lisa whisper to each other, "Gross," and then they snickered too.

Uncle Tin started laughing to himself, to let us know he also had a private joke. Judging by his preamble of snorts and leg slaps, I figured he must have practiced this joke many times: "I tell my daughter, Hey, why be poor? Marry rich!" He laughed loudly and then nudged Lisa, who was sitting next to him, "Hey, don't you get it? Look what happen. She gonna marry this guy here. Rich. 'Cause I tell her to, *marry Rich*."

"When *are* you guys getting married?" asked Vincent.

"I should ask you the same thing," said Waverly. Lisa looked embarrassed when Vincent ignored the question.

"Mom, I don't *like* crab!" whined Shoshana.

"Nice haircut," Waverly said to me from across the table.

"Thanks, David always does a great job."

"You mean you still go to that guy on Howard Street?" Waverly asked, arching one eyebrow. "Aren't you afraid?"

I could sense the danger, but I said it anyway: "What do you mean, afraid? He's always very good."

"I mean, he *is* gay," Waverly said. "He could have AIDS. And he is cutting your hair, which is like cutting a living tissue. Maybe I'm being paranoid, being a mother, but you just can't be too safe these days...."

And I sat there feeling as if my hair were coated with disease.

"You should go see my guy," said Waverly. "Mr. Rory. He does fabulous work, although he probably charges more than you're used to."

I felt like screaming. She could be so sneaky with her insults. Every time I asked her the simplest of tax questions, for example, she could turn the conversation around and make it seem as if I were too cheap to pay for her legal advice.

She'd say things like, "I really don't like to talk about important tax matters except in my office. I mean, what if you say something casual over lunch and I give you some casual advice. And then you follow it, and it's wrong because you didn't give me the full information. I'd feel terrible. And you would too, wouldn't you?"

At that crab dinner, I was so mad about what she said about my hair that I wanted to embarrass her, to reveal in front of everybody how petty she was. So I decided to confront her about the free-lance work I'd done for her firm, eight pages of brochure copy on its tax services. The firm was now more than thirty days late in paying my invoice.

"Maybe I could afford Mr. Rory's prices if someone's firm

paid me on time," I said with a teasing grin. And I was pleased to see Waverly's reaction. She was genuinely flustered, speechless.

I couldn't resist rubbing it in: "I think it's pretty ironic that a big accounting firm can't even pay its own bills on time. I mean, really, Waverly, what kind of place are you working for?"

Her face was dark and quiet.

"Hey, hey, you girls, no more fighting!" said my father, as if Waverly and I were still children arguing over tricycles and crayon colors.

"That's right, we don't want to talk about this now," said Waverly quietly.

"So how do you think the Giants are going to do?" said Vincent, trying to be funny. Nobody laughed.

I wasn't about to let her slip away this time. "Well, every time I call you on the phone, you can't talk about it then either," I said.

Waverly looked at Rich, who shrugged his shoulders. She turned back to me and sighed.

"Listen, June, I don't know how to tell you this. That stuff you wrote, well, the firm decided it was unacceptable."

"You're lying. You said it was great."

Waverly sighed again. "I know I did. I didn't want to hurt your feelings. I was trying to see if we could fix it somehow. But it won't work."

And just like that, I was starting to flail, tossed without warning into deep water, drowning and desperate. "Most copy needs fine-tuning," I said. "It's . . . normal not to be perfect the first time. I should have explained the process better."

"June, I really don't think. . . ."

"Rewrites are free. I'm just as concerned about making it perfect as you are."

Waverly acted as if she didn't even hear me. "I'm trying to convince them to at least pay you for some of your time. I know you put a lot of work into it. ... I owe you at least that for even suggesting you do it."

"Just tell me what they want changed. I'll call you next week so we can go over it, line by line."

"June—I can't," Waverly said with cool finality. "It's just not ... sophisticated. I'm sure what you write for your other clients is *wonderful*. But we're a big firm. We need somebody who understands that ... our style." She said this touching her hand to her chest, as if she were referring to *her* style.

Then she laughed in a lighthearted way. "I mean, really, June." And then she started speaking in a deep television-announcer voice: *"Three* benefits, *three* needs, *three* reasons to buy ... Satisfaction *guaranteed* ... for today's and tomorrow's tax needs ... "

She said this in such a funny way that everybody thought it was a good joke and laughed. And then, to make matters worse, I heard my mother saying to Waverly: "True, cannot teach style. June not sophisticate like you. Must be born this way."

I was surprised at myself, how humiliated I felt. I had been outsmarted by Waverly once again, and now betrayed by my own mother. I was smiling so hard my lower lip was twitching from the strain. I tried to find something else to concentrate on, and I remember picking up my plate, and then Mr. Chong's, as if I were clearing the table, and seeing so sharply through my tears the chips on the edges of these old plates, wondering why my mother didn't use the new set I had bought her five years ago.

The table was littered with crab carcasses. Waverly and Rich lit cigarettes and put a crab shell between them for an ashtray. Shoshana had wandered over to the piano and was banging notes out with a crab claw in each hand. Mr. Chong, who had grown totally deaf over the years, watched Shoshana and applauded: "Bravo! Bravo!" And except for his strange shouts, nobody said a word. My mother went to the kitchen and returned with a plate of oranges sliced into wedges. My father poked at the remnants of his crab. Vincent cleared his throat, twice, and then patted Lisa's hand.

It was Auntie Lindo who finally spoke: "Waverly, you let her try again. You make her do too fast first time. Of course she cannot get it right."

I could hear my mother eating an orange slice. She was the only person I knew who crunched oranges, making it sound as if she were eating crisp apples instead. The sound of it was worse than gnashing teeth.

"Good one take time," continued Auntie Lindo, nodding her head in agreement with herself.

"Put in lotta action," advised Uncle Tin. "Lotta action, boy, that's what I like. Hey, that's all you need, make it right."

"Probably not," I said, and smiled before carrying the plates to the sink.

That was the night, in the kitchen, that I realized I was no better than who I was. I was a copywriter. I worked for a small ad agency. I promised every new client, "We can provide the sizzle for the meat." The sizzle always boiled down to "Three Benefits, Three Needs, Three Reasons to Buy." The meat was always coaxial cable, T-1 multiplexers, protocol converters, and the like. I was very good at what I did, succeeding at something small like that.

I turned on the water to wash the dishes. And I no longer felt angry at Waverly. I felt tired and foolish, as if I had been running to escape someone chasing me, only to look behind and discover there was no one there.

I picked up my mother's plate, the one she had carried into the kitchen at the start of the dinner. The crab was untouched. I lifted the shell and smelled the crab. Maybe it was because I didn't like crab in the first place. I couldn't tell what was wrong with it.

After everybody left, my mother joined me in the kitchen. I was putting dishes away. She put water on for more tea and sat down at the small kitchen table. I waited for her to chastise me.

"Good dinner, Ma," I said politely.

"Not so good," she said, jabbing at her mouth with a toothpick.

"What happened to your crab? Why'd you throw it away?"

"Not so good," she said again. "That crab die. Even a beggar don't want it."

"How could you tell? I didn't smell anything wrong."

"Can tell even before cook!" She was standing now, looking out the kitchen window into the night. "I shake that crab before cook. His legs—droopy. His mouth—wide open, already like a dead person."

"Why'd you cook it if you knew it was already dead?"

"I thought . . . maybe only just die. Maybe taste not too bad. But I can smell, dead taste, not firm."

"What if someone else had picked that crab?"

My mother looked at me and smiled. "Only *you* pick that crab. Nobody else take it. I already know this. Everybody else want best quality. You thinking different."

She said it in a way as if this were proof—proof of something good. She always said things that didn't make any sense, that sounded both good and bad at the same time.

I was putting away the last of the chipped plates and then I remembered something else. "Ma, why don't you ever use those new dishes I bought you? If you didn't like them, you should have told me. I could have changed the pattern."

"Of course, I like," she said, irritated. "Sometimes I think something is so good, I want to save it. Then I forget I save it."

And then, as if she had just now remembered, she unhooked the clasp of her gold necklace and took it off, wadding the chain and the jade pendant in her palm. She grabbed my hand and put the necklace in my palm, then shut my fingers around it.

"No, Ma," I protested. "I can't take this."

"*Nala, nala*"—Take it, take it—she said, as if she were scolding me. And then she continued in Chinese. "For a long time, I wanted to give you this necklace. See, I wore this on my skin, so when you put it on your skin, then you know my meaning. This is your life's importance."

I looked at the necklace, the pendant with the light green jade. I wanted to give it back. I didn't want to accept it. And yet I also felt as if I had already swallowed it.

"You're giving this to me only because of what happened tonight," I finally said.

"What happen?"

"What Waverly said. What everybody said."

"Tss! Why you listen to her? Why you want to follow behind her, chasing her words? She is like this crab." My mother poked a shell in the garbage can. "Always walking sideways, moving crooked. You can make your legs go the other way."

I put the necklace on. It felt cool.

"Not so good, this jade," she said matter-of-factly, touching the pendant, and then she added in Chinese: "This is young jade. It is a very light color now, but if you wear it every day it will become more green."

* * *

My father hasn't eaten well since my mother died. So I am here, in the kitchen, to cook him dinner. I'm slicing tofu. I've decided to make him a spicy bean-curd dish. My mother used to tell me how hot things restore the spirit and health. But I'm making this mostly because I know my father loves this dish and I know how to cook it. I like the smell of it: ginger, scallions, and a red chili sauce that tickles my nose the minute I open the jar.

Above me, I hear the old pipes shake into action with a *thunk!* and then the water running in my sink dwindles to a trickle. One of the tenants upstairs must be taking a shower. I remember my mother complaining: "Even you don't want them, you stuck." And now I know what she meant.

As I rinse the tofu in the sink, I am startled by a dark mass that appears suddenly at the window. It's the one-eared tomcat from upstairs. He's balancing on the sill, rubbing his flank against the window.

My mother didn't kill that damn cat after all, and I'm relieved. And then I see this cat rubbing more vigorously on the window and he starts to raise his tail.

"Get away from there!" I shout, and slap my hand on the window three times. But the cat just narrows his eyes, flattens his one ear, and hisses back at me.

CULINARY ALCHEMY

"Taste as Nature has endowed us with it is still that one of our senses which gives us the greatest joy ... because it can mingle with all the other pleasures, and even console us for their absence."
   —Jean Anthelme Brillat-Savarin, *The Physiology of Taste*

EMILE ZOLA

THE CHEESE SYMPHONY

From *The Belly of Paris*

Translated by Ernest Alfred Vizetelly

MADEMOISELLE SAGET NOW hurriedly made her way across the Rue Rambuteau. Her little feet scarcely touched the ground; her joy seemed to carry her along like a breeze which fanned her with a caressing touch. She had at last found out what she had so much wanted to know! For nearly a year she had been consumed by curiosity, and now at a single stroke she had gained complete power over Florent! This was unhoped-for contentment, positive salvation, for she felt that Florent would have brought her to the tomb had she failed much longer in satisfying her curiosity about him. At present she was complete mistress of the whole neighbourhood of the markets. There was no longer any gap in her information. She could have narrated the secret history of every street, shop by shop. And thus, as she entered the fruit market, she fairly gasped with delight, in a perfect transport of pleasure.

"Hallo, Mademoiselle Saget," cried La Sarriette from her stall, "what are you smiling to yourself like that about? Have you won the grand prize in the lottery?"

"No, no. Ah, my dear, if you only knew!"

Standing there amidst her fruit, La Sarriette, in her picturesque disarray, looked charming. Frizzy hair fell over her brow like vine branches. Her bare arms and neck, indeed all the rosy flesh she showed, bloomed with the freshness of peach and cherry. She had playfully hung some cherries on her ears, black cherries which dangled against her cheeks when she stooped, shaking with merry laughter. She was eating currants, and her merriment arose from the way in which she was smearing her face with them. Her lips were bright red, glistening with the juice of the fruit, as though they had been painted and perfumed with some seraglio face-paint. A perfume of plum exhaled from her gown, while from the kerchief carelessly fastened across her breast came an odour of strawberries.

Fruits of all kinds were piled around her in her narrow stall. On the shelves at the back were rows of melons, so-called "cantaloups" swarming with wart-like knots, "maraîchers" whose skin was covered with grey lace-like netting, and "culs-de-singe" displaying smooth bare bumps. In front was an array of choice fruits, carefully arranged in baskets, and showing like smooth round cheeks seeking to hide themselves, or glimpses of sweet childish faces, half veiled by leaves. Especially was this the case with the peaches, the blushing peaches of Montreuil, with skin as delicate and clear as that of northern maidens, and the yellow, sun-burnt peaches from the south, brown like the damsels of Provence. The apricots, on their beds of moss, gleamed with the hue of amber or with that sunset glow which so warmly colours the necks of brunettes at the nape, just under the little wavy curls which fall below the chignon. The cherries, ranged one by one, resembled the short lips of smiling Chinese girls; the Montmorencies suggested the plump mouths of buxom women; the English ones were longer and graver-looking; the common black ones seemed as though they had been bruised and crushed by kisses; while the white-hearts, with their patches of rose and white, appeared to smile with mingled merriment and vexation. Then piles of apples and pears, built up with architectural symmetry, often in pyramids, displayed the ruddy glow of budding breasts and the gleaming sheen of shoulders, quite a show of nudity, lurking modestly behind a screen of fern-leaves. There were all sorts of varieties—little red ones so tiny that they seemed to be yet in the cradle, shapeless rambours for baking, calvilles in light yellow gowns, sanguineous-looking Canadas, blotched châtaignier apples, fair freckled rennets and dusky russets. Then came the pears—the blanquettes, the British queens, the Beurrés, the messirejeans, and the duchesses—some dumpy, some long and tapering, some with slender necks, and others with thick-set shoulders, their green and yellow bellies picked out at times with a splotch of carmine. By the side of these the transparent plums resembled tender, chlorotic virgins; the greengages and the Orleans plums paled as with modest innocence, while the mirabelles lay like golden beads of a rosary forgotten in a box amongst sticks of vanilla. And the strawberries exhaled a sweet perfume—a perfume of youth—especially those little ones which are gathered in the woods, and which are far more aromatic than the large ones grown in gardens, for these breathe an insipid odour suggestive of the watering-pot. Raspberries added their fragrance to the pure scent. The currants—red, white, and black—smiled with a knowing air; whilst the heavy clusters of grapes, laden with intoxication, lay languorously at the edges of their wicker baskets, over the sides of which dangled some of the berries, scorched by the hot caresses of the voluptuous sun.

It was there that La Sarriette lived in an orchard, as it were, in an atmosphere of sweet, intoxicating scents. The cheaper fruits—the cherries, plums, and strawberries—were piled up in front of her in paper-lined baskets, and the juice coming from their bruised ripeness stained the stall-front, and steamed, with a strong perfume, in the heat. She would feel quite giddy on those blazing July afternoons when the melons enveloped her with a powerful, vaporous odour of musk; and then with her loosened kerchief, fresh as she was with the springtide of life, she brought sudden temptation to all who saw her. It was she—it was her arms and neck which gave that semblance of amorous vitality to her fruit. On the stall next to her an old woman, a hideous old drunkard, displayed nothing but wrinkled apples, pears as flabby as herself, and cadaverous apricots of a witch-like sallowness. La Sarriette's stall, however, spoke of love and passion. The cherries looked like the red kisses of her bright lips; the silky peaches were not more delicate than her neck; to the plums she seemed to have lent the skin from her brow and chin; while some of her own crimson blood coursed through the veins of the currants. All the scents of the avenue of flowers behind her stall were but insipid beside the aroma of vitality which exhaled from her open baskets and falling kerchief.

That day she was quite intoxicated by the scent of a large arrival of mirabelle plums, which filled the market. She could plainly see that Mademoiselle Saget had learnt some great piece of news, and she wished to make her talk. But the old maid stamped impatiently whilst she repeated: "No, no; I've no time. I'm in a great hurry to see Madame Lecœur. I've just learnt something and no mistake. You can come with me, if you like."

As a matter of fact, she had simply gone through the fruit market for the purpose of enticing La Sarriette to go with her. The girl could not refuse temptation. Monsieur Jules, clean-shaven and as fresh as a cherub, was seated there, swaying to and fro on his chair.

"Just look after the stall for a minute, will you?" La Sarriette said to him. "I'll be back directly."

Jules, however, got up and called after her, in a thick voice:

"Not I; no fear! I'm off! I'm not going to wait an hour for you, as I did the other day. And, besides, those cursed plums of yours quite make my head ache."

Then he calmly strolled off, with his hands in his pockets, and the stall was left to look after itself. Mademoiselle Saget went so fast that La Sarriette had to run. In the butter pavilion a neighbour of Madame Lecœur's told them that she was below in the cellar; and so, whilst La Sarriette went down to find her, the old maid installed herself amidst the cheeses.

The cellar under the butter market is a very gloomy spot. The rows of storerooms are protected by a very fine wire meshing, as a safeguard against fire; and the gas jets, which are very few and far between, glimmer like yellow splotches destitute of radiance in the heavy, malodorous atmosphere beneath the low vault. Madame Lecœur, however, was at work on her butter at one of the tables placed parallel with the Rue Berger, and here a pale light filtered through the vent-holes. The tables, which are continually sluiced with a flood of water from the taps, are as white as though they were quite new. With her back turned to the pump in the rear, Madame Lecœur was kneading her butter in a kind of oak box. She took some of different sorts which lay beside her, and mixed the varieties together, correcting one by another, just as is done in the blending of wines. Bent almost double, and showing sharp, bony shoulders, and arms bared to the elbows, as scraggy and knotted as pea-rods, she dug her fists into the greasy paste in front of her, which was assuming a whitish and chalky appearance. It was trying work, and she heaved a sigh at each fresh effort.

"Mademoiselle Saget wants to speak to you, aunt," said La Sarriette.

Madame Lecœur stopped her work, and pulled her cap over her hair with her greasy fingers, seemingly quite careless of staining it. "I've nearly finished. Ask her to wait a moment," she said.

"She's got something very particular to tell you," continued La Sarriette.

"I won't be more than a minute, my dear."

Then she again plunged her arms into the butter, which buried them up to the elbows. Previously softened in warm water, it covered Madame Lecœur's parchment-like skin as with an oily film, and threw the big purple veins that streaked her flesh into strong relief. La Sarriette was quite disgusted by the sight of those hideous arms working so frantically amidst the melting mass. However, she could recall the time when her own pretty little hands had manipulated the butter for whole afternoons at a time. It had even been a sort of almond-paste to her, a cosmetic which had kept her skin white and her nails delicately pink; and even now her slender fingers retained the suppleness it had endowed them with.

"I don't think that butter of yours will be very good, aunt," she continued, after a pause. "Some of the sorts seem much too strong."

"I'm quite aware of that," replied Madame Lecœur, between a couple of groans. "But what can I do? I must use everything up. There are some folks who insist upon having butter cheap, and so cheap butter must be made for them. Oh! it's always quite good enough for those who buy it."

La Sarriette reflected that she would hardly care to eat butter which had been worked by her aunt's arms. Then she glanced at a little jar full of a sort of reddish dye. "Your colouring is too pale," she said.

This colouring-matter—raucourt, as the Parisians call it, is used to give the butter a fine yellow tint. The butter women imagine that its composition is known only to themselves, and keep it very secret. However, it is merely made from anotta; though a composition of carrots and marigold is at times substituted for it.

"Come, do be quick!" La Sarriette now exclaimed, for she was getting impatient, and was, moreover, no longer accustomed to the malodorous atmosphere of the cellar. "Mademoiselle Saget will be going. I fancy she's got something very important to tell you abut my uncle Gavard."

On hearing this, Madame Lecœur abruptly ceased working. She at once abandoned both butter and dye, and did not even wait to wipe her arms. With a slight tap of her hand she settled her cap on her head again, and made her way up the steps, at her niece's heels, anxiously repeating: "Do you really think that she'll have gone away?"

She was reassured, however, on catching sight of Mademoiselle Saget amidst the cheeses. The old maid had taken good care not to go away before Madame Lecœur's arrival. The three women seated themselves at the far end of the stall, crowding closely together, and their faces almost touching one another. Mademoiselle Saget remained silent for two long minutes, and then, seeing that the others were burning with curiosity, she began, in her shrill voice: "You know that Florent! Well, I can tell you now where he comes from."

For another moment she kept them in suspense; and then, in a deep, melodramatic voice, she said: "He comes from the galleys!"

The cheeses were reeking around the three women. On the two shelves at the far end of the stall were huge masses of butter: Brittany butters overflowing from baskets; Normandy butters, wrapped in canvas, and resembling models of stomachs over which some sculptor had thrown damp cloths to keep them from drying; while other great blocks had been cut into, fashioned into perpendicular rocky masses full of crevasses and valleys, and resembling fallen mountain crests gilded by the pale sun of an autumn evening.

Beneath the stall show-table, formed of a slab of red marble veined with grey, baskets of eggs gleamed with a chalky whiteness; while on layers of straw in boxes were Bondons, placed end to end, and Gournays, arranged like medals, forming darker patches tinted with green. But it was upon the table that the cheeses appeared in greatest profusion. Here, by the side of the pound-rolls of butter lying on white-beet leaves, spread a gigantic Cantal cheese, cloven here and there as by an axe; then came a golden-hued Cheshire, and next a Gruyère, resembling a wheel fallen from some barbarian chariot; whilst farther on were some Dutch cheeses, suggesting decapitated heads suffused with dry blood, and having all that hardness of skulls which in France has gained them the name of "death's heads." Amidst the heavy exhalations of these, a Parmesan set a spicy aroma. Then there came three Brie cheeses displayed on round platters, and looking like melancholy extinct moons. Two of them, very dry, were at the full; the third, in its second quarter, was melting away in a white cream, which had spread into a pool and flowed over the little wooden barriers with which an attempt had been made to arrest its course. Next came some Port Saluts, similar to antique discs, with exergues bearing their makers' names in print. A Romantour, in its tin-foil wrapper, suggested a bar of nougat or some sweet cheese astray amidst all these pungent, fermenting curds. The Roqueforts under their glass covers also had a princely air, their fat faces marbled with blue and yellow, as though they were suffering from some unpleasant malady such as attacks the wealthy gluttons who eat too many truffles. And on a dish by the side of these, the hard grey goats' milk cheeses, about the size of a child's fist, resembled the pebbles which the billy-goats send rolling down the stony paths as they clamber along ahead of their flocks. Next came the strong smelling cheeses: the Mont d'Ors, of a bright yellow hue, and exhaling a comparatively mild odour; the Troyes, very thick, and bruised at the edges, and of a far more pungent smell, recalling the dampness of a cellar; the Camemberts, suggestive of high game; the square Neufchâtels, Limbourgs, Marolles, and Pont l'Evêques, each adding its own particular sharp scent to the malodorous bouquet, till it became perfectly pestilential; the Livarots, ruddy in hue, and as irritating to the throat as sulphur fumes; and, lastly, stronger than all the others, the Olivets, wrapped in walnut leaves, like the carrion which peasants cover with branches as it lies rotting in the hedgerow under the blazing sun.

The heat of the afternoon had softened the cheeses; the patches of mould on their crusts were melting, and glistening with tints of ruddy bronze and verdigris. Beneath their cover of leaves, the skins of the Olivets seemed to be heaving as with the slow, deep respiration of a sleeping man. A Livarot was swarming with life; and in a fragile box behind the scales a Géromé flavoured with aniseed diffused such a pestilential smell that all around it the very flies had fallen lifeless on the grey-veined slab of ruddy marble.

This Géromé was almost immediately under Mademoiselle Saget's nose; so she drew back, and leaned her head against the big sheets of white and yellow paper which were hanging in a corner.

"Yes," she repeated, with an expression of disgust, "he comes from the galleys! Ah, those Quenu-Gradelles have no reason to put on so many airs!"

Madame Lecœur and La Sarriette, however, had burst into exclamations of astonishment: "It wasn't possible, surely!

What had he done to be sent to the galleys? Could anyone, now, have ever suspected that Madame Quenu, whose virtue was the pride of the whole neighbourhood, would choose a convict for a lover?"

"Ah, but you don't understand at all!" cried the old maid impatiently. "Just listen, now, while I explain things. I was quite certain that I had seen that great lanky fellow somewhere before."

Then she proceeded to tell them Florent's story. She had recalled to mind a vague report which had circulated of a nephew of old Gradelle being transported to Cayenne for murdering six gendarmes at a barricade. She had even seen this nephew on one occasion in the Rue Pirouette. The pretended cousin was undoubtedly the same man. Then she began to bemoan her waning powers. Her memory was quite going, she said; she would soon be unable to remember anything. And she bewailed her perishing memory as bitterly as any learned man might bewail the loss of his notes representing the work of a life-time, on seeing them swept away by a gust of wind.

"Six gendarmes!" murmured La Sarriette, admiringly; "he must have a very heavy fist!"

"And he's made away with plenty of others, as well," added Mademoiselle Saget. "I shouldn't advise you to meet him at night!"

"What a villain!" stammered out Madame Lecœur, quite terrified.

The slanting beams of the sinking sun were now enfilading the pavilion, and the odour of the cheeses became stronger than ever. That of the Marolles seemed to predominate, borne hither and thither in powerful whiffs. Then, however, the wind appeared to change, and suddenly the emanations of the Limbourgs were wafted towards the three women, pungent and bitter, like the last gasps of a dying man.

"But in that case," resumed Madame Lecœur, "he must be fat Lisa's brother-in-law. And we thought that he was her lover!"

The women exchanged glances. This aspect of the case took them by surprise. They were loth to give up their first theory. However, La Sarriette, turning to Mademoiselle Saget, remarked: "That must have been all wrong. Besides, you yourself say that he's always running after the two Méhudin girls."

"Certainly he is," exclaimed Mademoiselle Saget sharply, fancying that her word was doubted. "He dangles about them every evening. But, after all, it's no concern of ours, is it? We are virtuous women, and what he does makes no difference to us, the horrid scoundrel!"

"No, certainly not," agreed the other two. "He's a consummate villain."

The affair was becoming tragical. Of course beautiful Lisa was now out of the question, but for this they found ample consolation in prophesying that Florent would bring about some frightful catastrophe. It was quite clear, they said, that he had got some base design in his head. When people like him escaped from gaol it was only to burn everything down; and if he had come to the markets it must assuredly be for some abominable purpose. Then they began to indulge in the wildest suppositions. The two dealers declared that they would put additional padlocks to the doors of their storerooms; and La Sarriette called to mind that a basket of peaches had been stolen from her during the previous week. Mademoiselle Saget, however, quite frightened the two others by informing them that that was not the way in which the Reds behaved; they despised such trifles as baskets of peaches; their plan was to band themselves together in companies of two or three hundred, kill everybody they came across, and then plunder and pillage at their ease. That was "politics," she said, with the superior air of one who knew what she was talking about. Madame Lecœur felt quite ill. She already saw Florent and his accomplices hiding in the cellars, and rushing out during the night to set the markets in flames and sack Paris.

"Ah! by the way," suddenly exclaimed the old maid, "now I think of it, there's all that money of old Gradelle's! Dear me, dear me, those Quenus can't be at all at their ease!"

She now looked quite gay again. The conversation took a fresh turn, and the others fell foul of the Quenus when Mademoiselle Saget had told them the history of the treasure discovered in the salting-tub, with every particular of which she was acquainted. She was even able to inform them of the exact amount of the money found—eighty-five thousand francs—though neither Lisa nor Quenu was aware of having revealed this to a living soul. However, it was clear that the Quenus had not given the great lanky fellow his share. He was too shabbily dressed for that. Perhaps he had never even heard of the discovery of the treasure. Plainly enough, they were all thieves in his family. Then the three women bent their heads together and spoke in lower tones. They were unanimously of opinion that it might perhaps be dangerous to attack the beautiful Lisa, but it was decidedly necessary that they should settle the Red Republican's hash, so that he might no longer prey upon the purse of poor Monsieur Gavard.

At the mention of Gavard there came a pause. The gossips looked at each other with a circumspect air. And then, as they drew breath, they inhaled the odour of the Camemberts, whose gamy scent had overpowered the less penetrating emanations of the Marolles and the Limbourgs, and spread around with remarkable power. Every now and then, however, a slight whiff, a flutelike note, came from the Parmesan, while the Bries contributed a soft, musty scent, the gentle, insipid sound, as it were, of damp tambourines. Next followed an overpowering refrain from the Livarots, and afterwards the Géromé, flavoured with aniseed, kept up the symphony with a high prolonged note, like that of a vocalist during a pause in the accompaniment.

"I have seen Madame Léonce," Mademoiselle Saget at last continued, with a significant expression.

At this the two others became extremely attentive. Madame Léonce was the doorkeeper of the house where Gavard lived in the Rue de la Cossonnerie. It was an old house standing back, with its ground floor occupied by an importer of oranges and lemons, who had had the frontage coloured blue as high as the first floor. Madame Léonce acted as Gavard's housekeeper, kept the keys of his cupboards and closets, and brought him up tisane when he happened to catch cold. She was a severe-looking woman, between fifty and sixty years of age, and spoke slowly, but at endless length. Mademoiselle Saget, who went to drink coffee with her every Wednesday evening, had cultivated her friendship more closely than ever since the poultry dealer had gone to lodge in the house. They would talk about the worthy man for hours at a time. They both professed the greatest affection for him, and a keen desire to ensure his comfort and happiness.

"Yes, I have seen Madame Léonce," repeated the old maid. "We had a cup of coffee together last night. She was greatly worried. It seems that Monsieur Gavard never comes home now before one o'clock in the morning. Last Sunday she took him up some broth, as she thought he looked quite ill."

"Oh, she knows very well what she's about," exclaimed

Madame Lecœur, whom these attentions to Gavard somewhat alarmed.

Mademoiselle Saget felt bound to defend her friend. "Oh, really, you are quite mistaken," said she. "Madame Léonce is much above her position; she is quite a lady. If she wanted to enrich herself at Monsieur Gavard's expense, she might easily have done so long ago. It seems that he leaves everything lying about in the most careless fashion. It's about that, indeed, that I want to speak to you. But you'll not repeat anything I say, will you? I am telling it you in strict confidence."

Both the others swore that they would never breathe a word of what they might hear; and they craned out their necks with eager curiosity, whilst the old maid solemnly resumed: "Well, then, Monsieur Gavard has been behaving very strangely of late. He has been buying firearms—a great big pistol—one of those which revolve, you know. Madame Léonce says that things are awful, for this pistol is always lying about on the table or the mantelpiece; and she daren't dust anywhere near it. But that isn't all. His money—"

"His money!" echoed Madame Lecœur, with blazing cheeks.

"Well, he's disposed of all his stocks and shares. He's sold everything, and keeps a great heap of gold in a cupboard."

"A heap of gold!" exclaimed La Sarriette in ecstasy.

"Yes, a great heap of gold. It covers a whole shelf, and is quite dazzling. Madame Léonce told me that one morning Gavard opened the cupboard in her presence, and that the money quite blinded her, it shone so."

There was another pause. The eyes of the three women were blinking as though the dazzling pile of gold was before them. Presently La Sarriette began to laugh.

"What a jolly time I would have with Jules if my uncle would give that money to me!" said she.

Madame Lecœur, however, seemed quite overwhelmed by this revelation, crushed beneath the weight of the gold which she could not banish from her sight. Covetous envy thrilled her. But at last, raising her skinny arms and shrivelled hands, her finger-nails still stuffed with butter, she stammered in a voice full of bitter distress: "Oh, I mustn't think of it! It's too dreadful!"

"Well, it would all be yours, you know, if anything were to happen to Monsieur Gavard," retorted Mademoiselle Saget. "If I were in your place, I would look after my interests. That revolver means nothing good, you may depend upon it. Monsieur Gavard has got into the hands of evil counsellors; and I'm afraid it will all end badly."

Then the conversation again turned upon Florent. The three women assailed him more violently than ever. And afterwards, with perfect composure, they began to discuss what would be the result of all these dark goings-on so far as he and Gavard were concerned; certainly it would be no pleasant one if there was any gossiping. And thereupon they swore that they themselves would never repeat a word of what they knew; not, however, because that scoundrel Florent merited any consideration, but because it was necessary, at all costs, to save that worthy Monsieur Gavard from being compromised. Then they rose from their seats, and Mademoiselle Saget was burning as if to go away when the butter dealer asked her: "All the same, in case of accident, do you think that Madame Léonce can be trusted? I dare say she has the key of the cupboard."

"Well, that's more than I can tell you," replied the old maid. "I believe she's a very honest woman; but, after all, there's no telling. There are circumstances, you know, which tempt the best of people. Anyhow, I've warned you both; and you must do what you think proper."

As the three women stood there, taking leave of each other, the odour of the cheeses seemed to become more pestilential than ever. It was a cacophony of smells, ranging from the heavily oppressive odour of the Dutch cheeses and the Gruyères to the alkaline pungency of the Olivets. From the Cantal, the Cheshire, and the goats' milk cheeses there seemed to come a deep breath like the sound of a bassoon, amidst which the sharp, sudden whiffs of the Neufchâtels, the Troyes, and the Mont d'Ors contributed short, detached notes. And then the different odours appeared to mingle one with another, the reek of the Limbourgs, the Port Saluts, the Géromés, the Marolles, the Livarots, and the Pont l'Eveques uniting in one general, overpowering stench sufficient to provoke asphyxia. And yet it almost seemed as though it were not the cheeses but the vile words of Madame Lecœur and Mademoiselle Saget that diffused this awful odour.

"I'm very much obliged to you, indeed I am," said the butter dealer. "If ever I get rich, you shall not find yourself forgotten."

The old maid still lingered in the stall. Taking up a Bondon, she turned it round, and put it down on the slab again. Then she asked its price.

"To me!" she added, with a smile.

"Oh, nothing to you," replied Madame Lecœur. "I'll make you a present of it." And again she exclaimed: "Ah, if I were only rich!"

Mademoiselle Saget thereupon told her that some day or other she would be rich. The Bondon had already disappeared within the old maid's bag. And now the butter dealer returned to the cellar, while Mademoiselle Saget escorted La Sarriette back to her stall. On reaching it they talked for a moment or two about Monsieur Jules. The fruits around them diffused a fresh scent of summer.

"It smells much nicer here than at your aunt's," said the old maid. "I felt quite ill a little time ago. I can't think how she manages to exist there. But here it's very sweet and pleasant. It makes you look quite rosy, my dear."

La Sarriette began to laugh, for she was fond of compliments. Then she served a lady with a pound of mirabelle plums, telling her that they were as sweet as sugar.

MARCEL PROUST

FROM *SWANN'S WAY*

Translated by C. K. Scott Moncrieff

AT THE HOUR when I usually went downstairs to find out what there was for dinner, its preparation would already have begun, and Françoise, a colonel with all the forces of nature for her subalterns, as in the fairy-tales where giants hire themselves out as scullions, would be stirring the coals, putting the potatoes to steam, and, at the right moment, finishing over the fire those culinary masterpieces which had been first got ready in some of the great array of vessels, triumphs of the potter's craft, which ranged from tubs and boilers and cauldrons and fish kettles down to jars for game, moulds for pastry, and tiny pannikins for cream, and included an entire collection of pots and pans of every shape and size. I would stop by the table, where the kitchen-maid had shelled them, to inspect the platoons of peas, drawn up in ranks and numbered, like little green marbles, ready for a game; but what fascinated me would be the asparagus, tinged with ultramarine and rosy pink which ran from their heads, finely stippled in mauve and azure, through a series of imperceptible changes to their white feet, still stained a little by the soil of their garden-bed: a rainbow-loveliness that was not of this world. I felt that these celestial hues indicated the presence of exquisite creatures who had been pleased to assume vegetable form, who, through the disguise which covered their firm and edible flesh, allowed me to discern in this radiance of earliest dawn, these hinted rainbows, these blue evening shades, that precious quality which I should recognize again when, all night long after a dinner at which I had partaken of them, they played (lyrical and coarse in their jesting as the fairies in Shakespeare's *Dream*) at transforming my humble chamber pot into a vase of aromatic perfume.

Poor Giotto's Charity, as Swann had named her, charged by Françoise with the task of preparing them for the table, would have them lying beside her in a basket; sitting with a mournful air, as though all the sorrows of the world were heaped upon her; and the light crowns of azure which capped the asparagus shoots above their pink jackets would be finely and separately outlined, star by star, as in Giotto's fresco are the flowers banded about the brows, or patterning the basket of his Virtue at Padua. And, meanwhile, Françoise would be turning on the spit one of those chickens, such as she alone knew how to roast, chickens which had wafted far abroad from Combray the sweet savour of her merits, and which, while she was serving them to us at table, would make the quality of kindness predominate for the moment in my private conception of her character; the aroma of that cooked flesh, which she knew how to make so unctuous and so tender, seeming to me no more than the proper perfume of one of her many virtues.

But the day on which, while my father took counsel with his family upon our strange meeting with Legrandin, I went down to the kitchen, was one of those days when Giotto's Charity, still very weak and ill after her recent confinement, had been unable to rise from her bed; Françoise, being without assistance, had fallen into arrears. When I went in, I saw her in the back-kitchen which opened on to the courtyard, in process of killing a chicken; by its desperate and quite natural resistance, which Françoise, beside herself with rage as she attempted to slit its throat beneath the ear, accompanied with shrill cries of "Filthy creature! Filthy creature!" it made the saintly kindness and unction of our servant rather less prominent than it would do, next day at dinner, when it made its appearance in a skin gold-embroidered like a chasuble, and its precious juice was poured out drop by drop as from a pyx. When it was dead Françoise mopped up its streaming blood, in which, however, she did not let her rancour drown, for she gave vent to another burst of rage, and, gazing down at the carcass of her enemy, uttered a final "Filthy creature!"

I crept out of the kitchen and upstairs, trembling all over; I could have prayed, then, for the instant dismissal of Françoise. But who would have baked me such hot rolls, boiled me such fragrant coffee, and even—roasted me such chickens? And, as it happened, everyone else had already had to make the same cowardly reckoning. For my aunt Léonie knew (though I was still in ignorance of this) that Françoise, who, for her own daughter or for her nephews, would have given her life without a murmur, showed a singular implacability in her dealings with the rest of the world. In spite of which my aunt still retained her, for, while conscious of her cruelty, she could appreciate her services. I began gradually to realize that Françoise's kindness, her compunction, the sum total of her virtues concealed many of these back-kitchen tragedies, just as history reveals to us that the reigns of the kings and queens who are portrayed as kneeling with clasped hands in the windows of churches, were stained by oppression and bloodshed.

ALICE B. TOKLAS

MURDER IN THE KITCHEN

COOK BOOKS HAVE always intrigued and seduced me. When I was still a dilettante in the kitchen they held my attention, even the dull ones, from cover to cover, the way crime and murder stories did Gertrude Stein.

When we first began reading Dashiell Hammett, Gertrude Stein remarked that it was his modern note to have disposed of his victims before the story commenced. Goodness knows how many were required to follow as the result of the first crime. And so it is in the kitchen. Murder and sudden death seem as unnatural there as they should be anywhere else. They can't, they can never become acceptable facts. Food is far too pleasant to combine with horror. All the same, facts, even distasteful facts, must be accepted and we shall see how, before any story of cooking begins, crime is inevitable. That is why cooking is not an entirely agreeable pastime. There is too much that must happen in advance of the actual cooking. This doesn't of course apply to food that emerges stainless from deep freeze. But the marketing and cooking I know are French and it was in France, where freezing units are unknown, that in due course I graduated at the stove.

In earlier days, memories of which are scattered among my chapters, if indulgent friends on this or that Sunday evening or party occasion said that the cooking I produced wasn't bad, it neither beguiled nor flattered me into liking or wanting to do it. The only way to learn to cook is to cook, and for me, as for so many others, it suddenly and unexpectedly became a disagreeable necessity to have to do it when war came and Occupation followed. It was in those conditions of rationing and shortage that I learned not only to cook seriously but to buy food in a restricted market and not to take too much time in doing it, since there were so many more important and more amusing things to do. It was at this time, then, that murder in the kitchen began.

The first victim was a lively carp brought to the kitchen in a covered basket from which nothing could escape. The fish man who sold me the carp said he had no time to kill, scale, or clean it, nor would he tell me with which of these horrible necessities one began. It wasn't difficult to know which was the most repellent. So quickly to the murder and have it over with. On the docks of Puget Sound I had seen fishermen grasp the tail of a huge salmon and lifting it high bring it down on the dock with enough force to kill it. Obviously I was not a fisherman nor was the kitchen table a dock. Should I not dispatch my first victim with a blow on the head from a heavy mallet? After an appraising glance at the lively fish it was evident he would escape attempts aimed at his head. A heavy sharp knife came to my mind as the classic, the perfect choice, so grasping, with my left hand well covered with a dishcloth, for the teeth might be sharp, the lower jaw of the carp, and the knife in my right, I carefully, deliberately found the base of its vertebral column and plunged the knife in. I let go my grasp and looked to see what had happened. Horror of horrors. The carp was dead, killed, assassinated, murdered in the first, second, and third degree. Limp, I fell into a chair, with my hands still unwashed reached for a cigarette, lighted it, and waited for the police to come and take me into custody. After a second cigarette my courage returned and I went to prepare Mr. Carp for the table. I scraped off the scales, cut off the fins, cut open the underside, and emptied out a great deal of what I did not care to look at, thoroughly washed and dried the fish, and put it aside while I prepared

CARP STUFFED WITH CHESTNUTS

For a 3-lb. carp, chop a medium-sized onion and cook it gently in 3 tablespoons butter. Add a 2-inch slice of bread cut into small cubes which have previously been soaked in dry, white wine and squeezed dry, 1 tablespoon chopped parsley, 2 chopped shallots, 1 clove of pressed garlic, 1 teaspoon salt, $\frac{1}{4}$ teaspoon freshly ground pepper, $\frac{1}{4}$ teaspoon powdered mace, the same of laurel (bay) and of thyme, and 12 boiled and peeled chestnuts. Mix well, allow to cool, add 1 raw egg, stuff the cavity and head of the fish, carefully snare with skewers, tie the head so that nothing will escape in cooking. Put aside for at least a couple of hours. Put 2 cups dry white wine into an earthenware dish, place the fish in the dish, salt to taste. Cook in the oven for 20 minutes at 375°. Baste, and cover the fish with a thick coating of very fine cracker crumbs, dot with 3 tablespoons melted butter, and cook for 20 minutes more. Serve very hot accompanied by noodles. Serves 4. The head of a carp is enormous. Many continentals consider it the most delectable morsel.

NOODLES

Sift 2 cups flour, 1 teaspoon salt, and a pinch of nutmeg, add the yolks of 5 eggs and 1 whole egg. Mix thoroughly with a fork and then knead on a floured board, form into a ball, wrap in a cloth, and put aside for several hours. Divide into three parts. Roll each one in turn on a lightly floured board to tissue-paper thinness. Dry for $\frac{1}{2}$ hour, roll up, and cut into strips $\frac{1}{4}$ inch wide. Bring 1 quart water with 1 teaspoon salt to a hard boil. Place noodles a few at a time into boiling water, stir gently with a fork, reduce heat, and boil slowly for 10 minutes. Drain off all the water and add 3 tablespoons melted butter. These noodles are very delicate. Serves 4.

It was in the market of Palma de Mallorca that our French cook tried to teach me to murder by smothering. There is no reason why this crime should have been committed publicly or that I should have been expected to participate. Jeanne was just showing off. When the crowd of market women who had gathered about her began screaming and gesticulating, I retreated. When we met later to drive back in the carry-all filled with our marketing to Terreno where we had a villa I refused to sympathize with Jeanne. She said the Mallorcans were bloodthirsty, didn't they go to bullfights and pay an advanced price for the meat of the beasts they had seen killed in the ring, didn't they prefer to chop off the heads of innocent pigeons instead of humanely smothering them which was the way to prevent all fowl from bleeding to death and so make them fuller and tastier. Had she not tried to explain this to them, to teach them, to show them how an intelligent humane person went about killing pigeons, but no they didn't want to learn, they preferred their own brutal ways. At lunch when she served the pigeons Jeanne discreetly said nothing. Discussing food which she enjoyed above everything had been discouraged at table. But her fine black eyes were eloquent. If the small-sized pigeons the island produced had not achieved jumbo size, squabs they unquestionably were, and larger and more succulent squabs than those we had eaten at the excellent restaurant at Palma.

Later we went back to Paris and then there was war and after a lifetime there was peace. One day passing the *concierge*'s *loge* he called me and said he had something someone had left for us. He said he would bring it to me, which he did and which I wished he hadn't when I saw what it was, a crate of six white pigeons and a note from a friend saying she had nothing better to offer us from her home in the country, ending with, But as Alice is clever she will make something delicious of them. It is certainly a mistake to allow a reputation for cleverness to be born and spread by loving friends. It is so cheaply acquired and so dearly paid for. Six white pigeons to be smothered, to be plucked, to be cleaned, and all this to be accomplished before Gertrude Stein returned for she didn't like to see work being done. If only I had the courage the two hours before her return would easily suffice. A large cup of strong black coffee would help. This was before a lovely Brazilian told me that in her country a large cup of black coffee was always served before going to bed to ensure a good night's rest. Not yet having acquired this knowledge the black coffee made me lively and courageous. I carefully found the spot on poor innocent Dove's throat where I was to press and pressed. The realization had never come to me before that one saw with one's fingertips as well as one's eyes. It was a most unpleasant experience, though as

I laid out one by one the sweet young corpses there was no denying one could become accustomed to murdering. So I plucked the pigeons, emptied them, and was ready to cook

BRAISED PIGEONS ON CROÛTONS

For 6 pigeons cut $\frac{1}{2}$ lb. salt pork in small cubes, place in Dutch oven with 6 tablespoons butter, place pigeons in oven, brown slightly, cover and cook over low flame for 1 hour turning and basting frequently. While pigeons are cooking wash and carefully dry 2 lb. mushrooms. Chop them very fine, and pass through a coarse sieve, cook over brisk fire in $\frac{1}{4}$ lb. butter until liquid has evaporated. Reduce flame and add 1 cup heavy cream sauce and $\frac{1}{2}$ cup heavy cream. Spread on 6 one-half-inch slices of bread that have been lightly browned in butter. Spread the *purée* of mushrooms on the *croûtons*. Place the pigeons on the *croûtons*. Skim the fat from the juice in the Dutch oven, add 2 tablespoons Madeira, bring to a boil, and pour over pigeons. Salt for this dish depends upon how salty the pork is. Serves 6 to 12 according to size of pigeons.

The next murder was not of my doing. During six months which we spent in the country we raised Barbary ducks. They are larger than ordinary ducks and are famous for the size of their livers. They do not quack and are not friendly. Down in the Ain everyone shoots. Many of the farmers go off to work in the fields with a gun slung over a shoulder and not infrequently return with a bird or two. Occasionally a farmer would sell us a pheasant or a partridge. An English friend staying with us, astonished to find farmers shooting, remarked, When everyone shoots no one shoots. Our nearest neighbour had a so-called bird dog, mongrel she certainly was, ruby coat like an Irish setter but her head was flat, her paws too large, her tail too short. We would see Diane on the road, she was not sympathetic. The large iron portals at Bilignin were sometimes left open when Gertrude Stein took the car out for a short while, and one morning Diane, finding them open, came into the court and saw the last of our Barbary ducks, Blanchette, because she was blue-black. Perhaps innocently perhaps not, opinion was divided later, she began to chase Blanchette. She would come running at the poor bewildered duck from a distance, charge upon her, retreat, and recommence. The cook, having seen from the kitchen window what was happening, hastened out. The poor duck was on her back and Diane was madly barking and running about. By the time I got to the court the cook was tenderly carrying a limp Blanchette in her arms to the kitchen. Having chased Diane out of the court, I closed the portals and returned to my work in the vegetable garden supposing the episode to be over. Not at all. Presently the cook appeared, her face whiter than her apron. Madame, she said, poor Blanchette is no more. That wretched dog frightened her to death. Her heart was beating so furiously I saw there was but one thing to do. I gave her three tablespoonfuls of *eau-de-vie*, that will give her a good flavour. And then I killed her. How does Madame wish her to be cooked. Surprised at the turn the affair had taken, I answered feebly, With orange sauce.

There was considerable talk in the hamlet. While we were walking along the road someone would say, What a pity, or Your beautiful bird! to which we would answer that we would have had to be eating her soon anyway. But Diane's master did not know what attitude to take until I sent his wife a basket of globe egg plants, almost white and yellow tomatoes, and a few gumbos (okra), none of which she had seen before. Then he came to thank us for his wife and presented a large pot of fresh butter she had sent us. He knew our cook felt that his dog had caused the death of our duck. We wiped out the memory of the misadventure in thanking each other for the gifts. So Blanchette was cooked as

DUCK WITH ORANGE SAUCE

Put the bird aside and cook the rest of the giblets including the neck in 2 cups water with 1 teaspoon salt, $\frac{1}{4}$ teaspoon pepper, 1 small onion with a clove stuck in it, a shallot, $\frac{1}{2}$ laurel leaf, a sprig of thyme, and a small blade of mace. Cover and cook slowly. When the juice has reduced to 1 cup put aside. Cut 1 peeled orange into half a dozen pieces and put inside the duck. Cut the orange peel into small pieces and boil covered in $\frac{1}{2}$ cup water for 10 minutes. Roast the duck in a 400° oven in a pan with 3 tablespoons butter for $\frac{1}{2}$ hour, basting and turning the duck three times. Put the orange peel and the liver in a mortar. Moisten with $\frac{1}{3}$ cup of the best white curaçao and crush to an even paste. Add to this the cup of giblet juice and the juice in the pan from which the fat has been skimmed. Heat thoroughly but do not allow to boil, strain and serve in preheated metal sauce boat. Place very thinly sliced unpeeled oranges on the duck and serve. Sufficient for 4.

GÜNTER GRASS

FROM
THE FLOUNDER

Translated by Ralph Manheim

"THE LAST MEAL"

First built in 1346 as a bastion to the High Gate and subsequently enlarged as the need for prison cells, torture chambers, and business premises increased, the Stockturm, whose dungeon keeps were reputed to be dry, was rebuilt in 1509, when city architects Hetzel and Enkinger added two stories and capped the tower. Thereafter it stood empty and unused until King Sigismund of Poland, responding in April 1526 to the call of Mayor Eberhard Ferber, occupied the city, posted Counter Reformation statutes in the seven principal churches, and haled all the leaders of the uprising against the patrician council, except for the fugitive preacher Hegge, before a court of aldermen, which sentenced the six ringleaders to death by beheading, including the blacksmith Peter Rusch, whose daughter had recently been appointed abbess of Saint Bridget's—an imposing woman of controversial reputation who flattered the taste of all parties with her conventual cookery, took her cut on every transaction, and even in times of general ruin (war, plague, and famine) made a profit.

And because Mother Rusch was not without influence, she was able to obtain, if not her father's pardon, at least the right to cook one last meal for him. Highly placed persons accepted her invitation. Mayor Ferber, deposed and banished to his starosty in Dirschau by the rebellious guilds but now restored to office, and Abbot Jeschke of the Oliva Monastery repaired to the Stockturm in fur-trimmed brabant, quite willing to join blacksmith Rusch in spooning up his favorite dish. Executioner Ladewig was also invited, and came. The cooking abbess had put her full kettle on the hearth the night before in the kitchen of the executioner (and knacker), and the smell penetrated to every last dungeon of the now fully occupied Stockturm.

Who will join me in a dish of tripe? It soothes, appeases the anger of the outraged, stills the fear of death, and reminds us of tripe eaten in former days, when there was always a half-filled pot of it on the stove. A chunk of the fat paunch and the limp, honeycombed walls of the second stomach— four pounds for three fifty. It's the widespread distaste for innards that makes beef heart and pork kidneys, calf's lung and tripe cheap.

She took her time. She pounded the pieces and brushed them inside and out, as though some beggar's sweaty rags had found their way to her washboard. She removed the wrinkled skin, but she spared the belly fat, for tripe fat has a special quality—instead of hardening into tallow, it dissolves like soap.

When a last meal was prepared for blacksmith Rusch and his guests, seven quarts of water seasoned with salt, caraway seed, cloves, ginger root, bay leaf, and coarsely pounded peppercorns were set over an open fire. The limp pieces, cut into finger-long strips, were added until the pot was full, and when the water came to a boil the scum was skimmed off. Then the daughter covered her father's favorite dish and let it boil for four hours. At the end she added garlic, freshly grated nutmeg, and more pepper.

The time it takes. Those are the best hours. When the

tough has to be made tender, but can't be hurried. How often Mother Rusch and I, while the billowing tripe kept the kitchen stable-warm, sat at the table pushing checkers over the board, discovering the sea route to India, or catching flies on the smooth-polished table top, and telling each other about the tripe of olden times, when we were Pomorshian and still heathen. And about older than olden times, when elk cows were the only source of meat.

Later on, after the daughter had cooked her father's last dish of tripe, she cooked for rich coopers at guild banquets, for Hanseatic merchants who cared about nothing but Öresund tolls, for fat abbots and King Stephen Batory, who wanted his tripe sour and Polish. Still later Amanda Woyke, in her farm kitchen, cooked up tripe with turnips and potatoes into a soup that she seasoned with lovage. And still later Lena Stubbe taught the patrons of the Danzig-Ohra soup kitchen to enjoy proletarian cabbage soups made with (cut-rate) tripe. And to this very day Maria Kuczorra, canteen cook at the Lenin Shipyard in Gdańsk, makes a thick soup once a week out of *kaldauny* (tripe).

When you are feeling cold inside—try the walls of the cow's second stomach. When you are sad, cast out by all nature, sad unto death, try tripe, which cheers us and gives meaning to life. Or in the company of witty friends, godless enough to sit in the seat of the scornful, spoon up caraway-seasoned tripe out of deep dishes. Or cooked with tomatoes, Andalusian-style with chickpeas, or à la Portugaise with kidney beans and bacon. Or if love needs an appetizer, precook tripe in white wine, then steam it with diced celery root. On cold, dry days, when the east wind is banging at the windowpanes and driving your Ilsebill up the wall, tripe thickened with sour cream and served with potatoes in their jackets will help. Or if we must part, briefly or forever, like the time I was a prisoner in the Stockturm and my daughter served me a last meal of peppered tripe. . . .

Even when the bowls were empty for the fourth time, the blacksmith and his guests had not yet spooned up sufficient peppered and caraway-seeded tripe. Accordingly Mother Rusch ladled fifth helpings out of her deep kettle and poured black beer into mugs. She also went on mumbling her table talk: hints smothered in local gossip, threats stirred into her usual nunnish chatter. But if patrician Ferber and Abbot Jeschke had not been too stuffed to listen, they might have had something to think about, for Mother Rusch quite transparently detailed her plans for settling accounts with both of them. Which plans she also carried out, for three years later she smothered the rich Eberhard Ferber in bed under her double hundredweight; and fifty years later—for Fat Gret lived to a ripe old age for her vengeance—she fattened Abbot Jeschke to death: he died over a bowl of tripe.

Blacksmith Rusch may have gathered the gist of his daughter's projects from her table talk and understood how she meant to avenge his death, for the poor devil grinned broadly over his empty bowl. Indeed, something more than the warm feeling of having filled his belly one last time may have accounted for his satisfaction. He sang his daughter's praises, and there his talk became rather confused, for he brought in a fish, whom he referred to as the "Flounder in the sea," and thanked him for having advised him, at a time when his hair was still brown, to send his youngest daughter, whose mother was dying of the fever, to a convent, for there, so the Flounder had assured him, she would become shrewd and crafty, so as to manage her female flesh independently and have hot soup in daily readiness for her father in his old age.

Then he, too, fell silent, replete with tripe. After that, belches were accompanied only by an occasional word or half sentence. Ferber dreamed of his life in the country; far from all strife, he would live in the midst of his art collection, culling wisdom from books. After eating so much tripe, Abbot Jeschke could think only of the tripe he hoped to spoon up in the future, peppered just the way the abbess did it. But by then Lutheranism would—by drastic measures if necessary—have been eradicated from the world. Executioner Ladewig anticipated several articles of the "Newly Revised Ordinance." He would have liked to place with the local coopers an order for the barrels needed to clean up the city. For every barrel emptied he would charge only ten groschen. Blacksmith Rusch, on the other hand, predicted that the patrician council would be faced forever and ever with unrest and insurrectionary demands on the part of the guilds and lower trades, and his prophecy came true in December 1970. The lower orders have never ceased to rebel against patrician authoritarianism and to risk their necks for a little more civil rights.

Then, full fed, the guests left. Ferber said nothing. Jeschke delivered himself of a Latin blessing. Ladewig took the five emptied bowls with him. The pigeons in the window hole were silent. The torches had almost burned down in their holders. Peter Rusch sat in his chains and shed a few tears for his last supper. Laden right and left with the kettle and the empty beer keg, his daughter resumed her mumbling on her way out: "You'll soon be out of your misery now. You'll soon be a lot better off. They'll give you a nice cozy place in the heavenly guildhall. And you'll always have plenty of tripe. So stop worrying. Your Gret will settle up with them. It may take time, but I'll fix them good."

Then Mother Rusch admonished her father to hold his curly gray head erect the next day and not to fling curses at anyone whomsoever. He should kneel unbowed before the executioner. He could rely on her vengeance. The taste of it would linger in her mouth like Indian pepper. She wouldn't forget. No, she wouldn't forget.

Peter Rusch did as his daughter had bidden. He must have had a goodly portion of tripe half digested in his innards when, next day in the Long Market, facing the Artushof, where the patricians and prelates stood as though painted around Sigismund, king of Poland, he (fourth of the six candidates) silently let his head be severed from his shoulders. No bungling. You could count on executioner Ladewig. The abbess looked on. A sudden shower of rain made her face glisten. And addressing the Women's Tribunal, the Flounder said, "In short, dear ladies, vigorously as Margarete Rusch pursued her aims, perseveringly as she raked in her gains, slow as she was in settling her account—on June 26, 1526, when blacksmith Peter Rusch was executed along with the other ringleaders, a daughter wept for her father."

T. C. BOYLE

SORRY FUGU

"LIMP RADICCHIO."

"Sorry fugu."

"A blasphemy of baby lamb's lettuce, frisee, endive."

"A coulibiac made in hell."

For six months he knew her only by her by-line–Willa Frank—and by the sting of her adjectives, the derisive thrust of her metaphors, the cold precision of her substantives. Regardless of the dish, despite the sincerity and ingenuity of the chef and the freshness or rarity of the ingredients, she seemed always to find it wanting. "The duck had been reduced to the state of the residue one might expect to find in the nether depths of a funerary urn"; "For all its rather testy piquancy, the orange sauce might just as well have been citron preserved in pickling brine"; "Paste and pasta. Are they synonymous? Hardly. But one wouldn't have known the difference at Udolpho's. The 'fresh' angel hair had all the taste and consistency of mucilage."

Albert quailed before those caustic pronouncements, he shuddered and blanched and felt his stomach drop like a croquette into a vat of hot grease. On the morning she skewered Udolpho's, he was sitting over a cup of reheated espresso and nibbling at a wedge of hazelnut dacquoise that had survived the previous night's crush. As was his habit on Fridays, he'd retrieved the paper from the mat, got himself a bite, and then, with the reckless abandon of a diver plunging into an icy lake, turned to the "Dining Out" column. On alternate weeks, Willa Frank yielded to the paper's other regular reviewer, a big-hearted, appreciative woman by the name of Leonora Merganser, who approached every restaurant like a mother of eight feted by her children on Mother's Day, and whose praise gushed forth in a breathless salivating stream that washed the reader out of his chair and up against the telephone stand, where he would dial frantically for a reservation. But this was Willa Frank's week. And Willa Frank never liked anything.

With trembling fingers—it was only a matter of time before she slipped like a spy, like a murderess, into D'Angelo's and filleted him like all the others—he smoothed out the paper and focused on the bold black letters of the headline:

UDOLPHO'S: TROGLODYTIC CUISINE IN A CAVELIKE ATMOSPHERE

He read on, heart in mouth. She'd visited the restaurant on three occasions, once in the company of an abstract artist from Detroit, and twice with her regular companion, a young man so discerning she referred to him only as "The Palate." On all three occasions, she'd been—sniff—disappointed. The turn-of-the-century gas lamps Udolpho's grandfather had brought over from Naples hadn't appealed to her ("so dark we joked that it was like dining among Neanderthals in the sub-basement of their cave"), nor had the open fire in the massive stone fireplace that dominated the room ("smoky, and stinking of incinerated chestnuts"). And then there was the food. When Albert got to the line about the pasta, he couldn't go on. He folded the paper as carefully as he might have folded the winding sheet over Udolpho's broken body and set it aside.

It was then that Marie stepped through the swinging doors to the kitchen, the wet cloth napkin she'd been using as a dishrag clutched in her hand. "Albert?" she gasped, darting an uneasy glance from his stricken face to the newspaper. "Is anything wrong? Did she—? Today?"

She assumed the worst; and now he corrected her in a drawl so lugubrious it might have been his expiring breath: "Udolpho's."

"Udolpho's?" Relief flooded her voice, but almost immediately it gave way to disbelief and outrage. "Udolpho's?" she repeated.

He shook his head sadly. For thirty years Udolpho's had reigned supreme among West Side restaurants, a place impervious to fads and trends, never chic but steady—classy in a way no nouvelle mangerie with its pastel walls and Breuer chairs could ever hope to be. Cagney had eaten here, Durante, Roy Rogers, Anna Maria Alberghetti. It was a shrine, an institution.

Albert himself, a pudgy sorrowful boy of twelve, ridiculed for his flab and the great insatiable fist of his appetite, had experienced the grand epiphany of his life in one of Udolpho's dark, smoky, and—for him, at least—forever exotic banquettes. Sampling the vermicelli with oil, garlic, olives, and forest mushrooms, the osso buco with the little twists of bow-tie pasta that drank up its buttery juices, he knew just as certainly as Alexander must have known he was born to conquer, that he, Albert D'Angelo, was born to eat. And that far from being something to be ashamed of, it was glorious, avocation and vocation both, the highest pinnacle to which he could aspire. Other boys had their Snider, their Mays, their Reese and Mantle, but for Albert the magical names were Pellaprat, Escoffier, Udolpho Melanzane.

Yes. And now Udolpho was nothing. Willa Frank had seen to that.

Marie was bent over the table now, reading, her piping girlish voice hot with indignation.

"Where does she come off, anyway?" Albert shrugged. Since he'd opened D'Angelo's eighteen months ago the press had all but ignored him. Yes, he'd had a little paragraph in *Barbed Wire*, the alternative press weekly handed out on street corners by greasy characters with straight pins through their noses, but you could hardly count that. There was only one paper that really mattered—Willa Frank's paper—and while word of mouth was all right, without a review in *the* paper, you were dead. Problem was, if Willa Frank wrote you up, you were dead anyway.

"Maybe you'll get the other one," Marie said suddenly. "What's her name—the good one."

Albert's lips barely moved. "Leonora Merganser."

"Well, you could."

"I want Willa Frank," he growled.

Marie's brow lifted. She closed the paper and came to him, rocked back from his belly, and pecked a kiss to his beard. "You can't be serious?"

Albert glanced bitterly around the restaurant, the simple pine tables, whitewashed walls, potted palms soft in the filtered morning light. "Leonora Merganser would faint over the Hamburger Hamlet on the corner, Long John Silver's, anything. Where's the challenge in that?"

"Challenge? But we don't want a challenge, honey—we want business. Don't we? I mean if we're going to get married and all—"

Albert sat heavily, took a miserable sip of his stone-cold espresso. "I'm a great chef, aren't I?" There was something in his tone that told her it wasn't exactly a rhetorical question.

"Honey, baby," she was in his lap now, fluffing his hair, peering into his ear, "of course you are. The best. The very best. But—"

"Willa Frank," he rumbled. "Willa Frank. I want her."

There are nights when it all comes together, when the monkfish is so fresh it flakes on the grill, when the pesto tastes like the wind through the pines and the party of eight gets their seven appetizers and six entrées in palettes of rising steam and delicate colors so perfect they might have been a single diner sitting down to a single dish. This night, however, was not such a night. This was a night when everything went wrong.

First of all, there was the aggravating fact that Eduardo—the Chilean waiter who'd learned, à la Chico Marx, to sprinkle superfluous "ahs" through his speech and thus pass for Italian—was late. This put Marie off her pace vis-à-vis the desserts, for which she was solely responsible, since she had to seat and serve the first half-dozen customers. Next, in rapid succession, Albert found that he was out of mesquite for the grill, sun-dried tomatoes for the fusilli with funghi, capers, black olives, and, yes, sun-dried tomatoes, and that the fresh cream for the frittata piemontese had mysteriously gone sour. And then, just when he'd managed to recover his equilibrium and was working in that translated state where mind and body are one, Roque went berserk.

Of the restaurant's five employees—Marie, Eduardo, Torrey, who did day-cleanup, Albert himself, and Roque—Roque operated on perhaps the most elemental level. He was the dishwasher. The Yucatano dishwasher. Whose responsibility it was to see that D'Angelo's pink and gray sets of heavy Syracuse china were kept in constant circulation through the mid-evening dinner rush. On this particular night, however, Roque was slow to accept the challenge of that responsibility, scraping plates and wielding the nozzle of his supersprayer as if in a dream. And not only was he moving slowly, the dishes, with their spatters of red and white sauce and dribbles of grease piling up beside him like the Watts Towers, but he was muttering to himself. Darkly. In a dialect so arcane even Eduardo couldn't fathom it.

When Albert questioned him—a bit too sharply, perhaps: he was overwrought himself—Roque exploded. All Albert had said was, "Roque—you all right?" But he might just as well have reviled his mother, his fourteen sisters, and his birthplace. Cursing, Roque danced back from the stainless-steel sink, tore the apron from his chest, and began scaling dishes against the wall. It took all of Albert's 220 pounds, together with Eduardo's 180, to get Roque, who couldn't have weighed more than 120 in hip boots, out the door and into the alley. Together they slammed the door on him—the door on which he continued to beat with a shoe for half an hour or more—while Marie took up the dishrag with a sigh.

A disaster. Pure, unalloyed, unmitigated. The night was a disaster.

Albert had just begun to catch up when Torrey slouched through the alley door and into the kitchen, her bony hand raised in greeting. Torrey was pale and shrunken, a nineteen-year-old with a red butch cut who spoke with the rising inflection and oblate vowels of the Valley Girl, born and bred. She wanted an advance on her salary.

"Momento, momento," Albert said, flashing past her with a pan of béarnaise in one hand, a mayonnaise jar of vivid orange sea-urchin roe in the other. He liked to use his rudimentary Italian when he was cooking. It made him feel impregnable.

Meanwhile, Torrey shuffled halfheartedly across the floor

and positioned herself behind the porthole in the "out" door, where, for lack of anything better to do, she could watch the customers eat, drink, smoke, and finger their pastry. The béarnaise was puddling up beautifully on a plate of grilled baby summer squash, the roe dolloped on a fillet of monkfish nestled snug in its cruet, and Albert was thinking of offering Torrey battle pay if she'd stay and wash dishes, when she let out a low whistle. This was no cab or encore whistle, but the sort of whistle that expresses surprise or shock—a "Holy cow!" sort of whistle. It stopped Albert cold. Something bad was about to happen, he knew it, just as surely as he knew that the tiny hairs rimming his bald spot had suddenly stiffened up like hackles.

"What?" he demanded. "What is it?"

Torrey turned to him, slow as an executioner. "I see you got Willa Frank out there tonight—everything going okay?"

The monkfish burst into flame, the béarnaise turned to water, Marie dropped two cups of coffee and a plate of homemade millefoglie.

No matter. In an instant, all three of them were pressed up against the little round window, as intent as torpedoers peering through a periscope. "Which one?" Albert hissed, his heart doing paradiddles.

"Over there?" Torrey said, making it a question. "With Jock—Jock McNamee? The one with the blond wig?"

Albert looked, but he couldn't see. "Where? Where?" he cried.

"There? In the corner?"

In the corner, in the corner. Albert was looking at a young woman, a girl, a blonde in a black cocktail dress and no brassiere, seated across from a hulking giant with a peroxide-streaked flattop. "Where?" he repeated.

Torrey pointed.

"The blonde?" He could feel Marie go slack beside him. "But that can't be—" Words failed him. *This* was Willa Frank, doyenne of taste, grande dame of haute cuisine, ferreter out of the incorrect, the underachieved, and the unfortunate? And this clod beside her, with the great smooth-working jaw and forearms like pillars, *this* was the possessor of the fussiest, pickiest, most sophisticated and fastidious palate in town? No, it was impossible.

"Like I know him, you know?" Torrey was saying. "Jock? Like from the Anti-Club and all that scene?"

But Albert wasn't listening. He was watching her—Willa Frank—as transfixed as the tailorbird that dares look into the cobra's eye. She was slim, pretty, eyes dark as a houri's, a lot of jewelry—not at all what he'd expected. He'd pictured a veiny elegant woman in her fifties, starchy, patrician, from Boston or Newport or some such place. But wait, wait: Eduardo was just setting the plates down—she was the Florentine tripe, of course—a good dish, a dish he'd stand by any day, even a bad one like ... but the Palate, what was he having? Albert strained forward, and he could feel Marie's lost and limp hand feebly pressing his own. There: the veal piccata, yes, a very good dish, an outstanding dish. Yes. Yes.

Eduardo bowed gracefully away. The big man in the punk hairdo bent to his plate and sniffed. Willa Frank—blonde, delicious, lethal—cut into the tripe, and raised the fork to her lips.

"She hated it. I know it. I know it." Albert rocked back and forth in his chair, his face buried in his hands, the toque clinging to his brow like a carrion bird. It was past midnight, the restaurant was closed. He sat amidst the wreckage of the kitchen, the waste, the slop, the smell of congealed grease and dead spices, and his breath came in ragged sobbing gasps.

Marie got up to rub the back of his neck. Sweet, honey-completed Marie, with her firm heavy arms and graceful wrists, the spill and generosity of her flesh—his consolation in a world of Willa Franks. "It's okay," she kept saying, over and over, her voice a soothing murmur, "it's okay, it was good, it was."

He'd failed and he knew it. Of all nights, why this one? Why couldn't she have come when the structure was there, when he was on, when the dishwasher was sober, the cream fresh, and the mesquite knots piled high against the wall, when he could concentrate, for christ's sake? "She didn't finish her tripe," he said, disconsolate. "Or the grilled vegetables. I saw the plate."

"She'll be back," Marie said. "Three visits minimum, right?"

Albert fished out a handkerchief and sorrowfully blew his nose. "Yeah," he said, "three strikes and you're out." He twisted his neck to look up at her. "The Palate, Jock, whatever the jerk's name is, he didn't touch the veal. One bite maybe. Same with the pasta. Eduardo said the only thing he ate was the bread. And a bottle of beer."

"What does he know," Marie said. "Or her either."

Albert shrugged. He pushed himself up wearily, impaled on the stake of his defeat, and helped himself to a glass of Orvieto and a plate of leftover sweetbreads. "Everything," he said miserably, the meat like butter in his mouth, fragrant, nutty, inexpressibly right. He shrugged again. "Or nothing. What does it matter? Either way we get screwed."

"And 'Frank'? What kind of name is that, anyhow? German? Is that it?" Marie was on the attack now, pacing the linoleum like a field marshal probing for a weakness in the enemy lines, looking for a way in. "The Franks—weren't they those barbarians in high school that sacked Rome? Or was it Paris?"

Willa Frank. The name was bitter on his tongue. Willa, Willa, Willa. It was a bony name, scant and lean, stripped of sensuality, the antithesis of the round, full-bodied Leonora. It spoke of a knotty Puritan toughness, a denying of the flesh, no compromise in the face of temptation. Willa. How could he ever hope to seduce a Willa? And Frank. That was even worse. A man's name. Cold, forbidding, German, French. It was the name of a woman who wouldn't complicate her task with notions of charity or the sparing of feelings. No, it was the name of a woman who would wield her adjectives like a club.

Stewing in these sour reflections, eating and no longer tasting, Albert was suddenly startled by a noise outside the alley door. He picked up a saucepan and stalked across the room—What next? Were they planning to rob him now too, was that it?—and flung open the door.

In the dim light of the alleyway stood two small dark men, the smaller of whom looked so much like Roque he might have been a clone. "Hello," said the larger man, swiping a greasy Dodgers' cap from his head, "I am called Raul, and this"—indicating his companion—"is called Fulgencio, cousin of Roque." At the mention of his name, Fulgencio smiled. "Roque is gone to Albuquerque," Raul continued, "and he is sorry. But he sends you his cousin, Fulgencio, to wash for you."

Albert stood back from the door, and Fulgencio, grinning and nodding, mimed the motion of washing a plate as he stepped into the kitchen. Still grinning, still miming, he sambaed across the floor, lifted the supersprayer from its receptacle as he might have drawn a rapier from its scabbard, and started in on the dishes with a vigor that would have prostrated his mercurial cousin.

For a long moment Albert merely stood there watching, barely conscious of Marie at his back and Raul's parting gesture as he gently shut the door. All of a sudden he felt redeemed, reborn, capable of anything. There was Fulgencio, a total stranger not two minutes ago, washing dishes as if he were born to it. And there was Marie, who'd stand by him if he had to cook cactus and lizard for the saints in the desert. And here he was himself, in all the vigor of his manhood, accomplished, knowledgeable, inspired, potentially one of the great culinary artists of his time. What was the matter with him? What was he crying about?

He'd wanted Willa Frank. All right: he'd gotten her. But on an off-night, the kind of night anyone could have. Out of mesquite. The cream gone sour, the dishwasher mad. Even Puck, even Soltner, couldn't have contended with that.

She'd be back. Twice more. And he would be ready for her.

All that week, a cloud of anticipation hung over the restaurant. Albert outdid himself, redefining the bounds of his nouvelle Northern Italian cuisine with a dozen new creations, including a very nice black pasta with grilled shrimp, a pungent jugged hare, and an absolutely devastating meadowlark marinated in shallots, white wine, and mint. He worked like a man possessed, a man inspired. Each night he offered seven appetizers and six entrées, and each night they were different. He outdid himself, and outdid himself again.

Friday came and went. The morning paper found Leonora Merganser puffing some Greek place in North Hollywood, heralding spanakopita as if it had been invented yesterday and discovering evidence of divine intervention in the folds of a grape leaf. Fulgencio scrubbed dishes with a passion, Eduardo worked on his accent and threw out his chest, Marie's desserts positively floated on air. And day by day, Albert rose to new heights.

It was on Tuesday of the following week—a quiet Tuesday, one of the quietest Albert could remember—that Willa Frank appeared again. There were only two other parties in the restaurant, a skeletal septuagenarian with a professorial air and his granddaughter—at least Albert hoped she was his granddaughter—and a Beverly Hills couple who'd been coming in once a week since the place opened.

Her presence was announced by Eduardo, who slammed into the kitchen with a drawn face and a shakily scrawled cocktail order. "She's here," he whispered, and the kitchen fell silent. Fulgencio paused, sprayer in hand. Marie looked up from a plate of tortes. Albert, who'd been putting the finishing touches to a dish of sauteed scallops al pesto for the professor and a breast of duck with wild mushrooms for his granddaughter, staggered back from the table as if he'd been shot. Dropping everything, he rushed to the porthole for a glimpse of her.

It was his moment of truth, the moment in which his courage very nearly failed him. She was stunning. Glowing. As perfect and unapproachable as the plucked and haughty girls who looked out at him from the covers of magazines at the supermarket, icily elegant in a clingy silk chemise the color of béchamel. How could he, Albert D'Angelo, for all his talent and greatness of heart, ever hope to touch her, to move such perfection, to pique such jaded taste buds?

Wounded, he looked to her companions. Beside her, grinning hugely, as hearty, handsome, and bland as ever, was the Palate—he could expect no help from that quarter. And then he turned his eyes on the couple they'd brought with them, looking for signs of sympathy. He looked in vain. They were middle-aged, silver-haired, dressed to the nines, thin and stringy in the way of those who exercise inflexible control over their appetites, about as sympathetic as vigilantes. Albert understood then that it was going to be an uphill battle. He turned back to the grill, girded himself in a clean apron, and awaited the worst.

Marie fixed the drinks—two martinis, a Glenlivet neat for Willa, and a beer for the Palate. For appetizers they ordered mozzarella di buffala marinara, the caponata D'Angelo, the octopus salad, and the veal medallions with onion marmalade. Albert put his soul into each dish, arranged and garnished the plates with all the patient care and shimmering inspiration of a Toulouse-Lautrec bent over a canvas, and watched, defeated, as each came back to the kitchen half eaten. And then came the entrées. They ordered a selection—five different dishes—and Albert, after delivering them up to Eduardo with a face of stone, pressed himself to the porthole like a voyeur.

Riveted, he watched as they sat back so that Eduardo could present the dishes. He waited, but nothing happened. They barely glanced at the food. And then, as if by signal, they began passing the plates around the table. He was stunned: what did they think this was—the Imperial Dinner at Chow Foo Luck's? But then he understood: each dish had to suffer the scrutiny of the big man with the brutal jaw before they would deign to touch it. No one ate, no one spoke, no one lifted a glass of the Château Bellegrave, 1966, to his lips, until Jock had sniffed, finger-licked, and then gingerly tasted each of Albert's creations. Willa sat rigid, her black eyes open wide, as the great-jawed, brush-headed giant leaned intently over the plate and rolled a bit of scallop or duck over his tongue. Finally, when all the dishes had circulated, the écrevisses Alberto came to rest, like a roulette ball, in front of the Palate. But he'd already snuffed it, already dirtied his fork in it. And now, with a grand gesture, he pushed the plate aside and called out in a hoarse voice for beer.

The next day was the blackest of Albert's life. There were two strikes against him, and the third was coming down the pike. He didn't know what to do. His dreams had been feverish, a nightmare of mincing truffles and reanimated pigs' feet, and he awoke with the wildest combinations on his lips— chopped pickles and shad roe, an onion-cinnamon mousse, black-eyed peas vinaigrette. He even, half-seriously, drew up a fantasy menu, a list of dishes no one had ever tasted, not sheiks or presidents. La Cuisine des Espèces en Danger, he would call it. Breast of California condor aux chanterelles; snail darter à la meunière; medallions of panda alla campagnola. Marie laughed out loud when he presented her with the menu that afternoon–"I've invented a new cuisine!" he shouted—and for a moment, the pall lifted.

But just as quickly, it descended again. He knew what he had to do. He had to speak to her, his severest critic, through the medium of his food. He had to translate for her, awaken her with a kiss. But how? How could he even begin to rouse her from her slumber when that clod stood between them like a watchdog?

As it turned out, the answer was closer at hand than he could have imagined.

It was late the next afternoon—Thursday, the day before Willa Frank's next hatchet job was due to appear in the paper—and Albert sat at a table in the back of the darkened restaurant, brooding over his menu. He was almost certain she'd be in for her final visit that night, and yet he still hadn't a clue as to how he was going to redeem himself. For a long while he sat there in his misery, absently watching Torrey as she probed beneath the front tables with the wand of her vacuum. Behind him, in the kitchen, sauces were simmering, a veal loin roasting; Marie was baking bread and Fulgencio stacking wood. He must have watched Torrey for a full five minutes before he called out to her. "Torrey!" he shouted over the roar of the vacuum. "Torrey, shut that thing off a minute, will you?"

The roar died to a wheeze, then silence. Torrey looked up.

"This guy, what's his name, Jock—what do you know about him?" He glanced down at the scrawled-over menu and then up again. "I mean, you don't know what he likes to eat, by any chance, do you?"

Torrey shambled across the floor, scratching the stubble of her head. She was wearing a torn flannel shirt three sizes too big for her. There was a smear of grease under her left eye. It took her a moment, tongue caught in the corner of her mouth, her brow furrowed in deliberation. "Plain stuff, I guess," she said finally, with a shrug of her shoulders. "Burned steak, potatoes with the skins on, boiled peas, and that—the kind of stuff his mother used to make. You know, like shanty Irish?"

Albert was busy that night—terrifically busy, the place packed—but when Willa Frank and her Palate sauntered in at nine-fifteen, he was ready for them. They had reservations (under an assumed name, of course—M. Cavil, party of two), and Eduardo was able to seat them immediately. In he came, breathless, the familiar phrase like a tocsin on his lips—"She's here!"—and out he fluttered again, with the drinks: one Glenlivet neat, one beer. Albert never glanced up.

On the stove, however, was a smallish pot. And in the pot were three tough scarred potatoes, eyes and dirt-flecked skin intact, boiling furiously; in and amongst them, dancing in the roiling water, were the contents of a sixteen-ounce can of Mother Hubbard's discount peas. Albert hummed to himself as he worked, searing chunks of grouper with shrimp, crab, and scallops in a big pan, chopping garlic and leeks, patting a scoop of foie gras into place atop a tournedo of beef. When, some twenty minutes later, a still-breathless Eduardo rocked through the door with their order, Albert took the yellow slip from him, and tore it in two without giving it a second glance. Zero hour had arrived.

"Marie!" he called, "Marie, quick!" He put on his most frantic face for her, the face of a man clutching at a wisp of grass at the very edge of a precipice.

Marie went numb. She set down her cocktail shaker and wiped her hands on her apron. There was catastrophe in the air. "What is it?" she gasped.

He was out of sea-urchin roe. And fish fumet. And Willa Frank had ordered the fillet of grouper oursinade. There wasn't a moment to lose—she had to rush over to the Edo Sushi House and borrow enough from Greg Takesue to last out the night. Albert had called ahead. It was okay. "Go, go," he said, wringing his big pale hands.

For the briefest moment, she hesitated. "But that's all the way across town—if it takes me an hour, I'll be lucky."

And now the matter-of-life-and-death look came into his eyes. "Go," he said. "I'll stall her."

No sooner had the door slammed behind Marie, than Albert took Fulgencio by the arm. "I want you to take a break," he shouted over the hiss of the sprayer. "Forty-five minutes. No, an hour."

Fulgencio looked up at him out of the dark Aztecan

slashes of his eyes. Then he broke into a broad grin. "No entiendo," he said.

Albert mimed it for him. Then he pointed at the clock, and after a flurry of nodding back and forth, Fulgencio was gone. Whistling ("Core 'ngrato," one of his late mother's favorites), Albert glided to the meat locker and extracted the hard-frozen lump of gray gristle and fat he'd purchased that afternoon at the local Safeway. Round steak, they called it, $2.39 a pound. He tore the thing from its plastic wrapping, selected his largest skillet, turned the heat up high beneath it, and unceremoniously dropped the frozen lump into the searing black depths of the pan.

Eduardo hustled in and out, no time to question the twin absences of Marie and Fulgencio. Out went the tournedos Rossini, the fillet of grouper oursinade, the veal loin rubbed with sage and coriander, the anguille alla veneziana, and the zuppa di datteri Alberto; in came the dirty plates, the congested forks, the wineglasses smeared with butter and lipstick. A great plume of smoke rose from the pan on the front burner. Albert went on whistling.

And then, on one of Eduardo's mad dashes through the kitchen, Albert caught him by the arm. "Here," he said, shoving a plate into his hand. "For the gentleman with Miss Frank."

Eduardo stared bewildered at the plate in his hand. On it, arranged with all the finesse of a blue-plate special, lay three boiled potatoes, a splatter of reduced peas, and what could only be described as a plank of meat, stiff and flat as the chopping block, black as the bottom of the pan.

"Trust me," Albert said, guiding the stunned waiter toward the door. "Oh, and here," thrusting a bottle of ketchup into his hand, "serve it with this."

Still, Albert didn't yield to the temptation to go to the porthole. Instead, he turned the flame down low beneath his saucepans, smoothed back the hair at his temples, and began counting—as slowly as in a schoolyard game—to fifty.

He hadn't reached twenty when Willa Frank, scintillating in a tomato-red Italian knit, burst through the door. Eduardo was right behind her, a martyred look on his face, his hands spread in supplication. Albert lifted his head, swelled his chest, and adjusted the great ball of his gut beneath the pristine field of his apron. He dismissed Eduardo with a flick of his hand, and turned to Willa Frank with the tight composed smile of a man running for office. "Excuse me," she was saying, her voice toneless and shrill, as Eduardo ducked out the door, "but are you the chef here?"

He was still counting: twenty-eight, twenty-nine.

"Because I just wanted to tell you"—she was so wrought up she could barely go on—"I never, never in my life ... "

"Shhhhh," he said, pressing a finger to his lips. "It's all right," he murmured, his voice as soothing and deep as a backrub. Then he took her gently by the elbow and led her to a table he'd set up between the stove and chopping block. The table was draped with a snowy cloth, set with fine crystal, china, and sterling borrowed from his mother. There was a single chair, a single napkin. "Sit," he said.

She tore away from him. "I don't want to sit," she protested, her black eyes lit with suspicion. The knit dress clung to her like a leotard. Her heels clicked on the linoleum. "You know, don't you?" she said, backing away from him. "You know who I am."

Huge, ursine, serene, Albert moved with her as if they were dancing. He nodded.

"But why—?" He could see the appalling vision of that

desecrated steak dancing before her eyes. "It's, it's like suicide."

A saucepan had appeared in his hand. He was so close to her he could feel the grid of her dress through the thin yielding cloth of his apron. "Hush," he purred, "don't think about it. Don't think at all. Here," he said, lifting the cover from the pan, "smell this."

She looked at him as if she didn't know where she was. She gazed down into the steaming pan and then looked back up into his eyes. He saw the gentle, involuntary movement of her throat.

"Squid rings in aioli sauce," he whispered. "Try one."

Gently, never taking his eyes from her, he set the pan down on the table, plucked a ring from the sauce, and held it up before her face. Her lips—full, sensuous lips, he saw now, not at all the thin stingy flaps of skin he'd imagined—began to tremble. Then she tilted her chin ever so slightly, and her mouth dropped open. He fed her like a nestling.

First the squid: one, two, three pieces. Then a pan of lobster tortellini in a thick, buttery saffron sauce. She practically licked the sauce from his fingers. This time, when he asked her to sit, when he put his big hand on her elbow and guided her forward, she obeyed.

He glanced through the porthole and out into the dining room as he removed from the oven the little toast rounds with sun-dried tomatoes and baked Atascadero goat cheese. Jock's head was down, over his plate, the beer half gone, a great wedge of incinerated meat impaled on the tines of his fork. His massive jaw was working, his cheek distended as if with a plug of tobacco. "Here," Albert murmured, turning to Willa Frank and laying his warm, redolent hand over her eyes, "a surprise."

It was after she'd finished the taglierini alla pizzaiola, with its homemade fennel sausage and chopped tomatoes, and was experiencing the first rush of his glacé of grapefruit and Meyer lemon, that he asked about Jock. "Why him?" he said.

She scooped ice with a tiny silver spoon, licked a dollop of it from the corner of her mouth. "I don't know," she said, shrugging. "I guess I don't trust my own taste, that's all."

He lifted his eyebrows. He was leaning over her, solicitous, warm, the pan of Russian coulibiac of salmon, en brioche, with its rich sturgeon marrow and egg, held out in offering.

She watched his hands as he whisked the ice away and replaced it with the gleaming coulibiac. "I mean," she said, pausing as he broke off a morsel and fed it into her mouth, "half the time I just can't seem to taste anything, really," chewing now, her lovely throat dipping and rising as she swallowed, "and Jock—well, he hates *everything*. At least I know he'll be consistent." She took another bite, paused, considered. "Besides, to like something, to really like it and come out and say so, is taking a terrible risk. I mean, what if I'm wrong? What if it's really no good?"

Albert hovered over her. Outside it had begun to rain. He could hear it sizzling like grease in the alley. "Try this," he said, setting a plate of spiedino before her.

She was warm. He was warm. The oven glowed, the grill hissed, the scents of his creations rose about them, ambrosia and manna. "Um, good," she said, unconsciously nibbling at prosciutto and mozzarella. "I don't know," she said after a moment, her fingers dark with anchovy sauce, "I guess that's why I like fugu."

"Fugu?" Albert had heard of it somewhere. "Japanese, isn't it?"

She nodded. "It's a blowfish. They do it sushi or in little fried strips. But it's the liver you want. It's illegal here, did you know that?"

Albert didn't know.

"It can kill you. Paralyze you. But if you just nibble, just a little bit, it numbs your lips, your teeth, your whole mouth."

"What do you mean—like at the dentist's?" Albert was horrified. Numbs your lips, your mouth? It was sacrilege. "That's awful," he said.

She looked sheepish, looked chastised.

He swung to the stove and then back again, yet another pan in his hand. "Just a bite more," he coaxed.

She patted her stomach and gave him a great, wide, blooming smile. "Oh, no, no, Albert—can I call you Albert?—no, no, I couldn't."

"Here," he said, "here," his voice soft as a lover's. "Open up."

JOHN LANCHESTER

A WINTER MENU
From *The Debt to Pleasure*

WINSTON CHURCHILL WAS fond of saying that the Chinese ideogram for "crisis" is composed of the two characters which separately mean "danger" and "opportunity."

Winter presents the cook with a similar combination of threat and chance. It is, perhaps, winter which is responsible for a certain brutalization of the British national palate, and a concomitant affection for riotous sweet-and-sour combinations, aggressive pickles, pungent sauces, and ketchups. More on this later. But the threat of winter is also, put simply, that of an overreliance on stodge. Northern European readers will need no further elaboration: the "stodge" term, the stodge concept, covers a familiar universe of inept nursery food, hostile saturated fats, and intentful carbohydrates. (There is a sinister genius in the very *name* Brown Windsor Soup.) It is a style of cooking which has attained its apotheosis in England's public schools, and though I myself was spared the horrors of such an education—my parents, correctly judging my nature to be too fine-grained and sensitive, employed a succession of private tutors—I have vivid memories of my one or two visits to my brother during his incarceration in various gulags.

I remember the last of these safaris with particular clarity. I was eleven years old. My brother, then seventeen and on the brink of his final expulsion, was resident in a boarding school my father described as "towards the top of the second division." I think my parents had gone to the school in an attempt to persuade the headmaster not to expel Bartholomew, or perhaps he had won some dreary school art award. In any case, we were "given the tour." One of its most impressing features was the dormitory in which my brother slept. This was heated by a single knobbly metal pipe, painted black in ignorance of the laws of physics or in a conscious attempt to defy them, or in a deliberate effort to make the room even colder. The pipe had no effect whatsoever on the ambient temperature—Bartholomew and the nineteen other boys in the dormitory would regularly wake to find a generous layer of ice on the inside of windows—but was itself so hot that any skin contact resulted instantaneously in severe burns. The fact that school-uniform socks were mandatorily only of ankle length meant that the possibility of flesh-to-pipe contact was formidably high, so that (according to Bartholomew) the smell of burnt epidermis was a familiar feature of school life.

We had been invited to lunch. A long, low, panelled room, perfectly decent architecturally, housed a dozen trestle tables, each of which held what seemed to be an impossibly large number of noisy boys. The walls were hung with bad sludge-coloured paintings of defunct headmasters, a procession interrupted only by the most recent portrait, which was a large black-and-white photograph of a handsome sadist in an ermine-rimmed MA gown; and the one before it, which suggested either that the artist was a tragicomically inept doctrinaire cubist, or that Mr. R. B. Fenner-Crossway MA was in reality a dyspeptic pattern of mauve rhomboids. A gong was struck as we entered; the boys stood in a prurient scrutinizing silence as my parents and I, attached to a straggling procession of staff members, progressed the length of the hall to the high table, set laterally across the room. My brother was embarrassedly in tow. I could feel sweat behind my knees. A hulking Aryan prefect figure, an obvious thug, bully, and teacher's favorite, spoke words of Latin benediction into the hush.

We then sat down to a meal which Dante would have hesitated to invent. I was seated opposite my parents, between a spherical house matron and a silent French *assistant*. The first course was a soup in which pieces of undisguised and unabashed gristle floated in a mud-coloured sauce whose texture and temperature were powerfully reminiscent of mucus. Then a steaming vat was placed in the middle of the table, where the jowly, watch-chained headmaster presided. He plunged his serving arm into the vessel and emerged with a ladleful of hot food, steaming like fresh horse dung on a cold morning. For a heady moment I thought I was going to be sick. A plate of *soi-disant* cottage pie—the mince grey, the potato beige—was set in front of me.

"The boys call this 'mystery meat,'" confided the matron happily. I felt the *assistant* flinch. Other than that I don't remember (I can't imagine) what we talked about, and over the rest of the meal—as Swinburne's biographer remarked, *à propos* an occasion when his subject had misbehaved during a lecture on the subject of Roman sewage systems—"the Muse of history must draw her veil."

There is an erotics of dislike. It can be (I am indebted to a young friend for the helpful phrase) "a physical thing." Roland Barthes observes somewhere that the meaning of any list of likes and dislikes is to be found in its assertion of the fact that each of us has a body, and that this body is different from everybody else's. This is tosh. The real meaning of our dislikes is that they define us by separating us from what is outside us; they separate the self from the world in a way that mere banal liking cannot do. ("Gourmandism is an act of judgment, by which we give preference to those things which are agreeable to our taste over those which are not."—Brillat-Savarin) To like something is to want to ingest it, and in that sense is to submit to the world. To like something is to succumb, in a small but contentful way, to death. But dislike hardens the perimeter between the self and the world, and brings a clarity to the object isolated in its light. Any dislike is in some measure a triumph of definition, distinction, and discrimination—a triumph of life.

I am not exaggerating when I say that this visit to my brother at St. Botolph's (not its real name) was a defining moment in my development. The combination of human, aesthetic, and culinary banality formed a negative revelation of great power, and hardened the already burgeoning suspicion that my artist's nature isolated and separated me from my alleged fellowmen. France rather than England, art rather than society, separation rather than immersion, doubt and exile rather than yeomanly certainty, *gigot à quarante gousses d'ail* rather than roast lamb with mint sauce. "Two roads diverged in a wood, and I—I took the one less travelled by / And that has made all the" (important word coming up) "difference."

This might seem a lot of biographical significance to attribute to a single bad experience with a shepherd's pie. (I have sometimes tried to establish a distinction between cottage pie, made with beef leftovers, and shepherd's pie, made with lamb, but it doesn't seem to have caught on so I have abandoned it. They order these things differently in France.) Nevertheless I hope I have made my point about the importance of the cook's maintaining a proactive stance vis-à-vis the problem of the winter diet. Winter should be seen as an opportunity for the cook to demonstrate, through the culinary arts, his mastery of balance and harmony and his oneness with the seasons; to express the deep concordances of his own and nature's rhythms. The tastebuds should be titillated, flirted with, provoked. The following menu is an example of how this may be done. The flavours in it possess a certain quality of intensity suitable for those months of the year when one's tastebuds feel swaddled.

> *Blinis with Sour Cream and Caviar*
> *Irish Stew*
> *Queen of Puddings*

Of the many extant batter, pancake, and waffle dishes—*crêpes* and *galettes*, Swedish *krumkakor*, *sockerstruvor*, and *plättar*, Finnish *tattoriblinit*, generic Scandinavian *äggvåffla*, Italian *brigidini*, Belgian *gaufrettes*, Polish *nalesniki*, Yorkshire pudding—blinis are my personal favourite. The distinguishing characteristics of the blini, as a member of the happy family of pancakes, is that it is thick (as opposed to thin), nonfolding (as opposed to folding), and raised with yeast (as opposed to bicarbonate of soda); it is Russian; and like the Breton sarrasin pancake, it is made of buckwheat (as opposed to plain flour). Buckwheat is not a grass, and therefore not a cereal, and therefore does not fall under the protection of the goddess Ceres, the Roman deity who presided over agriculture. On her feast day, in a strangely evocative ceremony, foxes with their tails on fire were let loose in the Circus Maximus; nobody knows why. The Greek equivalent of Ceres was the goddess Demeter, mother of Persephone. It was in Demeter's honour that the Eleusinian mysteries were held, a legacy of the occasion when she was forced to reveal her divinity in order to explain why she was holding King Celeus's baby in the fire—no doubt a genuinely embarrassing and difficult to explain moment, even for a goddess.

Blinis. Sift 4 oz. buckwheat flour, mix with $\frac{1}{2}$ oz. yeast (dissolved in warm water) and $\frac{1}{4}$ pint warm milk, leave for fifteen minutes. Mix 4 oz. flour with $\frac{1}{2}$ pint milk, add 2 egg yolks, 1 tsp. sugar, 1 tbs. melted butter and a pinch of salt, whisk the two blends together. Leave for an hour. Add 2 whisked egg whites. Right. Now heat a heavy cast-iron frying pan of the type known in both classical languages as a *placenta*—which is, as everybody knows, not at all the same thing as the caul or wrapping in which the fetus lives when it is inside the womb. To be born in the caul, as I was, is a traditional indication of good luck, conferring second sight and immunity from death by drowning; preserved cauls used to attract a premium price from superstitious sailors. Freud was born in the caul, as was the hero of his favourite novel, David Copperfield. Sometimes, if there is more than one sibling in the family, one of them born in the caul and the other not, the obvious difference between them in terms of luck, charm, and talent can be woundingly great, and the fact of one of them having been born in the caul can cause intense jealousy and anger, particularly when that gift is accompanied by other personal and artistic distinctions. But one must remember that while it is disagreeable to be on the receiving end of such emotions it is of course far more degrading to be the person who experiences them. To claim that one's five-year-old brother pushed one out of a treehouse, for instance, and caused one to break one's arm, when in fact one fell in the course of trying to climb higher up the tree in order to gain a vantage from which one could spy into the nanny's room, is a despicable way of retaliating for that younger brother's having charmed the nanny by capturing her likeness with five confident strokes of finger paint and then shyly handing the artwork to her with a little dedicatory poem (This is for you, Mary-T / Because you are the one for me) written across the top in yellow crayon.

When smoke starts to rise out of the pan add the batter in assured dollops, bearing in mind that each little dollop is to become a blini when it grows up, and that the quantities given here are sufficient for six. Turn them over when bubbles appear on top.

Serve the pancakes with sour cream and caviar. Sour cream is completely straightforward and if you need any advice or guidance about it then, for you, I feel only pity. Caviar, the cleaned and salted roe of the sturgeon, is a little more complicated. The surprisingly un-German, Wisconsin-born sociologist Thorstein Veblen formulated something he called "the scarcity theory of value," to argue that objects increase in value in direct proportion to their perceived rarity rather than their intrinsic merit or interest. In other words, if Marmite was as hard to come by as caviar, would it be as highly prized? (Of course, there is an experimentally determinable answer to this, because we know that among British expatriate communities commodities such as Marmite and baked beans have virtually the status of bankable currency. When my brother was living near Arles he once, in the course of a game of poker with an actor who had retired to run a shop targeting nostalgic Englishpeople, won a year's supply of chocolate digestive biscuits. In the ensuing twelve months he put on ten pounds which he was never to lose.) Lurking in this idea is the question of whether or not caviar is—not to put too fine a point on it—"worth it." All I can say in response to that is to point to the magic of the sturgeon, producer of these delicate exotic rare expensive eggs, and one of the oldest animals on the planet, in existence in something closely resembling its current form for about two hundred million years. The fish grows to twelve feet in length, and has a snout with which it roots for food underneath the sea bed; when you eat caviar you are partaking of this mysterious juxtaposition of the exquisite and the atavistic. And spending a lot of money into the bargain, of course. Caviar is graded according to the size of its grains, which in turn vary according to the size of the fish from which they are taken: *beluga* being the biggest, then *ossetra*, then *sevruga*; *ossetra*, whose eggs span the spectrum of colours from dirty battleship to occluded sunflower, is my roe of choice. Much of the highest grade caviar carries the designation *malassol*, which means "lightly salted."

The process by which the correct level of salting is applied to Volga caviar is insufficiently well known. The master taster—a rough-and-ready seeming fellow he is likely to be, too, with a knit cap on his head, a gleam in his eye, and a dagger in his boot—takes a single egg into his mouth and rolls it around his palate. By applying his almost mystically fine amalgam of experience and talent, he straightaway knows how much salt to add to the sturgeon's naked roe. The consequences of any inaccuracy are disastrous, gastronomically and economically (hence the dagger). There are analogies with the way in which an artist—I am not thinking only of myself—can judge the quality of a work of art with a rapidity that appears instantaneous, as if the acts of visual apprehension and of critical estimation are simultaneous, or even as if the judgment infinitesimally precedes the encounter with the artwork, as in one of the paradoxes of quantum physics, or as in a dream one constructs an elaborate narrative, expanding confidently across time and space and involving many fragmentations of person and object—a deceased relative who is also a tuba, an airplane flight to Argentina which is also a memory of one's first sexual experience, a misfiring revolver which is also a wig—before coming to a terrifying climax with the noise of the siren ringing out across London to announce the imminent outbreak of nuclear war, a sound which resolves itself into the banal but infinitely reassuring domestic event that somehow contained within it the whole of the preceding story: the happy jangling of an alarm clock, or the arrival at the front door of one's favourite postman, carrying an inconveniently large parcel.

Caviar is sometimes eaten by chess players as a way of rapidly consuming a considerable quantity of easily digestible protein, without any of the stupefying effects of a bona fide meal. It is an excellent cold weather food. It is not available on cross-channel ferries such as this one, though in many respects it would be an ideal mid-journey picnic. There is, however, a deliriously vulgar "caviar bar" at Heathrow Terminal Four, just to the right of the miniature Harrods.

The chemistry of yeast, incidentally, has not yet been entirely deciphered by scientists. I take this to be a reminder that there are still some mysteries left, some corners and crevices of the universe, which are still opaque to us. For me, this dish, perhaps because of its connection or nonconnection with Demeter (for, as Buddhism teaches us, nonconnection can be a higher form of connection), is irrevocably bound up with the idea of mystery. I must confess to taking some pleasure from the fact that if it is not possible to diminish the magic of rising yeast then perhaps there are one or two corners of poetry left in a world that at times seems depleted and diminished by explanation. I myself have always disliked being called a "genius." It is fascinating to notice how quick people have been to intuit this aversion and avoid using the term.

With liberal additions of sour cream and caviar the above recipe—I prefer the old-fashioned spelling "receipt," but it was pointed out to me that "if you call it that nobody will have a f***ing clue what you're talking about"—represents adequate quantities for six people as a starter, providing several blinis each. Perhaps I have already said that. It is only sensible to construct an entire meal out of blinis if one is planning to spend the rest of the day out on the *taiga*, boasting about women and shooting bears.

Irish stew is uncomplicated, though none the less tasty for that. It is forever associated in my mind (my heart, my palate) with my Cork-born, Skibbereen-raised nanny, Mary-Theresa. She was one of the few fixed points of a childhood that was for its first decade or so distinctly itinerant. My father's business interests kept him on the move; my mother's former profession—the stage—had given her a taste for travel and the sensation of movement. She liked to live not so much out of suitcases as out of trunks, creating a home that at the same time contained within it the knowledge that this was the *illusion* of home, a stage set or theatrical redescription of safety and embowering domesticity; her wall-hung carpets and portable bibelots (a lacquered Chinese screen, a lean, malignly upright Egyptian cat made of onyx) were a way of saying "Let's pretend." She would, I think, have preferred to regard motherhood as merely another feat of impersonation; but it was as if an intermittently amusing cameo part had gruellingly protracted itself, and what was intended to be an experimental production (King Lear as a senile brewery magnate, Cordelia on rollerskates), had turned into an inadvertent *Mousetrap*, with my mother stuck in a frumpy role she had only taken on in the first place as a favour to the hard-pressed director. To put it another way, she treated parenthood as analogous to the parts forced on an actor past his prime or of eccentric physique who has been obliged to specialize in "characters."

She was ironic, distracted, and self-pitying, with a way of implying that, now that the best things in life were over, she would take on *this* role. She would check one's fingernails or take one to the circus with the air of someone bravely concealing an unfavourable medical prognosis: the children must never know! But she also had a public mode in which she played at being a mother in the way that a very *very* distinguished actress, caught overnight in the Australian outback (train derailed by dead wallaby or flash flood), is forced to put up at a tiny settlement where, she is half-appalled and half-charmed to discover, the feisty pioneers have been preparing for weeks to put on, this very same evening, under powered electric lights, a production of *Hamlet*. Discovering the identity of their newcomer (via a blurred photograph in a torn-out magazine clipping brandished by a stammering admirer) the locals insist that she take a, no *the*, starring role; she prettily demurs; they anguishedly insist; she becomingly surrenders, on the condition that she play the smallest and least likely of roles—the gravedigger, say. And gives a performance which, decades later, the descendants of the original cast still sometimes discuss as they rock on their porches to watch the only train of the day pass silhouetted against the huge ochres and impossibly elongated shadows of the desert sunset ... that was the spirit in which my mother "did" being a mother. To be her child during these public episodes was to be uplifted, irradiated, fortune's darling. But if this, as has recently been observed to me, "makes her sound like a total nightmare," then I am omitting the way in which one was encouraged to collude in her role-playing, and was also allowed great freedom of manoeuvre by it. With a part of oneself conscripted to act the other role in whatever production she was undertaking—duet or ensemble, Brecht or Pinter, Ibsen or

Stoppard or Aeschylus—a considerable amount of one's emotional space was left vacant, thanks to her essential and liberating lack of interest.

So travel and the condition of itinerancy did not bother my mother, which is just as well as it was a fundamental aspect of my father's business activities. I therefore had a mobile childhood in which the rites of passage were geographically as well as temporally distinct. Thus I have somewhere a maltreated red leather photograph album with a picture in it of me holding my mother's hand; I am looking into the camera with an air of suppressed triumph as I proudly model my first-ever pair of long trousers. The proliferation of out-of-focus yacht masts in the background gives less of a clue than it should: Cowes? Portofino? East Looe? Another picture shows a view from the outside of the high-windowed, difficult-to-heat ground-floor flat in Bayswater (still in my possession) where my father provided the first external reflection of the inner vocational light I felt glimmering within me: he picked up a watercolour I had made that afternoon (hothouse mimosa and dried lavender in a glass jar) and said, "D'you know, I think the lad's got something." That memory brings with it the smell of the parquet flooring which, on otherwise unoccupied afternoons, I used to dig up with my fingers, less for the pleasure of vandalism than for the heady and magically comforting odour of the gummy resin that bound the oblong blocks in place. When you'd dug up a tile, however carefully you put it back, it somehow never looked the same again. That parquet pattern, arranged so that the four-tile squares were aligned with the corners of the room in the shape of a squat diamond, had an air of interpretability, of cabalistic significance; as if, gazed at long enough or hard enough, it would be bound eventually to yield a meaning, a clue. Or our flat in Paris, off the rue d'Assas in the 6ème, still vivid to me as the location for my first encounter with the death of a pet: a hamster called Hercule who had been placed in my brother's charge by our sinister concierge's grandson during their August visit to relatives in Normandy. My father wore a black tie when he went downstairs to break the news.

In these early years Mary-Theresa was a constant presence, in the first instance as a nanny and subsequently as a *bonne* or maid-of-all-work. Although cooking was not central to her function in the household, she would venture into the kitchen on those not infrequent occasions when whoever was employed to be our cook—a Dostoevskian procession of knaves, dreamers, drunkards, visionaries, bores, and frauds, every man his own light, every man his own bushel—was absent; though she *had* left our employ by the most memorable of these occasions, the time when Mitthaug, our counterstereotypically garrulous and optimistic Norwegian cook with a special talent for pickling, failed to arrive in time to make the necessary preparations for an important dinner party because (as it turned out) he had been run over by a train.

In these circumstances Mary-Theresa would, with an attractive air of ceremonial determination, don the blue-fringed apron she kept for specifically this emergency, and advance purposefully into the kitchen to emerge later with one of the dishes which, after extensive intrafamilial debates, she had been trained to cook: fish pie, omelette, roast chicken, and steak and kidney pudding; or alternatively she would prepare her *spécialité*, Irish stew. As a result the aroma of this last dish became something of a unifying theme in the disparate locations of my upbringing, a binding agent whose action in coalescing these various locales into a consistent, individuated, remembered narrative—into my story—

is, I would propose, not unlike the binding action supplied in various recipes by cream, butter, flour, arrowroot, *beurre manié*, blood, ground almonds (a traditional English expedient, not to be despised), or, as in the recipe I am about to give, by the more dissolvable of two different kinds of potato. When Mary-Theresa had to be dismissed it was perhaps the smell and flavour of this dish that I missed most.

Assemble your ingredients. It should be admitted that authorities differ as to which cut of meat to use in this dish. I have in my time read three sources who respectively prefer "boned lamb shanks or leftover lamb roast," "middle end of neck of lamb," and "best end of neck lamb chops." My own view is that any of these cuts is acceptable in what is basically a peasant dish (a comment on its history, not its flavour). Mutton is of course more flavoursome than lamb, although it has become virtually impossible to obtain. There used to be a butcher who sold mutton not far from our house in Norfolk, but he died. As for the preference expressed by some people for boned lamb in an Irish stew, I can only say that Mary-Theresa used to insist on the osseous variation, with its extra flavour as well as the beguiling hint of gelatinousness provided by the marrow. Three pounds of lamb: scrag or middle of neck, or shank, ideally with the bone still in. One and a half pounds of firm-fleshed potatoes: Bishop or Pentland Javelin if using British varieties, otherwise interrogate your grocer. One and a half pounds of floury potatoes, intended to dissolve in the manner alluded to above. In Britain: Maris Piper or King Edward. Or ask. There used to be a very good grocer at the corner of rue Cassette and rue Chevalier in the 6ème, but I don't suppose he's there anymore. (Science has not given us a full account of the difference between floury and waxy potatoes. If the reader is having a problem identifying to what category his potato belongs, he should drop it into a solution containing one part salt to eleven parts water: floury potatoes sink.) One and a half pounds of sliced onions. A selection of herbs to taste—oregano, a bay leaf, thyme, marjoram. If using dry varieties—about two teaspoons. Salt. Trim the lamb into cutlets and procure a casserole that's just big enough. Peel the potatoes and slice them thickly. Layer the ingredients as follows: layer hard potatoes; layer onions; layer lamb; layer soft potatoes; layer onions; layer lamb; repeat as necessary and finish with a thick layer of all remaining potatoes. Sprinkle each layer with salt and herbs. You will of course not be able to do that if you have been following this recipe without reading it through in advance. Let that be a lesson to you. Add cold water down the interstices of meat and vegetables until it insinuates up to the top. Put a lid on it. Cook for three hours in an oven at gas mark two. You will find that the soft potatoes have dissolved into the cooking liquid. Serves six trencherpersons. The ideological purity of this recipe is very moving.

The broad philosophical distinction between types of stew is between preparations that involve an initial cooking of some kind—frying or sautéing or whatever it may be—and those that do not. Irish stew is the paladin of the latter type of stew; other members of the family include the Lancashire Hot Pot, which is distinguishable from Irish stew only by the optional inclusion of kidneys and the fact that in the latter stages of cooking the British version of the dish is browned with the lid off. The similarity between the two dishes testifies to the close cultural affinities between Lancashire and Ireland; it was in Manchester that my father "discovered" Mary-Theresa working, as he put it, "in a blacking factory"—in reality through a business colleague who had hired her in advance of his wife's parturition, going so far as to employ a private detective to check her references, and then dismissing her when it turned out that his spouse was undergoing a phantom pregnancy. Boiled mutton is a cousin to these preparations, and an underrated dish in its own right, being especially good when eaten with its time-honoured accompaniment ("It gives an epicure the vapours / To eat boiled mutton without capers"—Ogden Nash); one should also take into account the hearty, Germano-Alsatian dish *backenoff*, made with mutton, pork, beef, and potatoes; soothing *blanquette de veau*, exempted from initial browning but thickened by cream at the last moment; and of course the twin classic *daubes à la Provençale* and *à l'Avignonnaise*. In France, indeed, the generic name for this type of stew—cooked from cold—is *daube*, after the *daubière*, a pot with a narrow neck and a bulging swollen middle reminiscent of the Buddha's stomach.

In the other kind of stew, whose phylum might well be the sauté or braise, the ingredients are subjected to an initial cooking at high temperature, in order to promote the processes of thickening and binding (where flour or another such agent is used) and also to encourage a preliminary exchange of flavours. As Huckleberry Finn puts it: "In a barrel of odds and ends it is different; things get mixed up, and the juice kind of swaps around, and things go better." Notice that the initial cooking does not "seal in the juices," or anything of the sort—science has shown us that no such action takes place. (I suspect that this canard derives from the fact that searing often provides a touch of browned, burnt flavour gratifying to the palate.) Stews of this sort include the justly feared British beef stew, as well as the beery Belgian *carbonade Flamande*; the *gibelottes*, *matelotes*, and *estouffades* of the French provinces; *navarin* of young lamb and baby vegetables, with its sly rustic allusion to infanticide; the spicy, harissa-enlivened *tagines* of North Africa; the warming *broufado* of the Rhône boatmen; the *boeuf à la gardiane* beloved by the Camargue cowboys, after whose job it is named; the homely international clichés of *coq au vin* and *gulyas*; surprisingly easy to prepare Beef Stroganoff, so handy for unexpected visitors; all types of *ragout* and *ragu*; *stufatino alla Romana*; *stufato di manzo* from northern Italy; *estofat de bou* from proud Catalonia. I could go on. Notice the difference between the things for which French aristocrats are remembered—the Vicomte de Chateaubriand's cut of fillet, the Marquis de Béchameil's sauce—and the inventions for which Britain remembers its defunct eminences: the cardigan, the wellington, the sandwich.

One authority writes: "Whereas the soul of a *daube* resides in a pervasive unity—the transformation of individual quantities into a single character, a sauté should comprehend an interplay among entities, each jealous of distinctive flavours and textures—but united in harmony by the common veil of sauce." That is magnificently said. One notes that in the United States the now-preferred metaphor to describe the assimilation of immigrants is that of the "salad bowl," supplanting the old idea of the "melting pot," the claim being that the older term is thought to imply a loss of original cultural identity. In other words the melting pot used to be regarded as a sauté, but has come to be seen as a daube.

My choice of pudding is perhaps more controversial than either of the preceding two courses. Queen of Puddings is an appropriately wintry dish, and considerably easier to make than it looks. Mary-Theresa would always serve it after the Irish stew, and it was the first dish I was ever taught to make for myself. Bread crumbs, 5 oz. thereof; 1 tbs. vanilla sugar; the grated rind of a lemon; 2 oz. butter and a pint of hot milk; leave to cool; beat in four egg yolks; pour into a greased shallow dish and bake at gas mark four until the custard is barely set. Gently smear two warmed tablespoonfuls of your favourite jam on top. Are you a strawberry person or a blackcurrant person? No matter. Now whisk four egg whites in a copper bowl until the peaks stand up on their own. Mix in sugar, whisk. Fold in a total of 4 oz. sugar with the distinctive wrist-turning motion of somebody turning the dial of a very big radio. Put this egg-white mixture on top of the jam. Sprinkle a little more sugar on top and bake for a quarter of an hour. One of the disappointing features of this pudding is that it is almost impossible, in writing about or discussing it, to avoid the double genitive "of" which used so to upset Flaubert. But one of the charms of Queen of Puddings (see!) is that it exploits both of the magical transformations the egg can enact. On the one hand, the incorporation of air into the coagulating egg white proteins—the stiffening of egg whites up to eight times their original volume, as exploited in the *soufflé* and its associates. On the other hand, the coagulation of egg yolk proteins—as in custard, mayonnaise, hollandaise, and all variations thereof. Always remember that the classic sauces of French cooking should be approached with respect but without fear.

The first time I made Queen of Puddings was in the cramped, elongated kitchen of our Paris *appartement*. The almost untenable lateral constriction of space in the scullery (which is what it really was) was compensated for, or outwitted by, an ingenious system of folding compartments for storing crockery and utensils. Beyond this room was a small larder from which Mary-Theresa would emerge red-faced, lopsidedly carrying a gas canister, like a milkmaid struggling with a churn. She always insisted on installing a full canister before she began to cook, the legacy of an earlier incident in which she had run out of gas halfway through a stew and had to change canisters in the middle of the process. In the course of doing so she made some technical error, which led to a small explosion that left her temporarily without eyebrows. There was known to be a gremlin in that kitchen who specialized in emptying canisters which by all logic should have been full: the supply had a tendency to run out in the middle of elaborate culinary feats. My father once remarked that all you had to do to run out of gas was merely utter the word "koulibiac."

"It's time for you to learn about cooking," Mary-Theresa said, pressing a metal implement into my palm and holding my hand as we together enacted the motions of whisking, at first using my whole arm and then isolating the relevant movement of the wrist. I experienced for the first time the divinely comforting feeling of wire on copper through an intervening layer of egg, a sound to me which is in its effect the exact opposite (though like most "exact opposites" in some sense generically similar) to the noise of nails on a blackboard, or of polystyrene blocks being rubbed together. (Does anybody know what evolutionary function is served by this peculiarly powerful and well-developed response? Some genetic memory of—what? The sound of a sabertoothed tiger scrabbling up a rockface with unsheathed claws? Woolly mammoths, pawing the frozen earth as they prepare their halitotic and evilly tusked stampede?)

It was my mother, oddly, who was most upset by the revelation of Mary-Theresa's criminality. I say "oddly" because relations between them hadn't been entirely without the usual frictions between employer and employee, added to which were elements of the war (eternal, undeclared, like all the hardest fought wars—those between the gifted and the ordinary, the old and the young, the short and the rest) between the beautiful and the plain, an extra dimension to this conflict being supplied by the fact that Mary-Theresa's looks, slightly lumpy and large-pored, with the ovoid-faced sluggish solemnity of the natural mouth breather, were perfectly calibrated to set off my mother's hyacinthine looks: her eyelashes were as long and delicate as a young man's; her subtle colouration was thrown into relief by the over-robust blossoming of Mary-Theresa's country complexion; and the expressive farouche beauty of her eyes (more than one admirer having blurtingly confessed that until meeting her he hadn't understood the meaning of the term "lynx-eyed") was only emphasized by the exophthalmic naiveté of Mary-Theresa's countenance, which had a look that never failed to be deeply bullyable. Furthermore, there was also a tension of the type—mysterious and uncategorizable but immediately perceptible, as present and as indecipherable as an argument in a foreign language—that occurs between two women who do not "get on." This was apparent in the certain *ad feminam* crispness with which my mother gave Mary-Theresa instructions and issued reprimands, as well as Mary-Theresa's demeanour, with just the faintest bat-squeak of mimed reluctance as she acted on my mother's ukases, her manner managing to impute an almost limitless degree of willfulness, irrationality, and ignorance of basic principles of domestic science on the part of the spoiled chatelaine of the chaise longue (perhaps I paraphrase slightly). All this was underscored by the contrast with Mary-Theresa's attitude to what my mother would call "the boys," meaning my father (never boyish, incidentally, not even in the blazered photographs of his youth, which admittedly record a period before most people felt entirely unselfconscious in front of a camera) and me and my brother: Mary-Theresa's manner with us always having a friendly directness that my mother, with finer perceptive instruments than we possessed, I think saw as not being wholly free of all traces of flirtatiousness. (Has any work of art in any medium ever had a better title than *Women Beware Women*?) All this, of course, would be apparent (or not apparent) in dialogues which, if transcribed, would run, in full; as follows:

MOTHER: Mary-Theresa, would you please change the flower water.
MARY-THERESA: Yes ma'am.

—the live flame of human psychology having flickered through this exchange like the sparrow flitting through the hall in Bede's history. (There is an erotics of dislike.) Anyway, notwithstanding that, my mother reacted badly to what happened. It began one sharp morning in April. My mother was at her mirror.

"Darling, have you seen my earrings?"

Remarks of this nature, usually addressed to my father but sometimes absentmindedly to me or my brother, more as local representatives of our gender than as full paternal surrogates, were a routine occurrence. My father was in the small dressing room next door that opened off their bedroom, engaged in the mysteries of adult male grooming (so much more evolved and sophisticated than the knee-scrubbing, hair-combing, and sock-straightening that my brother and I would quotidianly undertake): shaving (with a bowl and jug full of hot water drawn from the noisy bathroom taps and then thoughtfully carried to his adjoining lair in order to make way for the full drama and complexity of my mother's toilette), eau-de-cologning, tie-tying, hair-patting, cuff-shooting, and collar-brushing.

The earrings in question were two single emeralds, each set off by a band of white gold, in my view possessing the unusual quality of being vulgar through understatement. They were the gift of a mysterious figure from my mother's early life, the love-smitten scion of a Midlands industrial family, who (in the version that emerged through veils of "This weather reminds me of someone I was once very fond of" and "I always wear it today because it was a special day for someone I'd prefer not to speak about") had refused to accept the earrings back when she attempted to return them, and had subsequently run away to join the Foreign Legion. His relatives managed to catch him in time because he was struck down in Paris (in the course of what was supposed to be his last meal as a free man) by a polluted *moule*. In later life he was knighted for services to industry before dying in a Caribbean seaplane crash. The gleaming banks of seafood on display at the great Parisian brasseries are like certain politicians in that they manage to be impressive without necessarily inspiring absolute confidence.

"Which earrings?"

"No, darling, Maman is busy"—this to me—"the emeralds."

"Not in the morning!"

"I wasn't going to wear them, darling—I'm looking in the box."

"Have you tried the box?"

The formulaic, litanic quality of these exchanges is perhaps perceptible in that reply of my father's.

"Of *course* I wouldn't wear them now I'm not an *idiot*," said my mother.

The discovery of the earrings hidden under Mary-Theresa's mattress in the traditional little attic room of the *bonne* was, to my mother especially, a shock. It was the gendarmes who found the cherished jewelry—the gendarmes whom my father had called, reacting to my mother's insistence at least partly in a spirit of exhausted retaliation, a cross between an attempt to show up my mother's as-he-said hysteria and an *après-moi-le-déluge* desire to give up and let the worst happen (the worst being, in his imagination, I don't know quite what; I think he thought either that the emeralds would turn up somewhere they had been irrefutably left by my mother—beside the toothpaste, down the side of a chair—or that they would have been stolen by the concierge, an especially grim widowed Frenchwoman *du troisième âge*, about whom my father observed that "it's very hard to imagine what Madame Dupont's husband must have been like, once one accepts that circumstances can be shown to rule out Dr. Crippen"). But I think my father had underestimated the French seriousness about property and money. The young gendarme to whom he made the initial report, filling out a form of great complexity, was genuinely and visibly affected by news of the value of the missing items, and turned up at our flat the next day, good-looking and polite, with his *képi* clutched in front of him in a gesture which made him look like a schoolboy apologizing for being late. The policeman, very fair, with the flaxen hair of some Normans, had the air and the manners of being too nobly born for his job—a *vicomte*'s younger son, perhaps, putting in his year or two on the beat (*noblesse oblige* being one of those expressions whose Frenchness is not accidental) before leapfrogging to some glamorously deskbound job in the apparat, tipped for the top. He first sequestered himself in the drawing room with my mother, who ordered tea. And then, before beginning his search, he spoke to my brother and me, first together, with our mother present, and then separately (this arrangement, and my mother's scented departure, smiling and glancing reassuringly and perfect-motherishly backward, being conveyed between the two of them with an apparently wordless complicity that in another context would have seemed tinglingly adulterous). The general overwhelmingness of the occasion was augmented by the feeling that the imputation of theft, once aired, had somehow taken on a life of its own—as if the allegation, when voiced, was, like magnesium, spontaneously combustible when exposed to oxygen. As indeed it turned out to be, though as so often happens with adult dramas that take place in front of children, the first stages were hidden and offstage, perceptible only through the distortions that affected our day. These began when, after potterings and meanderings around the flat on the part of the gendarme—while we sat by the drawing room with Mary-Theresa and our mother, my brother as usual daubing away with an indoor easel and myself reading, I happen to remember, *Le Petit Prince*—he came back into the room and, avoiding all our gazes, asked my mother if he could speak to her alone for a moment.

And now I have to admit to feeling a considerable degree of relief. (There is no more powerful emotion.) These meditations on winter food have been written—and I set down these words with a sense of rabbit-brandishing, curtain-swishing-aside, non-sawn-through-female-assistant-displaying bravura—as the introductory note attested they would be, in midsummer, at the start of my "hols." To disclose the truth in full, I have been dictating these reflections on board a ferry during an averagely rough crossing between Portsmouth and St-Malo, a journey I must admit to having often found frustratingly intermediate in length—neither the hour-long hop to Calais, allowing time merely for a cup of bad coffee, the crossword, and a couple of turns of the deck, nor the day-long full-dress crossing of Newcastle to Göteborg or Harwich to Bremerhaven, which at least offer a gesture in the direction of a proper sea voyage. Portsmouth–St-Malo does, however, have the benefit of depositing one in the most satisfactory, or least unsatisfactory, of the French port towns (an admittedly uncompetitive title, given that Calais is unspeakable, that Boulogne has seen the planners finish what the Allied bombardment began, that Dieppe involves an unthinkable departure from Newhaven, that Roscoff is a fishing village, and that Ostend is in Belgium). With the aid of a seductively miniaturized Japanese dictaphone I have been murmuring excoriations of English cooking while sitting in the self-service canteen amid microwaved bacon and congealing eggs; I have spoken to myself of our old flat in Bayswater while sitting on the deck and admiring the dowagerly carriage of a passing Panamanian supertanker; I have pushed through the jostling crowd in the video arcade while cudgelling myself to remember whether Mary-Theresa used jam or jelly in her Queen of Puddings, before it struck me (as I tripped over a heedlessly strewn rucksack outside the *bureau de change*) that she had indeed used jam but had insisted on its being sieved—a refinement which, as the reader will not have been slow to notice, I have decided to omit. In all memory there is a degree of fallenness; we are all exiles from our own pasts, just as, on looking up from a book, we discover anew our banishment from the bright worlds of imagination and fantasy. A cross-channel ferry, with its overfilled ashtrays and vomiting children, is as good a place as any to reflect on the angel who stands with a flaming sword in front of the gateway to all our yesterdays.

The sea's summer glitter is made tolerable by my newly

acquired pair of sunglasses, a proprietary brand of which you have almost certainly heard. Today's breeze is a degree or two cooler than one might in all justice expect it to be, though the chill is kept off by the unfamiliar warmth of my new deerstalker, which I am currently wearing with the earflaps lowered but with the chinstrap untied. I now feel the need to take a stretch around the promenade and inhale deep drafts of sea air through the slight tickle of my false moustache.

ERICA BAUERMEISTER

LILLIAN

LILLIAN HAD BEEN four years old when her father left them, and her mother, stunned, had slid into books like a seal into water. Lillian had watched her mother submerge and disappear, sensing instinctively even at her young age the impersonal nature of a choice made simply for survival, and adapting to the niche she would now inhabit, as a watcher from the shore of her mother's ocean.

In this new life, Lillian's mother's face became a series of book covers, held in place where eyes, nose, or mouth might normally appear. Lillian soon learned that book covers could forecast moods much like facial expressions, for Lillian's mother swam deeply into the books she read, until the personality of the protagonist surrounded her like a perfume applied by an indiscriminate hand. Lillian was never sure who would greet her at the breakfast table, no matter that the bathrobe, the hair, the feet were always the same. It was like having a magician for a mother, although Lillian always suspected that the magicians she saw at birthday parties went home and turned back into portly men with three children and grass that needed mowing. Lillian's mother simply finished one book and turned into the next.

Her mother's preoccupation with books was not an entirely silent occupation. Long before Lillian's father had left them, long before Lillian knew that words had a meaning beyond the music of their inflections, her mother had read aloud to her. Not from cardboard books with their primary-colored illustrations and monosyllabic rhymes. Lillian's mother dismissed the few that entered their house under the guise of gifts.

"There's no need to eat potatoes, Lily," she would say, "when four-course meals are ready and waiting." And she would read.

For Lillian's mother, every part of a book was magic, but what she delighted in most were the words themselves. Lillian's mother collected exquisite phrases and complicated rhythms, descriptions that undulated across a page like cake batter pouring into a pan, read aloud to put the words in the air, where she could hear as well as see them.

"Oh, Lily," her mother would say, "listen to this one. It sounds green, don't you think?"

And Lillian, who was too young to know that words were not colors and thoughts were not sounds, would listen while the syllables fell quietly through her, and she would think, *This is what green sounds like.*

After Lillian's father left, however, things changed, and she increasingly came to see herself simply as a mute and obliging assistant in the accumulation of exceptional phrases, or, if they happened to be somewhere public, as her mother's social cover. People would smile at the vision of a mother nurturing her daughter's literary imagination, but Lillian knew better. In Lillian's mind, her mother was a museum for words; Lillian was an annex, necessary when space became limited in the original building.

Not surprisingly, when it came time for Lillian to learn to read, she balked. It was not only an act of defiance, although by the time kindergarten started, Lillian was already feeling toward books private surges of aggression that left her both confused and slightly powerful. But it wasn't just that. In Lillian's world, books were covers and words were sound and movement, not form. She could not equate the rhythms that had insinuated themselves into her imagination with what she saw on the paper. The letters lay prone across the page, arranged in unyielding precision. There was no magic on the page itself, Lillian saw; and while this increased Lillian's estimation of her mother's abilities, it did nothing to further her interest in books.

It was during Lillian's first skirmishes with the printed word that she discovered cooking. In the time since Lillian's father had left, housework had become for Lillian's mother a travel destination rarely reached; laundry, a friend one never remembered to call. Lillian picked up these skills by following her friends' mothers around their homes, while the mothers pretended not to notice, dropping hints about bleach or changing a vacuum bag as if it were just one more game children played. Lillian learned, and soon her home—at least the lower four and a half feet of it—developed a certain domestic routine.

But it was the cooking that occurred in her friends' homes that fascinated Lillian—the aromas that started calling to her just when she had to go home in the evening. Some smells were sharp, an olfactory clatter of heels across a hardwood floor. Others felt like the warmth in the air at the far end of summer. Lillian watched as the scent of melting cheese brought children languidly from their rooms, saw how garlic made them talkative, jokes expanding into stories of their days. Lillian thought it odd that not all mothers seemed to see it—Sarah's mother, for instance, always cooked curry when she was fighting with her teenage daughter, its smell rocketing through the house like a challenge. But Lillian soon realized that many people did not comprehend the language of smells that to Lillian was as obvious as a billboard.

Perhaps, Lillian thought, smells were for her what printed words were for others, something alive that grew and changed. Not just the smell of rosemary in the garden, but the scent on her hands after she had picked some for Elizabeth's mother, the aroma mingling with the heavy smell of chicken fat and garlic in the oven, the after-scent on the couch cushions the next day. The way, ever after, Elizabeth was always part of rosemary for Lillian, how Elizabeth's round face had crinkled up into laughter when Lillian had pushed the small, spiky branch near her nose.

Lillian liked thinking about smells, the same way she liked the weight of Mary's mother's heavy saucepan in her hands, or the way vanilla slipped into the taste of warm milk. She remembered often the time Margaret's mother had let her help with a white sauce, playing out the memory in her head the way some children try to recover, bit by detail, the moments of a favorite birthday party. Margaret had pouted, because she was, she declared stoutly, never allowed to help in the kitchen, but Lillian had ignored all twinges of loyalty and climbed up on the chair and stood, watching the butter melt across the pan like the farthest reach of a wave sinking into the sand, then the flour, at first a hideous, clumping thing destroying the image until it was stirred and stirred, Margaret's mother's hand over Lillian's on the wooden spoon when she wanted to mash the clumps, moving instead slowly, in circles, gently, until the flour-butter became smooth, smooth, until again the image was changed by the milk, the sauce expanding to contain the liquid and Lillian thought each time that the sauce could hold no more, that the sauce would break into solid and liquid, but it never did. At the last minute, Margaret's mother raised the cup of milk away from the pot, and Lillian looked at the sauce, an untouched snowfield, its smell the feeling of quiet at the end of an illness, when the world is starting to feel gentle and welcoming once again.

When Lillian reached the age of eight, she began to take over the cooking in her own household. Her mother raised no objections; food had not disappeared along with Lillian's father, but while it was not impossible to cook while reading, it was problematic, and because of Lillian's mother's tendency to mistake one spice for another if a book was unusually absorbing, meals had become less successful, if also occasionally more intriguing. All the same, the transfer of cooking duties from mother to daughter was met with a certain amount of relief on both sides.

The passing of the culinary torch marked the beginning of years of experimentation, made both slower and more unusual by Lillian's blanket refusal to engage with the printed word, even a cookbook. Learning the ins and outs of scrambled eggs, following such a pedagogical approach, could take a week—one night, plain eggs, stirred gently with a fork; the next, eggs whisked with milk; then water; then cream. If Lillian's mother objected, she made no note of it as she accompanied Lillian on her quests for ingredients, walking down the aisles reading aloud from the book of the day. Besides, Lillian thought to herself, scrambled eggs five nights in a row seemed a fair exchange for a week otherwise dominated by James Joyce. Maybe she should add chives tonight. *Yes I said yes I will yes.*

As Lillian's skills progressed over the years, she learned other, unexpected culinary lessons. She observed how dough that was pounded made bread that was hard and moods that were equally so. She saw that cookies that were soft and warm satisfied a different human need than those that were crisp and cooled. The more she cooked, the more she began to view spices as carriers of the emotions and memories of the places they were originally from and all those they had traveled through over the years. She discovered that people seemed to react to spices much as they did to other people, relaxing instinctively into some, shivering into a kind of emotional rigor mortis when encountering others. By the time she was twelve, Lillian had begun to believe that a true cook, one who could read people and spices, could anticipate reactions before the first taste, and thus affect the way a meal or an evening would go. It was this realization that led Lillian to her Great Idea.

"I am going to cook her out," Lillian told Elizabeth as they sat on her friend's front stoop.

"What?" Eight months older than Lillian, Elizabeth had long ago lost interest in cooking for a more consuming passion for the next-door neighbor, who, even as they spoke, rode and then launched his skateboard dramatically from a ramp set up in front of Elizabeth's gate.

"My mom. I'm going to cook her out."

"Lily." Elizabeth's face was a mix of scorn and sympathy. "When are you going to give up?"

"She's not as far gone as you think," said Lillian. She started to explain what she had been thinking about cookies and spices—until she realized that Elizabeth was unlikely to believe in the power of cooking and even less likely to see its potential to influence Lillian's mother.

But Lillian believed in food the way some people do religion, and thus she did what many do when faced with a critical moment in their lives. Standing that evening in the kitchen, surrounded by the pots and pans she had collected over the years, she offered up a deal.

"Let me bring her out," Lillian bargained, "and I'll cook

for the rest of my life. If I can't, I'll give up cooking forever." Then she put her hand on the bottom of the fourteen-inch skillet and swore. And it was only because she was still at the tail end of twelve and largely unversed in traditional religions, that she didn't realize that most deals offered to a higher power involved sacrifice for a desired result, and thus that her risk was greater than most, as it meant winning, or losing, all.

As with many such endeavors, the beginning was a disaster. Lillian, energized by hope, charged at her mother with foods designed to knock the books right out of her hands—dishes reeking with spices that barreled straight for the stomach and emotions. For a week the kitchen was redolent with hot red peppers and cilantro. Lillian's mother ate her meals as she always did—and then retreated into a steady diet of nineteenth-century British novels, in which food rarely held a dramatic role.

And so Lillian drew back, regrouped, and gave her mother food to fit the book of the day. Porridge and tea and scones, boiled carrots and white fish. But after three months, Charles Dickens finally gave way to what appeared to be a determination on her mother's part to read the entire works of Henry James, and Lillian despaired. Her mother may have changed literary continents, but only in the most general of senses.

"She's stuck," she told Elizabeth.

"Lily, it's never going to work." Elizabeth stood in front of her mirror. "Just boil her some potatoes and be done with it."

"Potatoes," said Lillian.

A fifty-pound sack of potatoes squatted at the bottom of the steps in Lillian's basement, ordered by her mother during the

Oliver Twist period, when staples had begun appearing at the door in such large quantities that neighbors asked Lillian if she and her mother had plans for guests, or perhaps a bomb shelter. If Lillian had been younger, she might have made a fort of food, but she was busy now. She took her knife and sliced through the burlap strings of the bag, pulling out four oblong potatoes.

"Okay, my pretties," she said.

She carried them upstairs and washed the dirt from their waxy surfaces, using a brush to clean the dents and pockets. Elizabeth always complained when her mother made her wash the potatoes for dinner, wondering aloud to Lillian and whoever else was near why they couldn't just make a smooth potato, anyway. But Lillian liked the dips and dents, even if it meant it took more time to wash them. They reminded her of fields before they were cultivated, when every hillock or hole was a home, a scene of a small animal battle or romance.

When the potatoes were clean, she took down her favorite knife from the rack, cut them into quarters, and dropped the chunks one by one into the big blue pot full of water that she had waiting on the stove. They hit the bottom with dull, satisfying thumps, shifting about for a moment until they found their positions, then stilled, rocking only slightly as the water started to bubble.

Her mother walked into the kitchen, the *Collected Works of Henry James* in front of her face.

"Dinner or an experiment?" she asked.

"We'll see," replied Lillian.

Outside the windows, the sky was darkening. Already cars were turning on their headlights, as the light filtered gray-blue through the clouds. Inside the kitchen, the hanging lamps shone, their light reflecting off the bits of chrome, sinking quietly into the wooden countertops and floor. Lillian's mother sat down in a red-painted chair next to the kitchen table, her book open.

"*I remember,*" Lillian's mother read aloud, "*the whole beginning as a succession of flights and drops, a little see-saw of the right throbs and the wrong. . . .*"

Lillian, listening with half an ear, bent down and took out a small pot from the cabinet. She put it on the stove and poured in milk, a third of the way up its straight sides. When she turned the dial on the stove, the flame leaped up to touch the sides of the pan.

"*There had been a moment when I believe I recognized, faint and far, the cry of a child; there had been another when I found myself starting as at the passage, before my door, of light footsteps. . . .*"

The water in the big blue pot boiled gently, the potatoes shifting about in gentle resignation like passengers on a crowded bus. The kitchen filled with the warmth of evaporated water and the smell of warming milk, while the last light came in pink through the windows. Lillian turned on the light over the stove and checked the potatoes once with the sharp end of her knife. Done. She pulled the pot from the stove and emptied the potatoes into a colander.

"Stop cooking," she said under her breath, as she ran cold water over their steaming surfaces. "Stop cooking now."

She shook the last of the water from the potatoes. The skins came off easily, like a shawl sliding off a woman's shoulders. Lillian dropped one hunk after another into the big metal bowl, then turned on the mixer and watched the chunks change from shapes to texture, mounds to lumpy clouds to cotton. Slices of butter melted in long, shining trails of yellow through the moving swirl of white. She picked up the smaller pan and slowly poured the milk into the potatoes. Then salt. Just enough.

Almost as an afterthought, she went to the refrigerator and pulled out a hard piece of Parmesan cheese. She grated some onto the cutting board, then picked up the feathery bits with her fingers and dropped them in a fine mist into the revolving bowl, where they disappeared into the mixture. She turned off the mixer, then ran her finger across the top and tasted.

"There," she said. She reached up into the cabinet and took down two pasta bowls, wide and flat, with just enough rim to hold an intricate design of blue and yellow, and placed them on the counter. Using the large wooden spoon, she scooped into the potatoes and dropped a small mountain of white in the exact center of each bowl. At the last minute, she made a small dip in the middle of each mountain, and then carefully put in an extra portion of butter.

"Mom," she said, as she carefully set the bowl and fork in front of her mother, "dinner." Lillian's mother shifted position in her chair toward the table, the book rotating in front of her body like a compass needle.

Lillian's mother's hand reached for the fork, and deftly navigated its way around the *Collected Works* and into the middle of the potatoes. She lifted the fork into the air.

"*It was the first time, in a manner, that I had known space and air and freedom, all the music of summer and all the mystery of nature. And then there was consideration—and consideration was sweet. . . .*"

The fork finished the journey to Lillian's mother's mouth, where it entered, then exited, clean.

"Hmmmm . . . " she said. And then all was quiet.

* * *

"I've got her," Lillian told Elizabeth as they sat eating toast with warm peanut butter at Elizabeth's house after school.

"Because you got her to stop talking?" Elizabeth looked skeptical.

"You'll see," said Lillian.

Although Lillian's mother did seem calmer in the following days, the major difference was one that Lillian had not anticipated. Her mother continued to read, but now she was absolutely silent. And while Lillian, who had long ceased to see her mother's reading aloud as any attempt at communication, was not sorry to no longer be the catch-pan of treasured phrases, this was not the effect she had been hoping for. She had been certain the potatoes would be magic.

On her way home from school, Lillian took a shortcut down a narrow side street that led from the main arterial to the more rural road to her house. Halfway down the block was a small grocery store that Lillian had found when she was seven years old, on a summer afternoon when she had let go of her mother's hand in frustration and set off in a previously untraveled direction, wondering if her mother would notice her absence.

On that day years before, she had smelled the store before she saw it, hot and dusty scents tingling her nose and pulling her down the narrow street. The shop itself was tiny, perhaps the side of an apartment living room, its shelves filled with cans written in languages she didn't recognize and tall candles enclosed in glass, painted with pictures of people with halos and sad faces. A glass display case next to the cash register was filled with pans of food in bright colors—yellows and reds and greens, their smells deep and smoky, sometimes sharp.

The woman behind the counter saw Lillian standing close to the glass case, staring.

"Would you like to try?" she asked.

Not where is your mother, not how old are you, but would you like to try. Lillian looked up and smiled.

The woman reached into the case and pulled out an oblong yellow shape.

"Tamale," she said, and handed it on a small paper plate to Lillian.

The outside was soft and slightly crunchy, the inside a festival of meat, onions, tomatoes, and something that seemed vaguely like cinnamon.

"You understand food," the woman commented, nodding, as she watched Lillian eat.

Lillian looked up again, and felt herself folded into the woman's smile.

"The children call me Abuelita," she said. "I think I hear your mother coming."

Lillian listened, and heard the sound of her mother's reading voice winding its way down the alley. She cast her eyes around the store once more, and noticed an odd wooden object hanging from a hook on one of the shelves.

"What is that?" she asked, pointing.

"What do you think?" Abuelita took it down and handed it to Lillian, who looked at its irregular shape—a six-inch-long stick with a rounded bulb on one end with ridges carved into it like furrows in a field.

"I think it is a magic wand," Lillian responded.

"Perhaps," said Abuelita. "Perhaps you should keep it, just in case."

Lillian took the wand and slid it into her coat pocket like a spy palming a secret missive.

"Come back anytime, little cook," Abuelita said.

Lillian had returned to the store often over the years. Abuelita had taught her about spices and foods she never encountered in Elizabeth's or Margaret's houses. There was avocado, wrinkled and grumpy on the outside, green spring within, creamy as ice cream when smashed into guacamole. There were the smoky flavors of chipotle peppers and the sharp-sweet crunch of cilantro, which Lillian loved so much Abuelita would always give her a sprig to eat as she walked home. Abuelita didn't talk a lot, but when she did, it was conversation.

So when Lillian walked into the store, a week after making mashed potatoes for her mother, Abuelita looked at her closely for a moment.

"You are missing something," she noted after a moment.

"It didn't work," Lillian replied, despairingly. "I thought I had her, but it didn't work."

"Tell me," said Abuelita simply, and Lillian did, about cookies and spices and Henry James and mashed potatoes and her feeling that perhaps, in the end, food would not be the magic that would wake her mother from her long, literary sleep, that perhaps in the end, sleep was all there was for her mother.

After Lillian ended her story, Abuelita was quiet for a while. "It's not that what you did was wrong; it's just that you aren't finished."

"What else am I supposed to do?"

"Lillian, each person's heart breaks in its own way. Every cure will be different—but there are some things we all need. Before anything else, we need to feel safe. You did that for her."

"So why is she still gone?"

"Because to be a part of this world, we need more than

safety. Your mother needs to remember what she lost and want it again.

"I have an idea," Abuelita said. "This may take a few minutes."

Abuelita handed Lillian a warm corn tortilla and motioned for her to sit at the small round table that stood next to the front door. As Lillian watched, Abuelita tore off the back panel from a small brown paper bag and wrote on it, her forehead furrowing in concentration.

"I am not a writer," she commented as she finished. "I never thought it was worth much. But you will get the idea."

She put down the paper, picked up another small grocery bag, and began gathering items off the store shelves, her back to Lillian. Then she folded the paper, placed it in the top of the bag, and held the bag out to Lillian.

"Here," she said, "let me know how it goes."

At home, Lillian opened the bag and inhaled aromas of orange, cinnamon, bittersweet chocolate, and something she couldn't quite identify, deep and mysterious, like perfume lingering in the folds of a cashmere scarf. She emptied the ingredients from the bag onto the kitchen counter and unfolded the paper Abuelita had placed on top, looking at it with a certain reserve. It was a recipe, even if this one was in Abuelita's writing, each letter thick as a branch and almost as stiff. Lillian's hand itched to throw the recipe away—but she hesitated as her eyes caught on the first line of the instructions.

Find your magic wand.

Lillian stopped.

"Well, okay, then," she said. She pulled a chair up to the kitchen counter and stood on it, reaching on top of the cabinet for the small, red tin box where she kept her most valued possessions.

The wand was close to the bottom of the box, underneath her first movie ticket and the miniature replica of a Venetian bridge her father had given her not long before he departed, leaving behind only money and his smell on the sheets, the latter gone long before Lillian learned how to do laundry. Underneath the wand was an old photograph of her mother holding a baby Lillian, her mother's eyes looking directly into the camera, her smile as huge and rich and gorgeous as any chocolate cake Lillian could think of making.

Lillian gazed at the photograph for a long time, then got down off the chair, the wand gripped in her right hand, and picked up the recipe.

Put milk in a saucepan. Use real milk, the thick kind.

Abuelita was always complaining about the girls from Lillian's school who wouldn't eat her tamales, or who asked for enchiladas without sour cream and then carefully peeled off the cheese from the outside.

"Skinny girls," Abuelita would say with disdain, "they think you attract bees with a stick."

Make orange curls. Set aside.

Lillian smiled. She felt about her zester the way some women do about a pair of spiky red shoes—a frivolous splurge, good only for parties, but oh so lovely. The day Lillian had found the little utensil at a garage sale a year before, she had brought it to Abuelita, face shining. She didn't even know what it was for back then, she just knew she loved its slim stainless-steel handle, the fanciful bit of metal at the working end with its five demure little holes, the edge scalloped around the openings like frills on a petticoat. There were so few occasions for a zester; using it felt like a holiday.

Lillian picked up the orange and held it to her nose, breathing in. It smelled of sunshine and sticky hands, shiny green leaves and blue, cloudless skies. An orchard, somewhere—California? Florida?—her parents looking at each other over the top of her head, her mother handing her a yellow-orange fruit, bigger than Lillian's two hands could hold, laughing, telling her "this is where grocery stores come from."

Now Lillian took the zester and ran it along the rounded outer surface of the fruit, slicing the rind into five long orange curls, leaving behind the bitter white beneath it.

Break the cinnamon in half.

The cinnamon stick was light, curled around itself like a brittle roll of papyrus. Not a stick at all, Lillian remembered as she looked closer, but bark, the meeting place between inside and out. It crackled as she broke it, releasing a spiciness, part heat, part sweet, that pricked at her eyes and nose, and made her tongue tingle without even tasting it.

Add orange peel and cinnamon to milk. Grate the chocolate.

The hard, round cake of chocolate was wrapped in yellow plastic with red stripes, shiny and dark when she opened it. The chocolate made a rough sound as it brushed across the fine section of the grater, falling in soft clouds onto the counter, releasing a scent of dusty back rooms filled with bittersweet chocolate and old love letters, the bottom drawers of antique desks and the last leaves of autumn, almonds and cinnamon and sugar.

Into the milk it went.

Add anise.

Such a small amount of ground spice in the little bag Abuelita had given her. It lay there quietly, unremarkable, the color of wet beach sand. She undid the tie around the top of the bag and swirls of warm gold and licorice danced up to her nose, bringing with them miles of faraway deserts and a dark, starless sky, a longing she could feel in the back of her eyes, her fingertips. Lillian knew, putting the bag back down on the counter, that the spice was more grown-up than she was.

Really, Abuelita? she asked into the air.

Just a touch. Let it simmer until it all comes together. You'll know when it does.

Lillian turned the heat on low. She went to the refrigerator, got the whipping cream, and set the mixer on high, checking the saucepan periodically. After a while, she could see the specks of chocolate disappearing into the milk, melting, becoming thicker, creamier, one thing rather than many.

Use your wand.

Lillian picked up the wand, rolling the handle musingly between the palms of her hands. She gripped the slender central stick with purpose and dipped the ridged end into the pan. Rolling the wand forward and back between her palms, she sent the ridges whirling through the liquid, sending the milk and chocolate across the pan in waves, creating bubbles across the top of the surface.

"Abracadabra," she said. "Please."

Now add to your mother's coffee.

One life skill Lillian's mother had not abandoned for books was making coffee; a pot was always warm on the counter, as dependable as a wool coat. Lillian filled her mother's mug halfway with coffee, then added the milk chocolate, holding back the orange peels and cinnamon so the liquid would be smooth across the tongue.

Top with whipping cream, for softness. Give to your mother.

"What is that amazing smell?" her mother asked, as Lillian carried the cup into the living room.

"Magic," Lillian said.

Her mother reached for the cup and raised it to her mouth, blowing gently across the surface, the steam spiraling up to meet her nose. She sipped tentatively, almost puzzled, her eyes looking up from her book to stare at something far away, her face flushing slightly. When she was finished, she handed the cup back to Lillian.

"Where did you learn to make that?" she said, leaning back and closing her eyes.

"That's wonderful," said Abuelita when Lillian recounted the story to her the next day. "You made her remember her life. Now she just needs to reach out to it. That recipe,"

Abuelita said in answer to Lillian's questioning face, "must be yours. But you will find it," she continued. "You are a cook. It's a gift from your mother."

Lillian raised an eyebrow skeptically. Abuelita gazed at her, gently amused.

"Sometimes, *niña*, our greatest gifts grow from what we are not given."

Two days later, Lillian headed straight home after classes. The weather had turned during the night, and the air as Lillian left school that day had a clear, brittle edge to it. Lillian walked at a fast pace, to match the air around her. She lived at the edge of town, where a house could still stand next door to a small orchard, and where kitchen gardens served as reminders of larger farms not so long gone. There was one orchard she particularly liked, a grove of apple trees, twisted and leaning, growing toward each other like old cousins. The owner was as old as his trees and wasn't able to take care of them much anymore. Grass grew thick around their bases and ivy was beginning to grasp its way up their trunks. But the apples seemed not to have noticed the frailty of their source, and were firm and crisp and sweet; Lillian waited for them every year, and for the smile of the old man as he handed them to her across the fence.

He was in among the trees when she walked by and called out to him. He turned and squinted in her direction. He waved, then turned and reached up into one of the trees, checking first one apple then the next. Finally satisfied, he came toward her, an apple in each hand.

"Here," he said, handing them to her. "A taste of the new season."

The sky was already darkening by the time Lillian got home, and the cold air came in the door with her. Her mother sat in her usual chair in the living room, a book held under a circle of light made by the reading lamp.

"I have something for you, Mom," Lillian said, and placed one of the apples in her mother's hand.

Lillian's mother took the apple and absentmindedly pressed its smooth, cold surface against her cheek.

"It feels like fall," she commented, and bit into it. The sharp, sweet sound of the crunch filled the air like a sudden burst of applause and Lillian laughed at the noise. Her mother looked up, smiling at the sound, and her eyes met her daughter's.

"Why, Lillian," she said, her voice rippling with surprise, "look how you've grown."

JIM CRACE

#45
FROM *THE DEVIL'S LARDER*

THE CELEBRATED RESTAURANT is a short walk from the transport stores, westwards, towards the empty tenements. Just ask the way if you get lost or muddled in the yards and alleyways. A magazine article—with the headline "Simply the Best"—has said it serves the finest soup in the region and "merits the detour." So for a month or two, its tables are reserved by detourists, as we call them, and regulars like the Fiat garage workers and the women from the trade exchange must eat elsewhere.

The menu is a simple one. It has not changed for seven years at least and will not change until she dies, the owner says. Each diner gets a hock of bread, some butter, and some salt, a spoon, an ashtray, and a glass. There are sometimes three soups to choose from. One made with fish, of course. The port is nearby and fish is plentiful. Another's made with vegetables, according to the season. And, occasionally, there is a third, prepared from either beef or chicken. But most days there are only two, fish soup or vegetable. A glass of beer or water is included in the price. There is no point in asking for an omelette or some wine. The restaurant can't cope with such variety. The best you'll get is soup and beer and smoke. There's also little point in asking what the fish is for that day, or what fresh vegetables were used. The owner usually says, "You'll have to wait and see," because, to tell the truth, she's not entirely sure.

You could not say the place is celebrated for its ambiance.

It's just a corner house converted forty years ago into a lunchery, at a time when there were countless families living in this quarter of the town and employed in the naval joineries and engineering shops. It's modest, then, and not entirely clean. It's two rooms up and one room down, with plastic tablecloths and kitchen chairs to make you feel at home. It's cheap in there and cramped, and unusually for a celebrated restaurant these days, it's heavy with tobacco smoke.

If not the ambiance, then what? You find out when you lift the soup spoon to your lips. The soups are never liquidized into a smooth consistency, but even with their nuggets and morsels of flesh and vegetable, the substrate ballast of lentils, peas, and beans, the broth is so delicate and light, so insubstantial and so resonant, that taste and smell precede the near lip of the spoon and leap across the thin air to your mouth. You've heard of aftertaste? This is the opposite. This is a soup that's full of promises. We're not surprised. We're used to it.

These detourists, however, are perplexed as they depart between the crowded tables and step out through the narrow door into the diesel-smelling streets. They tip like kings and queens. Their tips are stiffer than the bill. It can't be right, they think, to dine so well and simply and be so cheaply satisfied. And, oh, such soup, such soup! The magazine has said the owner has a secret formula, an additive she will not name. So now they try to guess what they have tasted, other than the finest recipe not only in the region but in the world. What is the conjuring trick?

We have the answers, should they ask. When we have drunk a beer or two, then we will gladly tease the cook, the celebrated chef, with theories to explain the newfound eminence of her restaurant. Her secret is the sewer truffles that she adds to every pot of soup. She grows them in her cellar. Her secret is seawater: two parts of that to every three parts taken from the tap. Seaweed. Sea mist. The secret is the heavy pan she uses, made for her out of boiler iron by a ship's engineer as a token of his devotion. Its metal is not stable, but leaks and seeps its unrequited love into the soup. Her secret is the special fish that's caught for her by an old man, at night. He rows out beyond the shipping lanes, anchors in the corridor of moonlight, and scoops them from the water in a kitchen colander. Or else the magic's in the vegetables. Or in some expensive, esoteric spice.

Why all the fuss, she asks, as the visitors depart. Is not all soup the same?

Yet now, at night, when we are going home, we sometimes smell the putrefying truffles from the street or catch a glimpse of moonlit rowing boats or look into her kitchen at the back end of the house to see her lifting her lovelorn sailor's pan onto the hob or hear the tidal rhythms of the sea as two-parts brine goes by its secret route into her soup. We find her carrying something—skeins?—across the room. They could be wool or seaweed skeins. We cannot tell. We see her fingers in the steam, adding magic touches to the stock. We see her sleight of hand, the charms she uses to entice these strangers to her rooms.

So, for a month or two—for fame is brief and fashions only fleeting—our tables at the celebrated restaurant are taken by new visitors to town. And we must wait—yes, wait and see—until its reputation fades, until there's room again for us to sit and smoke, to dine and feel at home, to dip our spoons and bread into this new and famous mystery.

ACKNOWLEDGMENTS

ERICA BAUERMEISTER: "Lillian" from *The School of Essential Ingredients*, published by Berkley/Penguin.

T. C. BOYLE: "Sorry Fugu" from *If the River Was Whiskey* by T. Coraghessan Boyle, copyright © 1989 by T. Coraghessan Boyle. Used by permission of Viking Books, an imprint of Penguin Publishing Group, a division of Penguin Random House LLC.

If the River Was Whiskey by T. Coraghessan Boyle. Copyright © 1990 by T. Coraghessan Boyle. Reprinted by permission of Georges Borchardt, Inc., on behalf of the author.

JEAN ANTHELME BRILLAT-SAVARIN: "On the Pleasures of the Table: Sketch" from *The Physiology of Taste* by Jean Anthelme Brillat-Savarin, translated and edited by M. F. K. Fisher, translation copyright © 1949 by the George Macy Companies, Inc., copyright renewed 1976 by The Heritage Press. Used by permission of Alfred A. Knopf, an imprint of the Knopf Doubleday Publishing Group, a division of Penguin Random House LLC. All rights reserved.

ANTON CHEKHOV: "On Mortality: A Carnival Tale" from *The Undiscovered Chekhov: Thirty-Eight New Stories*, translated by Peter Constantine. Translation copyright © 1998 by Peter Constantine. Reprinted with the permission of The Permissions Company, Inc., on behalf of Seven Stories Press, www.sevenstories.com.

JIM CRACE: Excerpt from *The Devil's Larder* by Jim Crace.

Copyright © 2001 by Jim Crace. Reprinted by permission of Farrar, Straus and Giroux, LLC.

The Devil's Larder by Jim Crace, © Jim Crace, 2002, reprinted with permission from David Goodwin Associates.

ISAK DINESEN: "Babette's Feast" from *Anecdotes of Destiny and Ehrengard*, published by Vintage.

GERALD DURRELL: "Owls and Aristocracy" from *Birds, Beasts and Relatives* by Gerald Durrell, copyright © 1969 by Gerald Durrell. Used by permission of Viking Books, an imprint of Penguin Publishing Group, a division of Penguin Random House LLC.

First published in the UK by William Collins 1969, © 1969 Gerald Durrell.

NORA EPHRON: "Potatoes and Love" from *Heartburn*, published by Vintage.

M. F. K. FISHER: "A Kitchen Allegory" from *Sister Age* by M. F. K. Fisher, copyright © 1964, 1965, 1972, 1973, 1978, 1980, 1982, 1983 by M. F. K. Fisher. Used by permission of Alfred A. Knopf, an imprint of the Knopf Doubleday Publishing Group, a division of Penguin Random House LLC. All rights reserved.

GÜNTER GRASS: "The Last Meal" from *The Flounder* by Günter Grass, translated from the German by Ralph Manheim. English translation copyright © 1979 by Houghton Mifflin Harcourt Publishing Company. Reprinted by permission of Houghton Mifflin Harcourt Publishing Company. All rights reserved.

SHIRLEY JACKSON: "Like Mother Used to Make" from *The Lottery* by Shirley Jackson. Copyright © 1948, 1949 by Shirley Jackson. Copyright renewed 1976, 1977 by Laurence Hyman, Barry Hyman, Mrs Sarah Webster and Mrs Joanne Schnurer. Reprinted by permission of Farrar, Straus and Giroux, LLC, and the Estate of Shirley Jackson.

JOHN LANCHESTER: "A Winter Menu" from *The Debt to Pleasure*, copyright © John Lanchester, 1996. Reissued by Picador, 2015. Published with permission from Macmillan.

GUY DE MAUPASSANT: from *Bel Ami*, translated by Ernest Boyd (Knopf, 1923; Vintage reissue 2010).

ELISSA SCHAPPELL: "Joy of Cooking". Reprinted with the permission of Simon & Schuster, Inc. from *Blueprints for Building Better Girls* by Elissa Schappell. Copyright © 2011 Elissa Schappell.

"Joy of Cooking" from *Blueprints for Building Better Girls* by Elissa Schappell. Reprinted by permission of The Joy Harris Literary Agency, Inc.

ISAAC BASHEVIS SINGER: "Short Friday" from *The Collected Stories* by Isaac Bashevis Singer. Copyright © 1982 by Isaac Bashevis Singer. Reprinted by permission of Farrar, Straus and Giroux, LLC.

AMY TAN: "Best Quality" from *The Joy Luck Club* by Amy Tan. Used by permission of G. P. Putnam's Sons, an imprint of Penguin Publishing Group, a division of Penguin Random House LLC.

ALICE B. TOKLAS: Excerpt from pp. 37–43, including 4 recipes [2525 words] from *The Alice B. Toklas Cook Book* by Alice B. Toklas. Copyright 1954 by Alice B. Toklas. Copyright renewed 1982 by Edward M. Burns. Foreword copyright © 1984 by M. F. K. Fisher. Publisher's Note copyright © 1984 by Simon Michael Bessie. Reprinted by permission of HarperCollins Publishers.

"Murder in the Kitchen" short story / 2525 words from *The Alice B. Toklas Cook Book* by Alice B. Toklas (Michael Joseph, 1954) copyright © Alice B. Toklas, 1954. Reproduced by permission of Penguin Books Ltd.

LARA VAPNYAR: "A Bunch of Broccoli on the Third Shelf"

from *Broccoli & Other Tales of Food and Love*, published by Anchor.

EVELYN WAUGH: From *The Complete Stories* by Evelyn Waugh. Copyright © 2011 by the Estate of Evelyn Waugh. Used by permission of Little, Brown and Company. All rights reserved.

"The Manager of the Kremlin" short story / 2000 words from *The Complete Short Stories* by Evelyn Waugh (Penguin Classics 2001). Copyright © The Estate of Laura Waugh, 2011. Reproduced by permission of Penguin Books Ltd.

VIRGINIA WOOLF: Chapter 17 from *To the Lighthouse* by Virginia Woolf. Copyright 1927 by Houghton Mifflin Harcourt Publishing Company. Copyright © renewed 1954 by Leonard Woolf. Reprinted by permission of Houghton Mifflin Harcourt Publishing Company. All rights reserved.

Any third-party use of material published by Penguin Random House LLC, outside this publication, is prohibited. Interested parties must apply to Penguin Random House LLC for permission.